THE YEARS OF FIRE

A Novel

YVES
BEAUCHEMIN

TRANSLATED BY WAYNE GRADY

A DOUGLAS GIBSON BOOK

McCLELLAND & STEWART

Original title: Charles le téméraire
Copyright © 2007 by Éditions Fides
Published under arrangement with Éditions Fides, Montreal, Quebec, Canada
English translation copyright © 2007 by McClelland & Stewart Ltd.

Translated from the French by Wayne Grady
This translation comprises the second half of *Charles le Téméraire: Un temps de chien*.

Library and Archives Canada Cataloguing in Publication

Beauchemin, Yves, 1941-
[Saut dans le vide. English]
The years of fire / Yves Beauchemin ; translated by Wayne Grady.

Translation of volume 2 in the Charles the bold trilogy: Un saut dans le vide.
ISBN 978-0-7710-1149-8

I. Grady, Wayne II. Title.

PS8553.E172S3813 2007   C843'.54   C2006-904214-4

We acknowledge the financial support of the Government of Canada through the
Book Publishing Industry Development Program and that of the
Government of Ontario through the Ontario Media Development
Corporation's Ontario Book Initiative. We further acknowledge the support of the
Canada Council for the Arts and the Ontario Arts Council for our publishing program.

Typeset in Minion by M&S, Toronto
Printed and bound in Canada

A Douglas Gibson Book

This book is printed on acid-free paper that is 100% recycled,
ancient-forest friendly (100% post-consumer recycled).

McClelland & Stewart Ltd.
75 Sherbourne Street
Toronto, Ontario
M5A 2P9
www.mcclelland.com

1 2 3 4 5   11 10 09 08 07

THE STORY SO FAR

CHARLES THIBODEAU, born in 1966 in the east end of Montreal, experienced a hard early life. His mother, Alice, died when he was four. A few years later, his father, Wilfrid, a carpenter with a drinking problem, treated him so badly that, with the help of a local notary, he was taken in by kind neighbours, Lucie and Fernand Fafard. This was a godsend for Charles and his dog, Boff, since the Fafard children, Henri (a boy of his age) and his younger sister, Céline, were fond of Charles, as was his good friend Blonblon.

Charles is very bright and a keen reader, but by the time he begins classes at Jean-Baptiste-Meilleur Secondary School, his adventures have already earned him the nickname "Charles the Bold."

There was no student revolt at Jean-Baptiste-Meilleur School, at least not at mid-term. The school's principal, Monsieur Robert-Aimé Doyon, was a small, lively man with piercing eyes, a firm jaw, and even firmer ideas, which were as integrated with each other as bricks in a wall. He wanted his school to be a bastion of discipline, hard work, and cleanliness. He considered the establishment of such a cult his personal duty, and he imposed it upon everyone who passed through his school, whether regularly or only occasionally. His subdued but steely voice drew instant attention and respect. He forbade his teachers to wear beards or moustaches, had metal flanges screwed to the stair handrails to discourage anyone from sliding down them, and flew into such cold rages at the sight of a poorly swept hallway or a scrap of paper lying on the grounds that the caretaker had become a ghostly insomniac who made tours of inspection in the middle of the night. The poor travelling salesman who stood before him with a shirt button unfastened, or his tie knot slightly askew, or his shoes less than impeccably polished had his attention politely but firmly drawn to his deficiency at the start of any meeting. And if the same salesman was so imprudent as to adopt some of the overly familiar sales strategies that were practised in America – calling the client by his first name, for example, or resting a hand on his shoulder while telling an off-colour joke – the principal would fix him with his famous cold stare and ask, icily, "I'm sorry, do we know each other?"

It was therefore not a good idea to be sent to Robert-Aimé Doyon's office on any disciplinary matter. Students who entered his precinct did so with the pallor of a French nobleman climbing the steps to the guillotine, and left looking overwhelmed, and with a fairly full timetable. As a result, the teachers at Jean-Baptiste-Meilleur felt no particular warmth towards their principal, though each was well aware that the man's despotic approach made their jobs a lot easier.

The students were no less keen to get through their time at Jean-Baptiste-Meilleur and move on to their next level of education. Pierre-Dupuy High School was just down the street, and was a stark contrast to their own school; it was co-ed, for one thing, and seemed possessed of an infinitely more relaxed attitude. The fascination the high school exerted on the younger students had increased when a fire broke out in the building the previous winter, caused by a student with an acetylene torch, and completely demolished the building's fifth floor. And then there were the stories told about the high school's famous shower rooms, in which students were obliged to shower in groups, naked, whether they liked it or not.

After class, the students of Jean-Baptiste-Meilleur would gather discreetly on rue Fullum, across from Pierre-Dupuy, to watch the "big kids" leaving their enviable school. It was a way of preparing themselves for the new life that awaited them. They would observe the expressions, learn the swear words, and study the behaviours that were current among high school students. Thus it was that one afternoon Charles received his first hormonal shock.

The large, rubber-boned student whose ego had received a bruising in the scuffle with Charles at the Sacred Heart statue earlier in the year had slowly developed a kind of friendship with him. He had the somewhat picturesque name of Steve Lachapelle, and he lived with his mother and two sisters (his father having taken off several years before). Like many of his fellow students, Lachapelle came to school two out of three days with an empty stomach, a mouth full of saliva, and his attention scattered to the four winds. Charles and Henri had noticed this and from time to time shared their lunches with him. Despite his name, Lachapelle was a real devil. He was in school only because the law forced him to be, and so all he wanted to do was play tricks on his comrades, have a few laughs, and get out as soon as he was legally able to get a "good job" that paid "lots of dough" so he could buy himself some "wheels" and "pick up chicks." His physical development was a bit ahead of Charles's, whose own interest in the opposite sex existed somewhere out on the fringes of his consciousness.

One afternoon after class, however, Lachapelle invited Charles up to Dupuy to "check out the action" leaving school. The two friends stationed themselves in front of the Grover Building, a textile factory across from the high school that, day and night, filled the entire neighbourhood with a low hum. With their school backpacks on the sidewalk, they pretended to be engaged in an animated discussion, but their eyes constantly scanned the flood of students pouring into the street. Lachapelle was excitedly eyeing the "chicks," and Charles was imitating him. They were, however, being discreet about it, since it was well known that any "babies" from Jean-Baptiste-Meilleur caught hassling their elders on rue Fullum were liable to get a shit-kicking.

Suddenly, moving through the throng of people and the clouds of cigarette smoke, Charles saw a beautiful, young, black girl of about fourteen or fifteen, dressed in a black leather miniskirt and a blouse the colour of liquid aluminum, with a black spiderweb pattern over her incredible breasts. His astonished eyes didn't know where to come to rest: on her aristocratic face, illuminated by angelic eyes the whites of which seemed almost phosphorescent? On her legs, which were long and fine and magnificently bronzed in the caressing light? On her feet, with their mauve toenails encased in black, high-heeled sandals? On her supple, mobile waist? On her hips, her forehead, her slightly red-tinted hair? Adopting a vaguely disdainful air, she moved with regal slowness through the crowd like a goddess risen from the sacred depths of the jungle for the sole purpose of being admired for her beauty in the dust of Faubourg-à-la-Mélasse.

Charles was thunderstruck. He stood with his mouth hanging open as though he had seen a ghost, staring at her with such intensity that Steve elbowed him in the ribs, worried that he would draw unfavourable attention from the high-schoolers. Charles hardly noticed. For the first time in his life he had seen Woman, the Great Temptress, the bulging Cornucopia from which flowed the water that turned the great wheels of life.

Finally, fearing trouble, Steve grabbed his friend by the arm and dragged him quickly towards rue Ontario. Like a sleepwalker, Charles let himself be led off without a word. Two or three times he looked back, but the black girl had disappeared, no doubt on the arm of one of the high-schoolers. What boy would be good enough for her?

"Holy shit, that tarbaby sure turned your crank, didn't she?" exclaimed Steve, after a prolonged silence from his companion.

Charles stopped. "Watch your mouth, you jerk!" he said, furious. "She's not a tarbaby! You're not good enough to lick the sidewalk she walks on!"

And he began walking again, his head held stiffly and his eyes staring directly ahead of him.

After a moment Steve hurried contritely after him. "All right, she wasn't bad. Not bad at all. I'd screw her, for sure. But did you see that blonde walking beside her, the one with the huge tits and the great ass on her?"

Still engrossed in his vision, Charles wasn't listening. He was savouring the memory of his Black Goddess as he would hold a candy in his mouth, savouring the juice.

That night after supper he went into the garage workshop with Blonblon to help with an emergency repair job. He tried to describe his experience of the afternoon as best he could. Blonblon listened with a surprised smile, then suddenly put his finger to his lips: Céline was leaning against the wall outside the shed, near the open doorway, listening to their conversation. Charles turned and saw the edge of her skirt.

"Céline," he said sternly.

She appeared in the doorway, her hands on her hips.

"What? I've got a right to be in my own yard, haven't I? It's not my fault if you're always telling your stupid stories!"

Her scorn was so obvious that Charles broke out laughing. She ran off, stifling a sob.

He turned back to Blonblon, his mouth screwed up in perplexity. Blonblon sighed loudly and went back to his work.

"What's up with her?" Charles asked after a moment's silence.

Blonblon looked up calmly, with that look of wisdom that had always set him apart from other boys his age. He explained that Céline's anger probably stemmed from her feelings of jealousy. "And when you are jealous of someone, it's usually because you're in love with them."

"Céline? In love with me?" exclaimed Charles, stunned. "But she's like my sister!"

"No accounting for love, my friend," said Blonblon. "You're in love with your Black Goddess, and you haven't even spoken a word to her yet."

Blonblon's revelation troubled Charles for several minutes. Then he told Blonblon that for all his philosophy he didn't know what he was talking about. How could a little eleven-year-old girl fall in love with a boy of thirteen?

When he saw Céline again that evening, she seemed to have forgotten the scene at the garage. She barely paid attention to him at all. He decided that Blonblon was wrong and that he, Charles, was right. He finished his history homework, breezed through his math (with only middling success), and took his evening shower. In the warm, stinging water he gave himself the kind of treatment he would have liked to have enjoyed with the beautiful black girl.

■ ■ ■

The next day he was at his post on rue Fullum, ready to worship the Goddess. He barely caught a glimpse of her before she moved off with a group of other girls. The next time he took Henri with him, having let him in on the fact that he'd fallen head over heels for Black Beauty; Steve had refused to go because he found it too risky. But the Goddess didn't appear. Several days went by. Sometimes he saw her, sometimes he didn't. His frustratingly Platonic love made him walk around with eyes like a mooncalf. He stood off by himself in secluded places, hands in pockets, lost in reverie, sighing deeply, counting the hours that separated him from Linda (he had managed to find out her first name). Among his other faults, Steve Lachapelle was also a leaky bucket when it came to confidences, and soon everyone at school was making fun of Charles's passion. A few well-aimed punches kept most of them at bay.

Finally, one afternoon, his perseverance as a love-starved puppy drew the attention of two high school students. They crossed the street and asked him what newspaper he worked for. Charles opened his mouth, uttered two or three inarticulate sounds, and took off, but not before receiving a solid kick that left a large bruise on his buttock. The incident put a stop to his long-distance, anonymous idolatry.

Two weeks later, Charles came face to face with the beautiful Linda as he was coming out of a grocery store.

He stood stock-still, blocking the doorway, a bag of groceries in his arms, too enchanted to speak.

"Why are you looking at me like that?" Black Beauty asked in surprise.

His face felt blistered and his air passages became completely blocked. He looked from side to side for an escape route. Then suddenly, as though someone had come up and pushed him from behind, he moved forward, haltingly, and looked straight into her magnificent eyes.

"Because I think you're really beautiful."

Had she noticed him before this? Had someone told her of his passion for her, a passion that made him burst into flame?

"That's sweet," she said, laughing. "It's always nice to hear that. . . . But you better run home and drink up your soup, little guy. You still got some growing to do. Maybe we'll meet again in a couple of years . . ."

Still laughing, but with a gentle, tender laugh that made her look more beautiful than ever, she patted him on the shoulder and continued into the grocery store. Charles took off at a run, both delighted and humiliated. He never spoke of this encounter to anyone. And the few times he saw Linda after that, he made a point of avoiding her.

■ ■ ■

Charles excelled in all his subjects except mathematics, in which his performance was only mediocre. In November, at the suggestion of his French teacher, Jean-René Dupras, he began tutoring two of his fellow students, Steve Lachapelle and Olivier Giammatteo, both of whom delighted in torturing both spelling and syntax and were well on their way to the ambivalent land of illiteracy. It was known as the "help with homework" system, based on the observation that the transfer of knowledge often went more smoothly between members of the same peer group, who spoke more or less the same language, than when it came down from above, and it usually produced excellent results. The sessions took place during the lunch hour or after class and were entirely voluntary.

Charles was proud of his new role. He put a lot of effort into it and showed himself to be a good teacher. His skill was highly appreciated by his fellow students as well as by the faculty. Beneath his flippant exterior there lurked a seriousness not often found in thirteen-year-olds, especially those who had gone through as many difficult experiences as Charles had.

After several weeks the number of errors in Lachapelle's and Giammatteo's homework began to decrease to the point that they were actually fewer than the total number of words they had written. This was hailed as a vast improvement.

However, it was because of this generous assistance that Charles was to undergo a painfully humiliating experience.

At the tail end of one afternoon the trio was working away in a classroom. They'd been going at it for half an hour when Olivier Giammatteo, brought to the end of his tether by the rules of agreement of past participles, decided to break a different set of rules by lighting up a cigarette. He even succeeded in convincing his two colleagues to join him; Charles did so mostly to stay on his good side.

That was the moment destiny decided to bring Robert-Aimé Doyon onto the scene. The principal's infallible sense of smell immediately detected the forbidden odour. He opened the door of the classroom, surprised the culprits, and, his face brick-red, ejected them from the building. In a few harsh, clipped words he ordered them to appear in his office the first thing next day. The affair, it seemed, had assumed in his mind the proportions of the attack on Pearl Harbor, the Saint Bartholomew's Day Massacre, or the October Crisis.

The next morning the three students were subjected to a long sermon on the cumulative effects of nicotine and insubordination and were ordered to spend the next three afternoons, from four o'clock until six, cleaning out the school basement, which was a junk heap of dusty, useless items that the caretaker had never found the time to chuck into the garbage bin.

Robert-Aimé Doyon had always believed in combining the requirements of discipline with administrative efficiency.

On the second day, Steve Lachapelle, between a sneeze and a fit of coughing, stumbled on an old cardboard box jammed between two eviscerated desks. It contained books.

"Hey, Thibodeau! Look at this! I found something for you!"

Charles looked in the box and took out the books. Along with stacks of old health manuals and moral guides for Catholic youth, he found an illustrated edition of Defoe's *Robinson Crusoe*, the complete plays of Corneille (in two volumes), a copy of *The Other World, or The States and Empires of the Moon* by Cyrano de Bergerac, and *The Comic Novel* by Scarron. Except for the first, most of the titles meant little to him. After flipping through them, however, he set them aside to take home, assuming that they, like everything else in the basement, were meant to be thrown out.

Fifteen minutes after the three students had left, Robert-Aimé Doyon went down into the basement to inspect their work. His eye fell on the cardboard box, which they had placed on a pile of old boards. Curious, he opened the box and was surprised to see that some of the books were still covered in dust but others had been wiped almost clean. His instinct told him that these last had been handled, and that others had no doubt been liberated. The identity of the thief was not hard to guess. It wasn't so much the taking of the books that bothered him as that they had been taken without his permission. Everything in the school belonged to the school, and nothing must be allowed to leave the school without official authority and due consideration.

The next morning, as Charles was entering his classroom, a student came up and told him that the principal wished to speak to him. Surprised and worried, he knocked on the office door.

"Come in!" came the muffled, imperious voice.

Monsieur Doyon was seated at his desk, his chin resting on his joined fingers. He was wearing a black suit and tie because later that morning he was going to the funeral of one of his aunts, but the effect was to accentuate the hollowness of his eyes, making them seem like a killer's as they shot icy looks around him.

Charles stood in the middle of the room and felt his mouth become dry.

"How are you this morning, Thibodeau?" the principal asked with fake friendliness.

"Fine."

"Fine, *sir.*"

"Fine, sir," Charles repeated submissively.

"Your marks are satisfactory, or so I hear, despite the fact that you can be . . . disruptive, at times."

"Yes, sir."

"You're doing well enough in French to be tutoring some of your fellow students. You have my congratulations."

"Thank you, sir."

"You're welcome, I'm sure. I'm curious to know how it is that you do so well in French."

"Because I work at it, sir."

"Yes, of course. Nothing can be accomplished without work. It's one of the laws of nature. Is there not another reason, though, Thibodeau?"

"Maybe because I also like to read," Charles said, after thinking about it for a moment.

"Yes, yes, that doesn't surprise me . . . I would have bet both my ears and the tip of my nose that you were a book-lover. To the extent, I would also wager, that when you see a book your head begins to spin so much that you no longer know quite what you're doing. Am I correct?"

Charles's face began turning a telltale red.

"Am I not correct, Thibodeau?" the principal repeated, smiling a pitiless smile. "Answer me! Am I not correct?"

"I thought they were going to be thrown in the garbage, sir."

"You thought *what* were going to be thrown in the garbage?" asked the principal, feigning surprise.

"The books I found in the basement yesterday afternoon, sir. Isn't that what you called me in to talk about?"

"Oh? You found some books in the basement, did you? And what did you do with them?"

Charles stared at a small crack in the base of a plinth at the far end of the principal's office. He would have liked to have been able to shrink, like Alice, and escape through the crack forever, and never again have to see this terrifying man who was taking so much pleasure in his humiliation.

"I took them home," he said, barely able to speak. Then added, when there was no response from Doyon, "Sir."

"You took them home?" said the principal, holding his chin in his two open hands, a gesture Charles hadn't seen him use before and which made him look both clownish and menacing. "I'm afraid I don't understand."

"I just told you, sir. I thought the books were going to be thrown out, so I thought I might as well –"

"Let me see if I'm getting this right," the principal interrupted. "It seems to me there's still something I don't understand. Hmm. I wonder what it could be. Is it, by any chance, that your father has bought the school and no one bothered to tell me about it?"

Charles said nothing. A drop of sweat slid slowly down his left cheek. He felt as though his feet had caught fire and were swelling up and splitting his shoes. His stomach churned.

"Answer me, Thibodeau. I'm awaiting your response."

"He has not bought the school, sir."

"No, I hadn't thought so. So then nothing in this school belongs to you, or to him, except of course your own personal effects. Is that right, Thibodeau?"

"Yes, sir. That's right."

"In other words, you stole those books."

Charles stared at the floor, his fists clenched. His teeth grated against one another, emitting loud cracking sounds that echoed in his head.

"Answer me, Thibodeau."

"Yes, sir, I stole them."

"Good. Now we know exactly where we stand, do we not? Where do you live?"

"Nineteen-sixty-seven rue Dufresne, sir."

"Go home and get them. You've got ten minutes. I suggest you hurry."

Seven minutes later, Charles was back in Doyon's office, completely winded. He set a paper bag on the principal's desk. To his great relief the house had been empty, saving him from having to give embarrassing explanations.

The principal examined the bag's contents. Slowly his expression softened. As he had little interest in reading, none of the books was familiar to him, but their old, worn condition and the names of some of the authors, which conjured in his mind vague scholarly memories, suggested to him that they belonged in the category of "serious literature," even though all that meant to him was that they were stuffy and boring. It was also clear to him that they might as well have been thrown in the fire, since they were of no conceivable use to the school. Doyon raised his head and an incredulous smile spread across his thin lips.

"And you say you were going to read these things?"

Charles nodded, looking thoroughly fed up.

The principal continued examining the books and following his own reflections. But the dust made him sneeze, and with a brusque gesture he shoved them to the edge of his desk. Then he spent a long time clearing his throat. Suddenly his eyes lit up and began rolling wildly, a sign that he had hit upon a pedagogical opportunity.

"In principle, Thibodeau," he said, stretching out his hands and leaning forward in his chair, "I have no objection to your reading these books. But remember one thing, my friend: trying to educate yourself through theft, as you have just done, is like trying to nurture a plant by pouring boiling water on it. It won't work. Are you with me?"

Charles nodded in agreement.

"Good. Here's what we're going to do," he went on, picking up one of the volumes of Corneille and flipping through it. "You are going to study, hmm, let's see, *Le Cid*, a very good play, in verse, and tomorrow afternoon, at four o'clock, instead of going down to work in the basement with your two friends, you're going to come up here to my office and recite to me, from memory, the first one hundred lines."

Charles's head and shoulders slumped.

"The first hundred lines?" he murmured, horrified.

"The first hundred lines. By tomorrow at four o'clock. Now you may return to your class."

Charles, however, did not move. He seemed not to have heard the principal. The hundred lines flooded through his brain like an ocean too vast to drink.

A surge of anger suddenly welled up from somewhere deep within him, fury against this imbecilic dictator who amused himself by torturing his students, as his own father had tortured him for years; the anger rose and swelled with such relentless force that it swept away his fear like so much dust. Charles turned scarlet, and he shot at the principal a look that the latter had never, in his eighteen-year career, seen aimed at him before by a student. It was not a look of fear or resentment, it was an unleashing of the most scathing contempt. He opened his mouth to put this young imp of a student back in his place, but before he could speak Charles stepped forward, placed his hands on the desk, and spoke in a stifled, trembling voice.

"This is stupid, sir. I have an exam tomorrow afternoon. I won't have time to study for it, and I'll fail."

For a few seconds, Doyon felt as though his head were full of bubbles. The bubbles bounced crazily around, tumbled into each other, and burst, leaving nothing but emptiness. Nothing like this had ever happened to him before.

But his calm quickly returned. His lower lip protruded until it almost touched his moustache, and a fierce expression appeared on his face.

"What's that you say, Thibodeau? I didn't understand you."

"I said that it's a stupid idea," Charles repeated, in a somewhat less confident voice.

"Stupid, is it? Hmm. That's the first time anyone has spoken to me in such a manner. But I suppose you have your reasons. I might even concede the point. In fact, the more I think about it, the more I believe you to be right, at least in this case. Of course your studies must come first. As you say, it was stupid of me to deprive you of the time to prepare for your exam. I will therefore change your punishment. You will have three days to memorize your lines. But you will memorize three hundred lines, not a hundred, and instead of reciting them here in my office, you will give a little performance of them to the entire school, in the auditorium. On stage, naturally. That will be much more . . . amusing, don't you think? I'll make the arrangements. Now get out of here."

And he handed Charles the Corneille.

■ ■ ■

It was a deflated Charles who returned to his class. He was so caught up in his anguish that he didn't hear a word spoken by his math teacher, Monsieur Tousignant, who had to call his name three times to get his attention, to the great amusement of the other students. So great was his need to unburden his heart that after class he went up to Monsieur Tousignant, a large, boring man with the eyes of a dead fish and a completely monotonous voice, and told him what had happened. Monsieur Tousignant listened to his story carefully without making a single comment, but by his expression it was clear that he found Charles's punishment cruel and out of proportion.

"I'll speak to the principal later," he promised the boy. "But next time, keep a rein on that tongue of yours."

Doyon had a great deal of respect for the math teacher, whom he deemed to be "serious and businesslike." But he bridled with anger nonetheless when the teacher began speaking on Charles's behalf, threatening to add another hundred lines if he heard any more interference from the staff.

The next day Charles blew his geography exam like a complete dunce, because he'd spent the entire night studying *Le Cid*. The fear of humiliating himself in front of the entire school gave him cramps from his stomach down to his calves. He knew that that was the real goal of the principal's punishment: public humiliation. He saw himself standing on the stage, trying to give his lines despite the howls of laughter coming from the assembled students, and he was overcome by a kind of vertigo that robbed him of all his strength. But he lowered his head, forced himself to be calm, and applied himself to memorizing the play.

CHIMÈNE

Elvire, is what you've told me now th'entire truth?
Have you kept back nothing of what my father said?

ELVIRE

Indeed are all my own senses yet amazed;
He esteems Rodrigues as much as you do love him;
And unless I'm much deceiv'd in how I read his soul,
He will command you to respond in kind to his love.

At first it all seemed like so much gibberish, and he despaired of ever being able to memorize something he couldn't understand. Gradually, however, he began to make inroads into the text. He guessed that "flame" was another way of saying "love," and that "lovers" were simply people in love with each other. He was amazed to learn that at that time in Spain the father chose a husband for his daughter, and that an Infante (the daughter of a king) could cause a lot of trouble by falling in love with a simple knight, even though he was the most handsome, intelligent, and courageous knight in the world.

Finally the quarrel between Count Gormas and Don Diego impressed itself on his mind like a scene from a cloak-and-dagger movie. He began to hate the jealous count who was wicked enough to challenge a poor, old man who'd been given a position he wanted for himself. Certain of Corneille's lines, despite their somewhat bizarre turns of expression, began to resonate in his head like bronze gongs being banged together.

The greatest kings, alas, are made the same as we:
They can be in the wrong as all humanity.

Oh God! My strength, worn out by all this care, departs!

– Rodrigue, have you the heart?
  – So much so that my father
  Will discover when the time is come . . .

– Then I'll say no more. Revenge me, revenge thyself;
Show thee a worthy son of such a man as I.
Hounded by troubles wherever destiny sends me,
I'll rout them all. Go, run, fly, and revenge us both.

In his effort to memorize the lines, he didn't realize that the heroes of the play were in fact Rodrigue and Chimène (what an odd name!), and that the play was a love story. Often the impassioned spirit that ran through *Le Cid* took hold of him. But so many words to learn! So many plot twists to untangle! Such a torrent of curses falling on the head of Doyon, who was resting in his comfortable bungalow a few dozen blocks away in Cité-Jardin.

Charles spent the whole weekend stuffing his head with the three hundred lines, which formed the whole of Act I. Five or six times a day he would leave his room and grab the first victim he came across; whoever it was had to drop everything, sit down in front of him with a copy of *Le Cid*, and be his prompter. He became a stranger to them; he'd turned sour, his mouth twisted, and he jumped at the slightest sound. He even aimed a kick at Boff, the first time he'd ever done anything of the sort, then fell on the poor dog in tears and begged his pardon, while the rest of the household looked on in stunned silence.

Sunday night for Charles was a series of sudden awakenings, deep sighs, and groans. Corneille's lines cut through his head like the blade of a circular saw. Sitting up in bed he repeated them over and over, eyes wide with nervousness, seeing himself standing on the stage, legs shaking, voice thin as a piece of string. He'd told Blonblon, Henri, and Steve about his misadventure; the whole class was behind him. But what good would that be when the rest of the school was mocking him?

In the morning, during breakfast, Lucie found him calmer, imbued with a kind of stoicism. He'd spoken in the hallway to Henri, who had replied with great, approving nods of the head, and the two had gone down into the basement and come up with a large paper bag into which no one was allowed to look.

"Leave them alone," Fernand advised his wife. "What do you think they have in there? A bomb? Let them have their fun . . . within limits, of course."

And he looked warningly at the two boys. Then he leaned over and whispered to Lucie, "That damned principal has gone a bit far, if you ask me. He must have Nazi blood or something . . ."

"Good luck, Charles," murmured Céline, taking his hand.

"Bah! Nothing to worry about," he boasted. "It'll be fun."

And he opened the door for her with a chivalric flourish, as he imagined Rodrigue would open it for Chimène. But his throat was as tight as a noose and his heart was thumping in his chest as he walked to school with Henri, who did his best to comfort him. His worst nightmare was the appearance of his horrible "fish-face" twitch in front of the entire assembly of fellow students. If that happened, he decided he would leave the stage immediately, come what may.

Three or four of his classmates were waiting for him by the Sacred Heart statue, and they clapped him on the back encouragingly.

"I've worked it out with Steve and Robert Parent's gang," Blonblon whispered to him. "We're going to applaud like mad. What's that in the bag?"

"A surprise," Charles said, moving towards the class.

The principal, standing outside the door to his office, plucked him out of the hallway and told him that his presentation would take place after lunch, at one o'clock sharp. Charles spent French class plunged in Corneille, with the tacit approval of Jean-René Dupras. Some teasing came his way from time to time from the others in the class, but generally the students laid off, as though they wanted to help the unhappy actor prepare for his performance.

■ ■ ■

"My dear friends," began Robert-Aimé Doyon in a voice meant to imply humour but which inspired only dislike, "as an exception to the rule, I have assembled you here today in the auditorium because I want you to admire the talent – and, I hope, the memory – of our friend Thibodeau."

Here he turned towards Charles, who was standing on the stage next to him, his face drawn and pale, but staring firmly at the audience nonetheless. When he had walked onto the stage his courage had failed him momentarily, and he had dropped his paper bag in the wings.

"As many of you may know, our friend Thibodeau here has a certain facility for language – even, at times, impolite language. But still, in order to help him improve his vocabulary, I have asked him to learn a great number of new words by heart – all of them polite words – in the hope that in the future, such as the next time he is addressing a figure of authority, he'll have a better pool of polite words to draw from and will not have to rely on coarse language. Our friend Thibodeau is therefore going to recite from memory the first three hundred lines of a very beautiful and very old play. That is to say, from Corneille's play *Le Cid*."

"What's a 'cid'?" some wag called out. "You mean, like in Sydney, Nova Scotia?"

"Or acid indigestion?" replied a rival.

Ripples of laughter ran through the assembly. A student made a loud farting sound with his lips. Another began singing "Only You" in the voice of a young male in full rut. Steve Lachapelle contorted his body so violently that he jabbed an elbow into one of the teachers and had to say "Excuse me." Ordinarily punctilious in matters of protocol, Doyon merely smiled, arms crossed on his chest, while Charles, obviously terrified, hung his head like a felon awaiting execution.

"You will notice," continued the principal, "that the characters in the play always express themselves in an extremely polite fashion, even when they disagree with one another. I hope that will serve as an example to certain people. All right, Thibodeau, you may begin."

He left the stage and took a seat directly in front of Charles, in the first row.

Elvire, is what you've told me now th'entire truth?
Have you kept back nothing of what my father said?

"Louder!" came a cry from the audience.

"We can't hear!"

Charles shut his eyes, took a deep breath, and, seeing that he had nothing further to lose, decided to throw himself into the text like a swimmer caught in a riptide that was trying to drag him out into the ocean. He recited for two minutes. Calmness was slowly restored to the room. The students were amazed at the confidence with which their comrade delivered lines that might as well have been in Chinese as far as they were concerned. They looked at one another and nodded in admiration.

A frown began to spread across Doyon's lips. This little upstart was acquitting himself with distinction. This wasn't punishment. He suddenly saw himself having to get up on the stage to congratulate the little bugger in public. He felt a hand on his shoulder.

"You're wanted on the phone, sir," his secretary whispered. "It's urgent."

When Charles saw the principal leave the room, he stopped reciting, suddenly overcome with a wild joy.

"Just a minute!" he called to the audience.

He ran to the wings, retrieved his bag, and returned with a huge, plumed, felt hat left over from an old Hallowe'en costume, which he placed on his head. It had been Henri's idea, a way to get the scoffers on Charles's side.

Charles had come to his favourite passage: the altercation between Count Gormas and Don Diego, the central exchange of the whole drama.

COUNT
    Everything I deserved, you have taken from me.
DON DIEGO
    If that is so, I am the more deserving one.
COUNT
    He who puts it to best use is worthier still.
DON DIEGO
    Not to have taken it would have boded ill.

He jumped to the left, then to the right, changing positions and voice with each line, taking off and replacing his hat to give the illusion that there were two actors on the stage. A profound silence ruled the auditorium. Even little Lamouche, usually incapable of staying still and quiet for more than thirty seconds at a time, as though coffee ran through his veins instead of blood, sat staring at Charles with his mouth hanging open, paralyzed by surprise and admiration.

COUNT
    Your impudence,
    You bold, old man, shall be your recompense.
    (*Slaps him.*)
DON DIEGO
    (*Drawing his sword.*)
    Have at! And kill me after giving such affront,
    The first mark my race has suffered from another.
COUNT
    (*Disarming him easily.*)
    What thought you to accomplish with such feebleness?
DON DIEGO
    O God! My strength, worn out by all this care, departs!

Charles, his hat askew, was contemplating an imaginary sword lying on the ground when Doyon re-entered the room and saw at a glance the measure of his defeat. Silently he took his place in the first row and watched the young adolescent on the stage, carried away by a kind of drunkenness, certain now of turning the trial that the principal had so maliciously imposed upon him into a veritable triumph, unaware even that his judge had returned to the room.

"That's enough!" Doyon suddenly shouted, pounding his fist violently on the stage. "What is the meaning of this ridiculous disguise, Thibodeau?"

Six hundred eyes were fixed on Charles. Some with amusement, others with anxiety, still others with a cheeky delight. Slowly, Charles removed the hat and let it slip from his hand: the feather could be heard brushing the stage floor as it fell.

"I . . . I thought . . ."

"You thought *what*, Monsieur Thibodeau?" spat the principal, whose empurpled forehead seemed to have sprouted a number of curious protuberances.

"I thought," babbled Charles, "that since the play . . . er . . . took place . . . uh . . . in the past . . . I mean, in the time of kings . . . well, I thought . . ."

"I'll tell you what you thought. I know exactly what was going through that stubborn head of yours, but which you now don't have the courage to admit, Thibodeau. You thought that turning your punishment into a farce would give you a fine opportunity to ridicule AUTHORITY. Well, I've had enough of your insolence!" And he banged his fist again on the stage, which was unfortunately once too often for his watch strap.

A light tremor, composed of desperately stifled giggles, ran through the room.

"So that you will have time to reflect on all this, my friend, I am inviting you to remain away from this school until next Monday. Do you understand? And as for you lot," he said, turning towards the students, who were becoming restless in their seats, "get back to your regular classes. Immediately!"

"That was bloody good," murmured Steve as he passed Charles. "You should be in the movies!"

"Way to go! That was the best!" called Blonblon, with a wink. Others surreptitiously shook his hand or clapped him heartily on the shoulder. He had become a hero. Henri would never have to defend him again. From now on, his status would be his shield.

He left the school still absorbed in the scene he'd been playing on the stage. He sat for a moment on the school's front steps, partly out of bravado but also because his legs were shaking and he needed a rest. It was the beginning of December. Although there was still no snow, the chill in the air soon made him stand up.

"You stupid old idiot!" he mentally shouted to the principal as he walked down the street. "You can keep me out of your stupid school for a month for all I care. Blonblon and Henri will lend me their notes, and it'll be a holiday!" He was filled with a sense of pride and freedom, which quickly gave way to a feeling of anxiety. How would Lucie and Fernand react to his being suspended from school? The hell with it. He'd tell them exactly what had happened, and the principal would appear as odious in their eyes as he already was in his.

2

In his haste to leave the school he had forgotten his gloves, and by the time he neared home his hands were numb from the cold. He saw an ambulance parked in front of Chez Robert, its roof light flashing, and a small group of people huddled around the entrance to the restaurant. He started to run, seized by sudden alarm. A wheeled stretcher came through the restaurant door, pushed by two ambulance attendants. He had time to make out Roberto's face on the stretcher, tomato-red, cheeks deeply creased, his head wobbling from side to side as though attached to his body by the thinnest of threads; his large, hairy arms also seemed to have been chopped off, so white were his bloodless hands even against the sheet.

"Rosalie!" Charles shouted when he saw her coming out onto the sidewalk. The bright, flowery print of her yellow dress was a painful contrast to the dismal scene. "What's happened?"

She climbed into the ambulance behind the stretcher and turned towards him with a defeated look. She seemed not to recognize him. Then the rear door closed and the vehicle pulled quickly away from the curb.

Charles hurried into the restaurant. Liette was crying and dabbing her eyes with her frilly apron, and Monsieur Victoire had his arm around her. The new waitress, Marie-Josée, was stroking Liette's hair while puffing on a cigarette, with a grave expression that made her round, open face seem curiously old.

"GIVE THE MAN SOME AIR! GIVE THE MAN SOME AIR!" yelped Edward the Parrot, perched on a shelf that was splattered with its droppings. "WHERE'S THE BLOODY AMBULANCE? NOT HERE YET! SON OF A BITCH!"

A customer Charles vaguely recognized was serving coffee all around with a tragic, important air. The kitchen door was partly open, and looking in Charles saw the multicoloured makings of a pizza trampled into a mess on the floor. Bits of pepperoni were stuck to the linoleum in front of the counter.

"Charles, my boy, come over here," called Monsieur Victoire, the taxi driver, still comforting the waitress as she wiped her nose with her apron.

And in his deep, solemn voice, seemingly able to soften even the most terrifying words, Monsieur Victoire told Charles of the tragic event.

Roberto had been complaining all morning of a pain in his stomach, saying it felt like a drill bit was boring into him. But he absolutely refused to be taken to the hospital, despite Rosalie's insistence. About eleven o'clock he said he was feeling a little better.

"You see, Lili?" he told her, holding up a bottle of Fermentol. "Nothing but a little indigestion. You women, you're always thinking the worst."

Meanwhile he'd got a bit behind in his work and lunch hour was coming on, so he began banging things around in the kitchen like a bull who'd just spotted the cow of his dreams.

Rosalie was still worried, though. She checked in on him two or three times, sticking her head into the kitchen and saying, "How do you feel now?"

"Fine, fine. Like I tole you."

But his voice was strained and a bit breathless, and it was clear he was not fine at all. Noon came. The restaurant filled with a happy roar, punctuated by the clinking of knives and forks on plates and the shrill calls of waitresses giving their orders. Customers ate and talked, exchanged greetings, flipped nervously through newspapers, excited by the smell of good food, looking enviously at the plates of those who'd already been served. Trays of food were trotted out of the kitchen in a steady stream. At the cash, Rosalie was her usual welcoming, motherly self.

Liette had just been coming along the counter with a tray piled high with plates of beef and veg when they heard a dull thud from the kitchen and felt the floor shudder. Setting her tray on the counter, she ran back through the door and let out a scream:

"Madame Guindon! Madame Guindon!"

A deathly silence settled over the restaurant. Everyone stopped talking or moving.

Rosalie had been handing change to a customer. She ran into the kitchen and a second later they heard another scream, this one even more hair-raising than the first.

"Mercy upon us, for the love of God! He's had a stroke! Roberto! Roberto!"

The poor man was lying on his stomach on the floor, his face in the pizza he'd just taken from the oven, making little gurgling sounds. Rosalie tried to lift him up as the doorway filled with heads staring mutely in. A few minutes later they heard the sinister sound of a siren, and the ambulance arrived. By this time Roberto had lost consciousness. They gave him an injection and put an oxygen mask over his face. Someone said the word "infarction" and Rosalie gave a groan of horror. Something about the word, the way it sounded like something broken or cracked, made her feel suddenly dizzy and she had to sit down.

Charles ran home to tell Lucie the bad news, not thinking for a second that his presence in the middle of the afternoon would cause her even more concern. But she wasn't there, probably out shopping. He wandered from room to room for a few minutes, tried to read, watched a bit of television, but his thoughts were scattered in all directions like a handful of dust tossed to the four winds. Not knowing what else to do, he went back to the restaurant.

But he found the door locked. A notice, hurriedly scrawled in large, red letters on a piece of cardboard, read:

CLOSED UNTIL FURTHER NOTICE
DUE TO ILLNESS

There was another surprise waiting for him at the end of the afternoon: Lucie had not been shopping earlier that day, she'd been working at the hardware store. She was going to be working there now, six days a week. Business at the store had continued to drop off, and Fernand had had to lay Clément off because he couldn't afford to pay his salary. Lucie was taking his place. They told Charles about it as though it were all a normal part of doing business, but Charles wasn't taken in. There was a distinctly sombre feeling in the house. Lucie, exhausted from her first day on the job, made a kind of back-of-the-fridge supper and, for the first time since coming to live with the Fafards, Charles pushed his plate away without finishing it. The meal was tossed into the garbage, and Fernand told his wife to go lie down in the living room while he cleaned up the kitchen. As he worked, he sang bits of an old hit of Fernand Gignac's:

> *Let me have some roses,*
> *Mademoiselle,*
> *Let me have some roses,*
> *I need them right away.*

But even he was preoccupied, his mind wandering and his voice taking on a wistful tone that pierced the heart; it was clearly not roses he wanted but something else, something more essential, and something that Fate was refusing to let him have.

Although Henri had been kind to Charles all afternoon, that evening he barely spoke to him. From time to time he would cast Charles a look that the latter found strange, almost malevolent, a kind of reproach. But for what? Charles wondered if Henri regretted having become his adoptive brother, since it meant that Fernand had had to pay five thousand dollars to that swine of a carpenter who had fathered him. The thought gave him such a stab of pain that he took Boff into his room and spent the rest of the evening lying on his bed, curled up with his dog in a state of despair that reminded him sharply of those terrible years he'd believed were behind him forever.

Céline knocked on the door and asked him to help her with her homework, but her voice sounded so worried that he knew it was only a pretext.

"Leave me alone, Céline," he sighed after a moment. "I don't feel like seeing anyone right now."

The day had started with such bravado, such glory, and now look how it was ending. In misery.

Steve happened to telephone him towards the end of the evening and, despite the lateness of the hour, managed to persuade him to go out. They rambled along rue Ontario for a while, pushed by a brisk wind; Charles told his friend about the unhappy incident at Chez Robert earlier that day, then confided his worries about the hardware store, which seemed headed inevitably into bankruptcy.

For once, Steve didn't try to turn everything into a joke. He listened to Charles gravely and attentively and did his best to raise his spirits. Then he stopped walking and turned to face his friend.

"You're really stressed out, man. That's not good. All those dark thoughts, they'll only bring you down. I've got something that'll fix you up."

Charles looked at him, taken aback.

"We've got to find us a quiet space, my man, where we can blow our minds. Know what I'm saying?"

And from the pocket of his windbreaker he took a small plastic bag filled with some kind of brown substance. Charles knew what it was immediately. He'd been seeing the stuff around for some time. He'd even been invited to "have a toke" a few times, but for some reason he'd always put it off.

"It's better than tobacco, Thibo, my man. Those dark thoughts will just vanish into thin air. You might even see things from a thousand light-years away. You'll be so laid back you won't believe it!"

Charles smiled nervously. He felt as though he'd already been to the moon and back that day, and he wasn't sure he wanted to go on another "trip." But Steve was insistent, and soon they found themselves on the bench in the little park on rue Coupal, which at that hour was dark and deserted.

Charles took a drag and started coughing. Steve teased him, then encouraged him to try again. Then before he knew it, all of life's difficulties seemed to have lifted from his shoulders. He was on a high plateau that extended smoothly and peacefully before him as far as he could see. He stood up and began walking, his nose to the wind, his hands thrust deep in his pockets, laughing at the way his feet moved.

■ ■ ■

On December 20th, 1979, the Lévesque government laid before the National Assembly the wording of the question for the referendum on Quebec sovereignty. The idea of a public referendum on separation had been feeding stormy debates within the Parti Québécois for some time. Many were of the opinion that the election of an openly separatist government had itself been enough justification for a declaration of Quebec's independence, and for the beginning of negotiations with Ottawa to bring it into effect. They were called the hard-liners. The moderate faction were diametrically opposed to this view, urging a much more gradual approach. According to them, the election of a sovereigntist government had to be followed by a period of good governance, in order to inspire confidence in the electorate. Once that confidence was gained, voters could be appealed to by means of a referendum to determine the political future of Quebec.

In 1973, Claude Morin, known as "the father of phasing-in," a former senior Quebec bureaucrat and a very influential figure among the *independentistes* (although revelations of his secret contacts within the Royal Canadian Mounted Police would discredit him a few years later), had presented the idea of a referendum to the Parti Québécois leadership, and it had been rejected. The next year, however, he had put the idea forward again and it had been adopted. From then on the referendum project had been an essential plank in the party's platform.

The hard-liners considered the moderates to be a bunch of wimps, hiding their lack of courage behind a smokescreen of complex stratagems and endless negotiations. The moderates, in turn, treated their adversaries as a gang of fanatics. Whatever the truth of the matter, it was the moderates who were carrying the day.

After having let the debate drag on year after year, René Lévesque's mandate was drawing to a close and he had finally come to a decision. And so, on December 20th, 1979, the referendum question was sent out to every newspaper in the province.

> Whereas the government of Quebec has made known its intention to come to a new understanding with the rest of Canada, based on the principle of the equality of all peoples;
> And whereas this understanding will allow Quebec to assume exclusive power to make its own laws, collect its own taxes and establish its own foreign relations, which is the definition of sovereignty, and, at the same time, to maintain an economic association with Canada, including the use of the same money;
> And whereas any change in political standing resulting from these negotiations will be submitted to the population by referendum;
> Do you therefore give the Quebec government a mandate to negotiate the above understanding between Quebec and Canada?

After having read the question three times while standing in an aisle of his hardware store, Fernand turned pale, then violently red, then gave a long groan that would no doubt have caused little stir in a jungle but which produced a very marked effect in the store. He then shut himself in his office and informed everyone that he was not to be disturbed under any circumstances.

He stayed there for three hours, and no one ever knew what he did. But that night at home he declared to Lucie that Quebec was being run by fools, and that he'd have to be a fool himself to let them go ahead on such a disastrous course of action without doing anything about it.

"There's a special meeting tonight in Claude Charron's riding," he said. "We don't live in that riding, but I'm going to go to that meeting, and I'd like to see anyone try to stop me!"

At eight-thirty he was already there, seated in the second row. Despite the fact that it was a bad time for political meetings, there was a large crowd present. Everyone was in high spirits, associating the coming emancipation of Quebec (of which they had no doubt whatsoever) with the upcoming Christmas and New Year's celebrations. Fernand shot surly glances at those around him and groaned, but quietly this time, because he felt quite alone surrounded by such naive people, with their delighted faces.

Minister Claude Charron arrived and was greeted by fists raised in triumph. He walked in smiling, calling out greetings, galvanizing the faithful. The meeting got underway. It obviously had to do with the referendum. Some attendees expressed misgivings, but most wanted the referendum to be held as soon as possible – even the next day. One old gentleman, an almost perfect replica of Colonel Sanders, with flowing white hair and white goatee, proposed holding a contest for the creation of a national anthem.

Claude Charron burst out laughing.

"Maybe we should wait until we have a nation," he said.

At nine o'clock, Fernand made his way to the microphone, his legs a little wobbly.

"Sorry to rain on your parade, but in my view this referendum question should be tossed into the garbage. Has anyone really read it? One hundred and fourteen words! By the time you get to the end of it, you've forgotten how it started! And complicated! It's asking people for permission to come back later and ask them for their permission. And all that after negotiations with Ottawa, and no one in the room knows how they'll turn out. In fact, with all due respect, Mister Minister, the whole thing smells of fear. Fear and petty-minded calculation. Just you wait: that whoreson Trudeau is going to accuse us of trying to pull the wool over the people's eyes. In this kind of dealing, Mister Minister, just like in all important things in life, you have to be clear and concise. These twistings and convolutions will kill the cause. That's all I have to say."

He sat down. The room had fallen glacially silent. Someone sniggered behind his back, and Colonel Sanders shot him a withering look, as though he had just assassinated the national mascot in the public square. Claude

Charron was slightly embarrassed (did he share some of Fernand's misgivings?); he cleared his throat and then, in that familiar, comforting, infinitely seductive voice for which he was famous, spoke to the assembly.

"I think, my friends, that you will all agree with me when I say that this is no longer the time for endless discussion and analysis. It's time to spit on our hands and get the job done! Of course nothing is perfect, of course we could go back to the drawing board and come up with a better way of explaining the problem of the future of Quebec to Quebeckers. But, as far as I'm concerned, that would be a case of spending so much time polishing the pot that we never have time to make soup . . . and we'd die of hunger! No, my friends, there's a fresh wind a-blowing, we've got one hell of a crew, and Canada has made it clearer than ever that the only way they want to see us Quebeckers is on our knees with our hands out. Well, now's the time to act! Let's go forward! And long live sovereignty!"

The hall broke out into delirious applause. In three minutes Fernand's intervention had been swept aside, forgotten. Despite his anger he stayed until the meeting was over. Leaving early would have drawn attention to his defeat. But he was also gnawed by doubts. What if he were wrong? But how could he be wrong when he was just using common sense? Could complicated arguments convince someone of such a simple thing?

When the meeting was over and as the hall was emptying he succeeded in having a few last words with Claude Charron.

"René Lévesque likes you, Monsieur Charron. Everyone knows he considers you next in line for premier. I'm begging you, get him to change the question before it's too late."

"Listen to me, my good man," replied the politician, smiling broadly. "This is politics, not Hollywood. You can't just rewind the film and start over. You have to keep going forward, doing the best you can with what you've got. If you're so unhappy with the question, well then, stay home on voting day. But I guarantee you," he said, taking Fernand's hand with a big smile, "that by then you'll be out there with the rest of us, voting YES!"

■ ■ ■

While an emaciated Roberto spent his days lying on a hospital bed, his face blank and dark, not speaking, not even opening his mouth except to say he was getting out of the restaurant business, Rosalie searched frantically for a new cook. They were coming up to Christmas and its incessant shopping, one of the most lucrative times of the year.

When she reappeared behind her counter, Charles thought she looked older, more worried and impatient. She took Liette to task for the least little thing, not letting her get away with the smallest error. Her new cook, Rémi Goyette, was a tall man with large ears that stuck out from his head. He had a taciturn manner, an expressionless face, and a thick moustache that made him look like a Tartar. He had learned his trade in lumber camps and knew how to conduct himself in front of a stove well enough, but he sometimes came to work drunk and would turn the kitchen into a circus! One morning, without warning, he didn't turn up at all. Rosalie managed as well as she could for the day by herself, and when he showed up the next morning, explaining that he'd had laryngitis and had had to stay in bed burning up with fever, she pretended to believe him and swallowed her anger as best she could. She needed him.

Three weeks later it happened again. This time she didn't say a word. She began looking for a replacement, and as soon as she found one she stopped the Tartar as he was going out the door one evening, and with a perceptibly shaking hand gave him an envelope and told him not to come back. He favoured her with a tight smile, took the envelope, and bowed her way without saying a word. As he was leaving, however, he stepped hard on her left foot and slammed the door so violently that the glass cracked and Mademoiselle Galipeau, who worked in a ladies' dress shop, spilled her tea on her lap, causing, as she complained endlessly to Rosalie for the next several weeks, a severe case of skin irritation on her thighs.

A black cloud seemed to have settled over Chez Robert. Hardly had the year 1980 begun than the new cook was seized by a bout of homesickness and decided to return to the Magdalen Islands. Rosalie found another, this one so terrible the customers started complaining. On February the 14th a cold snap hit Montreal and a water pipe burst, flooding the restaurant.

Two weeks later Roberto reappeared, looking grey and pale but smiling bravely, and, to the great delight of his wife and their customers, resumed his place in the kitchen. But his illness had greatly reduced his abilities, and after a few days they had to hire an assistant, which was an extra expense. Business, meanwhile, for them as for everyone else, was not what it had once been.

In fact, the country was in a recession that showed itself in a thousand depressing ways. The neighbourhood became poorer and shabbier as the more successful elements began to move out. Houses and storefronts became vacant, very suspicious fires broke out, and factories that had been operating since the turn of the century, even earlier, shut their doors.

There was less and less work for Charles at the restaurant. Rosalie shook her head sadly to see him sitting in a booth, sometimes for an hour or more, reading a newspaper or with his nose in a book, waiting for the telephone to ring with a delivery order and the usual tip.

One particularly slow Saturday evening, as he was watching the television suspended from the ceiling in a corner of the restaurant, trying with a couple of customers to whip up an interest in a particularly slow hockey game, she brought over a cup of hot chocolate and a plate of cookies and set them down on the table in front of him.

"You didn't have to do this, Madame Guindon," he said to her, smiling broadly. "I had a big supper."

"Bah!" she replied. "You need a few calories in you with this wind blowing outside. If you ever have to go outside, that is," she added with a frown. "Which doesn't look likely . . ."

She sat down heavily across from him, watching him attack his food.

"Charles," she said. "I need to speak with you."

Her serious tone made him look up quickly, his eyes wide with surprise.

"It might be best for you to start looking for a job somewhere else. I don't have a lot to offer you here, and it hurts me to see you wasting your time like this. You need to earn money just like the rest of us, after all."

Charles pursed his lips as if to contradict her and looked away, chewing.

"I'm serious, Charles."

The boy placed his hands on the edge of the table and looked at her with such gravity that it made her smile in spite of her worry.

"Madame Guindon," he said sternly, "you should be ashamed of yourself, talking like that. You should have more faith. Things will pick up around here, you'll see. Roberto has only been back for two weeks and there are still a lot of people who don't know that yet. Besides, I like working here. I feel as though this were my home. If you want me to go you're going to have to fire me, the way you did those cooks."

Rosalie took his hand and kissed it, a very unusual gesture for her; Monsieur Vlaminck, a retired plumber who had come down to get away from his wife for a few moments, was amazed by it.

But despite Roberto's efforts, the business did not get back on its feet. Even more serious, the cook began to find his work distasteful. "It's a killer; it'll lead to the graveyard before the year's out."

One morning in March as they walked to school, buttons announcing YES pinned proudly to their windbreakers, Charles and Henri saw a sign in the restaurant's window. Roberto and Rosalie had put the place up for sale. Charles stopped for a moment in stunned silence, then shrugged his shoulders and continued on his way.

"It's best to sell, don't you think?" Henri said, trying to console his friend. "Roberto can't take it any more. Would you rather he worked himself to death?"

"I'm sure it's never going to be like it was before," was all Charles could reply.

He was downcast for the rest of the morning.

■ ■ ■

The school year ended with no further fireworks between Charles and the principal. Doyon maintained his constant and meticulous surveillance over his student, but the latter had decided to knuckle down and play it safe, behaving as well and with as much discretion as was possible for a boy of thirteen in his first year of junior high school. There were a few clashes, but they were over things so minute that the principal found no excuse in them to awaken the full majesty and invoke the power of his authority.

Chez Robert closed its doors at the end of spring. Roberto had put aside a bit of money, and he decided to go on a long vacation with Rosalie in the Laurentians. They rented a cottage and put the sale of the business in the hands of an agent. On closing day they held a goodbye party for all their friends and regular customers; they gave out free beer and soft drinks and pizzas – the last pizzas, Roberto swore, that he would ever make in his life. There were a lot of teary eyes. Rosalie seemed tired but happy, and she bestowed kisses on everyone in the room. In his deep, resounding voice, Fernand delivered a comical eulogy to the departing couple, his attempt to turn a sad event into a cause for laughter. Monsieur Victoire took a different tack and veered off into lofty sentimentality. He stood between the cook and his wife, his arms around both, and with his sumptuous voice soon had most of the room in tears, and even choked out a few sobs himself. Charles sat alone in a corner, a can of pop in hand, contemplating the scene with a pensive eye.

Perhaps it was puberty. Blonblon had pretty much abandoned the appliance repair shop, thereby delivering a mortal blow to his associate's interest in their small business as well. He now preferred to spend his spare time ambling down the streets of the neighbourhood with Charles and Henri, a much less lucrative occupation but one that seemed to hold a great deal more interest. They drifted down rue Ontario and hung around the Frontenac metro station, checking out the telephone booths for forgotten coins, picking up returnable cans and bottles, falling into occasional conversations with strangers, and absorbing as much of what the street had to teach them as they possibly could. Lucie began worrying about this sudden change in Henri's and Charles's behaviour. She confided her concern to her husband, who thundered about the house, imposed stricter rules, issued threats, and pointed out moral consequences, all to very little effect. Afterwards he told himself that the boys' natural goodness, along with the penchant for reading that Charles still displayed, meant that things would sort themselves out eventually. On the other hand, he read with careful attention a long article in *The New Observer* on the dangers of drugs, which their friend the notary, Parfait Michaud, had passed on to him one evening with a significant look.

Truth to tell, poor Fernand no longer knew what to think about anything. Despite his best efforts, business continued to fall off. He who had always been able to make a good living could see the day coming when he would barely be able to scrape by.

"We'll just have to wait out the storm," he sighed each night when he climbed into bed with his wife. "All we can do is try to keep our heads above water."

He was powerfully affected by the defeat of the YES side in the referendum. A smirch on the honour of all Quebeckers, he said, and he declared to anyone who would listen that a people so in love with their own mediocrity that they refused to even ask for the freedoms owed to them deserved every kick in the backside, constitutional or otherwise, that anyone cared to give them. However, he added in the same breath, one mustn't be too hard on one's compatriots. Trudeau and his team of federal tricksters had trampled all over the law governing referendums in conducting a campaign parallel with that of the NO camp; the law allowed each camp to spend no more than two million, two hundred thousand dollars on its campaign, but Ottawa had spent an additional seventeen million urging Quebeckers to vote NO! Why had the party simply denounced the fact without doing anything about it? Why hadn't they laid the thing out before a commission of inquiry? Appealed to international authorities? Held a new referendum, this time one with a real chance of winning? But no! Instead, everyone simply sank into a stupid and humiliating depression, wanting nothing more than to be left alone to forget about it, at any price, and to give themselves over to all kinds of stupidities. What a bunch of potato-heads!

Despite his criticisms of the Quebec government's strategies, Fernand had worked his tail off during the campaign, partly out of loyalty to the cause, but also as a way of taking his mind off his own financial difficulties, which nonetheless made him bitter and kept him awake at night. He went door to door, organized kitchen meetings, spent entire nights on the telephone conducting polls or trying to convince voters to vote YES; a huge YES sign hung across the front of his house, and his wife practically had to throw a fit to stop him from putting a similar one in the window of the hardware store. Though no less fervent a sovereigntist than her husband, Lucie was more prudent; she warned him against making his political convictions so well known; it could only cost them more customers, and the Lord knew that was the last thing they needed!

"I don't need that kind of customer," Fernand replied with superb disdain.

But then the businessman in him resurfaced.

"Besides, you're worrying about nothing, my love. When the dust has settled – and we finally have a country like any other normal people have, for crying out loud! – they'll all come back to me, you'll see. The law of the best quality and lowest price always wins out in the end. In fact it's working now, as we speak. There may be a few hotheads in the neighbourhood crazy enough to spend an extra five bucks for a screwdriver at my competitor's simply because they don't like my ideas. But they're not going to make me rich or poor, and it gives me great pleasure to be sending them off to suck on Pierre Trudeau's toes!"

In early April, René Lévesque was touring the riding when he was informed of the courageous support Fernand was giving to the cause. Late in the afternoon he paid a visit to the hardware store, along with a bevy of local bigwigs.

All of Fernand's objections vanished in a puff of smoke. He felt that that day was the most beautiful day of his life.

"Monsieur Lévesque! What a great honour!" he babbled, blushing with pleasure, when he saw the premier coming through the door of his shop.

He hurried towards the great man, hand outstretched, accidentally stepping on the foot of a customer who had come rushing down an aisle.

"Careful, Monsieur Fafard," laughed the politician, "you might have just cost me a vote."

"It's nothing, nothing at all, Monsieur Lévesque," managed the customer, wincing with pain.

Just then Charles walked in, looking for a bolt for his bicycle. He was rooted to the spot, as though he had seen a vision of the Messiah. Fernand introduced him to the premier.

"Charles, my son. One of my two sons, in fact. I also have a daughter."

Lévesque shook the boy's hand and smiled broadly, looking him straight in the eye, and for a second Charles sensed that he was receiving the man's entire attention, burdened though he must have been with so many heavy responsibilities.

Fernand escorted the premier to every nook and cranny of the store and was amazed by the pertinence of the man's questions about the business. ("Really *intelligent* questions," he would later say, "the kind of questions only a brain would know how to ask.") Charles followed them closely, a few steps behind, drinking in the statesman's every word. Every so often he would raise his right hand and stare at it in amazement. *Just think, it has just shaken the hand of René Lévesque!* The hand had become almost sacred, a kind of holy relic. Too bad no one had thought to take a photo! His friends would go crazy with envy when he told them about it tomorrow.

For once there were a few people in the store. They gathered admiringly around the politician, who chatted with them amiably, relaxed, knowing that he was in friendly territory. From a slight distance, an elderly man observed the scene with lips pressed together in disapproval; when Lévesque approached him he turned his back and swept out of the store, wearing his hostility like a flag.

For a second a shadow passed through the store, but then someone said something funny, everyone laughed, and Lévesque made his little amused grimace, which was such an expressive part of his arsenal of charms.

"Well, there's one we won't have to convince," he said, shrugging his shoulders.

"Do you think we'll win, Monsieur Lévesque?" Fernand asked worriedly as the politician was about to leave.

"We all have to work hard, day and night, just as you've been doing," was all that the premier replied, giving the lively, penetrating look that didn't always reveal what was going on behind it. "If we do that, we'll win, I promise you."

On May 20th, sitting in the living room in front of the television with the rest of the family and a few neighbours, Charles followed the election results, first with passion, then with an anguish that was soon transformed into a sticky, sickening sadness. Everyone was silent. A tall young man who was sitting on the floor with a beer between his legs began to cry and mutter vague imprecations. Fernand, sitting straight up in his chair, stared at the screen, not bothering to wipe away the tears that streaked his face. Lucie had put her hand on his knee and patted it from time to time. Near the end of the coverage, Lévesque appeared on the stage at the Paul-Sauvé Arena, accompanied by his wife and the minister of state, Lise Payette, all of them dressed in black. Lévesque went to the microphone, a frail, little man, his face drained of colour, incapable, it seemed, of seeing beyond the defeat to the long road they had come down in spite of all the odds. He stood without speaking for several minutes while the crowd cheered wildly. Gradually, reluctantly, the people fell silent.

"If I understand you correctly," he said in a voice hoarse with exhaustion, "what you're telling me is: Until next time!"

Lucie gave a sob and bent over, reaching out to the television, exposing some of her ample chest.

"He looks so sad," she said. "I just want to hold him in my arms."

"Now would be a good time," groaned her husband.

3

Early that summer, Chez Robert changed its name to the Blue Bird. After lengthy and bitter negotiations that went on for three long weeks, the restaurant was acquired by Constantin Valiquette for "a reasonable price."

Valiquette was a thin, nervous man in his forties, of medium height, florid of face, with an oversized head; he walked with short, jerking steps, as though his ankles were tied together by a rope. He had thick, wet lips that looked as though they belonged to a fat woman, dark, cavernous nostrils large enough to accommodate a thumb, and small, prying eyes that were both inquisitive and distrustful; hardly a face to show sympathy or inspire friendliness. Which made sense, because Constantin Valiquette was neither a sympathetic nor a friendly man.

For most of his life, in fact, he had divided the world into two categories: prey and predators. He attributed his own suspicious nature to two major events in his life. The first had occurred in 1947 and resulted in the death of his father, also a restaurant owner, who had been getting on in years and was deaf. One day he'd hurried out of his restaurant, headed across the street without checking for traffic, and been run over by a truck. From this, Valiquette learned a valuable lesson: "You have to look where you're going." The second event, which had involved him directly, had taken place in 1953, in the restroom of the old Loew's Theatre on Sainte-Catherine, while he was still a student. Standing at the urinal with his leather briefcase on the floor between his legs, he'd been in the process of relieving an overfilled bladder when he felt something rubbing against his ankle.

"Hey!" he shouted. "Thief!"

But by the time he'd got himself tucked back into his pants and done up his zipper, the man had run out into the vast theatre lobby and disappeared into the darkness. From this misadventure he learned a second lesson: "Always watch your back." Since then the two lessons had stood by him like shining beacons, lighting up the sometimes obscure paths of his life.

On the 26th of June, 1980, a ladder truck pulled up in front of Chez Robert and the men went to work. They took down the sign that Charles had been so proud of and replaced it with a longer, larger sign that showed, on the left, a bluebird with its wings spread out, and, to the right, the words:

THE BLUE BIRD

painted in blue letters. Below that, in smaller, red letters, the sign said:

CANADIAN, ITALIAN AND CHINESE MEALS

Charles and Blonblon watched the operation from across the street. They thought the new sign was ridiculous and vowed never to set foot in the place again. Charles loudly declared that it would feel dishonourable to go in and offer the new owner his services.

For the next few weeks, however, he couldn't stop thinking about the five thousand dollars Fernand had had to give his father to make him forfeit his paternal rights. The whole thing made him feel more and more unhappy.

Conversations in the Fafard household were never directly about their financial difficulties, but they were always slightly coloured by it. The burbling joy that had once rung out through the house was now tinged with moments of sadness. It took very little to send Fernand into a raging temper; Lucie, now juggling her household duties with her work at the hardware store, went to bed exhausted each night at nine o'clock. Charles told himself that the five thousand dollars would come in very handy, and wondered if Fernand regretted having let the money go, since no one had been forcing him to give it up. How sweet it would be to one day stand before Fernand with five crisp, thousand-dollar bills in his hand, and to give them to Fernand, saying: "Fernand, you have been extremely generous to me. This is my way of saying thank-you!"

But there was no chance that that dream would come true in the foreseeable future. Charles had no source of income, and his bank account, once impressive for a boy of his age, had shrunk to less than a hundred dollars. The day was not far off when he would have to ask his adoptive parents for pocket money, which they had already been giving him from time to time.

So it was that early in the morning of July 8th, Charles went back on his fiery declaration and presented himself at the Blue Bird to offer his services to its owner as a delivery boy.

The restaurant's interior had been repainted (blue, of course) and the seats of the stools lining the counter had been replaced (the old ones had admittedly been ripped in several places). Marie-Josée walked past him carrying a large tray of dishes and gave him a big smile, which encouraged him to continue. Then he stopped again, intimidated by the sight of Constantin Valiquette, standing behind the cash, absent-mindedly fingering his lips. With a movement of his enormous head he gestured Charles to step forward.

"Hello, sir," said the adolescent. "Are you the owner?"

The head moved again. Charles introduced himself nervously, adding that he lived just down the street from the restaurant, on rue Dufresne.

"Oh yes? Glad to meet you, my lad," replied the owner, apparently without thinking it necessary to introduce himself. "What can I do for you?"

Charles was already regretting his boldness, but he went on. He said he'd worked as a delivery boy for the previous owners for nearly four years, knew the job very well, and could be quite useful.

"Well, well, well. A delivery boy, a delivery boy, eh?" muttered Valiquette, still tapping his lips. He began questioning Charles closely on the workings of the restaurant, how it had prospered, what the customers were like, what kind of food they preferred, whether the previous owners had had to change the menu over the years, what improvements they had had to make to the building, why Roberto had decided to sell the business, how he got along with the police and the health inspectors, and so on. Every now and then he excused himself to serve a customer. The interview went on for half an hour. Charles, torn between fear and hope, had no idea where the conversation was going but answered as best he could, casting an occasional glance through the window out onto the street.

Valiquette was busy for several minutes with a customer who thought he'd detected an error in his bill. Then he turned back to Charles.

"Sorry, my lad, but I don't need a delivery boy just now. But thanks for the information. Maybe another time, eh?"

And he shook Charles's hand with a huge smile.

■ ■ ■

"Happy birthday, Charles," said the notary, coming forward with a be-ribboned box in his hands. "Careful not to drop it. It's a bit heavy."

"Fourteen already!" murmured Amélie Michaud, with an expression that could have registered either joy or sorrow.

"Yes, fourteen!" cried Fernand. "Almost a man!"

Charles looked embarrassed.

"Fernand," he said, "stop talking as if I were a baby."

Turning red with emotion, he began unwrapping the gift. The party was taking place in the notary's living room, with members of the Fafard family as well as Blonblon, Steve Lachapelle, and – wonder of wonders! – Roberto and Rosalie, who had come down from the Laurentians especially for the occasion. Parfait Michaud had asked if he could throw the party because, as he said, "although I know you're not my son, you're the closest thing to it I have." Amélie had slaved most of the day to make a "really healthy menu," but had given it up in the end and called a caterer.

"Oh, isn't that *cute!*" cried Rosalie, with slightly forced enthusiasm, when she saw what was in the box: a bronze statue of a sitting dog, about thirty centimetres high, looking alert, ears erect, chest puffed out, with huge hind feet and its tail curled up on its back. It was, in fact, nothing special.

"Well, at least it's an original," said Roberto, tugging at his tie. He took a long drink from his glass of beer.

Steve, completely baffled by the notary and his strange wife, stretched out his thin hand and felt the statue. Boff, too, gave it a good, long sniff.

"It is, I'll have you all know," declared the notary, who could sometimes sound a trifle pompous, "a replica in miniature of Hachiko, a statue erected in the Shibuya Train Station in Tokyo in 1934. It was put there to invoke a very moving story of a dog and his master. Would you like to hear it? I'm going to tell it to you anyway, whether I have your permission or not. Hachiko belonged to a professor at Tokyo University. Every day the professor took the train to work from Shibuya. It was the dog's custom to accompany his master to the station in the morning, and then to come back in the evening to meet the professor on his return. Well, it so happened that one day, in May of 1925, the poor man died of a heart attack in his office. However, that day – and every day for *the next nine years*, that is, until his own death – the dog went to the station at the usual time in the evening, in the hope that his master would return. His loyalty so struck the station personnel and the other commuters that they got together and built a monument to him, which became famous throughout Japan; many people in Tokyo (who are called Tokyoites) still use the statue as a rendezvous point. And Hachiko has become the very symbol of fidelity. Lovers stand beside it pledging eternal faithfulness – imprudently, in my opinion, but we insist on believing that human nature is composed of such sentiments."

"Not yours, it seems," sniffed Amélie, looking daggers at her husband.

"I thought," continued the notary, ignoring her remark, "that this little statue would please you, since you've always been so fond of dogs."

"Oh yes, Monsieur Michaud, I think it's very beautiful. Thank you so much!"

He shook the notary's hand vigorously and then, finding the gesture somewhat inadequate to the occasion, threw himself into Michaud's arms.

Lucie burst out laughing.

"Goodness gracious," she said. "It's safe to say you guessed right, Monsieur Michaud. You've made him happy as a lark!"

"Parfait, Lucie, call me Parfait! I've begged you a thousand times!"

"Parfait! You're perfect, all right!" said Fernand with a mouthful of canapé. And he clapped Michaud so forcefully on the back that the notary's glasses jumped.

Blonblon was still running his hands over the bronze dog. "My dad would love to see this," he said quietly. "He's very interested in Japan."

The Michauds had placed a long table against one wall, and on it was a buffet such as Charles had never seen. Going over for his third helping of veal galantine, he noticed the tip of Boff's tail sticking out from under the white tablecloth. He bent over, thinking that the dog had found some food somewhere and was hiding under the table to eat it. But he was wrong. Boff was asleep, his muzzle between his paws, worn out by the sound of their conversations – two bottles of wine had been drunk, and many bottles of beer. Charles pulled the dog towards him, held his head between his hands, and stared into his eyes.

"Did you hear that, Boff? Loyalty is important. It's one of the most important things in the world. Don't forget that!"

Céline, curled up in a soft chair with a plate of sandwiches on her knee, watched Charles with a strange gravity and without moving a muscle.

At about nine-thirty, Lucie said she was tired and began talking about going home. The little group began to break up, to the great relief of Amélie, who was feeling a headache coming on, and was aware that her husband had had a lot to drink. Instead of going home, however, Charles went with Blonblon to Frontenac Towers, to show Hachiko to Blonblon's father.

■ ■ ■

Half an hour later, Charles was walking slowly along rue Ontario, the box weighing heavily in his arms. A dozen paces from the corner of rue Dufresne he suddenly stopped dead, overwhelmed by a sense of danger.

Ahead of him, under the yellowish glare of the street lights that hung their resigned heads above the deserted street, everything had suddenly taken on a curiously sinister aspect. Yet it was the same street as usual, with its oil stains, its cracked and wrinkled asphalt like a snake's sloughed skin, its dirty sidewalks, its barred shop windows filled with glaring light that showed how badly in need of a good dusting some of them were. He continued on his way towards rue Dufresne, trying to figure out what had happened, when he recalled the glimpse of a figure half seen out of the corner of his eye when he'd yawned, a shadow slipping behind the corner of a house. He stopped, intending to retrace his steps, but he was too late: Wilfrid Thibodeau stepped out in front of him, looking at him with feverish intensity as he rubbed nervously at the three-day beard on his chin.

"Hey there, kid. How's it goin'? Son of a gun, you're even bigger than the last time I saw you! You'll be taller'n me pretty soon, eh?"

Charles stared at him with his mouth half open, parched as a desert, in such anxiety that everything around him seemed suddenly to have started shaking. For a full second he thought of running, but it would have meant dropping Hachiko, and he didn't even have the strength to do that.

"So, what's new? You gonna speak to me or what?"

"Hello, Papa," he finally managed to get out.

"*Papa?*" The carpenter laughed. "You're still calling me that? I thought you had a different papa these days."

Charles went on staring at his father. Despite his fear, he couldn't help noticing that a profound change had come over the man. Stooped shoulders, wizened body; he seemed to be going through a rough patch, at least in terms of his physical health. Even his clothing gave him away: the frayed collar of his shirt, his jeans worn so thin Charles could see the skin of one knee through the cloth. And his breath, warm and heavy, smelled of alcohol and rotten teeth.

"It's your birthday today, ain't it? What are you, fourteen?"

"Yes . . . Papa."

"Well. Happy birthday!"

He offered Charles his hand, then brought it up to rub his chin, as though uncertain of what to say next. His eye fell on the box Charles was carrying.

"What you got in there?" he asked brusquely.

"A present."

"You gonna show it to me?"

Charles lifted it out of its wrapping paper.

"Statue of a dog! Jeez, you still got dogs on the brain, eh?" Then, without a transition, he continued, "I been waiting here half the night. I wanted to see you, since it's your birthday. I'm not as heartless as everyone seems to think I am," he sniggered. "I knocked on the door at nine, but no one answered. So then I says to myself I'll get a pizza at the corner restaurant – Roberto's sold out, eh? – and who do I see go by the front window but Fernand and his wife and two kids, a real procession, like the Three Wise Men, eh, bearing their gifts. Were they all for you? I saw them go up to their house and I thought you'd be comin' along pretty soon. But you took your goddamn sweet time about it . . ."

"What did you want to say to me?" Charles asked, trying to keep the meanness from his voice. And almost succeeding.

"Hey, you little shit, don't talk to me in that tone of voice. I'm not your father any more, but . . . well, I am, in a way, you know, like it or not. That's how nature works . . . at least that's how I see it . . ."

He took a deep breath and closed his eyes, and Charles watched all the air seep out of him. Now would be a good time to run, he thought, but he stayed where he was, anchored in place by a vague feeling of pity.

"Anyway, all I wanted was to say happy birthday, kid," the carpenter went on, as though suddenly remembering his son's question. "No harm in that, is there?"

He started laughing through his teeth, all the time eyeing the boy in an agitated way. Charles couldn't decipher the look, but he didn't like it. It was the look of a drunk, or of someone on drugs. As he knew from experience, anything could come of it, at any moment.

46

"Course, you're a man now, ain't you, a good looker, too. You gettin' it on with the girls yet? Okay, I went too far. Sorry, none of my beeswax. No, stay here," he snapped when Charles seemed to be on the point of turning away. He put a heavy hand on the boy's shoulder. "I . . . I got somethin' for you. Nothing much . . ." With his other hand he reached into one of his pockets and, with much effort, took out a cracked leather wallet that had come partly unstitched. "Here," he said, flipping the wallet open and handing Charles a worn five-dollar bill. "Take it. I'd give you more but that's all I got left. Don't spend it all in one place, as me old mom used to say. So, goodbye and good luck."

He gave Charles a wink that twisted his face into a grimace and took off down the street, looking down at his feet, dragging his heels and swinging his arms heavily.

"Thanks, Papa," Charles said after a moment's hesitation.

Thibodeau continued walking away without turning around. Maybe he hadn't heard. With the five-dollar bill crumpled in the palm of his hand, Charles watched him go. Suddenly his shoulders shook and he began to cry, but whether from rage or relief or pity he couldn't say. Perhaps it was from the unbearable feeling of helplessness that comes over us in cases of irreparable loss.

┌─────┐
│ 4 │
└─────┘

Fernand's Oldsmobile gave up the ghost on February the 10th, 1981, after eight years of faithful service. Buying a new car was out of the question, and so as soon as he arrived at the hardware store he began looking through the want ads for used cars. This occasioned a great deal of huffing and puffing.

That same day two events opposite in nature took place in Charles's life. Robert-Aimé Doyon relieved him of his duties as editor of the Jean-Baptiste-Meilleur newspaper because of a disrespectful remark that had appeared in it concerning the statue of the Sacred Heart; and the Lalancette Pharmacy hired him as a delivery boy at a salary of two dollars an hour.

His job at the drugstore came about as the result of a series of curious circumstances involving french fries.

Fire Station Number 19, at the corner of Fullum and Coupal, counted among its brave crew members a certain Romeo Pimparé, whom heaven had blessed with exceptional skill in the culinary arts. Give him an old turnip and a couple of wilted carrots, a bit of oil or butter, and some seasonings, and he would create a soup au gratin the aroma of which would draw half the station into the kitchen. But it was from french fries that he derived his greatest successes. His captain told anyone who would listen that he would gladly walk through three walls of flame for half a plateful of Pimparé's french fries. Crispy on the outside, mushy on the inside, fried to a golden hue but never greasy, salted to perfection, they melted in the mouth and made anyone who tasted them swear that Romeo's fries were the only food they would ever eat. Every Wednesday evening for eight years Romeo had been preparing his fries for his fellow firefighters, who devoured them with hamburgers or pineapple ham, or sometimes with chicken stuffed with apples and cubes of bread.

This particular Wednesday, at about seven-thirty in the evening, Pimparé was keeping a sharp eye on his deep-fryer, in which the peanut oil (*de rigueur* for fries) was just beginning to come to a boil. Suddenly the alarm bell began to ring wildly throughout the station, summoning the firemen to the trucks. A major fire had broken out in the rear of the Woolworth's store on rue Ontario and was threatening to spread to the neighbouring buildings, and it was essential that Station Number 19 arrive on the scene before Station Number 5, which for some time had been in fierce competition with Number 19 – ever since a certain report in the Montreal *Journal* had appeared after a fire in the basement of the Church of the Immaculate Conception on bingo night.

Within thirty seconds, Romeo Pimparé was booted, helmeted, wearing his asbestos gloves, and hanging off the side of the truck as it took a hard left in the glacial air of the winter night. Two minutes, twenty seconds later they arrived at the scene of the fire. Pimparé was busy attaching a hose to a fire hydrant when Captain Flibotte ran up to him through the suffocating smoke and yelled to him furiously.

"Never mind that! Hurry! We have to go back to the station! A fire's broken out in the kitchen, you bloody idiot!"

In his hurry to leave, the fireman had forgotten to turn off the gas burner under the deep-fryer, and flames were shooting joyously up through the window, as though in revenge for all the jets of water the firemen had inflicted on them over the years.

Is there anything more comical or tragic than a fire in a fire station? The news spread throughout the neighbourhood as though whispered from ear to ear by the Holy Spirit Himself, and there was a jeering crowd waiting for them in front of the building when they returned.

Monsieur Victoire had seen the clouds of smoke as he was on his way home and run across the street to tell the Fafards. Charles and Henri were home alone that night, and they decided to go with Monsieur Victoire to take in the show.

By the time they arrived on the scene the firemen almost had the fire under control, but it had caused a great deal of damage, not so much to the building as to the pride and reputation of the men in charge of it. Charles and Henri elbowed their way through the crowd until they were at the barrier the firemen had put up to keep the curious at bay, but even so a spark flew over and caught Charles on his left eyelid. He cried out sharply and rubbed his eye, but quickly forgot about the pain as he watched the embarrassed firemen, red with anger and chagrin. He laughed at the cruel jokes being shouted out around him, and even shouted out a few of his own, at which those around him laughed as well.

By eight o'clock there was nothing much left to see, and since their toes were nearly numb the boys decided to go home. They'd lost sight of Monsieur Victoire long ago; shortly after their arrival he'd gone off to chat up a pretty South American woman muffled up in a white, hooded coat.

They took a detour down rue Ontario. From time to time Charles raised his hand to his eye, since it had started hurting again. He wondered if he shouldn't go to the hospital. Henri took a look at it and said it looked serious, and he told Charles he should do something about it. They were just coming up to a pharmacy; the windows were lit up and it seemed to be still open. They went in and were welcomed by a smiling woman in her fifties with black hair tied up in a ponytail. The woman looked them over carefully. The store was otherwise deserted, except for a balding man with grey hair and a pair of glasses balanced at the end of his nose, who was scribbling something behind a counter.

Charles went up to him and, in his politest voice, asked for something to put on the burn on his eyelid. The man looked up and stared at him. For several seconds his deeply lined face remained entirely expressionless; it seemed to be reflecting an inner emptiness, which, admittedly, might have been a reflection of the lack of customers in the store.

"How did you do that?" he asked at length.

"I was watching the fire at the fire station a few blocks from here, and a spark flew at me."

The pharmacist continued looking at him blankly; he looked over at Henri, then back at Charles, then gave a long sigh. Was it because he was tired? Charles wondered. Or bored? Or had Charles, with his incautious curiosity, just provided him with yet another example of human stupidity?

Finally the man recommended an ointment. Charles took out his wallet, asked a few questions about how to apply it, paid the bill, and turned to leave.

"One minute," said the pharmacist. "What's your name?"

Charles, though surprised by the question, told him.

"Do you live far from here?"

"Just at the corner of Dufresne and Ontario."

"Hmm. Not far, then. . . . Are you working somewhere in your spare time?"

Charles shook his head and assumed the attentive, focused look that had so often gained him generous tips in his career as a delivery boy.

"It's just that I'm looking for someone to do deliveries on Thursday, Friday, and Saturday nights. Does that kind of work appeal to you? You look like a good worker."

The man gave a very faint smile, which still was like a firework going off in the face of a totem pole.

"Yes, of course, I'm very interested, sir," Charles replied, under the envious gaze of Henri. "When would you like me to begin?"

"Tomorrow, if that suits you. Get yourself here around five-thirty. I'll pay you two dollars an hour."

And so Charles became an employee of Henri Lalancette, pharmacist, a 1953 graduate from the University of Montreal, married, father of three (now grown and moved away), a taciturn man not normally given to fantastical notions, but dependable, a hard worker, and, all in all, an agreeable person to work for when accepted exactly as he was.

Beneath his hibernating-bear exterior, Lalancette had three hidden passions. The first was his daughter, Claire, whom by dint of patience and

51

kindness he had succeeded in rescuing from drug addiction when she was sixteen. She was now married and worked in a downtown travel agency; every Thursday evening he had dinner with her in a restaurant.

His second passion was diseases of the prostate gland, an interest he had had for many years. He and a former medical student, who now worked in the laboratory of a pharmaceutical company, had been conducting "experiments" on the beneficial effects of the dregs of port wine on such diseases, beneficial effects that he himself had experienced.

And thirdly, he was an inveterate collector of paintings, some of them of dubious quality, hinting perhaps too strongly of the bargain bin. His most precious acquisition was entitled "View from the *Montréal-Matin* Building, Nightfall, Winter's Day," painted in 1953 by John Little, which he had bought from a retired journalist. It reigned on the living-room wall above the settee, along with a few other works of lesser interest, and no one but he and he alone was allowed to so much as dust its frame.

The pharmacist congratulated himself on having hired Charles. He found the boy friendly, resourceful, and conscientious; after two weeks he raised Charles's salary to two dollars and twenty-five cents, to show how satisfied he was with his work. For his part, Charles quickly learned that, despite Monsieur Lalancette's dour expression, he was an interesting man with a sensitive heart, a man who could easily be taken advantage of (as his associate in prostate research knew very well). Claire came into the pharmacy one evening and talked for a while with Charles. She, too, found him charming, and said so to her father. Two days later, after closing time, Charles was favoured with a thirty-three-minute lecture on the dregs of port wine; the pharmacist expressed his regret that Charles was still an adolescent and therefore probably had a properly functioning prostate, otherwise he would be able to join his small group of guinea pigs. The following week he invited Charles to his home, to admire his collection of paintings.

Madame Lalancette, a small, portly, somewhat snobbish woman, was cool towards Charles at first, but was soon won over by his smile and good manners. She offered him a glass of milk and a piece of raspberry pie, cutting a large slice for herself as well, which she ate while telling him about the week-long vacation she and her husband had taken in Cuba at the beginning of the winter.

Within a month Charles was nicely settled into his new job. True, the atmosphere in the pharmacy was infinitely less entertaining than Chez Robert's restaurant had been. But the work would nonetheless draw him into a terrible experience.

■ ■ ■

Céline was busting out all over. Two impish bulges had appeared under her blouse that very morning, and far from being shy about them she paraded about the house as though to show them off. She kept her eyes lowered demurely, but there was a smile of satisfaction on her lips. Could they have appeared overnight? Hard to believe. And yet one day it had been difficult to see her as anything but a young girl, and all of a sudden she'd been mysteriously transformed into a young woman, easily overtaking both Charles and Henri on the road to maturity.

The stir she created that morning almost made Charles forget it was the last day of school and they were leaving Jean-Baptiste-Meilleur School – and its tyrannical principal – forever. At the breakfast table the boys teased Céline mercilessly (Charles asked her why she had two little puppies playing under her blouse). Their jokes, however, made not a dent in her good humour. She ate her cereal without saying a word, looking up occasionally to give them an indifferent glare, as though to say: "Puppies, are they? Well, they're pretty good-looking puppies! And what do they look like now?"

That night, as he slid beneath the covers, Charles realized that a new object of desire had entered his thoughts to join the Black Goddess with the bouncing aluminum blouse, and was even threatening to edge the latter off the stage of his fantasies altogether. He worked especially feverishly that night to bring himself the relief he needed in order to go to sleep.

Charles was ending his second year of junior high school relatively successfully, having come first in French, English, and History. But he came seventeenth in Math. Henri, who was not a particularly good student, did better than Charles in that subject, and aced Phys. Ed. and, oddly enough, Visual Art.

The summer began with a dismal week, filled with rain and cold wind. Charles lingered in bed in the mornings, reading an old, yellowed copy of the tales of Edgar Allan Poe, translated into French by Charles Baudelaire; at ten he got up and went to the pharmacy – Henri Lalancette had taken him on five days a week for the duration of the holidays. The health of Charles's credit union account began to improve rapidly. After each deposit he checked his bankbook with a satisfaction that was not unmixed with anxiety. Business at the hardware store was still plummeting. If Fernand hadn't owned the building and hadn't been receiving rent from the other four tenants, he would almost certainly have had to close the store. He came home some evenings looking so woebegone that Charles couldn't help thinking of the sacrifice he had made in order to keep his adopted son in the family. In fact it was still costing him, since Thibodeau had stopped sending money for Charles's support.

Charles had seen his father on the street two or three times, each time looking scrawnier and more hunched over. Whenever Thibodeau spotted Charles he would skulk off, as though afraid of having anything more to do with him, and Charles felt the old, familiar rage rising inside. One night he dreamed he'd cornered his father in a quarry, with two huge blocks of granite preventing him from escaping. Leaning over the edge of the quarry, Charles began pelting his father with stones. His father moaned and begged, but far from moving him to pity, his pleas merely served to increase Charles's hatred, and more stones flew through the air with a murderous, whistling sound (for some reason, he kept his eyes fixed on the ground, as though unable to stand the sight of his father). Suddenly, Wilfrid shouted in a deafening voice: "Okay! Take your money and for Chrissakes leave me alone!" The air around Charles immediately filled with a thick cloud of banknotes. He woke up suffocating, and sat up in bed with hot tears rolling down his cheeks.

On July 7th another bomb went off. Charles was on his way home for supper – it was just after six o'clock – and when he turned onto rue Dufresne he saw Henri leaning against the fence as though waiting for someone. As soon as he saw Charles he ran towards him in an obvious state of high excitement.

"Hey, you want to hear something cool? Blonblon's got himself a girl-friend!"

Henri had seen Blonblon an hour before in Médéric-Martin Park, walking hand in hand with a thin-legged girl he didn't recognize but who must have lived in Frontenac Towers.

Suddenly Charles understood why Blonblon had been acting so strangely lately, not answering any of his phone calls, walking around with that irritating air of mystery he affected on the rare occasions he came out to spend an hour or two with his friends. But why be so secretive about it? Was he doing something he was ashamed of? Or did he think Charles and Henri were too stupid to be taken into his confidence?

Charles, feeling hurt, called Blonblon's number as soon as he finished eating. The phone was answered by Madame Blondin.

"Michel?" she said. "He just left. He must be meeting Caroline some-where. We don't see much of him these days, I'm afraid, Charles. He hardly shows up for meals. He jumps out of bed in the morning, throws on some clothes, and he's gone! I'll tell him you called."

"What's the matter?" Fernand asked, taking a toothpick from his mouth. A shred of meat fell onto his trousers and he flicked it off with a finger.

"Bad news?" asked Lucie.

"No, no," Charles replied, laughing, "nothing like that. Don't worry, it's nothing."

But he looked worried as he walked to his room. He was surprised at the feeling of abandonment that Blonblon's defection had caused him. Was that what friends did, dropped you just like that without a word of warning? Stretched out on his bed, a book in his hand, but with no desire to read, he stared up at the ceiling and let his mind drift. A second question popped into his head, so new and unforeseen that he had no idea how to answer it. How did someone go about finding a girlfriend?

■ ■ ■

Boff was gripped by a violent hatred for the dog Hachiko. Of course he knew it wasn't a real dog. It didn't move a muscle all day, just sat in its corner of the bedroom, as cold and inert as the bed and the dresser. But every time Boff went into the room and saw it, sitting so arrogantly with its muzzle in the air, its huge forepaws looking as solid as two chunks of wood, its bronze fur shining in the light from the sun or the overhead fixture, a repressed rage began to bubble up in his chest; he would give a long, low growl, walk slowly up to it and bare his teeth at it, give it a few disdainful sniffs, then trot off more furious than ever, disgusted by the faint odour of metal that mingled with the scent of his beloved Charles.

And that was what he found the hardest to bear, those caresses his master bestowed each day on that stupid dog, the sweet words he whispered into its metallic ears. As though the thing were able to hear them! All it did was make him, Boff, feel as though it were he who was the lifeless toy.

One afternoon when Charles was out God-knew-where, without going to the trouble of taking him with him, as usual, Boff went into Charles's room, jumped up on the bed, and lay there staring at the dog. Every now and then he would shake his head and sneeze. Hachiko had declared war, and Boff had to put him in his proper place. He jumped off the bed, went over to the door to make sure no one was watching, and cocked an ear for any sounds coming from the house. All he heard was Lucie humming to herself as she stirred something in a saucepan in the kitchen.

He went over to Hachiko and seized the dog's snout between his teeth. It was hard as rock! He'd never battled anything as tough as this before! After ten minutes of chewing, his teeth were hurting so much he had to stop, and yet there were only a few barely visible scratches on the statue. The damned thing was laughing at him! His eyes narrowed to slits that shot out needles of fire. His nose wrinkled fiercely; his nostrils became two deep, pink-lined pits; his mouth took on a terrifying aspect, the bared gums seeming to show twice the normal number of teeth; he gave a low, deep growl that would have frightened Charles himself and went back to work on the dog with demented fury. After several minutes there was a loud crack followed by a metallic tinkling; Boff had defeated his enemy, but in the process had broken a tooth, and a piece of it had fallen into the base of the statue. He sat back to admire his handiwork; there were drops of blood on the floor and even on Hachiko's muzzle, which now had a hole in it about the size of a dime a few centimetres up from its nostrils. The hole gaped like a kind of evil eye, making the statue look strange and sinister. Boff carefully licked the blood off the floor, gave a triumphant howl, then went into the kitchen to ask to be let outside. He had a sudden impulse to hide. He knew he was in trouble, maybe trouble such as he had never known, and he wanted to put it off for as long as possible. When it came, though, he would accept it. Trouble was the price he was willing to pay for victory, a victory he'd been lusting after for weeks.

"What have you been up to, eh?" Lucie said, looking at him suspiciously. "What have you done to your mouth?"

She bent over and looked at his teeth.

"Would you like to tell me what you've been chewing on, you little devil? Your mouth is full of blood! And you've broken a tooth! Come on, show me, show me what you've done. Bad boy!"

Resigned to his fate, Boff led Lucie back to Charles's room. Lucie looked around but didn't see anything amiss. She checked the furniture in the rest of the house and, still finding nothing, let Boff go outside.

It was Charles who discovered the disaster at suppertime. There was no doubt who the perpetrator had been. Furious, he went outside to look for Boff, but the dog was nowhere to be found. He would have to go back to work at the pharmacy without giving Boff the punishment he deserved.

"Poor little Hachiko," he murmured, devastated. "How am I going to fix you up? And why did he do this to you, the bloody idiot? If Monsieur Michaud sees you like this he'll never give me another present!"

He made a few deliveries. An old woman on rue Wurtele, who hobbled to the door on legs that looked like two hams stuffed into a pair of brown sausage casings, gave him a fifty-cent tip, but he was so wrapped up in dark thoughts that he barely thanked her. At eight o'clock things began to wind down at the pharmacy and, swallowing his pride, he decided to phone Blonblon. He was the only one he could think of who could save Hachiko. For once, Blonblon was home. He kindly agreed to have a look at the bronze dog that very night, and the two boys arranged to meet at nine by the Frontenac station.

Two or three times as they were walking to his house, Charles came close to asking his friend how he had met Caroline, but since the young swain hadn't brought up the subject and hence offered no opening into which to insert such a question, he thought it best to keep his curiosity to himself.

"Hmm," said Blonblon after taking a long look at Hachiko. "He really mangled this thing. I wonder what got into him?"

"Who knows. The bugger hasn't shown his face around here since. He knows what he'll get when he does."

Blonblon continued his examination, then declared in a serious, thoughtful tone that he believed it would be possible to repair the statue with automobile body putty and a lick of paint, but that he couldn't do it without a photograph of the original. Maybe Monsieur Michaud would have one.

"I'll go ask him right away," Charles said.

Parfait Michaud was a great reader and an assiduous music- and film-lover, and always stayed up late, so there was no risk of bothering him by turning up on his doorstep at nine-thirty at night.

Charles hurried over to the notary's house while Blonblon and Céline went into the Fafards' backyard to look for Boff, whose absence was beginning to worry them.

Amélie opened the door wearing a turquoise kimono with pink tassels and a scarf that gave off a strong scent of camphor oil and lemon.

"He's out visiting a friend," she said, strangely reserved. "I don't know when he'll be back."

She put a hand to her head, heaved a deep sigh, and shut the door. Disconcerted, Charles stood on the porch for several seconds wondering if he had been wrong about coming over so late, then slowly made his way back home. The evening was ending the way it had begun – detestably.

At the corner of Gascon Avenue he automatically looked up at Médéric-Martin Park and thought he saw Boff in the distance, lying beside a chain-link fence. Could it be that his fear of being punished had made him run away from home? Ordinarily he never came this far from the neighbourhood. Charles called to him a few times, then, since the dog didn't move, he ran towards him. He hadn't gone twenty steps before the animal jumped up and ran to the other end of the park.

Charles ran after him. "Boff! Boff!" he called. "Come back here! I'm not going to hurt you!"

He was no longer certain that the dog was Boff. After a few minutes he stopped, out of breath. The dog had disappeared somewhere up rue de Rouen, which hummed faintly across from where he stood. Resuming the chase, he hurried to the street, arriving in time to see the dog, nose to the ground, disappear between two houses about fifty metres down. Charles called a few times without success, then recrossed the street, certain now that he had been mistaken. Boff would never have wandered this far away. He would have come home by now, penitent and excited, ready to take his punishment and trying to regain Charles's favour with pathetic little whimpers.

Charles continued along Gascon, which ran beside the park towards rue de Rouen. Across the street, a man and a woman came out of a house and began walking in his direction. He stopped, taken aback. He recognized the man as Monsieur Michaud. The tall, stooped body, that way of stepping as though afraid of crushing something or of getting his feet wet, could only belong to his friend and mentor the notary. He didn't know who the woman was. The couple were talking in a friendly, animated way, the way people do after two or three glasses of wine, and they had not yet seen him. Charles had the feeling that the notary would not be pleased to run into him at this moment, and, seeing a hedge to his right, he quickly hid behind it. And not a minute too soon, because the notary and his companion decided at that moment to cross the street and were headed straight for him. He studied the woman from his hiding place; she seemed much younger than Monsieur Michaud, pretty enough, but with a kind of sugary sweetness and a way of holding her elbows to her sides and swaying her hips that reminded Charles of an actress in a French comedy. She leaned into her companion and whispered something in his ear.

"Wonderful! Wonderful!" cried Michaud, giving a great laugh (Charles had never heard him laugh like that). "You always have such wonderful ideas, you know, my sexy little temptress!"

And, putting his arm around her waist, he planted a kiss on her cheek.

Charles waited until the two were gone, then slowly walked to his house, thinking furiously. Céline came up to him looking worried. Boff had not returned. Blonblon had gone home.

"I don't want to scare you, son," said Fernand, coming out of the living room with a newspaper in his hand (Trudeau and Chrétien smiling, looking down), "but it's possible someone has taken him."

"No, Papa, Boff is too smart for that!" said Henri, coming up behind his father. But even he didn't look convinced.

Charles put his hands on his hips. "I'll bet my bottom dollar he's out there hiding under the shed."

He went out into the yard and called. Several minutes went by, but no dog appeared.

"Boff!" he called, now becoming as alarmed as the others. "Come out from hiding, Boff! There's a good boy! I know you're out there. . . . I won't punish you . . . not much, anyway!"

He looked around the yard, then with a deep sigh bent down and put his head under the shed. No doubt about it, this had been a rotten day. And his encounter with the notary certainly hadn't improved it. He felt as though he'd been deceived, and it left a bad taste in his mouth. But at the same time, Monsieur Michaud's arch, somewhat humorous mannerisms, which Charles had known for many years and had grown quite fond of, now took on a mysterious importance. And that only troubled him more.

■ ■ ■

Boff was not seen again until ten o'clock the next morning. It must have been hunger that brought him home, unless it was the need to expiate his guilt. Charles and Henri were out taping notices to the telephone poles in the neighbourhood, giving Boff's description and their telephone number.

When Charles came home and saw him stretched out on his bed looking contrite, it was all he could do to stop himself from running to him with a cry of joy. But with a serious, theatrical gesture he seized the statue of Hachiko and waved it under the dog's nose.

"Boff, what's this? Why did you do this, eh? Don't you know what this statue means to me? I love Hachiko. And now I don't know if it can even be repaired!"

He then took Boff's muzzle in his hand, but all he did was give it a rough shaking. Céline, who was watching from the doorway, sympathized with Charles's leniency and showed it by coming over and rubbing his back, which sent a shiver all the way down to his heels.

That evening Blonblon showed up with a box of auto putty and a can of spray paint. He spent a long time repairing the statue, because the hole required a great deal of filling that was difficult to mask. A photo would have been useful, he said. Charles pretended that the notary hadn't had one. But after a while Hachiko looked as good as new, almost. Charles was happy with the result, and this time he put the statue on top of his dresser where he knew Boff couldn't get at it. Then the two friends went off to tour the neighbourhood on their bicycles.

The streets had been baking all day, and even though the sun had set an hour earlier, the walls, sidewalks, and pavement still radiated a stifling heat. Blonblon said he was thirsty and suggested stopping somewhere for a soft drink. They had turned their backs on the Blue Bird, feeling it was their duty to boycott the place, and so they headed to Villa Frontenac, a restaurant across from the metro station that had been famous for almost thirty years for serving the best smoked-meat sandwiches in Montreal East.

"My treat," Charles said, feeling glad to be with Blonblon again.

After their sandwiches and fries, Charles suggested a bowl of ice cream for dessert, and, after a brief moment of polite reticence, Blonblon accepted.

For a while the two boys ate in silence, absorbed in the pleasures of their dessert. From time to time Blonblon looked up and smiled at Charles, who gave a little smile of contentment in reply. But it was not unadulterated; Charles was feeling bad for having lied to Blonblon about Monsieur Michaud. Last night's unexpected meeting with the notary still haunted him, and he felt the urge to confide in someone. Who better to lend an ear than Blonblon?

After using his spoon to carefully scrape the last fragments of nuts and almonds from the far reaches of his bowl, then taking a long drink of his 7-Up, he let out a deep sigh and looked his friend in the eye.

"Blonblon," he said, "there's something I need to tell you. I didn't go to Monsieur Michaud's last night."

Blonblon gave him a surprised smile.

"I mean, I went there, but he wasn't home. But I did see him a short time later, in the street."

He gave Blonblon the details of his encounter.

"So what do you think, Blonblon? It makes me sick to think about it," he went on without waiting for an answer. "Cheating on his wife when she's home in bed with a migraine. That sucks, doesn't it? I never thought he was like that. He's done a lot for me, Blonblon – without him, who knows where I'd be right now? – and he has a lot of fine qualities, I know that as well as anyone. But to see him with his arms around that little . . . tart, I mean, jeez, what I mean is . . . I . . ."

He stopped talking, tears welling up in his eyes.

Blonblon chewed his lip thoughtfully, then he, too, scraped the bottom of his bowl with his spoon.

A man sitting in a booth across from them was listening in on their conversation. He was bald and thick-lipped and had a scar on his left cheek that would have suited a pirate in a B movie; he listened with a strange smile, and every so often he rubbed the tip of his nose.

"Well, Thibodeau," Blonblon said with a seriousness Charles hadn't seen in him before, "here's what I think..."

He pushed his bowl away and took a drink of his root beer, in which the bubbles had started to slow in their ascent to the surface.

"...I think that love is the strongest force in the universe. No, listen to me! I know what I'm talking about. That girl might have seemed like a tart to you, but Monsieur Michaud is Monsieur Michaud and you are you. When love hits you between the eyes, my friend, watch out, there's nothing you can do about it. You don't think. Common sense just flies out the window, believe me. I wouldn't have been saying this a month ago, but now I can. Did you know that I have a girlfriend, Charles?"

"Everybody knows."

"Henri saw us together, is that it? I thought so."

"Your mother told me, too."

"Oh yeah? It doesn't matter, I'm not trying to hide anything. Her name is Caroline. Caroline Maltais. I'll introduce you one day soon."

And with a quiver in his voice, as though his life depended on each word he was saying, he launched into the story of his love life.

The affair had got off to a bad start. Caroline Maltais lived on the same floor as he did, but at the opposite end. He didn't run into her very often, and truth be told he hadn't paid much attention to her. Then one day, about a month and a half ago, he'd been waiting for the elevator on the ground floor when she came into the lobby with three of her friends; the small group huddled in a corner whispering and he had the strong impression that they were talking about him. Two or three times a phrase made it to his ears, along with a few stifled giggles: "Goldilocks." They could have been referring to his hair, which was blond and fairly curly, but Goldilocks was also the name of a girl in a fairy tale his parents used to read to him when he was young, and that really cut him to the quick: could they possibly think he was effeminate? Then the elevator door opened and he entered it without even bothering to turn around, determined to snub these little idiots the next time he saw them.

That same evening, as he was on his way out to get something for his father, he ran into Caroline in the hallway. She looked oddly at him and, as she passed by, turned her head away. He hadn't had the presence of mind to come up with a cutting remark. Two days later, however, he saw her again, this time on the sidewalk with her three friends. They were all giggling and punching each other on the shoulder, and again he heard the word "Goldilocks." But this time he was ready for them, and when he came abreast of them he turned to Caroline and said, "Hi, there, Stringbean!" He wanted to draw attention to her height, and to the skinniness of her legs, and to her long neck, which made her look like a giraffe reaching into a tree for a mouthful of leaves. Her eyes widened, as did those of her companions, and he went on his way feeling triumphant and revenged.

He didn't see her for a while after that and had almost forgotten the whole thing when he ran into her one night on his way into a convenience store. She was alone. She pretended not to notice him and passed by with her nose in the air. That week he saw her a few more times, and each time she acted as though he were transparent, or had shrunk to the size of a flea. The whole thing was getting on his nerves, although, given the circumstances, he could hardly have expected anything else.

Then one night, about eight o'clock, as he was coming out of Frontenac Towers on his way to the Fafards, he saw her coming towards him balancing a small parcel on the tip of her finger. She was wearing a blue dress and black shoes and she had a large, blue headband holding back her hair, which was chestnut brown. The sun was just on the point of passing behind a building, but first it showered her with a spray of copper rays that transformed her into an incandescent vision of exquisite grace and lightness. He stopped, dumbstruck, and had to force himself to resume walking. She continued straight towards him, falling back into shadow but, strangely, remaining as lovely as she had been in the light. As he passed her he nodded and smiled – and she smiled back!

From that moment on she was never out of his thoughts; watching TV, having a conversation, riding his bike, taking a shower, getting up or going to bed, during meals, her image floated through his head. He would wonder where she was at any given moment, what she was doing, whether she was thinking of him, and he felt tortured, but in a tender way, a way he had never felt before. It was a strange kind of melancholy. He couldn't shake the feeling off, and in any case he didn't want to. It was pain and pleasure mixed together. He'd never been so happy to be feeling so sad, joyfully embracing this huge sorrow that had come from God-knew-where to tear up his insides. He'd be gripped in feverish agitation for hours on end, then suddenly fall into a morbid torpor and lie stretched out on his bed or on the sofa, barely able to breathe. He knew it couldn't go on. He had to speak to her.

A few days later he was at the Quintal Arena on de Maisonneuve Boulevard, where he'd gone to have a swim with Steve Lachapelle. Caroline was there with a girl with a large chin, someone he hadn't seen before, who turned out to be a cousin or something. Anyway, when she saw him she gave a shy wave; he waved back and made a spectacular dive into the pool, which astonished Steve because usually it took a great deal of vigorous (and unsolicited) coaxing to get him into the water. Surfacing from his dive, he swam across the pool to where she was talking to her cousin and took part in their conversation. After a minute she joined him in the water and they began to swim lengths together. The cousin sat on the edge of the pool with her mouth open, paddling her feet in the water, and Steve Lachapelle worked on his breast stroke by himself, every now and then casting curious looks at Blonblon, obviously feeling like a fifth wheel. Things improved slightly when Blonblon brought Caroline over and introduced her and her wide-eyed cousin, Lina, to Steve.

An hour later they all left the pool together and went to a pizzeria. Showing more animation than Steve had seen in him before, Blonblon made Caroline laugh so hard she sometimes had to rest her head on his shoulder. Even Lina began to show signs of a fleeting intelligence. It was while Steve was trying to pull Lina from her lethargy that Blonblon summoned all his courage and, thin-lipped with worry, slid his hand under the table and placed it on top of Caroline's. She responded by taking his hand and squeezing it.

"From that moment on I was a goner," he said. "The next afternoon I kissed her in the elevator. Then we went for a short walk in Médéric-Martin Park, and after that . . ."

His voice trailed off. He was unable to describe the undescribable. He was an initiate rendered speechless by his initiation. He could only smile, his eyes drifting off, as he relived the first entrancing kisses and caresses, swept away again by an emotion that made his penis pulse almost painfully against the front of his jeans.

"Her tongue, man, her tongue . . . if you could just . . . and the way she runs her hands up and down my back . . . oh, man!"

Charles smiled, flattered at being taken into Blonblon's confidence, but was struck at the same time by the sharp blade of envy. His face fell. He had just realized that the friendship that had bound the two of them together would never be the same again. Blonblon moved off, waving his hand wildly and telling Charles he should find a girl of his own with whom to embark on this amorous voyage into the unknown.

Sure, thought Charles, find a girl. But who would this girl be? He hadn't the slightest idea.

An image of Céline flashed through his mind, but it was gone almost before he noticed it.

┌─────────┐
│   5   │
└─────────┘

U nbelievable that two schools so close to one another and filled with pretty much the same students could nonetheless be so different. That, at least, was what Charles was thinking as he walked home from Pierre-Dupuy High School on a rainy afternoon in September 1981.

The difference had hit him the minute he'd stepped inside the school. First there were the hordes of students swarming everywhere, moving in waves, filling the stairwells with a dull roar. He'd never seen anything like it! "There must be fifteen hundred of us," he told himself. Jean-Baptiste-Meilleur hadn't had half that many. And he'd been one of the older kids in his former school, whereas here he felt about as small as a germ. And all those girls, laughing, chattering, swinging their hips, allowing themselves to be hugged or pushing someone away with an elbow or a knee, their eyes flashing angrily and their mouths twisting. . . . It was all heady stuff for a guy who had gone to a boys-only school for the past eight years! And the whiff of cigarette smoke floating through the air. Just inside the main entrance was a kind of café covered by a green canopy and separated from the corridor by a white picket fence. Students smoked freely, sitting at the tables, perched on chairs, even in the stairwells and the corridors. Teachers even had the right to smoke in class! At Jean-Baptiste-Meilleur, if anyone had lit a cigarette within the school walls there would have been an earthquake; the guilty student would have got five hours of detention.

But all that was nothing compared to what took place in class.

That morning, he'd heard Pierre Blanchard say to Réal Dionne, their math teacher: "Jesus H. Christ, you filthy son of a bitch!"

Exasperated by Blanchard's behaviour, Dionne had then made a remark that sent a ripple of laughter through the class. The teacher didn't take the insult too seriously, because he could see that Blanchard was not in great shape. The word in the school was that his father was a hard case who had his own way of getting his children out of bed in the mornings. At any rate, Blanchard went up to Dionne after class and the two of them talked in low voices for a long time before parting on friendly terms.

Charles would never have admitted the fact publicly, but he had a lot of respect for his teachers. They had to have nerves of steel to teach at Pierre-Dupuy! Half of each class was taken up trying to impose some kind of order. Rarely was there quiet for more than twenty seconds at a time. The students talked freely among themselves, dropped things on the floor, shuffled their feet, rearranged their chairs and desks, got up and walked around and even left the classroom without permission, asked the same questions over and over (because they rarely listened to the answers), threw wads of paper at each other, read books, or napped with their heads on their desks. They didn't behave that way out of spite; they simply couldn't help themselves. They were like young animals incapable of harnessing their energy.

The previous day Jocelyne Ouellette had, as usual, paraded in front of everyone just before class, showing off her breasts that filled her black cotton sweater, until the teacher had told her to sit down at her desk. As she'd passed Charles she'd brushed his cheek with the back of her hand. He got the message. It was an invitation (the second in three days) to "get it on," like the others. He'd been too standoffish. The girls had figured out that he was still a virgin. They seemed to have a nose for that sort of thing, despite his best efforts to make them think otherwise. Their sometimes ironic attitude and certain innuendos indicated that they saw through his pretence. If he didn't do something about the problem in the next few weeks, they would write him off as a hopeless twerp.

If only his Black Goddess were still there, the one he'd spent the summer dreaming of. He would have drummed up the courage to have a go at her, despite the difference in their ages! He might not even have had to work too hard at it; she might have simply gone to bed with him out of kindness, to make a man out of him. But she'd been out of school for some time. What was she doing now? he wondered. Working as a packer at Rose & Laflamme? A spinner at Grover's? A go-go dancer in a downtown disco?

Steve Lachapelle swore he'd seen her coming out of the Macdonald's Tobacco factory with a man much older than she was – may he rot in hell, the old pervert!

Since Blonblon had little time for anything but his affair with Caroline, Charles had begun hanging out with Steve Lachapelle, who was as scatter-brained as ever but still fun to be around. He convinced Charles to take up pool, which he said was "a real trip, man," as much for the game itself as for the kinds of places where it was played. Since school began, Charles had been working at the Lalancette Pharmacy only on Saturdays, and so he and Steve took to going to the Orleans Billiards Hall on rue Ontario. To get there they had to go through a tunnel under a railroad overpass, a dark, filthy place that stank of urine; its vaulted ceiling and massive concrete pillars looked vaguely Egyptian and gave the place an aura of defeat; it gave Charles the creeps, but since he didn't want Steve to think he was chicken he pretended it was the coolest place in the world. Every time they went through it they clowned around and sang dirty songs at the top of their voices while cars and trucks whizzed past their noses.

The Orleans Billiards Hall was, by comparison, like heaven itself. It was on the second floor of a huge, faceless building, above a supermarket. They had to climb a wide staircase with three right turns, as clean and shiny as a bank counter; the experience awakened a host of lively emotions in Charles. The pool hall pleased him very much the minute he entered it: huge and dark, the room contained some twenty pool tables with long lights suspended above them, only some of which were burning. Around these the players moved slowly, almost athletically, totally absorbed in their games. On the left was a long bar behind which worked a very pretty girl wearing blue jeans and a tight-fitting blouse that stopped just above her navel. She made quite an impression on Charles. Behind the cash sat a heavy-set man in his fifties, with thick salt-and-pepper hair and the look of someone who had seen everything twice. He kept writing down numbers in a book and looking up occasionally to have a word with two customers perched on stools at the bar, sipping their beers. Three more were sitting at a table farther back, playing cards.

The mysterious clicking of balls, the bright-green rectangles glowing in the darkened room, even the dimensions of the hall, in which all sounds and voices seemed to dissolve into a vast, shimmering emptiness, gave Charles the impression of intrigue and adventure, and the heady feeling that he had entered into the world of adults.

He turned to Steve and smiled, and Steve gave a grunt of satisfaction.

"Not bad, eh? But you ain't seen nothing yet. Follow me."

He walked quickly and confidently up to the cash and asked for a table.

"Number eight," the man said after looking him over for a second. "Be careful of the cloth, okay?" he added suspiciously.

Lachapelle frowned at him.

"You've never had a problem with me. I've been coming here nearly three months now. He's new," he added, nodding towards Charles, "but I'll show him the ropes, don't worry."

"Just watch the cloth," the man said again, going back to his notebook.

"He's always like that," Steve grumbled as they walked over to their table. "Nadine's a lot nicer. I wouldn't mind getting into her pants."

"Nadine?"

"The beauty behind the bar."

He put his hand between his legs and thrust his hips forward with a grimace of pleasure.

"Man, I'd give it to her in a minute, but the old guy's poking her, can you believe it? I guess when you're the boss . . ."

They started playing pool. Charles thought the game went on too long. The one or two ropes that Steve bothered to show him were short ones.

He taught himself how to follow through with his stroke, how to rebound, how to carom off another ball, how to put English on the cue ball, how to break. He also played with extreme caution, since a tear in the cloth would have cost them a lot of money and got them thrown out of the pool hall.

Around nine o'clock Charles began to get a headache and suggested they go to the Villa Frontenac for a smoked-meat sandwich. Just then a tall, balding man in a checked shirt and jogging pants with baggy knees came up to them, hands in his pockets, swaggering a bit like Charlie Chaplin in old silent films. He stood at the end of their table and watched them play. After a while he went up to Charles and, excusing himself politely, showed him a better way to bridge his cue, then gave him a few tips on improving his play, always speaking as though to an equal, someone he had known for a long time. Every now and then he said something to Steve, whom he apparently considered a regular, and Steve would reply in kind, eager to be seen to be on an equal footing with a man who was twice his age.

When the game was finished, the man invited the boys over to the bar and offered to buy them a beer.

"They're underage, these two, De Bané," said the owner, pointing at Steve and Charles.

"Aw, c'mon," said the man, his eyes widening. "One beer never hurt anyone!"

"Maybe not, but it would hurt my licence. Coke, 7-Up, coffee, or the street, your choice. You might like running after trouble, but I'd rather chase something else."

De Bané turned to his guests and shrugged, his body sagging, his face twisted into a grimace. Charles realized he bore an astonishing resemblance to Steve, as though the two of them were distantly related: the same raw-boned body, the same contortions, even the same penchant for clownish behaviour.

"What can you do?" the man said. "If he won't serve you, he won't serve you. I could twist his arm, but it wouldn't do any good."

"Coke," said Charles.

"7-Up," said Steve.

"I'll have an Ex, and make it cold as possible," said the man. "My buy."

The owner signalled to Nadine to serve them. He didn't seem to care much for the man in the checked shirt. Charles was hypnotized by Nadine's navel. He had to make an effort not to stare at it. She also had a way of moving her hips and lifting her arms and turning her head to give her hair a slight ripple that caused him a certain amount of sweet discomfort.

René De Bané didn't seem put off by getting the cold shoulder from the owner. He launched into an account of his day, which had been fairly eventful. It turned out he was a plumber.

"... So I get to this guy's house on rue des Érables and he shows me into the kitchen. 'The sink's plugged,' he says. 'I tried everything. I even poured battery acid down it. Nothing worked.' As for me, it wasn't the sink that bothered me, it was this huge, big-eared dog that was lying curled up in front of the stove, staring at me and growling. 'Oh, don't mind him,' the guy says, 'he's never bitten anyone. That's just his way of telling you this is his house. He wouldn't hurt a fly.' 'No problem,' I says to him. 'I've seen a few dogs in my day. They don't bother me.' And I go to work on the sink. I can tell right away I'm gonna hafta take off the trap. It was so goddamn rusted it looked like it'd been buried out in the garden for the past ten years. I try turnin' it with my pipe wrench, but it don't give an inch. Meanwhile the guy's gone off who knows where and there I am alone in the kitchen with this dog, which is still staring at me and growling.

"So anyways I brace my feet against the bottom of the counter and pull on the wrench as hard as I can. Suddenly there's this *crack!* and the trap gives and I fall on my back with my head two inches from the dog's mouth! Ay-yi-yi! I jump up pretty quick, you can bet on that! If I hadn't had a wrench in my hand that friggin' animal would've bit off half my face! 'Hey! What's-yer-face!' I call to the guy. 'Put your dog outside or I'm leavin'!' I'm calling and calling and – nothin'. No answer. I'm alone in the house with this friggin' dog. Can you believe it? I try to leave the kitchen, the dog blocks my way and starts barking its friggin' head off. Okay, I says, he'll calm down eventually, you never hear a dog bark for ten hours straight. I can wait. I got my wrench handy to give him a whack up the side'a the head if I hafta.

"Finally the mutt goes back and lays down in front of the stove, but he's still starin' right at me, right? Well, I says to myself, since I got the trap off I might as well clean it out, but I keep an eye behind me on that dog, you wanna believe it. Well, you shoulda seen what come outta that trap. Some kind of thick black goop full of lumps and chunks, and it didn't smell like anything the Baby Jesus might've left in his diaper, I can tell you that! You're not gonna believe this, but as soon as the dog sees that slimy mess he's up on his feet and waggin' his tail and comin' at me: he wants to scarf the goddamn stuff! 'Okay,' I says to him and I push the piece of crud towards him, 'go nuts, you dumb dog!' So all the time I'm reattachin' the trap, he's lickin' this mess up off the floor like it's a bowl of gourmet Gravy Train, doesn't leave a drop. I don't believe it!

"So then the guy comes back, eh, lookin' all cool, colour in his cheeks, face all calm, wants to see how I'm gettin' on with my work. And there's his dog laying there on the floor belchin' like an old wino, and I says to him, 'That's not a dog you got there, buddy, that's a friggin' garburator!' And I tell him what's just gone down. 'Why didn't you stop him?' the guy says, gettin' all hot and bothered. 'Stop him?' I says. 'Are you kiddin'? What with? He woulda taken my arm off, maybe both of them! Where were you? Didn't you hear him barkin' his head off a few minutes ago? They could probably hear him all the way to Verdun!' All the time we're yellin' at each other the dog's layin' there burpin' and his gut's ballooning out. I tell you, that was one sick puppy. As I was goin' out the door I'm pretty sure it was his death rattle I was hearin'. Good riddance, I say! The guy wants to sue me, go ahead! He'll hafta find me first!"

All the while De Bané was talking, Nadine was moving back and forth behind the counter, listening, sometimes shaking with laughter, while the owner merely lifted his shoulders as though he was hard of hearing. Suddenly Charles realized he was late getting home, so he thanked the plumber for the Coke and left, followed by Steve, who first made a date with De Bané for a game of pool the next evening at eight o'clock.

"Do you believe his story?" Charles asked his friend.

"Don't you?" Steve said, surprised. "Anyway, I thought it was hilarious! He's a great storyteller. Makes the time go by pretty quickly. And he always picks up the tab. If the owner hadn't been there we would've had us a beer."

And he began whistling as though he didn't have a care in the world.

■ ■ ■

Charles began hanging out at the Orleans Billiards Hall. He went there with Steve once or twice a week, and Saturday nights after work at the pharmacy. René De Bané invariably showed up early in the evening, hands thrust into the pockets of his baggy track pants, always with an amusing story to tell.

Destiny seemed to have reserved its zaniest adventures just for him. One day, when he was repairing the plaster walls on the ground floor of a house on rue Wolfe, he noticed that some of the cracks he'd just replastered had opened up again. After filling them in a second, and then a third time, only to see them start to yawn open once again, he decided he must have been using an inferior grade of plaster. He was just about to take it back to the hardware store and complain when he felt the floor start to vibrate, just a little, and then suddenly it dropped six inches. He barely had time to dive for the door before the entire ceiling came crashing down in a huge cloud of plaster dust.

"What address was that on Wolfe?" the owner asked caustically.

"Eighteen thirty-seven, my friend."

"I passed by there this morning. I didn't see anything."

"We were working at the back," De Bané replied, not in the least disconcerted. "You can't see it from the street."

That was how Charles discovered that De Bané was not only a plumber, but also a plasterer. After a while he learned that the true extent of the man's talents, according to the man himself, was almost without limit.

De Bané knew all the pool hall regulars. Most of them laughed at his far-fetched stories and took him for a harmless crackpot, albeit a generous and good-natured one; others, however, regarded him with a certain restraint, as though they suspected that his hail-fellow-well-met act hid some darker aspect of his personality, one they would rather not get to know. All agreed that he was a good pool player and had won his share of tournaments, and he set about passing on what he knew to Charles, who made rapid progress under his tutelage. Charles also succeeded in becoming a heavy smoker, thanks to the ready packet of cigarettes the plasterer-plumber made available to him at all times.

Charles's new interest took him a few steps farther from his friendship with Blonblon, who was already caught up in his own love life. They saw a great deal of each other in school and accompanied each other to and from Pierre-Dupuy, at least when Caroline's timetable didn't permit her to walk home with her boyfriend. Charles did his best to persuade Blonblon to take up pool, but the latter showed no interest in the game whatsoever, saying that places like pool halls were generally held in fairly low esteem since they attracted a lot of low-lifes and good-for-nothings.

"You've met some of these people?" Charles asked him mockingly.

"No I haven't, because I've never set foot in a pool hall. But one hears things, you know. You don't have to actually go to war to know that wars are dangerous."

"So in your opinion the Orleans Billiards Hall is a dangerous place?" Charles pressed, smiling cruelly.

"Don't mess with my head, Charlie me boyo. I'm sure you've met a few bizarre types there, people who don't necessarily tell you everything they do during the day."

"Gee, you really know a lot about things, Blonblon. I can't wait to see what you're like when you're thirty. You'll no doubt go to mass every morning, surrounded by bodyguards in case one of the priests tries to mug you. You think the Orleans is dangerous? That's a laugh! It's about as dangerous as sticking your tongue out at a blind man. Ask Steve, if you don't believe me."

At the mention of Steve, Blonblon smiled but said nothing. He hated speaking ill of anyone, and in any case, he liked the big oaf who was

75

always willing to help others and who had a decided knack for making his friends laugh.

■ ■ ■

By the end of November, Fernand and Lucie were beginning to worry about Charles's infatuation with pool. It was keeping him away from the house and also interfering with his studies. Not to mention the smell of tobacco that had impregnated his clothes, which told the hardware-store owner – who had a delicate nose and a horror of cigarettes – that, like so many other adolescents, his adopted son had fallen prey to the lure of nicotine.

One night after supper he took Charles aside in the living room.

"We don't see much of you any more, Charles," he said by way of preamble in his "this is an important occasion" voice. "You always seem to be busy, yet for no good reason I know of."

"I try to keep busy," Charles replied drily, "so I don't get bored."

"Yes . . ." said Fernand, nodding his head and smiling. "Hard to argue with that kind of logic."

"Why would you want to argue with it?" Charles shot back.

There followed a moment of silence during which Fernand went over in his mind the careful strategy he had worked out during dinner.

"You've developed an interest in billiards, I believe," he said, after a session of rubbing his palms on his trouser legs.

"Yes."

"Is this Orleans place above board?"

"Yes."

"No low-lifes in it, by any chance?"

"None."

"You're sure of that?"

"Yes."

"I'm only asking," said Fernand, stifling a show of impatience, "because it's the kind of place where gangsters like to hang out."

"I don't know any gangsters."

"They don't advertise that they're gangsters."

"I suppose not."

Fernand took a deep breath through his nose, closed his eyes, ran his hand under his chin, then managed to smile.

"Charles, everyone knows that it's in places like the Orleans that people sell drugs, get together to plan robberies, and meet up with prostitutes . . ."

"It's perfectly obvious that you've never set foot in a pool hall," Charles said, disdain dripping from his voice. "Those're all just a lot of old wives' tales."

"Don't talk to me in that tone of voice!" Fernand thundered, banging his fist on the arm of his chair. (Boff, who was lying outside the room in the hallway, raised his head and looked threateningly at the living-room door.) "You're not speaking to your dog here, you're speaking to your father . . . at least, that's how I see myself . . . unless you have any objections? I'm only trying to warn you. You must understand that it's for your own good, for crying out loud, Charles! That's all Lucie and I ever want, your own good. Do you imagine for one second that I'm saying this for the good of my own health . . . ?"

And on he went with the usual banalities that parents hand out to their children in the naive conviction that experience is something that can be transmitted from one generation to the next, and that the fact that they are right is all the justification they need to impose their views on their offspring.

In the end, Fernand asked Charles to stay away from the pool hall during the week, before his studies – to say nothing about other aspects of his life – began to suffer. Charles argued that he was in the top percentile at Pierre-Dupuy, that he was getting good marks, and that it wasn't as if hanging around the house every night would make his marks go up. Pool halls were not healthy places for kids to hang out, Fernand objected. They were for layabouts and welfare bums and people with shady pasts. The only things he would learn there were bad habits – like smoking, for example, he added with a bitter smile, which, though it was probably the least damaging thing he could pick up, would sooner or later ruin his health.

His health was his business, Charles countered, he had the right to do with it what he wanted. And as for those kinds of people Fernand spoke of, he'd never seen anyone like that in the Orleans. He invited Fernand to come and judge for himself what kind of place the Orleans was.

"Nothing to be done," sighed Fernand when he joined his wife in the kitchen. "Everyone has to make their own mistakes, I guess, if they're going to learn about life. I just hope the mistake he's making isn't too serious."

"Who says he's going to make mistakes?" Lucie said. "You always let your temper get the better of you, my poor Fernand. You go flying off the handle, you say things you don't mean, and you get people's backs up. Does it make you feel any better? Let him do what he has to do, at least for a while. He'll get over it. He has a good brain in his head. Have a bit of confidence in him. We'll keep an eye on him, of course. There'll always be time to grab him by the scruff of the neck if he starts doing anything foolish."

■ ■ ■

Morning break had just begun; students spread out in front of the school's main entrance were talking and smoking in the heavy rumble of the Grover factory working at top speed across the street. The ancient brick building with its enormous dusty windows seemed to vibrate at such times, as though it were about to explode from the sheer effort of expending so much energy.

Suddenly a large black cat with a gold collar came out from between two parked cars. It seemed disoriented. The end of its tail was broken and one ear was in tatters. After sniffing a tire for a few seconds, it ran out into the street in front of a speeding delivery truck. A shriek arose from several nearby students, and a small group gathered around the animal. Its hind leg had been crushed. Splayed out on the asphalt, it stared up at the onlookers with a bewildered eye as a trickle of blood ran down its side. One grinning student tossed an empty cigarette pack at its head.

"Hey! You idiot!" shouted Blonblon. "Leave the poor thing alone! Don't you think it has enough problems without you pestering it?"

Two or three girls muttered their agreement. Blonblon kneeled down before the cat, which reared up onto its three good legs and started spitting and growling at him, ferociously defending what little remained of its life. Blonblon pushed some of the students out of its way, giving it room to escape, and the cat dragged itself off.

Just then Charles came up, cigarette lighter in one hand and the other reaching into the inside pocket of his windbreaker. When he saw the gathering he stopped, curious to know what was going on. The smartass who'd thrown the cigarette pack was giving Blonblon a hard time, shouting at him and digging his finger into Blonblon's chest. Someone filled Charles in on what had happened. He looked around for the cat, which had disappeared between two buildings, and then went over and stepped between Blonblon and the smartass.

"Take a hike, man," he said to the latter. "I want to talk to him. It's important. You can pound the shit out of him later."

The smartass went on shouting for a few seconds, then went off in a huff with two of his comrades.

"Would you like to make a few bucks?" Charles asked Blonblon. "Monsieur Michaud has just bought a whole library. Nearly a thousand books. He wants us to move it for him and put it on shelves."

"When?"

"Tonight, if that's cool, or else over the weekend."

"Not tonight," Steve interrupted, joining the two boys and looking at Charles with a secretive smile. He seemed bubbling over with barely suppressed excitement. "Tonight, my friend, we're going to play pool, you and I, and I don't think you'll want to miss it. No, I don't think you'll want to miss one minute of it, may my dick fall off if I'm wrong!"

And he laughed as though already enjoying the fun that was in store for Charles. Charles looked at him in surprise and some irritation, wondering what clever trick Lachapelle had up his sleeve. But the latter took himself off, still laughing, after telling Charles to be at the Orleans at seven-thirty.

Blonblon had already wandered off to look for the cat. Ever since he'd been struck by lightning he hadn't had much time for the frivolities of this world. All he cared about was love. The cat was nowhere to be found.

For the rest of the day Charles scratched his head trying to figure out what it was that Steve had lined up. It could only be some kind of trick. At three o'clock, the biology teacher, Monsieur Belzile, noticing Charles's preoccupied air, asked him to come up to the board and write down the principal functions of the liver. Charles stood at the board for a long time, completely befuddled, which delighted his classmates, then went back to his desk, smiling bravely but blushing to the roots of his hair, knowing for the first time in his life what it was like to be a complete dunce.

He walked into the pool hall around seven. As usual, Nadine gave him a big smile from behind the bar, filling him (also as usual) with a quivering, timid rapture. Obviously she thought he was attractive and that the three years that separated their ages did not in theory mean they couldn't go out together (provided, of course, that he could somehow supplant the owner). But he was paralyzed by her beauty. On top of which, and causing him no small amount of confusion, there was a certain hardness in her mannerisms and in her expression that told him that, despite her youth, she had already seen her share of life, and she was not afraid of it. As a result, when he was around her he felt he was still a bit of a child.

He looked around the room. Only three of the tables were being used, and Steve hadn't arrived yet. But just then he heard Steve's voice coming up the stairs. High-pitched, excited, slightly weird. Who could he be talking to? There was a burst of laughter. A girl's laughter. Then Lachapelle stood at the door, bracketed by two plump brunettes who were about the same height as him, not bad-looking. Charles recognized them from school, but he couldn't remember their names.

"Hey, Thibodeau! Here already?"

He looked down at his companions, who were laughing as hard as they could.

"You know Marlene Jobidon? No? She's in the same class as Henri. And Agatha Forcier?"

"One of my uncles owns the Blue Bird," she said, as though that were one of her personality traits.

"Oh really? I didn't know that," Charles said, not knowing how else to respond.

They began chatting about this and that. Every now and then Charles looked questioningly at Steve, who assumed an innocent air and went on telling joke after joke, making the girls laugh and generally bringing them up to his own level of excitement. He explained that Marlene and Agatha had expressed an interest in learning how to play pool. "So I said that you and I were pretty good with our sticks" – here the girls broke into laughter again – "and we'd be happy if they joined us to make a foursome."

Renewed hilarity from Agatha and Marlene.

After discreetly ensuring that Charles was willing to split the cost, Steve went over to the cash to arrange for a table. Charles had never seen him in such a lively mood. He heard Nadine telling Steve that the owner had gone out for the evening.

"Far out!" said Steve. "Bring us four drafts."

But she refused him outright. If the pool hall lost its licence would he be able to get them a new one?

They started playing. Charles soon realized that teaching Marlene how to play pool was nothing but a pretext for bringing them together. Certain intimacies shared between Steve and Agatha suggested that their acquaintance was already fairly well advanced. Of the two, Charles would have preferred Agatha for himself. Marlene was altogether too pudgy: pudgy cheeks, pudgy chin, pudgy nose, pudgy behind, even the tips of her shoes seemed pudgy. But her skin was superb, like cream, and she had a frank, easy laugh that was a pleasure to listen to. There didn't seem to be anything complicated about her. Not wanting to appear ungrateful, Charles set about imitating his friend. When Marlene succeeded in putting a little backspin on the cue ball, however accidentally, he kissed her on the cheek. When she made a second decent shot, she let him kiss her lips.

Charles felt a strange sensation spread through him, a mixture of curiosity, lust, and fear. The others were obviously running the show, but it was without malice; clearly his companions wanted nothing more than to have a good time. But part of him would have liked his friend to leave him alone in his innocence, to let him go on being a child, instead of making him feel that his illusions were being shattered every minute by the gestures and pleasantries shared by Steve and the two girls.

The next day, during one of their final bike rides of the season (since snow would soon be putting a stop to them for a few months), Steve would tell him that Marlene had had her eye on him for a long time, and had even bet Agatha that she would pluck his cherry before the week was out. The two girls had talked to Vicky, Steve's stepsister, and she had passed the word on to Steve. The latter, after having spent a few highly enjoyable hours with Agatha at Marlene's place, had agreed to set something up, and the idea of a game of pool had seemed the best way to put their plan into action.

They had just racked the balls for a second game when René De Bané appeared. His arm was in a sling and his face looked as though it had been pummelled with a pair of baseball cleats. The surprising and, to some extent, unfortunate thing was that for once he appeared to have a real story to tell, but he was in much too foul and uncommunicative a mood to tell it. When she saw him, Nadine gave an exclamation of surprise and asked him what had happened.

"Nothing you'd be interested in," he muttered.

The look he gave her told her that if she pressed him she'd be sticking her head into a lion's mouth. He ordered a beer and took it over to a table by the bar, where he sat staring darkly into his glass.

One of the pool players saw him, went over to say hello, and also remarked on his devastated face. But before he could ask him about it, De Bané suggested he go outside and play in the traffic on Boulevard Metropolitain. After two or three beers, however, his mood seemed to lift a little; he stood up, beer in hand, and leaned against a pillar watching the somewhat lively game that Steve and Charles were playing with their two friends.

"René," Steve ventured, "what happened to you?"

"Accident at work," was all the jack-of-all-trades would say. In an obvious effort to change the subject, he added, "If you'd taken that last shot off the rail you'd have dropped the seven in the corner pocket, no sweat."

"What kind of accident, René?" Steve persisted. "You fall down a chimney or something? Did a bus suddenly decide to give you a peck on the cheek? I mean, shoot, you don't often see a face as mangled as yours."

"Accident at work, I told you. I'll tell you about it some other time. I don't want to talk about it just now. You kids," he went on, settling into a vaguely philosophical bitterness, "you don't know what it's like to work for a living. When you get to know a bit about life you'll realize it's not always a bed of roses. Pushing pencils all day, that's nothing. A pastime for pussies!"

"I've been working since I was eight years old," Charles said, irked.

"Oh yeah? So you don't just push pencils, you sharpen them from time to time, eh?"

Agatha and Marlene laughed.

"No, I delivered pizzas for Chez Robert, my friend. I also sold chocolate bars on the street, and now I'm working as a delivery boy for Lalancette Pharmacy."

At this news René De Bané abruptly changed his attitude. He congratulated Charles for his courage and energy, delivered a paean of praise for any youngster who at least partly paid his own way while still going to school, and questioned Charles assiduously about his work at the pharmacy. How long had he been working there? How did he like the owner? Did he get along well with him? Was business good? And so on.

"It's your shot, Charles," Marlene interrupted, taking him by the arm. In the process she managed to run her hand along his thigh.

"You're ruining our concentration, René," Steve said sourly.

"Sorry, guys, sorry . . . didn't mean to butt in. . . . Hey, who wants a beer? My round. Speak now or forever hold your peace!"

He went over to the bar and ordered five Molsons. Nadine refused him outright, knowing who they were for. De Bané protested, saying that if he felt like drinking ten beers in a row it was his business and no law could stop him as long as he conducted himself in a proper manner. Then to reinforce his argument he slapped a five-dollar bill on the counter. The owner's absence robbed Nadine of a major portion of her moral authority and reduced the strength of her convictions; in the end she gave in, grumbling, and De Bané returned to the pool table with the beer.

The atmosphere around the table picked up considerably. Charles had never liked beer much, but that night, for some reason, he drained his glass in three gulps. His nervousness soon vanished and he began taking great pleasure in this odd game of pool arranged for his benefit with two girls he barely knew. He began to see Marlene in a new light, and even though Agatha still seemed to him to be the sharper of the two, certainly the more lively and bubbly, Marlene was beginning to gain on her with her good humour, her warmth of spirit, and her overall easygoing, childlike manner. At a certain juncture, when he was trying to guide her arm for a particularly delicate shot, he leaned his body against hers and gently rubbed the back of her hand; she responded with a movement of her rear that left no doubt about where the evening was headed.

De Bané continued watching them, unstinting in his advice and his running commentary. He suddenly seemed to think Charles could do no wrong; he marvelled at Charles's skill, clapped loudly at each good shot, and Charles, despite the scorn that De Bané usually inspired in him with his constant bouncing and clowning around, couldn't help taking a certain pleasure in his approval. After all, De Bané was a good player.

"That calls for another round," De Bané cried when Agatha, who until then had seemed intent on tearing the felt to shreds, sank two balls in a row. And off he went, back to the bar.

"Let's drink them fast and get out of here," Steve said quietly. He seemed to be getting more and more resentful of De Bané's presence. "I can't stand looking at his hacked-up face, can you?"

Ten minutes later the four were making their way to the door after having warmly thanked their somewhat piqued benefactor. Charles hadn't been able to finish his beer; a strange dizziness was coming over him, bringing with it some unpleasant memories.

They clattered loudly down the stairs. Halfway down, Marlene stopped.

"Let's go to my place," she said. "My father's away for the weekend. We'll have the apartment to ourselves."

Agatha and Steve went on ahead, hand in hand and calling back, while Marlene gave Charles a long look, arms at her sides, hands held palms up towards him. He took her in his arms and it was there, half drunk and halfway down the staircase of the Orleans Billiards Hall, with the smell of Javex and cigarette smoke in his nostrils, that he experienced his first really sensual kiss.

Marlene lived on Prince George, a few doors down from the high school. They walked east along Ontario and Charles stopped her in the dripping, noisy tunnel under the railroad overpass for another kiss; he gave out an involuntary groan when she ran a practised hand down the front of his pants.

"Let's go, speed it up there, you two lovebirds!" Steve shouted. He seemed in a hurry to get to where they were going.

Prince George was a short, quiet cul-de-sac that butted up against the back of the Grover factory. Marlene and her father lived on the ground floor of an old, two-storey brick building with a fine mansard roof. The building contained twelve apartments. A few months earlier, Monsieur Jobidon, who was on good terms with the building's owner, a distant cousin of his, had managed to annex a room in the basement as a bedroom for Marlene.

"Smells funny in here," Steve said with a grimace when they entered the apartment.

He turned his head this way and that, sniffing the air with a look of distaste. They were in a room almost completely occupied by an enormous television, an armchair, and a huge sofa covered in crinkled black leather.

"Oh, it's our damned cat!" Marlene said, laughing. "He pissed in here yesterday. We leave him outside now."

She went into a long, involved story concerning their cat, Puffball. The previous week when she'd come home from school one afternoon she'd found three little brats who had trapped Puffy under the hood of a car and were scaring it to death with the horn. She heard the poor thing's desperate meows and ran out into the street. How long had it been going on? At least half an hour, according to a neighbour. And Puffy still wasn't completely over it. Half crazy and almost deaf, it wouldn't let anyone get anywhere near it, except maybe Monsieur Jobidon when he was home. It wandered up and down the neighbourhood all night, wailing like a banshee. Last night her father had managed to coax it into the apartment and give it something to eat, hoping that would calm it down. Puffy had always been so well behaved, but it had spent the night marking everything with its own smell and tearing up the arm of the sofa with its claws. In the morning her father had been so furious he'd thrown the animal outside, saying it'd never be allowed inside again.

"But he used to love his little Puffball," Marlene added, laughing. "One day I went into the bathroom thinking it was empty, and there he was on the throne, trying to wipe himself with one hand and pet the cat with the other! It was hilarious!"

Steve and Agatha laughed heartily and Charles tried to join in, but he was beginning to find Marlene a little coarse for his taste. Not that that detracted from her attractiveness.

"Can a guy get a beer in this place?" asked Steve. De Bané's generosity hadn't quenched his thirst.

"The fridge is full," Marlene replied.

"But we can't touch them," warned Agatha. "Your father probably counted them before he left, like he always does, and you'll be in big trouble, girl, if he comes back and there's any missing!"

Steve shrugged. "No problem, we'll score some later at the corner store. Won't we, Thibodeau?"

"They won't sell us beer."

"The one near our place will. No sweat."

With these assurances Marlene went into the kitchen and came back carrying four bottles. Charles didn't feel up to more drinking, but to go along with his friends and to avoid being teased he took a few mouthfuls. Marlene knelt in a corner in front of a portable record player, and a song by The Police filled the room. Charles took out his pack of smokes and offered them around, but Steve stopped him with a gesture.

"I've got something better," he said.

Picking up his jacket from the sofa, he took from the pocket a small plastic bag half filled with pot and a packet of cigarette papers. He rolled two joints, with the others looking on eagerly.

Wreaths of bluish smoke rose above their heads. After each toke, Charles concentrated on holding back a small, dry cough, each one more rasping than the last. This time, to his consternation, the weed was apparently having no effect on him. Then, after a few minutes, it seemed to him the music was becoming louder and taking on a new and quite wonderful dimension. His legs suddenly felt weak. Steve was staring off into space with a solemn, languid expression that made Agatha laugh. "He does look like a bit of an idiot," thought Charles. Then he felt Marlene's arm on his shoulder, and they were kissing so passionately he forgot to breathe. Every now and then he sneaked a look at Steve and Agatha, who were entwined on the sofa, hoping they would give him a clue as to what came next. He was completely clueless about his next move.

"Come on," Marlene whispered in his ear, "let's go down to my room."

Taking his hand, she led him into the kitchen. It was a very small room with grease-stained walls and an impressively high pile of dirty dishes in the sink. Beside the fridge a door stood open, disclosing a narrow staircase leading down to the basement. It was low-ceilinged, with a poured concrete floor. A purple runner led from the bottom of the stairs to a second door in a newly constructed wall.

"My bedroom," Marlene said proudly, taking him through the second door into a fairly large room. Everything in it was blue – the walls, the wall-to-wall carpet, the down-filled duvet on the bed – and the monotone was given added emphasis by a blue bulb in a lamp hanging in one corner. Above the bed was a high window covered with blue-flowered curtains, and on the bed itself sprawled an enormous chocolate-coloured teddy bear. Posters of Blondie, Joan Jett, and Jean Michel Jarre decorated the walls. A dresser burdened with trinkets stood in a corner beside a desk. The room was as tidy as a cell in a convent.

"You like?"

He nodded yes. But his excitement was beginning to wane, replaced by a strange sensation he had never felt before, a mixture of exaltation and terror, anguish and burning curiosity. He felt helpless in its grip. A thousand questions flew through his mind. What did Marlene expect him to do? Were there some things to avoid doing? Was it as great as everyone said it was? Maybe she didn't really want to make love. How would he know? He should have brought his beer with him. Mechanically he patted his pockets looking for his cigarettes.

She saw the trouble he was in and it made him seem even more desirable to her. What a treat to be the first for such a handsome specimen! She smiled at him, drew him to the bed, and they began kissing again. After a moment she saw that he wasn't making a move to undress her, so she gently pushed him back and began unbuttoning her blouse, still smiling sweetly. He undid the buttons of his own shirt. Something flashed in his head, as though all the beer he had drunk during the course of the evening suddenly began working at once. He stared at her breasts, large but firm and jutting out beautifully, the same creamy white as her face. Their supreme beauty engulfed him. He reached out shyly and touched them, then gently caressed them with his trembling hands. Then he leaned over and kissed them as she tried to take off her pantyhose. She laughed and pushed his head away.

"Slowly, slowly, you naughty boy! Take your clothes off first. . . . Don't you want me to see your ass? You don't need a safe," she added, in case he was worried, "I've just finished my period."

The next instant his jeans and her slip were on the floor, and he was on her.

"Take off your socks," she murmured. "I'm not a hooker."

He took them off, hardly aware that she was speaking. Her caresses sent flames shooting through his entire body. He squeezed and kissed her; she opened her legs and guided his hand but, misunderstanding what she wanted, he tried to penetrate her right away. In any case, it was too late. A spasm came over him and he squirted three whitish streams over her vagina and abdomen. Kneeling before her he looked up with a penitent smile.

"Not to worry," she said gently. "We'll have another go. . . . My, my, what a cute little thing you have there."

She stretched out her arm and, opening the drawer of her night table, took out a handful of Kleenex.

Meanwhile, Puffball had crept along the outside wall of the building and stretched itself out against the basement window. It had spent the afternoon lying beneath a balcony, licking the paw that earlier that day had been run over by a truck. It would have slept, but the pain was ferocious and spreading through the lower half of its body, giving it no respite. It was having difficulty breathing. Its mouth was dry and filled with the bitter taste of blood. It panted, changing position, repeatedly trying to get comfortable. Finally it had decided to return home in the hope that this time they would let it in.

Through a gap in the curtains it could see the blue duvet on which it had spent so many days sleeping. If it could only lie on it once more it was certain the pain would go away. The duvet had been pushed to the bottom of the bed, and two pairs of bare legs seemed to be kicking at it, as if trying to make it fall onto the floor. After a time the legs stopped moving, then they tangled themselves together.

Cold crept into Puffball's body and blended with the pain, a heavy, terrible coldness that inched towards its heart and began squeezing the breath out of it. It gathered up the last of its strength and gave out a long meow.

"What was that?" Charles said, jumping up.

"Just the cat," Marlene murmured, half asleep. "It wants in. But it has to stay out."

"Sounds as though it's at the window."

Charles stood up and opened the curtains.

"The cat doesn't look too good, Marlene . . . it might even be dying."

She gave a deep sigh, turned over a few times under the duvet, and then stood up as well. When she saw the animal lying stretched out against the window, its mouth half open, its pupils dilated as though filled with despair, she brought her hand to her mouth and said nothing.

"I'm going out to see how it is," said Charles. "We can't just leave it like that."

He dressed and went upstairs; the living room was empty. Marlene came up behind him wearing a robe.

"Where'd they go?" he asked, nodding at the sofa.

She shrugged. Charles went outside. Marlene sat on the sofa and hugged her legs.

"Bloody Agatha," she muttered. "How many times have I asked her not to go into my father's bedroom? If he ever found out I'd be good as dead." But her father would never find out. He spent every weekend with his girl-friend in Châteauguay and didn't come back until Monday morning, looking grey, and in a difficult mood. She paid for her two days of freedom with five days of tiptoeing around, still receiving her share of complaints and cuffing, not to mention the occasional punch. If only he could find work! That would help things a bit. She would take it for another two months, maybe three, but after that, if he was still at the house all day, she'd decided she would get an apartment with her friend Julie and go back to being a waitress.

The door opened.

"Your cat's dead," Charles said sadly. "Its hind leg was crushed. It must have died from loss of blood . . ." When she didn't reply, he said in surprise, "Doesn't it mean anything to you?"

"It wasn't my cat, more my father's," she said. "Having it around was a real drag sometimes. . . . But it had its uses, I guess," she added with a sigh. "Like when I was lying down, it'd come up and purr in my ear, and some-times I'd let it sleep with me."

"What do you want me to do with it? We can't just leave it there at the window."

"My father'll take care of it on Monday. Or I could put it in a garbage bag in the morning," she said, seeing the look on Charles's face. "Aren't you coming back to bed?"

They made love for the third time. Charles was beginning to take real pleasure from the act, as though as the novelty wore off he was able to get closer to his feelings. The presence of the cat above their heads put a damper on the evening, however. He felt vaguely guilty for the cat's death, but what did he have to feel guilty about?

He rolled over onto his stomach and closed his eyes, one arm resting on Marlene's shoulder. He felt wet between the cheeks of his bum and sweat glistened down the small of his back. His sleeping penis was blissfully numb. Everything was so new he felt as though he were inhabiting a new body and that he himself were someone else, someone both totally unknown and totally familiar. It was a pleasant feeling.

Marlene had brought a litre of milk and a bag of chocolate-chip cookies to her room. They ate the cookies and drank the milk, then lay down again beside each other.

"I wonder what they're doing upstairs," Charles said, curious about the silence that came from the ground floor.

Marlene burst out laughing. "The same as us, what do you think?" She raised herself on one elbow and looked him over. "You're a real hunk, you know."

"Thanks. You too. You're beautiful, I mean," he added, carefully.

"Me?" she said, with a rueful pout.

She went on with her examination.

"You have a nice ass," she said clinically. She sounded like an entomologist.

He looked at her in astonishment.

"But there's nothing special about it."

"Believe me. You have a nice ass."

He laughed, flattered in spite of himself. How many guys must she have slept with to have developed such an expert opinion? he wondered.

They heard steps upstairs followed by a long burst of laughter. It was Agatha. The door at the top of the stairs opened and Steve's voice called down.

"You two dead down there, you lovebirds?"

"No, not us," Charles thought, "but someone else has died." He and Marlene got dressed and left the bedroom.

"Man, I'm starving!" Steve exclaimed. "What about you?"

He looked at Charles as though to ask: Well, how did it go? Did you have a good time? Are you as deliriously happy as I am?

"We stuffed ourselves with chocolate-chip cookies," said Marlene. "I must have put on two pounds."

"Her cat just died, right outside her bedroom window," said Charles, surprised to realize what an impression the incident had left on him.

"What? Puffball?" cried Agatha. "What happened to him? Oh, I loved him so much, the poor little thing! He used to sleep on my lap sometimes when I was watching TV."

Marlene was standing at a mirror, arranging her hair. "What did you expect? When you let cats roam around like that they always end up getting run over."

Steve finally convinced the others to go with him to the Villa Frontenac for a smoked-meat sandwich. It was nearly one o'clock in the morning by the time they were back on the street. Agatha yawned and said she had a headache. Since they lived in opposite directions, they decided to part in front of the restaurant; Charles gave Marlene a hug so chaste it made Steve laugh.

"Don't forget to come and replace those beers tomorrow," Marlene reminded them as she left. "I'm counting on you!"

"Tomorrow, in the dawn's early light, I'll bring you a whole case," said Charles lightly.

"Your chum talks like a book," Agatha said to Marlene as they walked away. "Does he screw like a book, too?"

They both burst out laughing.

The two boys walked for a while without saying anything. Now that the excitement was over their legs seemed heavy and they were thinking of the warmth of their own beds, feeling pleasantly tired. A few tipsy customers came out of a bar waving their arms. A fat man leaned weakly against his car, digging in his pants pockets for his keys, while a woman with red, baggy cheeks wearing a fake-fur jacket spluttered angrily at him in a low voice. A big, lean, yellow dog ran across the road and Charles thought of Boff, at home waiting patiently for him at the foot of his bed. Steve started talking about his evening with Agatha, making fun of her deodorants and perfumes and her mania about putting on weight, but also speaking fondly of her enthusiasm once she got going. They slowed down when they reached the corner of Dufresne, where they were parting company.

"So," Steve said, suddenly serious. "Did you, uh, have a good time tonight?"

"Yeah, yeah, not bad. . . . She's cool, Marlene."

He almost added "Thanks!" but thought better of it. It would have made him look ridiculous and was disrespectful of Marlene.

"We'll be in touch tomorrow?"

They smiled and, without really knowing why, shook hands.

When he got to the house, Charles realized he wasn't the least bit sleepy. He pushed open the little gate and sat on the porch steps. Across the street and down he could see the staircase leading up to his old apartment. He hadn't checked it out for a while. The present tenants were an elderly, retired couple. They'd already leaned a snow shovel beside their door, ready for the winter that would soon be battering the city, a blue plastic shovel like the one his father had used to clean off the steps and the balcony. Maybe it was the same one, who knew? Monsieur Victoire's taxi wasn't parked anywhere. He often worked late on weekends, ferrying around the party-goers, strippers, prostitutes, and young couples who had decided to party on until dawn.

Shivering as he felt a sudden chill, Charles pulled up the zipper on his windbreaker and sighed. For the past few minutes he'd felt a dull emptiness opening up in his chest. On the outside he felt completely satisfied. A bit of a rocky start, but the evening had gone well. And they would no doubt continue to go well in the foreseeable future. From now on he'd be able to look any guy or any girl at Pierre-Dupuy straight in the eye, because he had *passed the big test*. Marlene would waste no time letting all and sundry know that he had left his virginity at the foot of her bed. Agatha would vouch for her. And that might make a few other girls sit up and take notice, you never knew. . . .

Then why this big hole? Why this little voice inside him saying over and over again, "Is that all there is to making love? Is that what everyone has been talking about so endlessly for so many thousands of years?" He thought of Blonblon and the way his eyes grew wide with wonder when he talked about Caroline. Blonblon was in love with Caroline, whereas he barely knew plump little Marlene, and deep down he wasn't much interested in getting to know her better. It was sad but true. Maybe he was missing something. But maybe not. In the books he'd read (he'd just finished *Anna Karenina*) making love was something you took terribly seriously, not at all the way he'd taken it that evening. But did books represent real life, or did they just try to console us for it?

In the silence of the autumn night, with the city huddling into itself in the damp and the cold, he felt sad and tired. If it hadn't been so late he wouldn't have minded two or three bowls of thick, creamy soup, or sinking into a good hot bath.

He stood up and entered the house. Hanging his windbreaker up in the hall, he noticed a light on in the living room. Someone was waiting up for him. He was pretty sure it was Fernand.

He opened the door and looked in. Fernand was sitting in an armchair with a newspaper folded in his hand, wearing his bathrobe, his two hairy legs plunked one beside the other like a pair of marble columns. Light from a lampshade printed a curious pattern on his bald head, like a thin slice of a phosphorescent tomato.

"Do you know what time it is?" he said, standing up and striding in Charles's direction.

"Of course I do. I have a watch."

Fernand turned scarlet, took a deep breath through his nostrils and let it out slowly. He looked angrily at Charles, who stiffened, ready for anything. A moment passed. Boff appeared in the hallway and sat down, observing the scene.

"I can see by your eyes that you've been drinking."

Fernand spread his legs wide, crossed his arms, and seemed to Charles to become even larger and more formidable than ever.

"You listen to me, young man," he went on, his voice heavy and filled with rage. "I didn't adopt you as my son so that you could grow up to be like your father."

When he saw the look in the boy's eyes he realized he had gone too far.

"All right. I shouldn't have said anything so stupid. Forget what I said. It just slipped out. Forget I said it. You'll never be like your father, no matter where you happen to be living, believe me. But you must understand, Charles, that coming home after one o'clock in the morning without telling us where you're going, it doesn't make a hell of a lot of sense! Lucie and I've been worried sick, for Chrissakes!"

"Why? If I can't look after myself when I'm fifteen years old, I'll never be able to. So you're wasting your time worrying about me."

He turned on his heels and, followed by Boff, shut himself in his room and locked the door. The unexpected quarrel had added to his sadness. He felt more alone and helpless than ever. When he lay down on the bed he felt like taking Simon the Bear in his arms, but Simon had long since been retired to the storage bin in the basement. Besides, Charles was much too old now to give in to such a childish longing. He was ashamed of himself for even thinking about it.

6

In early December, business at the hardware store was so bad that Fernand held a huge pre-Christmas sale, a strategy that violated every principle of good retail management, since everyone knew that such displays of goodwill were supposed to be reserved for cash-strapped customers after the holidays were over. The sale was only moderately successful, and Fernand's hair turned a little greyer. Charles was only one of his many headaches. Henri, for example, had been developing the irritating habit of leaving his things lying around everywhere in the house, was using his ghetto-blaster as a public-address system, grunted like a whole herd of pigs whenever he was asked to do the tiniest thing, and stayed up so late at night that the only time he got any sleep was in class the next day.

On the 16th of March, a sudden thaw melted nearly all the snow that was still on the ground, and rain fell steadily for ten hours. This was followed the next day by a sudden cold snap that coated the entire city in ice; walking home that night, Fernand twisted an ankle and had to see a doctor about it. When he finally arrived home, with an empty stomach and in a mood that would have made an artillery battalion run for cover, Charles announced that he was going to spend the weekend with some friends, and that Lucie had already said it was all right with her. There followed the stormiest discussion the house had known since its construction at the turn of the century. It ended with an understanding having been tentatively reached: from then on the number and duration of Charles's little excursions outside the house would be determined by his marks at school (which so far were highly satisfactory, it had to be admitted); the slightest drop in his scholastic achievement would occasion a corresponding increase in the amount of time he spent at home studying. This agreement was written down on paper and signed by both parties. Lucie drew up the text, every word of which was given the most minute possible examination, and it was duly signed by all concerned. Then Fernand, feeling he had arrived at the end of his negotiating rope, wolfed down an enormous plate of boiled ham and potatoes and spent the rest of the night watching television with his ankle wrapped in a plastic bag filled with ice water.

■ ■ ■

Weeks passed. Charles saw Marlene a few times. She had become a kind of bed-buddy, a role she played episodically with two or three other boys from school. It was a highly informal arrangement that suited everyone. He also briefly enjoyed Agatha's favours. She was fairly liberal with them – one had only to ask – but he soon gave them up out of loyalty to Steve, who was not at all into sharing, and also because he didn't like the way Agatha put on airs, or the way she was always comparing her sexual partners, attacking the reputations of those who had gone before with a mocking cruelty that gave Charles the willies. He marvelled at the turbulent sensations his new life entailed, but sometimes they frightened him.

He continued going to the Orleans Billiards Hall, to the consternation of Fernand and Lucie, who were afraid that the vices that had ruined his father's life would also ruin the son's. René De Bané showed up most nights, and almost always had a bizarre story to tell.

On the 6th of May, around nine o'clock, he arrived in an extraordinarily dismal mood, took a seat at the bar, and drank three beers without uttering a single word.

"What's up with you?" Nadine asked him.

The owner, who was busy arranging bottles in the refrigerator, looked over briefly and shrugged.

"Nothing," said De Bané.

"Yes there is. I can tell by the look on your face."

"I said there was nothing and I meant there was nothing! Go mind your own business!"

But the barmaid had nothing else to do, and she kept at him until he finally gave in and agreed to recount the source of his immeasurable pain. Nadine signalled to the regulars in the room; everyone crowded around, Charles and Steve in the front row, and, with the air of a Roman martyr about to have hot needles shoved under his fingernails, De Bané launched into a story of the unmitigated evil recently endured by one of his favourite uncles.

The uncle's name was Charlemagne Alarie. He had a bad leg and a big mouth and was a former police officer who, they say, had one day run up against none other than Machine Gun Molly herself. The previous night he'd asked De Bané to go with him to look at a boarding house he owned on rue Beaubien, saying the place needed some repairs. The two men had just stepped out of Alarie's car when a kind of wolf-dog with teeth like a Swiss Army knife leapt over a fence and started chasing them down the street, howling at their heels like a hound from hell. De Bané ran across the street and nearly got himself run over by a taxi, but the dog, realizing it couldn't chase them both at the same time, stuck with the one with the bum leg, who was hopping stiffly along like a madman trying to keep ahead of it. The animal was gaining on him. Then De Bané, keeping pace with them on the other side of the street, hoping he could somehow help his uncle (though he had no idea how), witnessed the most amazing thing he'd ever seen in his life. He saw, with his own eyes, how absolute terror transformed a cripple into an Olympic runner! Charlemagne Alarie, knowing that there were no more than a few centimetres between his ass and the dog's teeth, dug deep and came up with a reserve of strength that must have been hiding in there for years: he literally flew down that sidewalk! In a matter of seconds he was so far ahead of the dog that it stopped dead in its tracks, totally confused, and sat on its haunches in disbelief. The old man jumped – yes, jumped! – over a fence and ran up a set of spiral stairs, taking them four at a time. When he reached the balcony he banged on the door to ask for help. But it was too late! His heart, weakened by the valiant effort it had just made on the old man's behalf, gave out.

And it was there, clinging to a doorpost, his eyes turned heavenward and his mouth gaping open, that the poor man gave up the ghost, while his four-legged murderer sat down below on the sidewalk barking like it was trying to rip out its own throat.

De Bané stopped, his eyes moist, his lips trembling. To his grief at losing a much-loved uncle was added the pain of losing a contract, since he knew full well that whoever took over the ownership of the building would never take him on. There followed a moment of silence.

"Are you going to the funeral, René?" someone asked.

De Bané gave the questioner a look that clearly showed how pained he was by such a question.

"When is it?" asked another listener. "I'd like to go too."

"Family only," sniffed De Bané. "By his own request."

"What I find most amazing," Steve breathed in Charles's ear, "is that he believes his own bullshit."

Just then a group of kids burst loudly into the room and came up to the cash to get a table. Everyone went back to their games. De Bané smoked two or three cigarettes while pacing up and down beside the bar, then took a table himself. Telling the story seemed to have calmed him down. He even began humming to himself as he played.

The owner leaned on the bar and watched him for a while. Then, tauntingly, a bit scornfully, he called over to him.

"Tell me, René, doesn't anything normal ever happen to you? You know: you cross a street and don't get run over by Santa Claus, or you go to a movie and a fire doesn't break out in the theatre, things like that?"

"All the time, my friend." And he burst out laughing.

■ ■ ■

By dint of constant little attentions, an unlimited supply of cigarettes, judicious counselling in matters relating to pool, and endless rounds of beer, De Bané succeeded in winning, if not Charles's and Steve's friendship, at least their tolerance. He even took them and their girlfriends out for meals to a nearby restaurant famous for its club sandwiches. Charles couldn't figure out how someone who seemed to live hand to mouth had so much money to throw around.

"He must have a racket," Agatha said. "I'm going to try to get him to tell us about it."

But neither her cleverness nor her charms were able to pry anything out of him but evasive pleasantries. The pool-hall regulars she quizzed couldn't tell her much either. Out of desperation she sought out the owner, despite his reputation for having no time for gossip. His only reply was a smile and a slight shrug of his shoulders, with his eyes focused on an indefinite point somewhere in the middle of the room.

Charles worked at his game like a man possessed and was on the verge of becoming something of a shark. He'd been beating Steve regularly for some time, and he was at least as good as players who were twice his age, some of whom he'd already sent to the showers; a few of them had even suggested he register for the next tournament. At the Orleans he was considered a regular; Nadine sometimes gave him credit, and the distinct impression that with a little effort on his part she would gladly give him a lot more than that.

One night in early June, however, when a stretch of fine weather was keeping most of the regulars away, an event took place that knocked Charles out of his habitual routine. He was playing with Marlene, Steve, and De Bané when the downstairs door banged open and he heard the sound of heavy footsteps coming up the stairs. A man appeared in the doorway, red-faced, hair dishevelled, shirt half unbuttoned; he leaned against the door frame and his eyes swept the room as though he was looking for someone. When Charles saw him he turned pale and crouched down behind the pool table, to the astonishment of his companions.

"Go back and open the door to the storeroom," he whispered to Steve. "I'm going to sneak back between the tables. I don't want that man to see me."

His friend thought he was joking, but a hard punch on his thigh made him realize that Charles was serious.

Steve made his way to the back of the room, followed by Charles crawling on all fours between the tables. Marlene and De Bané, sensing the seriousness of the situation, went on playing as though nothing were amiss.

"What's going on, buddy?" Steve asked when they were alone in the back room with the door closed.

"That's my father who just came in. I don't want to speak to him."

A slight tremor passed through Charles's jaw, and his eyes began leaping frantically around the room from one object to another – old pieces of furniture, tables piled with cans of soup and bottles of cleaning products – as though he were looking for a crack to hide in. They could hear Wilfrid Thibodeau laughing loudly at the bar, his strange, high-pitched cackle breaking off sharply, making him sound pitiful.

"Your father?" Steve exclaimed, surprised. "He's the guy who owns the hardware store?"

"He's not my real father, that's him out there, I've already told you," replied Charles angrily. "Now go, hurry up, get out of here before the owner comes in. He might've seen us. Go and tell him I've got to hide here, and no one is to come looking for me, for the love of God! When my father leaves, come and knock on the door."

Wilfrid seemed to be in a jubilant mood that night. Recognizing a drinker sitting at the bar, he sat down beside the man and began talking and laughing loudly at everything, every so often banging his fist on the counter. He laughed so hard and so long that two of the players put down their cues and joined the party. De Bané, smelling fresh blood for his ludicrous stories, left Steve and Marlene and went over to the group, which was already settling in to do some serious drinking. Wilfrid's laughter cranked up a notch and filled the four corners of the pool hall so full the room could barely contain it. Marlene went home, put out by the way the evening had turned sour.

Sitting on a broken chair in the dark, Charles stared at the line of light coming in under the door and rubbed his mouth and jaw. He remembered his father as a taciturn man, always grumpy, hardly ever laughing except when he was drunk, and even when he'd had a skinful his brief bouts of hilarity would suddenly turn into fierce anger at the slightest word from his mother, who had done her best to be a good parent. Never had he heard his father laugh like this, so uncontrollably, almost dementedly. His laughter echoed in Charles's ears like a threat. After a few minutes he could barely stand listening to it, but he forced himself to remain seated, his eye fixed on the thin band of light, trapped in this storeroom that reminded him of the bleak day he'd survived only by acts of courage and ingenuity, and the kindness of little Alice, who had allowed him to follow her through Wonderland. Tonight, however, Alice would not be able to help him. Alas.

Wilfrid decided he wanted to play pool, and he challenged De Bané to a game. A bet was laid. The game was even for the first few shots, then De Bané began potting balls with a nonchalance that made a few of the onlookers start to chuckle. The carpenter remained silent, chewing his lips, becoming more and more sullen, and he tried to use all the skill left to him in his drunken state. Suddenly he became angry and began insulting his opponent and accusing him of cheating. When De Bané, supported by the spectators, denied the charge, Thibodeau broke his cue on the table and threw it at him. The next moment the owner was grabbing him by the shoulders and throwing him out. For several minutes they could hear him shouting down in the street. The mood in the pool hall seemed to have darkened.

"He's gone," De Bané announced, leaning out one of the windows. "He's a total pain, that one."

A few customers left. Steve knocked on the door of the storeroom. When there was no response he stuck his head in and was met by a current of fresh air. Charles had found a small window hidden at the back behind some boxes and had succeeded in getting it open and crawling outside, where a fire escape had let him climb down to the street.

■ ■ ■

Charles stayed away from the pool hall for the next two weeks. His excuse was that he had too much work at the pharmacy, and in fact Monsieur Lalancette had asked him to add Thursday nights to his work schedule. But no one believed this was the real reason. He had made Steve and Marlene promise to keep the scene at the Orleans a secret, not wanting anyone else to know what a loser he had for a father. The two friends kept their word, though as much from indifference as from friendship, since such situations were not uncommon in the neighbourhood and few people would have been surprised by this one.

To the great relief of Fernand and Lucie, Charles began spending more time at home, falling back into some of his old habits. Once again they would find him reading in his room, or in the living room, or even in the bathroom (which he monopolized with the egocentric insouciance of a typical adolescent); he spent Sunday nights watching TV in his pyjamas, often in the company of Céline. He went back to visiting Parfait Michaud, to borrow books or simply to chat when the notary wasn't swamped with paperwork or tied up with clients.

One thing Lucie and Fernand didn't know was that the day after the incident at the pool hall, Charles had gone to Amélie Michaud and asked her if he could spend a little time in the Christmas room. He was only in there for ten minutes. The sickly sweet, artificial atmosphere in the room failed to have its usual effect on him; the magic didn't work; he was bored by the whole thing. Greatly disappointed, even shaken, by this failure, he left the house and headed towards his old daycare in the hope that the soul of the little yellow dog would still be hovering above the ground near the cherry tree, and that it would help him to find himself again, to see himself clearly once more. But he stopped after two or three blocks. The idea was absurd. He thought about phoning Blonblon, who always had a sympathetic ear to lend to his friends, but he couldn't find the courage to talk about his troubles, so he returned home, more downcast than ever.

The incident at the pool hall had thrown him for a loop. Not so much because of his father's behaviour (he wasn't his father any longer, after all), but because of the similarities he had discerned between the carpenter and himself. It was no accident, he thought, that the two of them had found themselves in the same pool hall at the same time. If Charles were a bit older they might have met in a bar, or a tavern, or a nightclub. He'd been drinking beer fairly regularly for months now, and the distaste he had always had for it was wearing off bit by bit. He was even beginning to like it. Like father, like son, as the saying went. Was he sliding down the same slippery slope, one that would take him into the nether regions where Wilfrid was now festering? Would he share the fate of a man he detested and for whom he'd never felt anything but contempt? Was there an escape hatch somewhere? Who could he find to help him? And how?

Well, he could confide in Boff. Lying on his bed one night, his hands resting on the dog's flanks, and gazing deeply into his eyes, he talked in a quiet voice about the things that were tormenting him inside, things he had never been able to tell anyone else. He emptied his heart of everything that had been eating away at him. Forgotten memories resurfaced, and once again he was four years old sitting at the kitchen table with his father, his father's red face spitting curses at him as he tried to force him to eat a plate of reheated spaghetti, while Alice sobbed in her bedroom with the door closed. He was engulfed again by a terrible sadness, as intense as it had been at the time, and tears rolled down his cheeks. Boff regarded him with an air of powerless sympathy, then licked the end of his nose and the corner of his left eye.

Days went by. One afternoon after a biology class he waited until the classroom emptied, even looking out into the hall to make sure no one could hear him, then went up to the teacher, who was gathering his papers and putting them in his briefcase; a cigarette in his mouth, his throat tight, his ears burning, for the tenth time rewording the question he had resolved to ask, he waited for the teacher to look up.

"Yes, Thibodeau?" asked Léon Belzile. His voice was grave and a bit hoarse, but his look was friendly. He considered Charles to be one of his most brilliant students, even if he was a bit of a smart aleck. "What can I do for you?"

"I've got a strange question to ask you."

Belzile saw that Charles was genuinely troubled and guessed how difficult it had been for him to come forward. He assumed the nonchalant air usually employed to make timid people feel more at home.

"Strange questions are quite often the best kind. What's it about?"

"It's about . . . er, heredity, I guess, or something like that, anyway."

"Let's go for heredity."

"We know that if a man has a big schnozz there's a good chance his daughter will also have a big schnozz, right? The same with hair colour, body type, shape of the hands and feet, and certain diseases, like diabetes, for example . . ."

"Right. We know all that, Thibodeau. It's called the transference of physical traits via the genes. The subject is thoroughly covered, you may perhaps recall, in the fourth chapter of your biology text."

Charles hesitated. His eyes left the teacher's face and drifted over to a half-erased word on the blackboard.

"Is it the same for . . . a person's character?"

"Ah, well now, that's a bit more complicated, because, as we've known for some time, education and environment are important influences on character. If you take an Inuit baby living in poverty and transplant it to a family of millionaires in Arizona, it certainly wouldn't develop the same character as it would have if you'd left it to grow up among its own people."

He gave a short laugh, pleased with his example.

Charles nodded, thoughtful, but the expression on his face showed that he hadn't found the answer entirely satisfying. He tried to think of another way to pose the question, and suddenly it came out all at once.

"What about alcoholism, sir?" he asked, turning red. "Is that a heredi-tary disease?"

Belzile's eyes widened, his nostrils twitched, and he pursed his lips; the pain and anguish he saw behind the question were quite disconcerting.

"Hmm. How can I put this, Charles? To be honest, no one knows the answer to that. There are those who believe alcoholism to be a genetic deficiency, but so far I find their studies unconvincing. Let's say it's still at the hypothetical stage. Why, is there something worrying you?"

Charles took on a serious air. His troubled look had almost entirely dis-appeared, as though he felt better for having resigned himself to making a clean breast of it.

"My father is an alcoholic, sir. I mean my real father. I don't live with him, I live with another family, where things are fine. . . . I don't want to become like him, not at all. And yet I've been drinking beer for some time now. At first I didn't like the taste, it even made me sick. But lately it's like I've gotten used to it, and now . . ."

He gave a pitiful smile and looked away.

Belzile was touched in a way he hadn't been touched for a long time. He came around from behind his desk and put his hand on his student's shoulder.

"Don't worry, Charles. In my opinion, you're getting upset for nothing. In any case, the very fact that you're worried about it is reassuring. And of course, if you do discover that tendency in yourself, there's a solution, isn't there? You could . . . well . . . exercise your willpower, as it were, decide not to touch it again. Simple as that! I have a friend who used to have a terri-ble problem with alcohol, and I mean terrible. His wife left him, he lost his job, his health was starting to go down the tubes. No question, he was bottoming out, this friend of mine, the very bottom. . . . And then one day he decided to quit, and he took steps to break the habit. It's been ten years now since he touched a drop, and he's been living a normal life, as happy as I think it's possible to be in this world. Of course, you're not bottom-ing out yet, are you?" he added, patting Charles on the shoulder.

"No, I don't think so," Charles replied with a weak smile.

A feeling of relief washed over him and, at the same time, a strong desire to end this conversation, which he now regretted having started.

"Thank you," he said, making his way to the door.

Belzile lit a cigarette and watched him go, not knowing if what he had said had been enough. The problems that had driven his student to confide in him could very well be more serious than they seemed. Should he have got the boy to open up more?

"Charles . . ."

Charles stopped and turned, already thinking about something else; the look he gave his teacher was tinged with indifference.

"Don't be too hung up about it, eh?" he said with an embarrassed smile. "At the end of the day, we're all the masters of our own destinies. Good luck."

Charles's face brightened for a second. He gave a brief nod and left.

"Is that true, I wonder?" the teacher asked himself, stroking his chin and leaning against his desk. "Are we the masters of our own destinies?"

■ ■ ■

Charles lost much of his interest in playing pool and drinking beer – activities that even without his private fears had provided him with only a limited amount of pleasure. The fear of finding himself once again in the same room with his father, and worse, developing the same habits as his father, made him avoid hanging around with Steve, who took to calling him "Gramps" and "home-boy" and "a cool turd." But he still kept seeing Marlene. In a way, he couldn't help himself. He was fond of her, despite her crudeness, and didn't take offence at her sluttish ways, mostly because he benefited from them. But the pleasures of sex alone didn't account for his attraction to her.

Marlene possessed the evenness of temper and spontaneous generosity of all good-natured voluptuaries: uncomplicated, seeing only the surfaces of things, easily satisfied because they demanded so little of life. Charles liked her easy, rippling laugh, a laugh that reminded him of Christmas bells, and above all the heart she put into it. When he was with her, he found himself resorting to all sorts of buffoonery in order to hear her laugh. In short, he enjoyed her company immensely. She introduced him to the mysteries of the female anatomy in ways that he would remember for the rest of his life. She taught him how to cook, which he would also find useful later on. For her part, her contact with Charles refined her slightly. She no longer thought of Harlequin Romances as the *ne plus ultra* of literature. She had her first taste of wine with him – an inexpensive Valpolicella that Charles had had before at the Michauds' – and she no longer thought that men with a vocabulary of more than four hundred words were effeminate.

"I get the feeling the crisis has passed," Fernand said one evening as he and his wife were walking home together from the hardware store.

"There'll be others, Fernand, don't worry. No one becomes a man in six months . . ."

Without knowing it, Wilfrid Thibodeau had had a salutary effect on his son. But in a short while, and again without his being aware of it, he was going to plunge him into a real horror show.

7

S everal months went by. One night, in July 1982, after his last delivery
for the pharmacy, Charles helped Henri Lalancette decant two litres
of port dregs into small vials. The pharmacist had procured the dregs
through his acquaintance with the director of a laboratory run by the
Liquor Control Board of Quebec, and he was going to make use of them
in a series of (according to him, in any case) definitive experiments.
Afterwards, Charles left to meet Blonblon at the Frontenac metro station,
and the two young men sat for a moment on a bench by the entrance,
enjoying the delicious freshness of the air settling over the city after a blis-
tering, completely still day, a day when even the idea of doing anything
made sweat roll down the middle of one's back.

An old, partly crippled man appeared, looking stern and solemn in a
black suit and tie, and began hobbling across the square as though walking
barefoot on hot coals. Charles leaned towards his friend and whispered
something, and Blonblon burst out laughing. Realizing that they were
laughing at him, the man stopped and gave them a withering look, and
they laughed again, although more quietly this time. Then Blonblon suggested they watch *Apocalypse Now* on television; his father had just had
air-conditioning installed in their living room.

Both of them were going through a bad patch. Blonblon had split up
with Caroline two months before and was wallowing in prideful solitude,
obstinately refusing to say a word about the cause of their breakup, despite

the fact that he had heard so many of Charles's confidences. Charles was still seeing Marlene, off and on, but less and less. They had grown tired of each other; she had quit school and was working as a cashier in a Provigo supermarket, spending her time picking up clerks and customers. Charles had gone out with two or three other girls from school, but for the moment he preferred being alone, dreaming of the ideal woman.

He hardly saw Steve at all any more. Steve's family had moved to Pointe-Saint-Charles at the beginning of the summer, and it looked as though the day was fast approaching when they would be total strangers, with nothing whatsoever to say to each other.

Since the film wasn't coming on until late, Charles convinced his friend to take the metro with him to McGill Street, to a bookstore called the Palais du Livre, where he bought a used copy of *Gone With the Wind?* that was nearly falling apart; Blonblon picked up a copy of René Ducharme's *The Swallower Swallowed*, which Charles had praised to the skies.

The film lasted until one in the morning, and left them in such a disturbed state of mind that they sat talking in the little park in front of Blonblon's building until two-thirty. Charles walked home whistling "The Ride of the Valkyries," struck by the strange charm of the sleeping city and thinking with satisfaction that he would soon be turning sixteen, that his whole life was stretched out ahead of him, and that it would be filled with an incalculable number of perfectly wonderful nights like this one that was just coming to an end.

He quietly slipped his key into the lock, and closed the door carefully when he got into the hallway. There he took off his shoes and tip-toed along the corridor, keeping to the right, where the floorboards didn't squeak. A quiet return home avoided all sorts of excuses and explanations.

To his great surprise the kitchen door was closed and light was coming from underneath it. He took a few steps down the hall and stood at the door to his own room, listening. He heard a series of loud sighs followed by the clinking of glass, a sound that was all too familiar to him from his previous life. Someone was drinking himself into a foul mood. It could only be Fernand. A faint odour of rum, the hardware store owner's favourite drink, came to his nostrils. What was Fernand doing drinking rum in the kitchen at three o'clock in the morning?

What terrible thing had happened to him?

Charles was torn between going to bed (and lying awake all night, torturing himself with questions) and risking a conversation with a man who was drunk (the idea frightened and sickened him at the same time). Suddenly he heard a stirring and Lucie appeared, tying her bathrobe. He barely had time to withdraw into the shadows before the hallway was flooded with light as she pushed open the kitchen door. He heard her subdued voice, pleading and very worried, in the otherwise silent house.

"Fernand, come on, come to bed. Please, Fernand. What's the use of staying up the whole night like this?"

"I'm not sleepy."

"Come and curl up against me anyway. It'll be nicer that way, won't it?"

"I'm in no mood to curl up against anyone."

There followed a conversation that seemed to have taken place many times already. Fernand was unable to stop brooding over whatever it was that was tormenting him, and his bitterness continued to increase. Charles was riveted to the spot. Time stopped. How long did he stay there in the darkness, his eyes unfocused, his mouth trembling, trying to figure out what was going on? Ten minutes? Thirty?

Gradually, through the snippets of conversation he could overhear, he was able to piece the story together.

As if Fernand didn't have enough to worry about, a new problem had appeared, one much bigger than all the rest. Bigger and more appalling, because Charles was involved in it, in a way – a horrible way.

Wilfrid Thibodeau had gone to see Fernand two weeks before to ask him for more money. He hadn't worked in months and he was saddled with debts. The brief confrontation had taken place in the small warehouse beside the hardware store. Furious, Fernand had shown Thibodeau the door, and Thibodeau had threatened him: "I'll give you some time to think it over, my friend," he had said coldly, "but if you want my advice, you'd be wise to take out a lot of insurance on this place."

Grabbing the drunkard by the shoulders, Fernand had propelled him out of the warehouse and into the store, and then, to the astonishment of Lucie and three customers, who had turned at the sound of raised voices, he'd given Thibodeau the bum's rush to the door. There the carpenter had narrowly escaped the rough justice of Fernand's boot, which had just missed connecting with the seat of his pants; instead it brushed his back pocket and sent his frayed wallet flying into the air.

"I shouldn't have given up playing soccer," Fernand had quipped, his face flushed from his exertions. "I'm losing my touch."

Everyone had laughed, and after a few days Fernand had forgotten the incident. But when he'd arrived at the store that morning he'd found an empty gasoline can and a book of matches lying beside the wooden wall of the warehouse. It was a clear warning. Lucie had wanted to call the police. "And what good would that do, eh? Do you think they'll send a cop over to spend every night in our yard? Come on, use your head, you know how these things are. The police won't get involved until the firemen have watched the place burn to the ground!"

But in the end, at his wife's insistence, he'd filed a complaint against Thibodeau.

That afternoon an officer had come to the store, taken a look at the gas can without seeming very interested in it, made a few notes in his note-book, then left, saying the police would look into it. "Rooster feathers will be growing out of my ass before they look into anything," Fernand had grumbled disgustedly.

He had an electrician come and install two powerful spotlights in the yard. But he knew how easy it was to set fire to a building! Committing arson was safer than making candy; all proof of the arsonist's presence usually went up in smoke, gone, disappeared. Towards five o'clock Lucie had found Fernand in his office, a total wreck. "The only thing I can think of is to sell the place," he said. "If there's still time . . ."

In the kitchen, the two of them discussed the situation at length. Then Lucie angrily took the bottle of rum, emptied it into the sink, and convinced her husband to go to bed. Ten minutes later the bedroom was reverberating with his snores.

Charles lay on his bed, Boff stretched out along his leg, and watched the day approach through his window. He hadn't bothered to pull the blind, since he'd known he'd be awake all night. For a long while a star twinkled above the back alley, its solitary light courageously defying the immensity of the night; from time to time a dark, purplish cloud mass would obscure it from Charles's view, but it always managed to gain the upper hand simply by staying put. As the sky turned milky blue the star slowly faded, defeated at last by the light it had helped to shed. Translucent swaths of pink and pale green spread across the sky, and suddenly everything took on its normal shape. The alley became an alley, the brick wall and tiled roof of the house next door reappeared in all their familiar and reassuring details, the branch of the basswood tree reached out above the fence with its usual grace; the birds resumed their singing, cars and buses began their rumbling. A new day was starting, and he could either fill it with something useful or do nothing about it at all.

■ ■ ■

Charles got up and ate his breakfast hurriedly while Boff chomped his in the corner. Then he dressed and took Boff out for a walk. He couldn't sit still, and he had three whole hours to wait until the credit union opened. It was his turn to act. Fernand and Lucie had done their bit, now it was up to him to take over. But how was he going to go about it? He thought he had an approach to the problem, but actually going through with it was the most difficult part.

He walked for a long time, smoking cigarette after cigarette, and eventually found himself in Médéric-Martin Park, as deserted as a coral reef at this time of the day. Somewhere far off a church bell rang very slowly. Its muted, unassuming voice pealed with such calmness that it seemed to be inviting everyone to stop for a moment and reflect. Across rue Gascon

113

two women in grey hats, tall and straight in their dark dresses, walked carefully along the sidewalk, probably on their way to church. Suddenly Charles felt tired. He sank down onto a bench; Boff, conscious of the unusual nature of their outing, busied himself sniffing at everything in the vicinity.

"Come here, Boff. Stay close to me!" Charles called, but the dog seemed not to have heard him.

His throat burned from having smoked too many cigarettes, and his thoughts, which so far had seemed clear and almost too free-flowing, were becoming cloudier by the minute.

"What a drag!" he murmured to himself. "Why can't he just leave us alone, once and for all? Why doesn't he just get lost and go to hell? Do everyone a favour . . ."

He raised his hand to his cigarette pack, then thought better of it. His head sank onto his chest and he closed his eyes.

When he awoke, the sun was warming his legs. Two little girls in blue overalls were standing motionless in front of him, watching him gravely.

"Charlotte! Melanie! Come over here!" called a young woman's voice.

The two girls ran off.

He stretched, yawned, rubbed his back where it had been pressed against the bench, then jumped to his feet and looked around the park for Boff. The dog was sleeping under the bench.

"You gave me a fright, old friend," he said, kneeling down and shaking him. "Come on, get up, we've got to go."

Though his sleep had been filled with confused, agitated dreams, it had renewed his resolve. As he walked home, he managed to work out a plan of action.

At the house he found Céline in the kitchen, making toast. She was seated at the table, one foot raised on a chair rung, concentrating on wiping a spot of jam from the tablecloth with her finger. The back of her neck was a delicious caramel colour; it glowed softly through the strands of her black hair. Charles stood in the doorway, struck by her grace.

"Where've you been?" she said, looking up and smiling at him.

"I went for a walk."

"You were a real early bird. You're as bad as Papa. He left for work at seven, and Mama's just gone to join him. Poor man. This business has thrown him for a loop. We should help him, but what can we do? Do you want some toast?"

He said yes, just to prolong the moment. Sitting across from her, he continued to watch her surreptitiously. What was it about her? Had she grown even lovelier overnight? He found her more attractive than ever. She was like a squirrel, but a squirrel that had somehow, as though by magic, grown calm and affectionate. He wanted to touch her neck; perhaps some of her sweetness and gentleness would rub off on him. He could sure use a bit of sweetness and gentleness this morning!

"There's a fly on your neck," he said, brushing her warm, velvety skin with the tips of his fingers. He played with one of her curls.

She laughed, undeceived by his pretence.

"That tickles," she said. "What do you want on your toast?"

"Leave it, I'll do it."

"No, no, let me," she said happily, a tender, mischievous gleam in her eye.

He bit into the toast – it was soggy with butter and dripping with raspberry jam – and watched her do the same. Her nostrils dilated with pleasure, and she looked small in her too-large pyjamas. Her bare foot curved gently around the chair rung. Suddenly he felt his face turning red. She went on smiling at him.

"Boff!" he called, looking around. "Come and eat!"

The dog ran up to him and took the piece of toast.

"I'm going to try to do something for Fernand this morning," he announced suddenly, almost regretting his words before they were out. But he urgently wanted to be useful. "You have to promise you won't say anything to anyone. Promise, Céline?"

She listened to him in silence, crunching her toast, and the admiring expression that spread across her face as he described his plan chased away Charles's last fears and gave him a reckless desire to throw himself into action.

"I'm going to do it now," he said, standing up. "If Lucie or Fernand call, tell them I've gone over to Blonblon's, okay?"

She nodded and also stood up. Then, with a rapid, supple movement that froze him to the spot, she pressed herself against him and put her arms around him.

"Be careful, Charles. You're being very brave, and very good. I don't know anyone else like you. . . . Shouldn't someone go with you, though? Like Henri, maybe? He's as strong as a bull, you know."

"No," Charles replied coolly, disengaging himself from her. "This is my doing and I'll take care of it. Besides, there isn't time. I want to be back by supper."

■ ■ ■

He left the house and walked to the credit union on Fullum, where he emptied his account: the one thousand five hundred and fifty-five dollars and sixty-four cents, most of it in hundreds, made a satisfying bulge in his pocket.

Standing outside the building he looked across the street: to the left was his old school, Jean-Baptiste-Meilleur, where he had scored such a success with *Le Cid*; to his right, beside the school, was Saint-Eusèbe Church, where his mother's funeral had taken place. "Come on," he said to himself, shaking his head. "Get your ass in gear."

His next move was to find out where his father was living. It was probably somewhere in the neighbourhood. He returned to the park, where there was a telephone booth, and looked up his father's name in the phone book. It wasn't there, and the operator had no listing for it, either. It then occurred to him that if he checked out all the bars, brasseries, and taverns in the area he'd be bound to run into him, or else find someone who knew where he was living. He set off and went into the first place he came to, the Rivest Brasserie, on rue Ontario near Frontenac.

The brasserie was almost empty. It was an old, seedy-looking place. Two large men were sitting with a woman next to the counter, smoking and talking.

"You're not getting old, Émile," said one of the men, punching the other man lightly on the shoulder.

"Oh yes I am. I'm getting old," said the second man. "An' if you can't see it, it's because your eyesight's failing. I'm turning into an old fart."

Charles stood uneasily in the doorway, looking around the room. The walls were trying to hide their scars and bruises under a thick coat of bile-green paint. They must have seen generations of drinkers, he thought; it was as though all the shouting, the rattling of glasses and bottles, the scraping of boots on the floor, and the sounds of all the fights that had broken out had made the walls look cracked and broken.

The woman looked up and came towards him. Her long, blond hair and desiccated body made him grimace involuntarily.

"What can I do for you, young man?" she asked, in a voice that was both hard and inviting.

Charles explained that he was looking for a man named Wilfrid Thibodeau. Did she know him?

"Wilf? Sure I know him. He's in here all the time."

"Do you know where he lives?"

She turned to the two men at the table.

"Hey, any of you guys know Wilf's address?"

"This spring he was living on rue Préfontaine, down by the park," Émile said. "But he moved three weeks ago. I don't know where to."

The aging blonde smiled at Charles and shrugged her shoulders, as though to say: "You're a good-looking guy, dearie, but I'm afraid that's the best I can do for you this time."

"Thanks," Charles said, and left.

He made the rounds of the neighbourhood, going from tavern to bar, from bar to brasserie. A friendly sun was gently warming the city; the streets, swept as they were by a tepid breeze, seemed wider and more spacious than usual; there was a clarity in the air that made everything seem lighter. It was the kind of weather that seemed to make everyone look younger and enliven even the most modest corner. The light seemed to come from all directions at once, from the walls and the sidewalks, from the leaves on the trees, even from the hydro poles lining the streets. As occasionally happens for totally inexplicable reasons, the streets and sidewalks teemed with beautiful women, dressed and coiffed in a thousand exciting ways, each with her own particular beauty and her own small imperfections that only made her more desirable. They had ways of drawing attention to the fine line of their mouths, or to their eyes or breasts, the curves of their calves and thighs, the contours of their bare feet in expensive sandals, of leaving behind a phosphorescent trail of wistful looks. Moved by such exquisite abundance, Charles could hardly stop turning around and sighing. He regretted not having anyone to share his impressions with. In his mind he saw Céline's foot curved seductively on the chair rung, and his lips tingled with the desire to kiss it.

The city trembled with a furious joie de vivre that passed into him and blended in a bizarre way with the anger that was causing him to track Wilfrid down. Several times he was tempted to drop the whole thing, give himself over to this vague, sun-filled drunkenness that was rising within him, but he shrugged off the feeling with disdain. He had to find his father and cancel him out once and for all, with a positive equal to his father's negative, as though the whole thing were a simple algebraic equation; when you came right down to it, it was a problem of mathematics. That was no doubt how Fernand and Lucie saw it, and that was how he must see it, too.

Around eleven o'clock he decided to use the metro and buses to save time, since his fruitless quest was taking him farther and farther from his starting point. He went from place to place, sticking his head into bars and taverns, taking a quick look around, asking his question and always getting more or less the same answer: yes, they all knew Wilfrid Thibodeau, some vaguely, others quite well, but no, they didn't know where he was living at the moment. He wasn't the kind of guy who talked much about his personal life.

After a while he had the strange feeling of going into and out of the same place, over and over. Whether it was the Bienvenue Tavern on rue Amherst, or the Chez Baptiste Brasserie on Mont-Royal, or the Baudrias Tavern on Rachel, or the Donaldson Bar on Ontario, it was always the same decor: grey-tiled floor, captain's chairs, one pool table, varnished pine walls, yellowish light, air filled with smoke. It was Wilfrid Thibodeau's world, a checkerboard of identical squares through which his father made his way, performing exactly the same ritual each time: a large Molson's here, a Take-5-for-50-ale there, until the final belch brought up with its odour of fermented hops the soul of a drinker whose throat was perpetually dry.

At one o'clock he was tired, impatient, fed up with so many perfect legs and tanned shoulders, and starving. He went into the Famous Smoked Meat Restaurant at the corner of Saint-Denis and Mont-Royal, the "modern" facade of which was stuck brutally onto a beautiful, old, brick building.

He was just finishing his Cottage Pudding when he suddenly remembered that for a long time his father used to hang out at a bar with the grandiose name Les Amis du Sport. He checked the telephone book to make sure the place still existed, then paid his bill and headed for the metro. On his way he passed a second-hand shop, in the window of which was a small switchblade knife that caught his eye. He went in and bought it. It had a smooth leather-and-polished-wood handle that fit nicely into the palm of his hand. "Maybe it'll bring me luck," he said, rubbing it and slipping it into his pocket.

Les Amis du Sport was squeezed into the angle formed by the intersection of Logan and de Lorimier, near the Papineau metro station. It took Charles twenty minutes to get there. It seemed a notch or two above the level of the places he'd already visited that day. For once the grey-tiled floor was clean; the chairs had cushions and the arms were padded. Two ceiling fans circulated a measure of fresh air in the room, and a third fan installed in a wall expelled the stale air. Above the bar there was an imposing diorama in the style of the Bourgault brothers, depicting an old-time sugaring-off party. There were half a dozen customers in the bar, two sitting at one table, four others talking quietly at the counter. Charles didn't recognize any of them. Suddenly he felt like having a cold beer, and he sat at a table by the wall beside a varnished wooden drum, hoping no one would make a fuss about his age; above his head was a TV screen with the sound turned off, showing a baseball game. A young waitress came over. She had wide hips, round arms, and a cold eye, and she looked him over suspiciously.

"How old are you?" she said.

"Eighteen. You want to see my ID?" And he turned red, as though someone had just pulled his pants down.

She looked hesitant, then gave a slight shrug and took his order.

"And bring me a ham sandwich, too, please," he added, although he didn't feel the slightest bit hungry.

"Please" was a word she didn't often hear from customers, and she gave him a light smile. In a somewhat softer voice she asked if he would like mustard or mayonnaise.

"Mustard," he said.

"Hot or regular?"

"Hot."

She smiled again and went off to the kitchen with a spring in her step.

"She might be going to tell the owner," Charles thought, and his cheeks turned fiery red once more. He thought about running out, but that would have been acting like an idiot. Instead, he stretched out his legs and sat facing into the room.

Several minutes went by. Complicated business, he thought, making a ham sandwich.

"Robert Bourassa?" exclaimed one of the four men at the counter. "That's bullshit! I wouldn't have that guy for a doorman! A worm could teach him something about standing up for himself. He made me feel ashamed the whole time he was in power! And what did he leave behind when he got out? A few hydro dams in James Bay, and that's it! We need him like we need a hole in the head!"

Amused, Charles listened to their conversation. Then, looking up, he noticed that the wall was plastered with photographs of all the famous people who had been in the bar; one of them was of the businessman Pierre Péladeau, shaking hands with a man who had a kind of puzzled smile on his face.

The waitress placed his sandwich on the table, along with a glass and a bottle.

"Three-fifty," she said.

Charles paid her and took a bite of his sandwich before realizing he could hardly swallow it. Why on earth had he ordered the stupid thing? He felt miserable. He'd wasted five whole hours, and it was almost time for him to go to the pharmacy. Meanwhile, Fernand and Lucie were still worried sick. Maybe tonight would be the night the hardware store burned down. He looked feverishly about him, fighting for air.

Two tables away, an old man with yellowed, ill-fitting skin was reading a newspaper in a cloud of smoke. He had a cigar in his mouth and was wearing a wig that gave him the air of a much younger man. He looked ridiculous, but not formidable. Charles leaned towards him.

"Excuse me, sir, but have you been coming here for a long time?"

"Thirty-two years, my boy. Longer than you have, I'd say." He laughed.

"Yes, in fact this is my first time here. It seems like an okay place."

"It's got its good points," the old man agreed.

"Tell me," Charles said, after taking a drink of beer, "have you ever run into a man named Wilfrid Thibodeau?"

"He and I had a drink together in here just last night, my friend."

"Oh yeah? It's just that I'm trying to locate him."

A few minutes later, having replied in the vaguest possible terms to his curious neighbour's questions about why he was trying to track down the carpenter, Charles learned that his father had been living for the past two weeks in a small rooming house on rue Parthenais, across from the famous prison and not two minutes' walk from Les Amis du Sport. His amiable informant, whose name was Oscar Turgeon, even knew the address – he began fumbling through his pockets looking for his notebook – because he'd lent his car to Thibodeau when he was moving his things, "the back seat folded down, you see, there's a small tear in the fabric on the left side but it isn't too noticeable." Charles wrote the address on a paper napkin, thanked the man, and left the tavern, his heart pounding.

He walked along a row of modest, one-storey, brick buildings that seemed to be shrinking away from the enormous black rectangle that was the Parthenais Prison, a strange and hideous mass that had landed in the neighbourhood like a spaceship signalling an alien invasion. The idea that his father would be living across the street from it brought a furtive smile to his lips; it was a solution he heartily endorsed. But a tightness in his throat made him draw in his breath: he was standing in front of the building in which his father lived. In a few minutes it would all be over. If he had enough courage to go through with it.

8

Wilfrid Thibodeau had had a headache for the past three days. Nothing worked, not Aspirin, not hot and cold compresses, not even the huge, yellow pills the convenience store owner's wife had given him the night before that were supposed to perform miracles. A buzzsaw was cutting the top of his head off, and some sadist was pressing on the back of his neck, causing an oily sort of nausea that wouldn't let him eat enough to keep a bird alive. Alcohol worked, a bit, for a while, but since he had to meet a contractor later that afternoon who might have a job for him at a Jean Coutu pharmacy, he'd decided to stay off the booze until after the interview was over, just to improve his chances.

He was slumped over the kitchen table, vaguely listening to a song on the radio and begging for something to put an end to his torture, when a relatively happy thought entered his head. As it was the first in a long time, he let it hang around for a while.

The convenience store owner's wife had been friendly to him. He barely knew her, had hardly been civil to her until last night when she gave him the pills. But her friendliness could be useful to him. Her husband was a fat tub of lard who looked half asleep most of the time and muttered nothing but idiocies. She must have lost interest in him ages ago. Maybe she needed a man. And a woman who needed a man was easy on the purse strings when she found a man who could please her. She wasn't much to look at herself, mind, but so what? These were tough times, he couldn't afford to be choosy. He could look around for a younger chick when he had a bit of scratch in his pocket.

At that point the saw started buzzing through his head again. He should try not to think, turn himself into a board or a bag of cement. Or sleep. The goddamn pain had kept him awake most of the night. He folded his arms on the table and put his head down sideways, closed his eyes, and tried to relax. After a few minutes a kind of numbness began to dull the saw's teeth, and he was on the verge of falling asleep when the doorbell rang.

"Who the hell could that be?" he muttered, getting up. "I'm not expecting anyone."

Through the muslin curtain left on the door by some previous tenant he saw a tall young man standing on the porch, but he couldn't make out his face.

He opened the door and stood there for a few seconds without saying anything.

"Is it you?" he whispered, his voice sinking to the back of his throat. "Hello. What do you want?"

Charles made a strange sound, a mixture of surprise and pity, but said nothing. Then, finally, he said, "Can I come in? I want to talk to you."

From the tone of his voice, Thibodeau could tell whatever Charles had to say to him wouldn't be good. He frowned, then forced himself to smile, and slowly closed the door behind his son.

"I was on my way out. But I can give you a couple of minutes."

He shuffled back into the kitchen, slightly bent over, his arms hanging by his sides. "He's sick," Charles said to himself. "Maybe really sick. He's almost an old man. What I have to say to him isn't going to help much."

There was a yellow formica table with chrome legs at the centre of the tiny room, and three chairs covered with vinyl in the same colour. The bright light that reigned outside was hardly penetrating the greasy panes of the single window above the filthy sink. The counter was full of empty bottles, a few kitchen utensils, dirty plates, and a plastic bag in which some shirts were soaking in bluish-grey water. It was an allegory of chaos. The stink of burnt fat, cigarette smoke, and stale beer permeated the air.

Thibodeau pulled out a chair. "Have a seat," he said.

He sat down across the table with a deep groan.

"Okay, so what brings you here?"

Charles tried to think of a way to begin.

"You don't look very well. Are you okay?"

"Splitting headache. Three days now. It's killin' me, for Chrissakes."

"Go see a doctor. It's free."

Thibodeau nodded and his face twisted with pain. His eye clouded over and he rubbed his forehead. Then suddenly he looked up at Charles, his eyes clear, incisive, arrogant.

"I don't suppose you came here to talk about my health. Go ahead, spit it out."

Charles blushed and fidgeted in his chair.

"You know why I came to see you."

Thibodeau looked at him with a smile playing lightly on his lips. The shrunken sufferer was gone and had been replaced by a clever fox with dangerous teeth.

"The other day I heard you made some sort of threat to Fernand," Charles continued. "And then they found that gas can." His face hardened. "It made me feel sick! I couldn't believe you'd sunk so low!"

He stood up, shoved his shaking hand into his pocket, and took out his wallet: a small object fell out onto the floor, but neither of them noticed.

Thibodeau gave a low whistle. A pile of hundred-dollar bills had fallen onto the table with a faint rustle.

"You want money, go ahead, take it!" Charles cried theatrically. "You can have it all, everything I've got: fifteen hundred dollars. But that's the end of it! If you ever come back again, you'll have to answer to me."

A shudder went through his body and stuck in his throat, and he didn't think he could go on talking.

The carpenter remained seated and stared impassively at Charles. He stretched out his arms along the table as though to rake in the money, then, in a low voice full of calm disdain, he murmured, "You don't know what you're saying."

"And you," shouted Charles, shaking with anger and fear, "you don't know what you're doing."

A moment passed. In the apartment above them someone switched on a radio full-blast, then quickly shut it off.

"Take your money," Thibodeau said, his voice still calm, "and get the hell out of here."

"I'm not leaving until you promise to stop bothering Fernand."

He couldn't stop trembling, and his voice came out in sobs. The carpenter smiled again and, still sitting down, began counting the hundred-dollar bills. The sight of them seemed to be having a certain effect on him.

"My, my," he said, almost to himself. "You're right. Fifteen hundred smackeroos."

He placed them in a small pile to one side, stroked them thoughtfully for a moment with his forefinger, then took one bill from the pile and put it in his shirt pocket. He pushed the rest towards Charles.

"I'm keeping one to teach you a lesson about being polite, kid. You shouldn't talk to me like that. Now get out, I've had enough of you for now. Come back when you're in a better mood."

His eye fell to the floor and to the knife that had fallen out of Charles's pocket. He bent down and picked it up, then looked at it, smiling nastily.

"So, what do you know, a switchblade. . . . Nice one, too. . . . What were you going to do with it, stick it in my guts?"

"Give it back," murmured the adolescent, his voice hoarse.

Thibodeau flicked open the blade and slid the end of his index finger along the edge, then gently pushed the tip into the palm of his hand.

"A real nice little knife," he said, standing up. "Could come in real handy."

He turned the knife over and over in his hand, looking steadily at his son, who had become livid.

"I think I might keep this little baby too."

Suddenly Charles sprang at him, pushing him violently backward. The carpenter fell onto his chair and went over, hitting his head on the refrigerator door with a dull crack. Running around the table, Charles threw himself on the man and began pounding him with his fists as hard as he could. Thibodeau let out a shout of fury and punched at the boy's face with his free hand, kicking at him with his feet. The table overturned with a crash and banknotes fluttered everywhere. The two continued fighting, more and more violently. The carpenter, still unable to get back on his feet, cried out in pain and smashed his fist into his son's head. Charles didn't let up. The knife rolled onto the floor. Charles threw himself at it, then bounded for the door. The next instant he was running down the sidewalk, followed by demented shouts from his father, who was standing in the doorway shaking his fist.

Charles ran as far as de Maisonneuve, then slowed down, out of breath, avoiding an elderly couple with their Pekingese who had stopped to watch him. He made his way to Sainte-Catherine, saw a restaurant, went in, and locked himself in the men's washroom. His right cheek was red and beginning to swell, and a blue mark was appearing at the corner of his eye. Other than that he appeared to be in one piece. He made a compress with a wad of paper towels soaked in cold water and held it to his cheek, brushed his hair in place, and lit a cigarette. His heart pounded with despicable joy.

"Damn," he suddenly cried, looking at his watch. "I'm going to be late for work!"

His cheek didn't look too bad; it might have been caused by a severe toothache. He left the restaurant, hurrying past the complaints of the owner, who was standing behind the counter with a dishcloth in his hand grumbling about people who came in to use his washrooms without bothering to order so much as a cup of coffee, and went down into the Papineau metro station. The large ceramic fresco inside the station – with its strong, bold colours showing Louis-Joseph Papineau, the fiery politician with the distinctive tuft of hair, standing before a monument during a skirmish in the 1837 Rebellion – sent a surge of warmth to his face. He stopped, took a deep breath, stuck out his chest, and smiled. He, too, had triumphed. He had the knife in his pocket to prove it. And the hundred-dollar bills were in the kitchen with the old man. He would do even better than Papineau, he would see his victory through to the end, even though at the moment he had no idea what that end might be.

Sitting in the subway car, he rubbed his throbbing right temple and tried to think up a story to explain the state of his face to Monsieur Lalancette.

In the seat across from him a young woman in a black dress was showing off her splendid legs. They were pink and glowing with health. From time to time she wiggled her feet in their black open-toed shoes with enormous high heels. He watched her from the corner of his eye, her pretty face, her legs crying out for love and passion for life. He suddenly wanted to involve this woman in the victory he had just won over his father, but how he would do that he didn't know. Should he sit beside her and chat her up? Simply smile at her, or wink? Follow her off the metro and speak to her? His wounded cheek made the venture seem risky. A few seconds later he would arrive at the Frontenac station, where he had to get off. The train began to slow down, and the brakes came on.

Suddenly he was gripped by a transport of joy: he knew what he was going to do. He leaned forward on his seat, ready to leap up. The second the doors began to open he threw himself on the young woman, kissed her on both cheeks, and dashed off the train under the dumbfounded gaze of the other passengers; the car filled with bursts of laughter, and the victim, astonished, intrigued, and a little alarmed, began talking animatedly to a woman sitting beside her.

Charles, meanwhile, had reached the street level, once again out of breath. He checked to make sure no one was following him, then set off rapidly towards rue Ontario, looking around with great satisfaction. It had definitely been a good day. Couldn't have been better. Every obstacle in his way had melted before the sheer force of his will. A fierce joy seized him and he jumped in the air and clapped his hands, nearly frightening to death an old woman who had been shuffling along trying to remember the recipe for stewed rhubarb.

■ ■ ■

On the morning of November 7th, 1982, a neighbour who hadn't spoken three words to Madame Michaud in as many years suddenly felt compelled to stop her on the street to tell her that she had seen her husband the previous evening in the company of the former manager of the Woolworth's store on Mont-Royal, a woman who, one might say, was in no immediate danger of being made a saint. In any case, the way she'd been holding his arm and laying her head on his shoulder left not a shred of doubt as to the intimate nature of their relationship. Minutes later, Parfait Michaud was subjected to a raging torrent of abuse, during which accusations of infidelity and threats of revenge alternated with fits of weeping, great sobs, appeals for pity, and shortages of breath, all of which led up to the grand finale of a spectacular nervous breakdown. She calmed down slightly with the application of a cold compress and a few inhalations of Ventolin, after which she was able to drag herself off to bed, declaring, however, that she was in no condition to even think about making lunch, and in any case she had no intention of doing so.

Michaud sat at his desk, trying, without notable success, to concentrate on the will of an important businessman who had made his fortune manufacturing sexy lingerie. Certain clauses in the will had given him pause to reflect, just as certain phrases from Amélie's tirade were still ringing in his ears. He tried to look at himself objectively, and ended up considering himself by turns a hypocrite, a swine, a sexaholic, a lecher, a whoremonger, and a plethora of other epithets the delineation of which would be too shocking for sensitive ears.

His life with Amélie had begun with all the delights of young love, but they had long ago turned rancid. She had always had her little ways, unimportant in themselves. At first he had found them amusing; but eventually they had taken root and grown until they'd completely engulfed the personality of the young woman he had married when he was twenty-two, a woman full of imagination and spirit. They had turned her into a cranky hypochondriac, useless to herself and to others, and had made their last fifteen years together a waking nightmare. He had thought of leaving her many times, but he hadn't, whether out of pity, or fear, or laziness, he couldn't say.

In the end he had decided to lead a double life, as sad and banal as that solution seemed to him. In the parts of Montreal he frequented he'd heard himself referred to as "Notary Trop Chaud," a pun on his name that plunged him into a state of self-loathing; he felt as though it were not only his name but the honour of his profession that was being maligned, especially since it was a profession that he'd practised with such meticulous zeal. It reminded him of hearing a busker in the metro a few months before butchering Schubert's "Ave Maria" on a saxophone, giving it a lot of trills and splutters to a pre-recorded piano accompaniment. It was like seeing the Holy Virgin do a striptease. "Life is ugly," he sighed. "And I'm ugly! No wonder God has washed His hands of humanity. We're not worth the trouble . . ."

He stood up, went to the window, and stood looking out over rue Bercy with his hands behind his back. Three men walked by, two young and one old. The two younger men passed the older one without looking at him. All three seemed to him to be nondescript, vaguely grey in the face, undistinguishable, washed out, absorbed in their own petty thoughts. A young woman appeared at the corner pulling one of those small, wire shopping carts. She had a pretty mouth and lively eyes. He looked away; no more pretty women for him! It was time for him to develop other interests. "But you already have other interests, imbecile!" he scolded himself. "Music, books, your work. . . . They aren't enough, though, that's the problem . . . they never were enough. . . . Maybe you should have had . . . I'm only guessing here . . . children."

Which made him think of Charles. There was a time when he would have adopted Charles himself, if he'd been more forthright and had had enough presence of mind. He thought of the time about a year ago, when he had asked Charles and his friend Michel Blondin to help him shelve his new library. The two boys had worked very hard and very carefully, but Charles, who was ordinarily so talkative and warm, had seemed distant, hard to draw out of himself, and a few times the boy had given him an almost ironic look, as though he'd wanted to say something. Michaud had been intrigued.

When they were about to leave, Charles had stood in front of the shelves, examining each book in turn.

"Is he any good, Balzac?" he'd asked.

"Good?" Michaud had replied. "You absolutely must read him before you die, otherwise you go straight to Hell."

"*The Physiology of Marriage.* Is that a novel?"

"Umm . . . no. It's a sort of treatise, or pamphlet, if you like. Pretty strong stuff."

Charles had turned to him then, as though he'd been waiting for this moment for some time.

"There are those who think physiology is more important than marriage."

And he'd raked Michaud with the pitiless look that adolescents reserve for adults who have disappointed them.

"Yes, well. . . . That's how it goes sometimes," Michaud had babbled. "Human nature not being perfect . . ."

But he'd suddenly understood that Charles knew about his double life and had decided to confront him with it before he'd come to terms with his own anger.

Since that conversation he had had almost no contact with Charles. Two or three chance meetings in the street, cut short, and one other, a few months ago, when Charles had turned up at the house to borrow Louis Fréchette's *Legend of a People*, which he'd needed for an essay. He'd stayed no more than a couple of minutes. He apparently couldn't wait to leave.

And so, along with the ruin of his marriage, he had also watched his reputation suffer, a further ruin that risked costing him a friendship that meant the world to him. All for the futile and fleeting pleasures of being with women of uncertain virtue. The few times he'd met a woman of any worth, the affair had been brief . . .

Michaud paced back and forth in his office, hands thrust deep in his pockets, absently following a row of roses printed on his carpet. Then he sat again at his desk, looked at the bizarre document he'd been asked to go over, and tried to become absorbed in it. But soon he looked up, checked the clock, and sighed. Céline Fafard, Fernand's daughter, was going to be there in a few minutes. She'd called the night before to make an appointment, without saying why. He could still hear her thin, high voice on the phone. It was the first time a fourteen-year-old had asked to consult with him as a notary public. Of course it would be today (Fate again, the idiot), when he was so depressed he didn't know how he would be able to manage an interview that might well concern a matter of some delicacy, as he had quickly realized.

No use trying to read the will. He got up and went into the kitchen to make himself an espresso. Amélie was still snivelling in her bed, probably on the point of going to sleep. He raised his demitasse to his lips just as the doorbell rang.

"It's her," he said.

Minutes later she was sitting in front of his desk, smiling but evidently nervous. She was a pretty young woman already, with magnificent eyes, cheeks perhaps a little on the bright side, but a fine, graceful, small nose and an intelligent look about her. She appeared to be a lot more serious than most people her age. Two or three years from now, when her face filled out a bit and her features became firmer, when the sensual curve of her lips was more accentuated, she was going to make a lot of young men very happy indeed – or perhaps just one man, if that was what she wanted.

"I came because I wanted to talk to you about Charles," she began, coming directly to the point, blushing slightly but with a determined air about her.

"Charles," said Michaud, smiling and joining the tips of his fingers together under his chin. The coincidence surprised him, as he had just been thinking about Charles himself.

"It's . . . it's about a Christmas present I want to get him."

"Aha. I see you like to plan ahead. And you want me to chip in for it, is that it?"

"No, no, nothing like that!" she exclaimed, confused. "I have enough money. . . . I want to give him a book, but I don't know which one. I thought since you and he know so much about books, and you are always lending them to him, you could give me some advice. It's not easy to choose a gift for someone," she said seriously, "when you really want to make them happy."

"Yes, of course," agreed the notary, trying to be friendly and warm. "Often we give presents that would make us happy if we got them, and don't really think of what would make the other person happy. In other words, we remain egotists even when we're trying to be altruists."

"Exactly," Céline said, impressed by the elegant way he had put the problem.

Michaud was consumed by a salacious curiosity. "Do you give him presents like this every Christmas, Céline?" he asked.

"No. In fact, this is the first time. That's why I want to make sure it's the right present."

Her cheeks flushed pink again and she looked away.

"Would I be prying," replied the notary, in his most mollifying, paternal tone, "if I asked you why you want to give him a present this particular year?"

He took a swallow of coffee to give her time to think about her answer. But she replied instantly.

"Because I love him. And I want to show him that I love him."

The notary was jubilant. The conversation had lifted him into a state of happiness that made him forget the depths into which his day had plunged him.

"There are less . . . costly . . . ways of doing that," he said pleasantly.

Céline gave a little irritated pout.

"I'm not about to throw my arms around his neck, if that's what you mean," she said. "What would he think of me?"

"You know, my dear Céline, girls often forget how shy boys can be. I myself was very shy when I was Charles's age. Sometimes you have to give them a little nudge. Things often go well, after that."

Céline shook her head, annoyed.

"That's not like me," she said. "First I want to give him a present."

The notary agreed that in matters of the heart it was better to follow one's own inclinations. The best strategy, after all, was the one that came most naturally.

"How much money do you have to spend?"

"About thirty dollars."

She had to have been saving her pennies for months, he thought. She probably should keep some of it, but she seemed ready to spend everything she had to show Charles how much she loved him. Michaud was surprised and touched by the candour with which she was speaking to him.

"You love him that much?" he asked.

"I do," she said, her eyes filling with a dreamy sadness. "Ever since I was young . . . and especially since he came to live with us. I thought for a while I would get over it, but in fact the opposite has happened. So, what book do you think I should buy, Monsieur Michaud?"

The notary sat back in his chair. "That is the question, as our dear old Hamlet would say." And he stared at the ceiling, the picture of deep concentration.

But no ideas came into his head. He slid the candy dish towards Céline and offered her a caramel, which she accepted, then took one for himself and put it in his mouth. Then he got up from his chair and sauntered along the rows of books on his shelves, running his eyes over their titles, bending down and standing up with tiny exhalations of breath. Céline watched him, her hands clasped on her lap, with a faint smile of astonishment. She had never met anyone like him in her life. He was gentle, impressive, and a bit ridiculous, all at the same time.

"Got it!" he cried suddenly. "But it might be a tad expensive . . ."

"What is it?"

"*The Complete Short Stories of Guy de Maupassant*," he said. "The Albin Michel edition, in two volumes, printed on fine paper. It's beautiful, a real treasure. They might sell each volume separately. I remember Charles read *The House of Tellier*, a collection put out by Livre de Poche, and liked it very much. Shall I call a bookstore for you?"

He found what he wanted after three calls. The volumes were sold separately, for twenty-two dollars each.

"That's perfect, then," Céline decided. "I'll go get the first one right away. Could they hold it for me, please?"

Excited, she leaped to her feet in a transport of joy and ran her hands along the edge of the desk, as if she were caressing it.

"If you like, I could pick it up for you, my dear. I have to go downtown tomorrow anyway."

"Are you sure he'll like it? I mean, really like it?"

"I'm sure, yes," replied the notary, squeezing his eyes shut with a satisfied smile.

She thanked him effusively, reached into her pocket, and took out three ten-dollar bills. He took two of them.

"Keep some for yourself," he said. "I'll see if I can get a discount. I'm a regular customer at Champigny's, and they sometimes do me favours."

Céline was on her way to the door when she turned back, suddenly stricken by a horrible thought that brought down the corners of her mouth.

"You promise you won't tell him about my visit? He would laugh at me, I know it."

"Céline, my sweet little Céline," he replied gravely, placing a hand on her shoulder, "at my age one knows love when one sees it. There is nothing so beautiful – or so terrible. Do you think I'd be so mean as to do such a thing?"

■ ■ ■

Wilfrid Thibodeau hadn't been heard from for several months. It seemed he had disappeared from the neighbourhood. Had he left the city, or even the country? Charles told himself that the sacrifice of his money might not have been in vain after all. But thoughts of his father continued to haunt him. What hole was he hiding in? Had he gone back north to work? His victory still filled him with pride, but it was beginning to seem a little too easy. He couldn't believe that his father wasn't out there somewhere, planning his revenge.

One cold and windy Saturday in March he decided to go to the Amis du Sport, to see if he could find Oscar Turgeon, the elderly gentleman who had given him his father's address. He was pulling on his gloves in the vestibule, looking out at the gusts of snow sweeping down the street, when Céline came down the hallway, still in her pyjamas (she'd been sleeping in).

"Where are you going?"

Ever since Christmas, when she'd blushingly given him the Maupassant short stories (which he'd devoured in three days), there had been a pact of silence between them. Embarrassed at not having a Christmas present for her, he had waited until New Year's Day to give her, almost secretly, a handsome silver bracelet with inlaid agates that he'd bought her – after great deliberation and scrutiny and much consultation with Marlene – at Parchemin's Jewellery Store in the Berri-de Montigny metro station. Céline had worn it every day since.

"I'm going to find out what's happened to my father."

"Where?"

"A bar. The Amis du Sport, on Logan."

He'd told her about his encounter with his father. No one but she and Blonblon knew about the fight. He hadn't brought Henri in on the secret because he thought Henri was too much of a blabbermouth. Charles had made both Blonblon and Céline swear they'd never say anything about it to Fernand or Lucie; with his hotheaded temper, Fernand would no doubt run off to Thibodeau's place and force him to return what was left of his son's fifteen hundred dollars, if anything was left of it at all.

"I'll come with you," Céline said. "Give me a minute to jump into some clothes."

But Charles told her no, she was too young to be allowed into a bar.

Twenty minutes later it was he who was being ejected from the bar. As soon as he'd seen Charles enter, the owner had asked to see some ID, and after looking Charles over briefly he'd told him he couldn't be served.

"I didn't come here to drink," Charles declared, looking around the room. "I'm looking for someone. A Monsieur Turgeon, Oscar Turgeon."

"He never shows up here before two o'clock on Saturdays. Wait for him outside, my lad. The fresh air'll do you good."

And he'd bowed with an elegant, exaggerated arm movement that managed to hint at more direct methods of expulsion.

Charles left, shamefaced, but glad that he had not let Céline come along. According to his watch it was a quarter to one. There was nothing he could do but wait. The wind was blowing hard and pellets of snow were stinging his eyes. It was a damp, heavy wind, merciless and tenacious, freezing his cheeks and his earlobes and making him feel as though icy snakes were crawling all over his body, despite the thickness of his hood and toque and coat. He looked up and down the street, but there was no corner store or restaurant from which he could keep an eye on the bar. There was a bus shelter a few feet away and he stood in that. If he kept perfectly still and straight, with one shoulder leaning against the glass wall of the shelter in such a way that the skin of his legs touched as little of the icy material of his trousers as possible, then after a few minutes a kind of buffer of warm air built up between him and the glacial dampness.

Fifteen minutes passed. Three men entered the bar, one after the other, bent over against the wind and walking quickly, but none of them looked like Oscar Turgeon. Charles shivered but remained stoical. His shoulder was frozen where it touched the shelter wall. The cold chewed furiously at his toes. Maybe the bad weather was a warning, he thought. "Why are you chasing after your father, Charles? Nothing good has ever come from your contact with him."

A young woman came into the bus shelter with her three young children, numbed by the cold. She looked Arabic. She was wearing a long, heavy coat and her head was wrapped in brightly coloured shawls that encased her face like a shell. Then three adolescents came in, bare-headed, acting excited; one of them had a cat under his coat, which was looking about wildly. A bus stopped with a long squealing of brakes and Charles was alone again, feeling colder than ever. He hiked up his coat sleeve and looked at his watch: it was only twenty after one. His method of trapping calories by not moving was reaching the limit of its effectiveness. It wasn't working for his feet at all: he could no longer feel them except for a sort of tingling sensation in the heels. How much longer could he last?

Another bus came and stopped, but when Charles didn't move it left again with an angry growl, leaving behind the acrid stench of diesel fuel. He coughed, rubbed his frozen shoulder, thought about lighting a cigarette but didn't have the courage to get one out. "I'll count to three hundred," he decided, "and if he doesn't come by then, I'm out of here." The storm raged on more furiously than ever. It now had complete possession of the deserted streets. It was crazy to be waiting for someone outdoors in such weather.

He'd almost reached two hundred when a silhouette appeared in the distance, walking in his direction, surrounded by swirls of flying snow that made him stagger and sometimes come to a full stop; the figure disappeared completely in a white cloud, then appeared again on the move, hobbling along with jerky movements. The silhouette seemed familiar. It was a man, that much was clear. Whoever it was turned his back into the fury of the wind to catch his breath, and as he readjusted his hood Charles suddenly recognized him. He ran out of the bus shelter.

"Steve!" he shouted as loudly as he could. "Over here!"

The figure jumped, raised its arms in the air, tried to run but slipped and fell onto the sidewalk. A few seconds later he was sitting beside Charles on the bench inside the shelter.

"I was at loose ends," he said, brushing snow from his face, "so I thought I'd come downtown and see what was up. Céline told me where you were. . . . Christ, you sure picked a good day for it!"

And he gave Charles a big smile.

He persuaded Charles to leave the shelter, where they were certainly about to freeze to death, and warm themselves up in the nearest restaurant. His friend's arrival changed Charles's mood, and he no longer felt like fulfilling his quest. It had been a long time since he'd seen Steve. Stretched out on a chair, his feet pressed up against a radiator, he told Steve about his last encounter with his father, only slightly exaggerating his courage. Every now and then he cast a glance out the window, where the storm was building up into a huge spectacle. He'd come down to the Amis du Sport, he explained, because he wanted to be sure that his victory was definitive.

"Forget it," Steve said, with princely nonchalance. "Fifteen hundred bucks! Can't you imagine where he is? Curled up in the bottom of a bottle. You won't hear from him again, I'll bet my mother's butt on it! It cost you a bundle, but it was worth it. Bingo! So, what do you say we go down to the Orleans and play a little pool?"

Charles hadn't set foot in the pool hall since his friend had moved out to the suburbs. He liked the idea of a game. He needed to unwind, and with Steve, unwinding was easy. The guy seemed made for nothing else. They decided to split the cost of a taxi, and one arrived within half an hour.

"You're not going far, I hope," the driver said, giving them a suspicious look. "The streets will be totally blocked soon. You got enough money?" he added when Lachapelle gave him the address.

"If I don't have enough money for a cab, I walk," Steve said, piqued.

René De Bané was playing alone in the otherwise empty room. He welcomed Steve and Charles the way a castaway on a desert island might welcome a buxom blonde carrying a barbecued chicken and a case of wine.

"Holy cow!" he said. "A royal visit! It's been ages since I've seen you guys! You just get out of jail or something?"

"Yeah," said Charles. "We had your old cell."

After laughing heartily at Charles's repartee, De Bané asked them what was new, told them how good they were looking, thanked Fate for having sent them to him on such a miserable day, and went over to the counter to confer with Nadine. He came back with three bottles of beer, and the game began. It was an animated, enjoyable session, punctuated by hilarious jokes and spectacular shots that allowed each player to share the limelight in turn. Charles was delighted to have hooked up with Steve again. His friend still clowned around and acted on impulse, and the fact that he'd come into town on purpose to spend time with him felt good, especially since, as he reproached himself, he had almost forgotten about Lachapelle. As for De Bané, the man couldn't be friendly enough. He laughed at the smallest joke his companions made, marvelled at their skill, and was generous with his tips for playing championship pool, since, as he said, "you have to give a leg up to the next generation, especially when they're as talented as you two."

Around four o'clock they began to feel hungry, and De Bané, as usual, invited them to join him at a restaurant. He insisted on driving them to the Villa Frontenac, despite the weather, where they feasted on smoked-meat sandwiches, fries, ice cream, and chocolate cake.

"You must be rolling in dough, René," Charles said, leaning back in his chair, stuffed.

"It's not hard when you know how to use your head," De Bané replied with a secretive smile. "Coffee? Hot chocolate? Come on, drink up, it's on me!"

"Tell me something, René," Steve said, very directly. "Are you queer, or what?" He wiggled his hips like a belly dancer, holding his elbows above the table. "Because if you are, my ass isn't for sale."

"Nor mine," added Charles, becoming serious.

"You guys kidding me?" De Bané sputtered, almost choking on a mouthful of chocolate cake. When he got his breath back he assured them he was nothing of the kind, that he had fathered five children with three different women, that he liked a bit of poontang as much as they did, if not more, that nothing pissed him off more than running into one of those kiddie-diddlers, and he'd kicked the stuffing out of more than his share of them in bars and pool halls and other, similar places.

They finished their meal. De Bané suggested going back to the Orleans for another game, on him, of course, because he loved playing against really skilled opponents. But Charles and Steve declined his invitation, saying they had other things to do.

"You still working at that pharmacy, Charles?" he asked when Steve had left the table to make a phone call.

"Yup. I took today off, but normally I'm there every Saturday and one or two nights during the week."

Intrigued by the question, Charles looked at De Bané through partly closed lids.

"If you're interested, we could do some business, you and I," De Bané said.

"Business?"

"Business, yeah. Smooth as shit and twice as easy. You could make a lot of money, and do it with your eyes closed."

"Oh yeah? How?"

His suspicious and somewhat sarcastic tone brought a smile that split the pool shark's long face in two.

"Maybe this isn't the best time to talk about it. I don't want to keep you too long. But take a couple of days to think about my proposition, Charlie, my boy. If you're interested, let me know. You know where to find me."

"He's selling dope," Steve said when Charles told him about the conversation. "Watch yourself, buddy. You could end up in shit up to your neck."

Charles shrugged. "Thanks for the advice," he said. "I'll give it some thought."

The storm had nearly passed. Steve had called Louisa, his girlfriend from Haiti, whom he had met that summer in Pointe-Saint-Charles, and convinced her to come and join them. The three of them walked to Marlene's place; Charles hadn't seen her for nearly two weeks. She didn't seem to hold it against him, and gave him a long, wet kiss on the mouth. Louisa was a little bit of a thing, very bubbly and nervous. It was her first winter in Quebec. The snowstorm had sent her into a fit of ecstasy from which nothing could bring her down. She wanted to go outside and play. Marlene looked at her with a condescending smile.

"We could make a snow fort," Steve suggested, anxious to please his girlfriend.

"The snow won't stick," Marlene objected. "It's too cold."

"We just have to spray it with a hose," Charles said. "The fort will be there until spring. We could even sell it to Club Med!"

They frolicked in the snow until it was too dark to see, stacking blocks of snow and laughing like children. Every now and then they dashed into the apartment to warm up with cups of coffee. Finally, Louisa, exhausted by the cold, nearly fell asleep on the sofa.

So they devoted the rest of the night to other occupations.

141

┌─────────┐
│   9   │
└─────────┘

In the middle of the night of May 6th a fire broke out behind the storage shed at the Fafard hardware store. A chartered accountant, unable to sleep, was out walking his dog when he saw the plume of smoke rising above the courtyard and small, short flames flickering diabolically beneath a barred window. "Hey!" he shouted in indignation. He was the son, grandson, and great-grandson of firefighters, and so he came from a family that considered fire a hereditary enemy, the defeat of which was a moral duty. He therefore ran to the nearest front door and banged on it with his fist. When there was no response, he tried the handle and the door swung open.

"Fire! Fire!" he shouted, running into a darkened room. "Someone please call the Fire Department!"

He saw a wall-mounted telephone in the kitchen, faintly lit by the glow of a night-light. He ran to it and was performing his duty as a good citizen when he became aware of a small, old woman watching him from the doorway, trembling in her pink, cotton nightgown. He signalled to her to go to the window in the living room to see what was happening in the street, and then returned his attention to the phone. A second "Hey!" – muted this time – followed by "Have mercy on us, Sweet Jesus" told him that the reason for his unannounced intrusion into this woman's house was now sufficiently clear for there to be no disagreeable scene. He hung up, gently patted his involuntary hostess on the shoulder (her dentures clacking at the sight of so much smoke in the street), then went back outside and joined the small group of gawkers that had assembled in front of the store. Within minutes, sirens from the fire trucks were waking up the entire neighbourhood.

All this time, Fernand had been lying in his bed with his teeth clenched and his arms and legs held rigid, swerving violently back and forth at the wheel of a huge eighteen-wheeler on the Turcot Interchange, which hardly seemed a plausible thing to be doing, given that he'd never driven such a truck in his life. In any case, when Lucie woke him to tell him that the hardware store was on fire, he was already in the appropriate state of mind for receiving the news. He was outside the store in a matter of minutes, plunged in gloom, his wife at his side, along with his two children and Charles, whose expression of anger and distress attracted wondering glances from several of the onlookers.

Fernand never knew which good soul he had to thank for the speed with which the firemen had been called; by the time he arrived the fire was already well under control and the good soul in question had gone home to try to catch a couple of hours of sleep, exhausted by his efforts and satisfied that the Enemy had been delivered a crushing defeat.

The fire damaged one wall and destroyed some merchandise. It had been halted next to a flat of paints, solvents, and thinners, which, had it caught fire, would have turned the storage shed into a blazing inferno and the hardware store into a hazy memory. There was considerable water and smoke damage, however. The source of the fire had been destroyed as well, as often happens, theoretically removing the evidence that a crime had even been committed. The claims adjuster, when called in first thing in the morning, estimated the damage at ten thousand dollars and congratulated Fernand on his good fortune.

"Such as it is," muttered the hardware store owner darkly.

Lucie, her face pale and the cords in her throat standing out like those of an old woman, took her husband's arm encouragingly.

But Fernand was devastated. He might have been lucky this time, but there would surely be a next time, and fortune might not be so kind in the future. He walked through the store muttering unintelligibly to himself,

143

his face sagging, looking lost. Henri watched him in silence, visibly distraught. His father seemed to have aged ten years in a few hours; the barrel-chested colossus had changed into a broken shell of a man. Lucie sat on the counter, her legs dangling, her sandals hanging from her toes, wiping her eyes with a dustcloth, while Charles and Céline went out to clean up the storage shed.

Charles stopped suddenly in front of Céline, a dustpan piled with debris in his hand, his lower jaw protruding, and his face ugly with rage.

"He won't get away with this, Céline," he said in a strangled voice. "I'll make sure of that."

"What are you going to do?"

All he could do then was shake his head and go back to work in silence. Half an hour later, however, after hastily gulping down the breakfast Lucie had ordered from a nearby restaurant, he left for school. During the morning break he took Blonblon aside and told him what had happened; he had to speak to someone about it, if only to dilute his anger and his fear.

"I'll go look for him," Blonblon said, in a spirit of noble generosity. "I'm going to try to reconcile the two of you. Yes, Charles, we have to try. I don't like to get mixed up in your business, but it won't be hard for me to act as a kind of intermediary, try to negotiate some kind of . . . Charles! Listen to me, Charles, please: you've got to talk to him. It's always better to talk than to fight! The worst that can happen is that I waste my time. But fighting . . ." He shook his head sympathetically.

Charles heard him out, open-mouthed, touched by Blonblon's candour. But he turned the offer down flat.

"Please, Charles," Blonblon begged. "At least let me try. What have you got to lose?"

"Blonblon, you're getting on my nerves. You sound like a Jehovah's Witness or something. What, are you going door to door now? We're not in kindergarten any more, this isn't about settling a little set-to in the hallway. Smell the coffee, man! My father is a total asshole! He's already tried to kill me, or have you forgotten that little detail? It was thanks to him that I had to change families. He doesn't work because he's no longer capable of working. All he does is drink or take drugs, or both for all I know, and he needs money, lots of money, and he'll do anything he can to get it. He proved that last night, Blonblon. It's a miracle the store wasn't burned to the ground and Fernand isn't a ruined man. By going to see him, all you'll do is warn him that I'm coming after him. You'll make what I have to do twice as difficult."

"You're going at it the wrong way, Charles. And you'll regret it."

"I'd regret doing nothing even more."

"I know how to talk to people, Charles. You've seen me do it before. Just last Thursday, Laframboise wanted to punch Mathieu Laplante's face in because he thought Laplante had stolen his girlfriend. Well, I talked to him for fifteen minutes, quietly, explaining to him that you can't steal a girl from someone the way you steal a jackknife or a bicycle. I told him the real problem must have been between him and his girlfriend, and it was her he should talk to, ask her what went wrong. I told him, *ask* her what went wrong, don't try to strangle it out of her, or drag her down the street by the hair. You don't get anywhere by fighting. When you ask questions, you might get a few answers, you might learn something. Then you can fix whatever it is that isn't working."

"Where did you get that from, *The Watchtower*?"

"I didn't get it from anywhere, Charles. It came from my own head. And you know what Laframboise did? He took my advice. Phaneuf told me yesterday, he saw him and Doris in the Lafayette Restaurant, and things seemed to have been patched up. What do you have to say to that, Charles?"

"Laframboise is not my father."

"When you manage to find the right words, Charles, you can almost always reach what is good in a person – and there is some good in all of us, believe me."

"Not in my father, not any more. Once, maybe. But it's been completely eaten up by the bad stuff. He's an asshole, Blonblon."

And he ended the discussion by telling Blonblon that any attempted intervention between him and his father would be the end of their friendship. Blonblon bowed his head and sighed, and they went in to class.

That evening Charles went to the Orleans. He had no particular plan of action in mind. All he knew was that he was going to need a lot of money in a hurry. Nothing could get in his way.

René De Bané was sitting at a table, drinking beer. There were two young men with him, both with scraggly moustaches and bony faces. They looked like brothers. Charles hadn't seen them before. When De Bané saw Charles, he cheerfully waved his long monkey-arms.

"Charlie, my boy! Good ol' Charlie! Come over and have a beer with us!"

He introduced Charles to his two companions, who looked vaguely over at him and went on with their conversation.

"I wanted to talk to you," Charles murmured to De Bané as he took his place at the table.

"I could tell just by looking at you, Charlie boy, and I'm not in the least surprised. You're a smart kid, and a smart kid never lets a good opportunity pass him by. Sorry, boys," he said, turning to the two young men, "but I'm going to have to catch you later. Charlie and I have a few things to talk about."

"No problem, René," the two replied in unison, in a subservient tone that surprised Charles.

"I suddenly feel like a hot dog," De Bané announced as they were going down the stairs. "We could go across the street, if you like. It's usually fairly quiet this time of night."

The three main features of Angelo's Grill were:

1. Its pale-blue (when washed) linoleum floor, with one large, bare patch along the counter through which the subfloor could be seen, which was also partly worn through;
2. The interminable card game being played by a group of loud retirees every morning from eight to eleven, behind a cloud of cigarette smoke and amid the smell of hot grease; and
3. The almost total absence of customers in the evening, which, however, did not prevent its persevering owner from keeping it open, year after year, until ten o'clock, in the perpetually

unrealized expectation of a sudden change in the eating habits of the local citizenry.

As for its hot dogs, hamburgers, fries, and poutine, they were neither better nor worse than those of any other similar establishment.

De Bané ordered three hot dogs with mustard, relish, and ketchup – the bright, clean colours reminiscent of certain paintings of the German Expressionist school – and devoured them with the avidity of a crocodile swallowing a sparrow. Then he talked quietly to Charles, who was sitting across from him, looking intense yet vaguely morose. From time to time De Bané would turn his long, narrow face to make sure old Angelo was still nodding off at the end of his counter.

The interview lasted about half an hour, after which the two men left the restaurant and Charles went home, thinking hard as he walked. He had promised De Bané an answer the following day. He left rue Ontario after a block or two and found himself on a dark, deserted side street, corduroyed by speed bumps and bordered by tiny squares that were the backyards of two rows of houses. He longed for quiet and solitude – and also sleep. For some reason, his short conversation with De Bané had exhausted him.

As he made his way towards home, walking quickly with his head down, the sound of a gunshot caused him to look up. It had come through a half-opened window a few metres to his right. The curtains had been partly drawn, probably to allow some fresh air into the room, and a large man with white hair was splayed out on a sofa, his shirt unbuttoned, watching television; he appeared so hopeless and discouraged that Charles could hardly bear to look at him. He looked like a man who had been shipwrecked, left to die on an iceberg. Charles watched him with a kind of fascination. He would have liked to knock on the man's door and talk to him, comfort him, and be comforted by him, for the man seemed so much like himself. Abandoned. And adrift.

■ ■ ■

His sleep that night was so restless that for once Boff decided to spend the night in Henri's room. When Lucie saw his face in the morning she said he looked like death warmed over and asked him if he was feeling all right.

In a small, weak voice he assured her he was fine. Fernand, paging glumly through the sections of *Le Devoir*, looked up, studied him for a second, then went back to his reading. Leaning her head out of the bathroom door, Céline gave Charles a worried smile. He frowned back at her and went into his room to get a schoolbook. Hachiko was perched on the dresser, watching, unperturbed, as patches of sunlight lit up its body in shafts of fire. Charles looked back at the statuette. The play of light and shadow on its flanks made it look as though it were breathing. He walked over to the dresser and looked into the dog's bronze eyes.

"Does loyalty go that far, Hachiko?" he murmured under his breath. "Tell me, does it go so far?"

The statuette's lower jaw seemed to tremble, and Charles felt almost as though its mouth were going to open. But whatever Hachiko's thoughts were it kept them to itself and went on sitting impassively in the warm sun.

That day, although Charles was physically present in all his classes, had he been asked what any of them were about he wouldn't have had a clue. Cupidon Goulet, the chemistry teacher (who of course was called Cupid the Ghoul), exasperated by Charles's wool-gathering, asked him if he wanted to go home to sleep. Charles thanked him and said no, he was getting plenty of sleep where he was. The other students laughed, and Charles spent the rest of the class in the hallway, contemplating his sharp tongue.

During morning break, Blonblon tried two or three times to talk to him, but Charles managed to avoid being alone with him. Blonblon called the house that evening; Charles told him offhandedly that he was still "working on a solution" and changed the subject when Blonblon tried to pump him for more details. An hour later, feeling even more worried, Blonblon called again. Charles had Céline tell him that he had come down with a headache and had gone to bed, and that he'd see him the following day.

At ten o'clock, however, he left the house saying he needed some fresh air and went down to the pool hall. René De Bané was playing with one of the two young men with the scraggly moustaches who had been there the night before. Charles took De Bané aside.

"I'm going to take a pass," he told him. "I'm not interested."

"You're making a big mistake, boyo," De Bané said. "It's a golden opportunity I'm offering you, and there's no risk!"

"So you keep saying."

De Bané looked at him a moment, then put his hand in his pocket and took out his wallet, which he half opened to show Charles its contents. He fanned his thumb across a thick wad of bills, which made a delicate, fluttering sound.

"If business isn't as good as I say, where do you think I got so many of these brown babies?" he said. "Look at all the hundreds in there! Look at the twenties! It's a Cabinet minister's portfolio!"

Charles hesitated for a second. "I don't care," he said. "I don't want to get mixed up in it. It's dirty money."

De Bané passed a hand slowly over his long face, and his friendly manner changed suddenly into an icy stare.

"Whatever you say, Charlie, my boy. I'm not going to twist your arm. But I'm sure you know enough to keep all this to yourself, eh? People with big mouths sometimes lose their teeth . . ."

■ ■ ■

One June night after supper, when Lucie had asked Henri for the third time to put the dishes in the dishwasher and tidy up the kitchen because it was his turn, and Henri had refused, also for the third time, each time more insolently than the last, saying inaccurately that it had been his sister's job all week and she'd barely lifted a finger the whole time and therefore she should be the one to fill the dishwasher, Fernand awakened from his nap and appeared in the living room and told his son to shut up and get to work without another word.

"No way!" Henri replied, thrusting out his chin and looking at his father belligerently.

At which point Fernand picked Henri up bodily, dragged him to the back door, which he opened with a kick, and threw him into the yard, where fortunately he landed without injury.

"If you don't want to live by the rules of this house," Fernand bellowed in a barely recognizable voice, "go live somewhere else!"

Never in the history of the Fafard family, not even going back several generations, had anything like this happened before. Céline, Lucie, and Charles stared at Fernand in horror as he made his way back to his bedroom, lumbering down the hall like a bear that had been disturbed from his winter hibernation. Everyone understood then that there was something seriously wrong going on inside poor Fernand's head.

It was true that, the day before, one of his most important suppliers had told him the company was reducing his discount because of the continued decline in the number of orders Fernand had been making of late; and then the owner of the store next to the hardware had come in to say that the previous night she'd seen some dark, shadowy figure skulking about in the yard behind the storage shed.

Two hours later, Fernand apologized to his son. Henri, who had had quite a fright, accepted with good grace. Everyone breathed a sigh of relief and, closing the book on the incident, filed it away in the drawer labelled "Unhappy Memories."

The next day, however, Fernand refused to get out of bed to go to work, saying he was extremely tired and heartily sick of the things of this world. Lucie went to the store herself, and that night, when she returned home, found Fernand still in bed. Not even Parfait Michaud, who was called over to speak to his friend, was able to bring him around.

"It's like trying to get a telephone pole to sing," he told Lucie, holding up his long hands in a gesture of powerlessness. "Your husband is not well, my dear. You must call a doctor."

When she asked Fernand about it, he replied that, exhausted though he was, he would still find the strength to throw a doctor out of the house. "Just leave me alone, once and for all," he told her breathlessly, although his expression was ferocious. Nothing interested him any more, least of all his business, which was either going down the tubes or up in flames.

Charles understood then that he no longer had the luxury of indecision, and that he had to do whatever it would take to save this man from ruin. Fernand had generously come to Charles's aid when he needed it most, and now he must do the same for him. He left the house without saying a word and set off quickly for the pool hall.

He didn't even have to go that far, for it is a fact that it is far easier to grab the Devil by the tail than it is to escape his evil designs. De Bané, who had exchanged his powder-blue jogging pants for a fuchsia pair that created an even more curious effect, was standing on rue Ontario, a cigarette hanging from his lips, his back against the darkened window of a dry cleaner's, looking for all the world as though he were waiting for someone to come along and engage him in an intimate conversation.

Charles saw him first, paled slightly, then walked up to him.

"Aha! How's it going, there, Charlie boy?" said De Bané.

He moved about on his long legs in a kind of dance, as though he could tell from the expression on the adolescent's face that his patient efforts were about to bear fruit.

"I've had second thoughts about your offer," Charles declared, standing in front of De Bané. "I'm ready to roll."

"I knew it, I knew it," De Bané crowed jubilantly, although he kept his voice low in the approved style of a man of mystery. "I told myself you were too smart to let a chance like this slip through your fingers. When do you go back to work at the pharmacy?"

"Tomorrow."

"What time?"

"In the evening, just after seven."

"Okay, listen up. I'll be waiting right here for you at six-thirty with all the stuff you'll need. Bring your school bag with you. If your boss wants to know what it's for, tell him you need to do homework between deliveries or something, whatever, I don't care what you tell him as long as he buys it."

And he told Charles in minute detail exactly how he was to proceed.

151

10

In the early 1980s, psychotropic drugs hadn't yet appeared on the prescription drug market. The psychiatric pharmacopia consisted essentially of anxiety-reducing drugs, tranquilizers (notably Valium and Librium), which had been in use for two decades, long enough for plenty of people to have become hooked on them. Valium came in the form of pills and Librium in capsules. Placebos, which have more or less disappeared these days, existed for many of the drugs, to the greater profit of traffickers, who got hold of prescription drugs fraudulently from pharmacies and switched the real drugs with placebos. Capsules were easily opened, and drug dealers simply replaced the Librium with flour or starch, and Valium with fake pills.

The surest and simplest way to practise this low-level fraud was by working out an arrangement with a delivery person. Which is what René De Bané had just succeeded in doing, without any knowledge of the reason behind his success.

The following day at six-thirty he supplied Charles with a stapler and two hundred fake pills and capsules. All Charles had to do when he was on a delivery was to pry open the staples sealing the paper bag containing the medication, make the appropriate switch, and re-staple the bag. Since he usually made three or four deliveries of tranqs a day, and De Bané had told him he would pay him a dollar per capsule or pill, this had the potential to add up, easily and quickly, to a lucrative arrangement.

"But listen up, Charlie boy," warned the drug dealer, whose easygoing manner and air of buffoonery had suddenly changed to a chilly and commanding gravity. "If our little team effort is going to work out, you have to be able to use your head. Always keep your cool, take it very easy, capiche? Never take a chance, even if it looks tempting."

The adolescent, taken aback by this abrupt change of tone and feeling as though he were talking to a complete stranger, nodded a bit fearfully, already regretting that he had agreed to go along with such a proposition.

"One other thing: I depend on you, and you depend on me. If one of us trips up somewhere, the other goes down too. You got that? So we always have to think for two. If you start just thinking about yourself, some day you might get the idea that you can pull something over on me, you know what I'm saying? But just remember this, Charlie boy: I'm always gonna find out in the end – and the end will come a lot sooner than you might think, because I've got the nose of a bloodhound for that kind of stuff, believe me. And if that ever happens, Charlie, well, what can I say ...?"

He raised his hands and shrugged his shoulders as though to say that things would take their natural course and there wasn't much he could do about that.

Then he let loose a burst of laughter.

"So, good luck!" he said, slapping Charles on the shoulder. "We'll meet again next Wednesday at the Orleans. Eight o'clock sharp. Okay?"

■ ■ ■

Charles had no specific plan in mind regarding his father. The only thing he knew for certain was that he was going to need money, and lots of it. Was he going to try to buy his father off? Or would he pay someone to remove Thibodeau from the scene? This last option seemed horrifying to him, but he hadn't rejected it outright. He would put off making a decision until later. The haze that surrounded him was preventing him from thinking straight. He simply didn't have the strength to look down to the end of the road on which he had just embarked.

He had often seen Monsieur Lalancette scooping pills from the amber-coloured glass jars that contained the medication that so many turned to for the comfort they were unable to find by usual means. The pills had to be taken in moderation and with caution, the pharmacist had said, because their repeated use could lead to a strong dependency. And he had mentioned the amount of trafficking that took place, the nightmare it represented for all pharmacists, and the trap it had been for more than a few of them. Luckily, so far he himself had been shielded against such hooliganism, except for once, several years ago, when he had caught one of his delivery boys in the act of pocketing a prescription.

"I sent him packing. Oh, he cried, telling me it was the first time, he'd never do it again. But I told him to save his breath. I have no use for people like that, Charles, and I make sure they keep their distance from me. They make me sick."

A grimace of disgust crossed his face, which ordinarily was as expressionless as a block of wood.

This time the delivery boy was named Charles, but unlike his predecessor's, his descent into a life of crime was not motivated by personal gain, rather by generosity and gratitude. The result, however, was the same. From that day on he was a member of the ignoble fraternity of thieves, and knowing that made his hatred of his father even more intense.

It turned out to be a fruitful week: in three days he made a dozen deliveries of tranquilizers, which found their way into his backpack to be replaced by the blanks supplied by De Bané. Only twice did he not have the heart to make the substitutions.

The first time was when he made a delivery to Amélie Michaud, who had just been given a prescription for Valium. How could he bring himself to play such a low trick on that strange and fragile woman, who had always shown him such affection? He rang her doorbell and handed her the package, avoiding her eyes.

"Why are you blushing like that?" she asked him, surprised. "Is something wrong?"

"No, nothing at all," he stammered, pocketing his tip. He said goodbye and hurried off, saying he was swamped with work.

The second time was three days later, and had an even greater effect on him.

The customer lived in Frontenac Towers, and Charles was delivering to him for the first time. The man must have been hard of hearing, or perhaps asleep, because after three rings there was still no answer. Charles was about to leave when he heard the patter of footsteps and the door opened. An old man stood before him, looking so decrepit, his eyes filled with such anguish, that Charles was struck dumb.

"At last," the man croaked. "Not a minute too soon. How much do I owe you?"

Charles showed him the bill stapled to the bag, and reaching into his pocket the old man painfully withdrew an old, cracked, leather wallet with a brass clasp and tried to open it. But his hand trembled so much he couldn't manage it. He finally asked Charles to open the wallet for him and take the money.

"Take fifty cents for yourself," he said. "Yes, yes, take it, take it, you've earned it. Thank you, thank you so much."

He closed the door and Charles stood in the corridor without moving. He could hear the man's lightly flapping footsteps retreating into the apartment. Then he turned and made his way slowly to the elevator, deeply disturbed. The old man was clearly in a bad way. How would he manage without his medication? How long would his torment last? Who knew? Maybe without it he would become suicidal? It wasn't unusual with old people, Monsieur Lalancette had told him. Riddled with sickness and a dozen infirmities, very often alone in the world, one day they decide to end it all with a single stroke, and *Wham!* Just like that. Well, in this case the pills wouldn't do it, but he could slit his wrists, or throw himself from a window.

He mulled over these dark thoughts all the way to the lobby, then stopped, unable to take another step. The idea of leaving the man at the mercy of his illness drained the strength from his legs and made his stomach heave. He knew it would haunt him for days to come, and might even force him to give up his little fiddle. And he didn't want that!

A few minutes later he was ringing the old man's doorbell again.

"A mistake?" said the man, in alarm. "But I've already taken two pills!" He began to shake so violently that he had to lean against the doorpost.

"That's all right, sir," Charles assured him, trying to hide his confusion. "It was the right drug, but a weaker prescription. I just got the bills mixed up. I'm very sorry. I'll take back the ones I gave you, and I'll bring you the right pills right away. It won't take me ten minutes, I promise. Trust me."

The old man looked at him as though in a daze, his arms hanging down, his face twitching; he seemed on the verge of breaking down.

"Please, sir," Charles said, growing impatient. "Make up your mind, for heaven's sake. Do you want the right pills or don't you?"

"Yes, yes, I want them," the man babbled, and hurried back into the apartment. There came the sound of a heavy object falling, and then a deep groan, and then the man reappeared. The front of his trousers was wet.

"But . . . how did you . . . realize . . . ?" he asked, handing Charles the half-torn bag.

"I just did, that's all," Charles replied briskly, turning on his heels.

Now he wished he hadn't gone back. What would he tell Monsieur Lalancette if the old fool phoned the drugstore? You feel pity for someone you don't even know, and sure as hell you end up landing in trouble. Idiot!

He switched the pills in the washroom of a nearby restaurant and returned to the old man's apartment. This time the man took the bag without thanking him, muttering something about being sorry he'd given Charles such a large tip. But he didn't call the pharmacy, and the affair ended there. Charles, however, promised himself never again to give in to feelings of compassion – and he kept his promise.

■　■　■

Sometimes even scumbags keep their word. De Bané kept his. He paid Charles upon delivery of the merchandise, every cent he owed him. He didn't ask too many questions, seemed to be in an excellent frame of mind, but no longer invited Charles to eat with him in restaurants, saying that it wasn't a good idea for them to be seen together too often. Charles knew that there was another, simpler reason: Why keep hustling someone when you've already got what you wanted from him? In any case, he would have refused the invitation, since keeping company with the drug dealer had become repulsive to him and he tried to avoid it whenever possible. He had come to hate the sight of De Bané.

One day he asked himself who, among all the people he had known, had inspired the most hatred in him: Conrad Saint-Amour, the diddler? Gino Guilbault, who exploited young children in other ways? Robert-Aimé Doyon, the sadistic school principal? Or De Bané? De Bané came close to bumping Saint-Amour into second place. But he had an advantage over the pederast: thanks to De Bané, Charles's bank account was growing swiftly. By the beginning of July, he had already saved the handsome sum of six hundred dollars.

But there was another presence that weighed on him more and more, and it was one he was forced to endure: his own. Charles now had to consider himself as much a criminal as De Bané. Small-time, maybe, but a criminal nonetheless. Down there with pickpockets, counterfeiters, bootleggers, and people who hustled magic potions that guaranteed long life. The more he thought about it, the more he realized he was probably worse than those other figures of the underworld. Because of him, sick people were being deprived of their medications, and at the same time a lot of other people were becoming more and more addicted to tranquilizers. Monsieur Lalancette had often criticized the easy way such drugs were handed out; for several years doctors had been prescribing them for just about everything. It was a handy way for them to get rid of patients quickly, so they could see more in the course of a day and thereby increase their income. But for many people the sedatives were extremely necessary. And dear little Charles was depriving them of it. That his intentions were honorable had nothing to do with it; by doing what he was doing, he was dirtying his hands. As an old customer at Chez Robert had once told him, you can't walk in butter without getting grease on your feet.

One day, while returning from a delivery, he bumped into Jean-René Dupras, his old French teacher from Jean-Baptiste-Meilleur. Charles had always liked this man, who had helped him on the rocky road of his high school career. Dupras had married and already had two children. His face was a bit puffy, and there were crow's feet around his eyes, but he still looked young. He shook Charles's hand effusively, as though he were an adult, and even invited him to join him for a coffee in a nearby restaurant. They talked for twenty minutes, and Charles came within an ace of telling him about his problems, but his courage failed him. He didn't want to lower himself in his former teacher's eyes.

The very sight of pills, any pills, disgusted him. In the pharmacy he averted his eyes from the jars and tubes, which to him held nothing but reproaches. For some time now, Fernand had been taking sleeping tablets and multivitamins, in the hope of regaining some of his energy. Lucie kept them in one of the kitchen cupboards, next to the glasses and plates, a cupboard that was constantly being opened. Charles moved them to the spice drawer so that he wouldn't have to see them so often.

Lucie had been keeping an anxious eye on Charles. His natural and easy happiness were gone, buried under a heavy sadness. He barely spoke at the dinner table, sitting there with a sullen and closed expression on his face, and getting up with his plate barely touched, only to stuff himself with sweets later on. "I'll bet his father is back in the picture," she told herself one day. But she could not get him to talk about what was bothering him. He completely shut her out.

During the night he kept waking up with a jerk, seized by an inexpressible anguish. His stomach churned, his feet felt frozen, his heart pounded. He tossed in his bed feeling as though his room were just a thin shell spinning far out into interstellar space, beyond the possibility of return. He even thought about taking one of the pills that he'd been stealing from patients. Once, at the very edge of panic, he took a Librium. A delicious feeling of indifference spread through him, but in the morning he woke up in such a state of mental confusion that he promised himself he'd never touch another drug.

158

He was haunted by a terrifying thought: that his father would burn down the hardware store before he could contact him, leaving Charles burdened by the guilt of his odious actions without the solace of knowing that they were being put to some good use. He had to let his father know as soon as possible that he was working for him, and that the money he'd tried unsuccessfully to extort from Fernand would soon be falling into his lap. After their last encounter, however, Charles was afraid to go near him. And yet time was running out. He remembered Blonblon's offer to act as an intermediary. Reconciliation was impossible, of course, but he might ask Blonblon to go with him. With a witness present, his father might be forced to restrain himself and to listen.

Blonblon would surely be amazed to see how much money Charles had, and how much he expected to make in the future. It would be necessary to tell him where it came from – that he was selling drugs. Too risky? Not really. His friend would never betray him. He was as incapable of such an action as he was of flapping his arms and flying up into the sky. Several times Charles had been tempted to confide in Marlene, who was also a close friend, but each time he'd held back. Marlene was a nice girl, but she could never keep anything to herself. Blonblon, on the other hand, was correctness and generosity pushed to its ultimate extreme, which was innocence. If he'd been born thirty years earlier, he might have become a missionary in Africa or at the North Pole. And who was to say he might not yet end up like that? There were times when there seemed to be a kind of light emanating from his eyes, the kind that had doubtless suggested the haloes that were often depicted around the heads of saints. And if it weren't for the fact that he had fallen in love with a woman – and deeply in love – he could easily have been mistaken for a saint. Since he had started stealing drugs, Charles hadn't seen much of his friend. A kind of uneasiness had crept over their friendship. When there are things going on that friends can't talk to one another about, other words don't come easily. Luckily, ruptures healed quickly with Blonblon.

Half an hour later, as if summoned on some telepathic telephone, Blonblon knocked on Charles's door. Charles opened it joyfully and ushered

Blonblon into his room, where Boff, rudely awakened, shook himself mightily and, wagging his tail, jumped down from the bed to be petted.

"You're getting fat, poor thing," said Blonblon, scratching the dog behind the ears, "and you've got white hairs growing all over your chin."

Charles patted Boff's flank.

"He must be twelve years old," he said. "Almost an old man. But his teeth are still good, that's for sure. The other day he tore half of Céline's bathrobe to shreds when she refused to give him a piece of chicken."

Blonblon knelt in front of the dog and looked him in the eye.

"You're a bad boy, you know that. You ought to get a boot up your ass when you do things like that!"

"If I hadn't been there I think Fernand would have skinned him alive."

Sensing that he was being talked about, and not kindly, Boff whimpered quietly; his head filled with images of torn cloth, furious faces and waving hands, and the sound of his name being shouted, accompanied by cries and angry phrases; he stood and stared apologetically at the floor, waiting for Charles's and Blonblon's attention to move on to something else.

"How is Monsieur Fafard doing?" Blonblon asked.

"Not too well. The doctor says he's depressed. He hardly goes to the store any more. Lucie has to take care of everything, and the strain is beginning to show on her. I might have to drop out of school to give her a hand. Unless . . ."

Charles looked at a loss. He took out a pack of cigarettes and then slipped them back into his pocket, since it was absolutely forbidden to smoke in the house.

"In fact," he went on, "that's what I wanted to talk to you about, Blonblon. You're the only one I can turn to."

And sitting on the edge of his bed, he began to describe the curious rescue mission he had begun a month earlier. Blonblon listened, flabbergasted and struggling to control his indignation. He let Charles go on without a single interruption. Then, when Charles was finished his story, he merely let out a long sigh.

"You find the whole thing disgusting, don't you?" Charles said.

Blonblon scratched his knee, then the tip of his nose, searching for the right words. He was also trying to put some order to his thoughts.

"No, Charles," he said at last. "Not disgusting. That's not what disgusting means. You're an idiot! For Christ's sake, open your eyes! You're in shit up to your eyeballs, man! I wouldn't give two cents to be in your skin right now. This De Bané can do whatever he wants with you. Do you realize that? Do you realize you could go to prison, Charles? You can't help Fernand from prison! And if you're caught, who could help you? No one, my friend. No one."

Charles tried to convince his friend that there was no problem, that if De Bané tried to rat on him he would simply return the money, and if he didn't, once he'd made enough to pay off his father he'd give up stealing drugs.

Blonblon shook his head sadly.

"That's what they all say, Charles, that's what they all say."

Charles blushed and leapt to his feet.

"Yeah, well, I'm not just anyone, you know! I've seen what other people are like. When I decide to do something, I do it. I'm not going to let that asshole tell me what to do. I do what I want. And only what I want."

He sat down just as sharply as he had got to his feet, and a strange, pleading look came over his face.

"But I need your help, Blonblon, if I'm going to carry out my plan. I absolutely need you to help me. You can't refuse to do what I ask."

And he begged Blonblon to go with him to his father's. For a long time they continued their conversation, speaking in low voices. Boff, lying on the floor with his muzzle between his paws, watched the two of them with an anxious, puzzled look. He'd never seen them so serious, so tense. Every so often he beat his tail on the floor to bring a bit of levity back into the room, but neither of them noticed. He gave a deep sigh and went to sleep. He barely looked up when Charles and Blonblon left the room, merely half opening one eye in time to see that Charles looked relieved and Blonblon looked worried.

11

Fernand lay on his bed staring up at the ceiling. The heat and humidity filling the room had robbed him of whatever strength he'd been able to muster during the night. Outside the window a faint breeze gently stirred the branches of the basswood tree, and their shadows on the ceiling formed a black-and-white lacework pattern that he'd been studying with satisfaction for a long time.

At eight o'clock he'd eaten breakfast, then dressed, with the firm intention of going to the hardware store. He knew full well that Lucie was becoming exhausted after weeks of picking up his slack, and that it wouldn't be long before she reached the limit of her endurance. But the heat and the humidity had fallen so suddenly over the city, and the three cups of coffee he'd drunk to give himself a lift had had the opposite effect, completely draining his limited resources. Feeling like a huge barrel of boiling water, he'd decided the best thing he could do would be to go back to bed, take a load off his feet. He'd been fast asleep in seconds.

He'd been awakened by the sound of a door closing. He recognized the voices of Charles and his friend, Michel Blondin. They went into Charles's room and started a lengthy discussion, the details of which he couldn't catch. All he could make out was a low murmur, but there was something in their tone that told him they were talking about him. It was the tone people used when they talked about the recently dead, or someone whose business had just failed, or a pregnant woman who had just lost her baby. He listened, still unable to make out individual words, staring up at the pattern of light and shadow on the ceiling, and the certainty that he was completely and utterly finished came over him more strongly by the minute. If he had been told he had AIDS, that new sickness that was killing people by the thousands, the effect on him couldn't have been worse.

The boys finally left the house, and Fernand was once again alone. Totally alone. As alone as if the Earth had suddenly become depopulated, or as if he'd been sealed in a barrel and dropped to the bottom of the ocean. Unbearably alone. He realized now that he had always been like this, even when the frenetic activity that had become his way of life shielded from him the stultifying reality of his loneliness. He was alone and he was finished. The faint breeze that stirred the curtain, the damp mattress beneath him, the mahogany bedroom furniture, the delicate rose-coloured walls, the play of light and shadow on the ceiling, all of that was nothing but a delusion, a cruel deception, orchestrated by God-knew-who to keep him from grasping the lamentable futility of his situation.

He sat up on the bed, unable to breathe. He had to do something, it didn't matter what. He couldn't go on like this. A groan escaped his lips, a groan directed at no one because there was no one there to hear it. He stood up, wobbly on his feet, hands outstretched as though he were blind, and left the room. Boff appeared in the hallway and, when he saw Fernand, began emitting small, plaintive noises.

"Go away, dog," Fernand murmured under his breath.

He made his way to the kitchen and opened the door to the backyard. Boff followed him, and he booted the dog outside, which launched Boff into such a state of stupefaction that he urinated on the porch. Then Fernand went into the bathroom. He leaned both hands on the sink and breathed heavily, staring at himself in the mirror on the medicine cabinet. What he saw horrified him. Who was this? Not Fernand Fafard, surely? Not this foolish old man with the hollow cheeks, the forehead glistening with sweat, the dazed look of someone searching for something he had no hope of ever finding?

163

He flung open the cabinet door, which banged against the wall. His eyes swept the bottles of pills, feverishly looking for something that would give him some relief, any kind of relief; what he saw was a packet of razor blades.

A light went on in his head. He picked up the packet, opened it, and took out a blade. He held the blade up and examined it closely. Here was a way to put an end to his misery. Simple, nothing complicated about it, the choice of thousands; all it required was a bit of courage. Not even courage, really. Surely it took more courage to go on living the way he was!

Holding the blade firmly between his thumb and forefinger, he ran it gently, gently, across his wrist. He felt nothing but a slight tickling sensation. He repeated the gesture several times, to get used to the feeling and to prepare himself for the real thrust, the one that would surely make him feel pain.

Then suddenly, quickly, he slashed through the flesh. He felt a sharp burn, but a very localized one, something he could easily stand. Blood spurted out in small, crimson arcs and poured down into the sink, making tiny sounds that pulsed to the rhythm of his pounding heart. It wasn't nearly as messy as he would have expected. And it was so easy, as though this were something he was supposed to be doing. He watched his blood run into the sink with a kind of detached interest, only his throat a bit tight from the line of fire that was burning his wrist. He was astonished that such a thing could be accomplished so easily.

There was a small stepladder behind the door. Holding his left arm over the sink, he reached for the ladder with his right hand, opened it with a jerk, and sat on it. His legs were beginning to feel weak. In fact his whole body was beginning to sag. Black spots had begun to leap around him, as though thrown into some wild kind of dance. He understood that in a few more minutes he would be dead. What was it, this death? A one-way street. But leading where? No one knew. The only sure thing was that the choice he had just made superseded all the other choices he would ever make.

The burning on his wrist was almost gone, but the heaviness continued to weigh him down. It felt to him like a relentless pressure. The blood still trickled into the sink; it had made a sort of pink tulip shape at the bottom, lighter at the edges, very pretty, except that it was vibrating, constantly coming into and out of focus. It was his vision that was failing, he thought, and rapidly. A curious gurgling sound rose from the drain and blended with the pounding that now filled his eardrums.

He realized suddenly that it was himself that was running down that black hole, from which there now came a faintly disagreeable odour. He was going to vanish forever! A sense of horror gripped him, forced him to cry out, although weakly. He ran his right hand along the shelves of the medicine cabinet, knocking everything onto the floor. A Band-Aid, where were the Band-Aids? A kind of mist was filling the room, making his search more difficult. He finally found a roll of gauze and, grabbing it in both hands, unrolled a long strip and tried to tear it off with his teeth. This caused the blood to drip onto his shirt and down to the floor, where it landed with a series of dull splats. The gauze would not tear. Desperate now, he wound it around his wrist anyway and pulled it as tight as he could manage. His skin was slippery with blood and the gauze would not stay wound. He took a toothbrush and slid it under the gauze, then turned it like a tourniquet. Slowly the bleeding lessened. He stood up from the stepladder and left the bathroom, staggering, careening off the walls. The nearest phone was in the kitchen. He could barely see it. After every step he had to stop to catch his breath. "My God," he said to himself, "what have I just done?" A confused noise began to rise within him, turning into a small voice that told his head to start spinning dangerously. He found himself standing by a table with the television remote in his hand. He must have spun into the living room. The pressure had now reached his head, making any sort of thinking impossible. His fingers played awkwardly over the telephone buttons as they danced before his eyes. A woman's voice answered. He spluttered a few words, looked around for something to lean against and, not finding anything, crashed heavily to the floor. Outside, sensing something bad was happening, Boff began attacking the back door, sending up a spray of wood chips.

■ ■ ■

165

The two boys stood on the sidewalk and looked at the door.

"I hope he hasn't moved," Charles murmured, his voice tight. "He's always moving."

Blonblon walked up the minuscule cement steps and thrust his hand into the black metal mailbox. He took out an envelope.

"Well, Hydro-Québec has just sent him a bill, anyway."

Charles joined him, rang the bell, and coughed several times, a small, dry, nervous cough. Blonblon glanced at him, and seeing that Charles still looked strained, he began to whistle as a way of comforting him.

No one came to the door. Charles rang again and then noticed a small piece of paper taped to the inside of the window: "ENTER."

They opened the door and found themselves in the tiny kitchen. The damp heat exacerbated the rank smell of stale cigarette smoke, grease, and fresh paint.

"I'm in the bathroom, Liliane. I'll be out in a minute." It was his father's oily voice, the voice he used when he was talking to a woman. Charles had heard it when he was a child and the carpenter had been in a particularly good mood.

The boys looked at each other without speaking. Blonblon smiled and held a finger to his lips.

"It's not Liliane," Charles said after a moment's hesitation. "It's me."

There was a pause. They heard the sound of a toilet flushing, then a sigh, and the carpenter appeared in the doorway doing up his belt.

"So," he said quietly, his face serious. He looked at Blonblon, who was looking at him closely. "Who's he?"

"A friend."

"What's he doing here?"

Charles hesitated again. "He came with me," he said, unable to think of anything else to say.

Thibodeau laughed mockingly. "Afraid to come on your own?"

Charles looked again for a reply but none came, so he merely pursed his lips and crossed his arms.

"If you want to talk to me, tell him to get lost."

"We didn't come here to cause you any trouble, Monsieur Thibodeau," Blonblon said, with a warmth and ease that even Charles found surprising. "Charles wanted to talk to you about a few, er, delicate matters, and since there are no secrets between us, he thought maybe I could . . . help out in the discussion. That's all."

Thibodeau stared at him as though he had just turned into an Oriental prince, or a kangaroo. Obviously it was the first time anyone had addressed him in such a cordial manner. But he soon regained his composure.

"If you want to talk to me, tell him to get lost," he said again, this time with a degree of menace in his voice.

Charles frowned and shook his head.

Thibodeau walked behind them and opened the door to the street.

"Fine, then, get lost the both of you. Go on, get the hell out! This is my place and I'll let in who I want."

"You'll want to hear what I have to say, Papa. I've come to tell you something important."

"Important things are talked about one on one, man to man, no bloody eavesdroppers to go spreading our business around."

"He's not an eavesdropper. In any case –"

But he had to stop because his father was trying to push him through the door.

"If you want, Charles," Blonblon said, "I could wait for you outside."

Father and son stared at each other for a moment, then Charles turned to his friend and accepted his offer with a nod.

"If anyone calls for you," Blonblon said to Thibodeau with a smile, "I'll tell them you're busy."

Without acknowledging he had heard, the carpenter closed the door behind him with his knee.

As soon as he was on the sidewalk, Blonblon regretted his offer. He had made it only to be accommodating, but wasn't it also an act of cowardice? He had left his friend inside, alone and defenceless with an unpredictable, vindictive, and apparently unscrupulous man. How could he be of any possible use to him now?

He walked up and down the street in front of the door, his mouth set, a scowl on his face, telling himself over and over that the carpenter wouldn't dare hurt Charles knowing that one of his friends was waiting for him a few feet away. But he was also aware that with people like Thibodeau you never knew what would happen. If this Liliane person showed up, he wouldn't tell her that her boyfriend was busy. He'd let her ring the bell and go in. But no Liliane appeared. She'd seen the two boys through the corner store window and thought it better to postpone her visit to a more opportune time.

■ ■ ■

Henri Lalancette was taking advantage of a quiet moment in the pharmacy to leave things in the hands of his buxom, trusty cashier, Rose-Alma Bissonnette, while he went downstairs to spend some time in his laboratory. He had no qualms about doing this: Rose-Alma's green eyes were perfectly capable of spotting the most furtive of movements in any of the pharmacy's four corners, or all of them at once, for that matter, a quality that had earned her the hatred – and the fearful respect – of the neighbourhood shoplifters.

As soon as he entered the lab, his nostrils were assailed by a sickly sweet odour, like that of overripe figs. He quickly approached a counter on which stood an uncovered jar labelled "Port-Wine Dregs – Sample 83-44" and replaced the lid, then looked around irritably for signs of further negligence. There were none. He was in a medium-sized room, its windowless walls painted white, with the usual cupboards, tables, counters, and varieties of containers and other equipment made of glass, plastic, and stainless steel. In short, an ordinary-looking chemical workplace, but one in which for the past six years he had been conducting the experiment that had come to be his main interest in life.

He pulled up a chrome-legged stool and sat on it, issuing a grateful sigh. Being a pharmacist was beginning to take its toll on his legs. His heels had been burning for the past two hours, and his knees felt like jelly, while his calves seemed to have turned to concrete. But if advancing age was making itself felt in his lower extremities, the same could certainly not be said for his head, which fairly hummed like a factory. The delicious fruits of his long labours now hung mere centimetres from his outstretched fingertips. One or two more cross-checks and he would be ready to pluck them down and sink his teeth into them!

How his trials and tribulations had tested his patience, demanded his obstinate will to go on, dragged him willy-nilly into the heady regions of scientific adventure, through hair-raising rapids and gut-wrenching whirlpools, banishing boredom forever – that dull companion of the insignificant dunce!

No one, it seemed to him, was happy with his lot. The bus driver wanted to be a cook. The cook dreamed of being a pilot. The pilot knew in his heart he would be happier running a hotel. And the hotelier was born to be a boxer, it was as plain as the nose on his face, never mind that he had neither the courage nor the physique for it.

Henri Lalancette saw himself as a biological researcher. He'd opted to become a pharmacist at the last minute, for the purely prosaic reason that it was safer, easier, and more lucrative. But he had always regretted it, especially since exciting new drugs arrived at his pharmacy daily, mocking him for his lack of audacity. "If only we could have two lives!" he had once sighed, the banal refrain of all those dissatisfied people who feel they have blown their golden opportunities. The birth of his children and the demands of his occupation had drawn him farther and farther away from his dream, until it had almost vanished from his mind forever.

But on the 7th of June, 1976, all that had changed.

He had been vacationing in Portugal with his wife. On the day in question he was sprawled on a divan in the lobby of a small hotel in Lisbon, handkerchief in hand, sweat running down his forehead, trying to find the strength to get up and follow his guide out onto the city's red-hot cobblestones, when an old man who had been listening to their conversation came up to them and, in passable French, asked them what country they came from. He said he had been unable to place their accent. They fell into conversation and, deciding it was far too hot to play at being tourists and that their new acquaintance was a friendly enough fellow, Lalancette invited the latter to join them in a glass of port. The old man bowed his head with a faintly superior smile and accepted the invitation. Their choice of beverage was fortuitous, he said, for he had worked for many years for a port producer and would be happy, if they were interested, to introduce them to the intricacies of that marvellous fortified wine of Portugal.

Two hours later, the pharmacist, his wife, and Augusto Soares had drained a bottle, eaten a tray of hors d'oeuvres, and cemented a lasting friendship. The wine, the heat, the tranquility of the locale, and the friendly, florid faces of his new friends prompted the Portuguese gentleman to confide that, thanks to his former profession, he would probably live to be a hundred, and that in any case he was presently enjoying an incredibly youthful old age, one that showed not the slightest sign of diminishing. He owed this good fortune, he said, to his habit of drinking two small glasses of the dregs of port wine each day. He had been doing this for many years now, having picked it up from an old friend of his, who had been a cooper. Despite the fact that he was seventy-eight years old, he said, he could still piss a line as straight and strong as that of any young man, and he had lost none of his vigour in bed – as could be attested to by a number of his female friends (he had been widowed some fifteen years before), some of whom were quite young and were delighted by his unique combination of experience and virility.

Lalancette was intrigued, and he questioned Soares closely. It was clearly not a question of genetics: Soares's parents and three of his grandparents had died young, and his grandfather on his mother's side had been taken at the age of fifty-eight by prostate cancer. No, the prolongation of his youth was due solely to the dregs of port wine, affirmed the old man. It was a gift. And he advised the pharmacist, as he advised all his friends and acquaintances, to do as he did, which sometimes produced extraordinary results. They then ordered dinner, and drank a great deal with their meal, after which the old man brought them to his house and gave Lalancette a bottle of his precious dregs of port wine.

"This will last you about three months," he told the pharmacist, "after which you'll have to replace it. The effects go on for eight days after you take the last dose."

Upon their return to Quebec, Henri Lalancette began drinking a small glass of the dregs each morning. At first it was more or less as a joke, but after two months Augusto Soares had himself an ardent disciple – and Madame Lalancette, to her amazement and alarm, found herself with the husband she had not known since the early days of their marriage.

Lalancette had long been aware of the beneficial effects of some substances on benign tumours and hyperplasia, or the enlargement of certain cells: green tea, pygmy-palm bark, citrus seeds, soya, tomatoes, all of which contained high levels of zinc, flavoproteins, and lycopenes. But they were of limited effectiveness, and in any case were used mainly as preventatives. These dregs were a different thing altogether. They seemed to have rejuvenated his prostate by at least twenty years, and it was the prostate, after all, situated at the base of the bladder, whose smooth functioning was so indispensable not only to masculine comfort but also to masculine pleasure and pride.

He realized that Fate had given him a sign. He could take this empirical evidence supplied to him so fortuitously by an elderly Portuguese gentleman, submit it to the rigorous examination of science, and quite possibly come up with an important medical discovery. It would take a great deal of time and money, of course, and present almost insurmountable difficulties. How, for instance, would he be able to convince twenty or thirty patients with enlarged prostates or benign prostate tumours to undergo regular rectal examinations, over a period of several months, which were still the only way known to ascertain the state of their prostates?

He enlisted the aid of a former medical student named Igor Troelhen – a great lover of port wine – and the two men worked day and night for more than six months on the problem. They ran up against a thousand hurdles, managed to get over them all one by one, and now a blinding light was perhaps on the verge of being turned on – a light bright enough to place the name Henri Lalancette on the same stage as that of Louis Pasteur, or Albert Einstein, or, at the very least, Armand Bombardier.

He reached out, picked up a notebook, and became absorbed in the final report that Troelhen had dropped off that afternoon, after having kept him waiting for three days.

A faint smile of satisfaction softened the somewhat unprepossessing features of his face, which normally seemed to have been sculpted as an illustration of melancholy or indifference or simple ill humour. Everything was in place. In a few months people totally unaware of his existence today would be shaking his hand.

He placed the notebook in a drawer, sat back down on the stool, stretched out his legs, and wrapped his arms around himself, amazed at his own reaction. If everything was going so well, why was it that he felt so morose? What infernal *bête noire* was clawing at his entrails, preventing him from giving himself up for once in his life to unalloyed, trumpeting joy?

He heard the door of the pharmacy open upstairs, and someone ask:

"Is Charles here?"

There was such anxiety in the voice that Lalancette jumped to his feet, hurried up the stairs and down an aisle, almost toppling a pyramid of perfume bottles in his haste, and found himself standing before an unsavoury-looking young man whom he recognized as a friend of Charles's. He seemed on the verge of collapse.

"What is it, young man?"

"Do you know where I can find Charles?" the boy repeated.

"He doesn't work here today. I have no idea where he is."

"That's what I just told him," said Rose-Alma.

"Why?" Lalancette addressed the young man. "What's happened?"

"Something serious with his family," was all Steve Lachapelle would say. He turned and ran out of the pharmacy.

Lalancette went out onto the sidewalk and looked after him. The young man didn't seem to know where to go. Something serious must have happened indeed. But what could it have been?

"Hey!" he called. "Come back!"

But the young man didn't even turn his head. It was as though he didn't want to speak to the pharmacist.

Suddenly Lalancette spun on his heels, his mouth hanging open. Rose-Alma looked at him in alarm. He had just put his finger on what it was that had been clawing at him earlier, getting in the way of the full enjoyment of his long labours. It was Charles. Certainly he was the most resourceful, the most conscientious, the most agreeable delivery boy he had had since he'd gone into business. There was no denying the fact. But the boy had changed lately. It had taken the pharmacist this long to realize it because the change had announced itself only in small, almost imperceptible ways. His good humour had become slightly tarnished, his look furtive. He had moments of absent-mindedness, and at time flashes of sadness crossed his face, which he would dispel with a brisk shake of his head.

Something was going on with Charles that was making him unhappy. No doubt the arrival of this dishevelled young man had to do with whatever it was. Perhaps it even had something to do with Lalancette, or else why would the young man have refused to tell him about it? But what could it be?

All this flashed through his mind as he stood in the doorway, to the increasing astonishment of his cashier. A tall, extremely thin man, barely able to hold himself upright with the aid of a cane, was trying to squeeze himself in and was vexed at not being able to get past the massive body of the pharmacist.

"Someone's trying to get in, Monsieur Lalancette," Rose-Alma finally said.

Lalancette stood aside and excused himself. The tall man handed him a prescription and launched into a long, flowing litany of his multiple ailments. Other customers entered. Lalancette became busy behind the counter, filling tubes and bottles, deciphering prescriptions, writing out directions and dosages, assailed by questions, forcing himself to reply to each one as clearly and succinctly as possible, and doing his utmost to maintain a reserve of patience.

As soon as the rush was over he hurried into a room at the back of the shop in which his employees took their lunch and coffee breaks. It was furnished with a microwave oven, a table and several chairs, and three lockers for their personal effects. He opened the locker on the left and took out the rough, cotton backpack that Charles normally used when making his deliveries. He shoved his hand into the bag, removed it quickly and, with a look of surprise coming over his forlorn features, examined the tips of his fingers.

■ ■ ■

Charles and Blonblon were rushing towards the Papineau metro station. Charles was telling his friend about his meeting with his father. His face was pale, his features sagged as though from the effects of deep fatigue, and his voice was an octave higher than usual.

"What is it you want from me?" the carpenter had growled after glancing at the door to make sure Blonblon couldn't hear him. A fierce scowl jerked his mouth into a crooked line. "You come to give me some more dough? Or to break my wrist again? Or both, maybe, eh?"

"I broke your wrist?" asked Charles, surprised and embarrassed.

"As good as! Couldn't work for two weeks after that. . . . You're lucky I didn't grab you, you little bugger, I'd've shaken you like you never been shook before!"

Charles watched him without replying. Leaning on the corner of the table, his half-unbuttoned shirt revealing an abundance of robust, black chest hairs that somehow belied the thinness of his scrawny chest and neck, the carpenter took short, nervous puffs of his cigarette and stared at his son without expression. The adolescent decided there was no point beating around the bush; better to come right out with it, make it as brutal as possible.

"I know it was you who set fire to the hardware store two months ago."

Thibodeau laughed. His only other response was to shrug his shoulders and go to the refrigerator, take out a beer, and, without bothering to offer one to Charles, tip it back and take a long drink. When he was done he turned to Charles.

"Oh yeah? You don't say."

Charles paled and stared at him in silence.

"Is that why you came here? To tell me that?" Thibodeau said mockingly.

"I came to tell you to leave Fernand alone," Charles said, his voice shot through with barely controlled anger. "He's sick. He hardly goes to work any more. What good will it do you if he loses his business?"

Thibodeau took another guzzle of beer, sat down squarely on the table, his legs dangling over the edge, and looked at his son. He seemed infinitely pleased with the turn the conversation had taken.

"Listen to me, my boy. I'm going to tell you two things. First: somewhere around the beginning of June the police came here to question me about that bloody fire. They were here for three hours trying to get me to talk. They thought I'd hang myself with my own rope, but I goddamn well never told them nothing. They couldn't prove nothing against me because they didn't have squat, know what I mean? They couldn't prove I did it because I never had nothing to do with that business. You got that? So if you ever come around here again, find yourself another song, okay? That one goes in one ear and out the other."

Charles tried to say something but Thibodeau cut him off with a gesture.

"And the second thing I want to say is this," he went on. "You're wasting your breath trying to get me to feel sorry for Fernand Fafard. After the way he treated me the last time I saw him, I couldn't give a sweet goddamn if he lost his hardware store, his wife, and his kids to boot! You got that, too? So don't come here talking to me about Fernand Fafard either."

Thibodeau's tone had become threatening. Charles continued to watch him in silence, amazed to realize how unimpressed he was now by this dry, little man with the ravaged face and the fierce eyes. Was it because he knew Blonblon was just outside the door? But there wasn't much Blonblon could do, was there, other than be a witness after the fact. No, the reason was simple: since he'd moved into the Fafards' house, he had grown and his father had shrunk, diminished in every possible way. He had become transformed into a kind of hairy spider. He had made himself a fine web, it was true, but he could still be crushed underfoot. All Charles had to do to protect himself was keep his eye on him.

"All right, Papa, that's all very well, but we still have to talk about him, because that's the reason I came here."

His father gave him a long look, then sighed deeply and lit a cigarette.

"How much will it take for you to leave Fernand in peace?" Charles asked him.

"Nothing at all. Because I'm already leaving him in peace."

"Come on, Papa, no more fooling around. You're wasting my time. I came here to make you an offer. I've got money."

"Yeah, I saw that the last time you came here," Thibodeau snorted. "Where do you get it all?"

"That's my business."

A hideous expression of distrust and greed came over Thibodeau's face. He took another gulp of beer, rolled it thoughtfully around in his mouth before swallowing, then inhaled a long drag from the cigarette that was balanced lightly between his fingers. He exhaled in two long jets from his nostrils.

"How do I know this ain't a trap, eh?" he said finally, in a cocky manner.

Charles shook his head and ran his fingers through his hair.

"I'm not asking you to tell me about your life. I'm asking you how much you want."

"Right. And if I give you a number, you don't think later on you might take that for some kind of confession . . . ?"

"Listen, Papa, if there's no way we can talk to each other, then I might as well leave. I can easily find some other way to help Fernand."

This remark seemed to cast Thibodeau into deep reflection. Leaning with both hands on the edge of the table, cigarette jutting from the middle of his mouth – a pucker of purplish flesh that made him look grotesque –

he stared at the floor through billows of blue smoke. Charles had slid his hand into his pocket and was fingering his own pack of cigarettes, but he didn't bring them out. He balked at the idea of smoking with his father.

Thibodeau raised his head suddenly.

"So you're all grown up, eh, Charlie, my boy? You and I can have some serious conversations now, I guess . . ."

If Charles were looking for a warning, he would have found it in the softened tones of his father's voice, a voice filled with a dangerous languor, and in the honeyed smile that tried without success to soften the features of his shrunken face, formed as it had been by more brutal passions.

"So how much do you want?" Charles repeated quietly.

"Depends on how much you got."

"I have the money. And I can get more."

"Oh-ho! Who you working for these days, the Bank of Canada?"

"Come on, Papa. I'm in a hurry."

"If I mention a figure," Thibodeau said with the wiles of an old cat, "you understand it has nothing to do with any fire at the hardware store. We're agreed about that, right?"

"Yes, we're agreed about everything."

The carpenter maintained his silence for another moment, uncertain about his next move, and apparently spellbound by the incredible luck that had befallen him.

"Give me two thousand," he murmured at last, "and you'll never hear from me again."

"I can't give you that all at once."

"I'd be surprised if you could."

"I can give you four hundred a month. Some months maybe a bit less."

"Understood. Can you let me have some now?"

"No, I didn't bring any money with me. I'll come back tonight."

Thibodeau took a last drag on his cigarette and crushed the butt in a saucer. Then he gave his son a small salute. Charles was about to open the door when a sinister idea stopped him. He turned around and pointed a menacing finger at his father.

"Don't mess with me, you got that? If anything ever happens to the hardware store, I'll move heaven and earth to make sure you pay for it a hundred times over!"

The next thing that happened was so quick that he had trouble reconstructing it in his own mind, let alone for Blonblon. He felt a saucer whistle past his cheek and smash against the wall. A shard from it struck him on the neck, drawing blood.

The carpenter didn't move, as though even he was astonished at what he had done. Then a thin smile appeared on his lips.

"Nobody talks to me like that. It gets on my nerves, see? If I'd wanted to I could have sliced your face wide open. Next time, kid, keep a decent tongue in your head."

12

Charles was opening the gate to his front yard when Monsieur Victoire ran across the street to tell him that Fernand had just been taken to the hospital. He wouldn't say anything more. Charles ran into the house. Céline was mopping the bathroom floor and crying, and Henri, on his knees in the living room and moving with the slowness of a sleepwalker, was trying to wipe spots off the rug with a sponge. Lucie had gone with her husband to the hospital. When he saw the bathroom sink smeared with blood, Charles gave a cry of horror. He ran into the kitchen and threw up into the sink.

"He just lost his head," Henri said, speaking quietly, when Charles emerged from the kitchen. "It didn't last long. As soon as he realized what he'd done he made a sort of tourniquet and called for help. But he'd already lost a lot of blood . . ."

Céline was sobbing in her room, lying across her bed. Charles went in to see her. He sat beside her and stroked her hair.

"Oh, Charles, he could have died! Just think. And for nothing! The medics in the ambulance barely got here in time!"

No, it wasn't for nothing, Charles thought, shaking his head. *It was because of my father. When my father finds out what's happened he'll wet his pants with glee, the bastard.*

"He must be so sad! What could we have done to help him? Do you know, Charles?"

Yes, I do know, Charles thought. *I've already taken steps. And I'll see it through to the end. As much as it takes, Wilfrid. And if I have to throw you into the river to stop you, that's what I'll do.*

He bent his head over her and put his cheek against hers.

"The doctors are looking after him," he said. "Everything will be all right. And I'm going to help him. There'll be no more trouble, I promise."

Céline turned and held him in her arms, shuddering, and her tears ran down Charles's cheeks.

"I need you, Charles. I feel so alone. So small. I don't know what to do any more. I'm afraid . . ."

"No, no," Charles said gently, troubled by her desolation and her loss of control. "You're not alone. I'm here, right beside you. . . . And Lucie, she's here, and Henri . . . and Monsieur Michaud. We're all going to look after Fernand, you'll see, and in a month or two he'll be back at the hardware store, just like before . . ."

"No, Charles," she sobbed, "nothing will ever be like it was before."

He went on trying to console her, patiently, though he was as tortured by doubts and worries as she was.

Henri watched them silently from the doorway, his arms by his sides. Their intimacy surprised him, and he felt strangely like lashing out with a sharp word.

■ ■ ■

Charles could see Lucie sitting in a chair at the foot of the bed in the darkened room. She looked exhausted but calmly determined. She smiled up at him and motioned him to come closer.

He entered the room and stood beside the bed.

"Five minutes, no more," she said in a low voice. "Doctor's orders. He's very tired. Henri is downstairs in the cafeteria. You can go down and join him if you want."

He nodded, then saw that Fernand was looking at him hazily. If Lucie hadn't been there he might have doubted he was in the right room, so changed was the man lying before him. The Fernand he knew didn't look anything like this man, with his hollow cheeks, his flaccid face, his curiously bony, prominent nose. He seemed to have been transformed into something sinister.

Charles felt a constriction in his throat, and he had to wait before he could speak.

"Hello, Fernand," he finally managed.

Fernand continued to look at him without seeming to have heard. He looked lost, as though he belonged to a different world.

"Hello, Fernand," Charles said again, after looking anxiously at Lucie. A moment passed.

"Don't talk to me," Fernand said suddenly, his voice weak and hoarse.

Stunned, Charles looked again at Lucie, who had stood up and placed her hand on her husband's shoulder, looking down at him anxiously.

"You don't want me to . . . to speak to you?" Charles said with a painful frown of disbelief.

"That's what I said. Don't talk to me," Fernand repeated, more loudly this time. "I asked you not to talk to me."

Charles started to cry. The destruction of the Fernand he had known and loved was now complete. This man could die now, and nothing would change.

Lucie had come around the bed to take the young man in her arms.

"You can cry all you want," Fernand murmured bitterly. "You'll never cry enough."

And he turned his head away.

Lucie took Charles out into the hall and tried to console him.

"What did I do to him? What did I do to him?" he sobbed, his face pressed against her large bosom.

"Nothing, nothing, don't be silly. You can see for yourself he's not in his right mind. After what happened this morning, and all the drugs they've given him, he doesn't know what he's saying. He's not making any sense at all."

Ashamed of his weakness, Charles leaned back and looked into her eyes.

"He knows what he's saying," he said angrily. "And he's right not to want me to talk to him. If it weren't for me coming to live with you, none of this would have happened."

Lucie raised her hands in consternation and tried to respond, but Charles had already turned and was running down the hall, so lost in his own misery that he nearly knocked over a nurse carrying a tray of medications.

■ ■ ■

Henri Lalancette looked at the tips of his fingers, which were covered with a white powder. He sniffed them, but couldn't determine what it was. After frowning two or three times and uttering a few perplexed grunts, he cautiously touched his finger to the tip of his tongue. The substance tasted a bit sweet; maybe it was powdered sugar or something like that. But how would powdered sugar get in the bottom of his delivery boy's backpack?

He stood motionless before the open locker, the bag in his hand, somewhat ashamed of himself for resorting to subterfuge but still wracked by doubt, even though he could think of no good reason to be suspicious. He heard steps approaching. Quickly he slid the bag back into the locker and closed the door.

For the rest of the day he was even more taciturn than usual, which was saying a lot! During the afternoon, Rose-Alma asked him in a motherly way if he was suffering from indigestion, which was sometimes the case with him. He replied coolly that his stomach was working perfectly, and concentrated on his work.

But just before five, the need to confide in someone overcame his reticence, and after a few false starts he told his cashier about what he had found, and about the suspicions – so far baseless, he admitted – that the white powder had raised in his mind.

Rose-Alma laughed.

"Really, Monsieur Lalancette," she said, "the ideas that get into your head sometimes! You must have watched too many movies on TV this week!

I've been working behind a cash register for twenty-two years now, and I've seen a thing or two, but Charles? Involved in drug trafficking? You can't be serious! He probably bought a box of doughnuts at the bakery, he sometimes does that, and some of the icing sugar got into the bottom of his bag. That's all it will be . . ."

Her words reassured the pharmacist, and after a few hours he regained some of his quiet good humour. He even allowed himself a joke or two with his customers. But that night, lying in bed beside his sleeping wife, whose anti-aging cream smelled strongly of cucumbers and made the room smell depressingly like a cellar, his suspicions reasserted themselves, and sleep was a long time coming.

■ ■ ■

It took a lot of courage for Charles to return to the hospital. Squeezed into an elevator with a tightly packed group of secretaries in sundresses who were visiting a friend who had gone into labour, he chewed his lips, lost in thought and oblivious to their giddy, schoolgirl chatter and the abundance of bronzed flesh oozing pleasure and life.

It had been ten days since Fernand's suicide attempt. The previous night Lucie had come home with good news. Doctor Berthiaume's therapy sessions were beginning to bear fruit and Fernand was on the road to recovery. He had smiled three times, eaten his dinner without complaint, no longer talked of selling the hardware store, and was even beginning to find his stay in the hospital a tad overextended.

"You must go and see him," she'd said to Charles, with her mother-knows-best smile. "He asked me about you. He probably doesn't even remember what he said the other day."

Charles had given the matter some thought. He was torn between the desire to tell Fernand that from now on, thanks to him, there was no more danger of a fire breaking out at the hardware store, and his fear of having to tell him why that was so.

He pushed open the door to Room 6281 with a knot in his stomach and promised himself that he would keep a firm rein on his emotions. Fernand was sitting by the window, spreading his newspaper out in front of him with a loud crackle.

"Hello there," he said, looking sombrely at Charles as though trying to figure out what to say next.

"Hello, Fernand," Charles replied in a low voice. He stayed near the door, suddenly filled with apprehension and unable to walk farther into the room. "How are you feeling?"

"Not too bad."

He smiled faintly, and Charles felt relief wash over him. He stepped away from the door.

"Don't just stand there," Fernand said, indicating a chair. "You're going to grow roots down into the floor."

Charles laughed, not at the joke, which was an old one, but because of the joy he felt inside: Was Fernand getting better? Could it be that their friendship was still intact?

"You look good," he said, sitting down.

To be honest, it was the word "better" that had come to mind, but he substituted "good" as a way of encouragement. "Sick people recover faster," he thought, "if they think they look like there's nothing wrong with them."

"Well, that's not what my mirror told me this morning when I shaved, but thanks anyway. It's always nice to hear."

"No, I mean it," Charles insisted, almost convinced of it himself. "You look good."

Fernand nodded with a skeptical smile. He folded his newspaper in half and tossed it on the radiator.

Neither spoke for a time. This was what Charles had most feared. He searched his mind desperately for some way to start a conversation. Fernand sighed deeply.

"I'm told I said something stupid to you the last time you were here. I don't remember it, myself."

Charles smiled. "Neither do I," he said.

And he made a gesture to imply that as far as he was concerned the whole thing was of no importance at all.

"All those shots they gave me, my brain was like a bowl of pea soup. And I was in pretty bad shape. I didn't know where I was, everything was strange and sort of jumbled. I hope you didn't take me seriously, eh?"

"Don't even think about it, Fernand," Charles said, tears filling his eyes, and furious at not being able to keep his resolution not to cry.

He placed a hand on Fernand's knee.

Now he wanted to tell Fernand the good news; his natural caution was giving way slowly to the pleasure it would give him. Fernand, however, always embarrassed by shows of emotion, changed the subject by talking about the quality of the food he was being served. At least they were helping him to lose weight, he said. But he was getting the best of care, really remarkable care, and it was made all the better by the beauty of his two nurses, one of whom, a magnificent Filipina woman, seemed to have developed a crush on him.

"But it's mostly Doctor Berthiaume who has helped me get through all this," he added seriously.

He tapped his temple with his forefinger.

"He's helping me understand what was going through my head, Charles. I can't tell you everything because it's still very complicated and mixed up. But there's at least one thing I do understand, and that's that I have a problem with anger. I was full of rage against myself, against everything that wasn't going as well as I wanted it to, against Wilfrid, against the police, all that kind of thing. Anyway, instead of taking all that rage out on whatever it was I was angry at, and getting rid of all that negative energy, as they call it, and making myself feel better by pounding the living daylights out of whoever happened to deserve it, I was turning it against myself – which apparently was not a good thing. Sounds simple, doesn't it? But it never occurred to me that that's what I was doing."

Charles looked at him for a moment.

"Well, you don't need to pound the living daylights out of anyone, Fernand," he said. "I've done that for you."

Fernand looked at him like a dog who was hearing bagpipes for the first time.

"What's that?"

"I've taken care of it for you," Charles said, turning red.

"What do you mean?"

"I went looking for my father a few days ago. I had it out with him. He promised me we'll never hear from him again, ever."

Fernand let out an incredulous laugh.

"No, no, it's true," Charles continued, turning even redder. "It wasn't just a drunken promise. He has no choice, he's going to leave us in peace from now on. I've made sure of it."

"And how did you do that, may I ask? By sprinkling his forehead with holy water from St. Joseph's Oratory?"

Charles stood up, deciding that now was a good time to leave.

"I can't tell you just yet . . . maybe later. But from now on you can rest easy, cross my heart!"

He reached out to take Fernand's hand.

"Don't you believe me?"

"I'd like to, I'd like to," murmured Fernand without conviction. "Are you leaving so soon? We've hardly had a chance to talk."

His face had sunk as though from enormous fatigue. He seemed to have aged another ten years.

"I have to make a delivery," Charles said, looking away. "And you have to rest."

Pushing up on the arms of his chair, Fernand slowly rose to his feet.

"Rest," he said, sighing. "That's all I ever do around here."

He walked Charles to the door, and they shook hands again. He watched Charles thoughtfully, and with some concern, as he disappeared down the corridor. The Filipina nurse passed and said hello to him, smiling; normally he would have replied with a joke, but this time nothing came to him. He went back to his bed, and with the heavy slowness of an insect numbed by the cold, crawled between the sheets, his body shivering despite the stifling heat of the room.

"I wonder what he could have said to him," he murmured two or three times, until his eyes lost their focus and he slipped into a comfortable slumber.

■ ■ ■

When they were youngsters, Charles and Henri had been almost inseparable, but as their personalities and tastes developed they had grown away from one another, until now any sense of solidarity they shared was mostly from habit, from living in the same house, their former closeness having dissolved into indifference. They still got along well enough, but they ran into one another only occasionally outside the house or school. Each had his own friends and his own preoccupations. Which at least meant there were no problems having to do with rivalry.

Nonetheless, a kind of secret jealousy lingered in Henri. Charles's arrival in the family had ousted him from his position as the only son. Charles wasn't as physically strong as Henri, he wasn't as good in sports or much of a fighter, but he had charm, and more sparkle; Henri sometimes wondered if his parents didn't exhibit a preference for the newcomer. Obviously no such thoughts bothered Céline, though. On the contrary, it had been a very long time since Henri had shown as much affection for Charles as Céline did. Her feelings for Charles had made her the target of much teasing, and the subject of many quarrels.

Henri had also noticed that a change had come over Charles. He hadn't given it much thought until one day when he'd accidentally overheard the tail end of a conversation between Charles and Blonblon in a quiet corridor at Pierre-Dupuy High School. He'd heard only a few sentences, and he couldn't have said what they were about, but he had picked up the reproachful tone in which Blonblon was speaking to Charles, and the embarrassed, irritated way in which Charles replied, and he'd guessed that something serious was under discussion. He'd gone up to them as though he suspected nothing, and they'd immediately changed the subject.

From then on, however, he'd kept a closer eye on his adoptive brother.

One day, for example, Charles happened to take out his wallet when Henri was there; it was fat with a thick wad of bills.

"Holy cow! You're rolling in it. Where'd you get all that?"

"I saved it up," Charles replied insolently, but in a tone that failed to hide his embarrassment. And he quickly put his wallet back in his pocket and moved off.

■ ■ ■

Fernand returned from the hospital looking weak and thin, but apparently in good spirits. His hair was turning grey and the skin under his chin was loose. Before long he was back at the hardware store, at first for only a few hours a day, leaving in the middle of the afternoon looking tired and drawn. But before too long he was his old strong, vigorous, sometimes impatient self again. One evening, ever the dutiful neighbour, he helped the son of a friend who lived down the street move into his own apartment, amazing everyone with his bullish strength by moving a refrigerator single-handed. Although still somewhat worried, Lucie was happy to have her old Fernand back; the next day, however, he stayed in bed until ten o'clock, obviously exhausted by his effort, and made only a token appearance at the store.

Twice a week he went to his psychiatrist, Dr. Berthiaume, whom he considered his "saviour" and "such a genius he should run for the United Nations, maybe even for secretary-general." One Sunday at noon, during lunch, he declared that, in fact, he had two saviours, and he placed one hand on Charles's head with an affectionate, teasing smile.

"Believe it or not," he said, "this boy has taken care of the problem of those fires at the store. Don't ask me how, he doesn't want me to know. But it doesn't matter; one of these days, I'm going to nominate him for Fire Chief for the City of Montreal."

He was joking, but beneath the bantering tone lurked a sincere gratitude. Charles looked down at his plate, his face as red as a beet, and forced a kind of smile, not answering any of the questions that were put to him.

It wasn't difficult for Henri to make a connection between this mysterious episode, the conversation he'd overheard at Pierre-Dupuy, and Charles's thick wallet. That evening he voiced his suspicions to Charles, who reacted so angrily that Henri was certain he was correct. He began keeping an even closer eye on Charles than ever.

He soon noticed that Charles was making frequent trips to the credit union to make deposits. He didn't think the job at the pharmacy could be paying well enough to explain such an abundance of money. Then one night in September he saw Charles having a conversation on a street corner with a decidedly suspicious-looking individual, someone he'd seen a few times around the neighbourhood. Another connection was made in his mind, and he felt that the final revelation was not far off.

Shortly after that, he was leaving school with Charles one day when the latter suddenly said he had an errand to run. It was pouring rain; Henri said he thought it was an odd time to be running errands without an umbrella, and he pointedly offered to go with him. Charles made a face and said that if he'd wanted Henri's company he would have asked for it, and then hurried off. Henri waited impatiently for two or three minutes, then set off to follow him. He didn't have far to go.

Charles left rue Parthenais, on which the school was located, and turned onto rue Fullum, which ran parallel to it. He headed south, then almost immediately returned to Parthenais and rang the bell to a lodging almost directly across from the prison. His heart pounding with the thrill of his exploit, Henri hid behind a dumpster that was parked in front of a building being renovated, mindless of the drizzle that was soaking through his clothing.

After a few minutes, Charles reappeared and passed within a few feet of him, a worried look on his face, and turned off at the first corner. Whom had he gone to see? Henri left his hiding place, made a note of the address, and retraced his steps, uncertain as to what to do next. Ringing the doorbell himself didn't seem like a good idea. What reason could he give to whoever answered the door? He thought of taking up his vigil behind the dumpster again until the person came out, but that could take a long time. . . . Then he saw the corner convenience store. Maybe he could gather some information in there. A large, red-headed woman was smoking a cigarette behind the cash. She was in her fifties, still with remnants of her former beauty, though it apparently had been of a fairly cheap type. Her eyes were glued to a television set. He bought a chocolate bar and tore off the wrapper; his adventure had given him an appetite.

"Do you know who lives at number 1670?" he asked the woman, sounding as disinterested as he could manage.

She looked at him in surprise, and more than a bit suspiciously.

"Why do you want to know?" she asked.

"My mother asked me to deliver a letter to one of her aunts, but I'm not sure what her address is."

"It's a Monsieur Thibodeau who lives there. He lives by himself. What's her name, this aunt of your mother's?"

Henri barely registered the question. He left the store and walked down the sidewalk, whistling a merry tune to himself.

■ ■ ■

The picture was slowly taking shape. Charles had got himself involved in some way with a guy who dressed like a circus clown and paid him a lot of money, which he was giving to his father, who was obviously blackmailing him. Henri could already hear the congratulations heading his way. It wouldn't be long before everyone would know which of the two of them was the smartest! Or at the very least which one was more honest. There was only one problem to be solved: What was Charles selling to be making so much money? It had to be drugs. What else could it be? And he had to be getting the drugs from the pharmacy.

This idea gave him pause. By exposing Charles he ran the risk of getting him into serious trouble – he could even end up sending him to prison! His success at divining Charles's little secret was pleasing, but he had no desire to play the role of informer. That would dirty his reputation forever. Honesty was all well and good, but not when it took on the form of betrayal.

190

On the other hand, if Charles knew that his secret was now out in the open – or as good as – it might force him to give it up, and one day he might even thank Henri for it. At any rate, it was quite clear that it was up to Henri to make Charles clean up his act . . .

A week went by, and still Henri hesitated. He wouldn't admit it even to himself, but he was afraid of how Charles would react. Charles could be all over the map sometimes. And then there was Fernand; still fragile, the last thing he needed was something like this to add to his worries.

But then one evening the problem took care of itself.

It was a Saturday. For once, Charles and Henri were both home at the same time. Fernand had gone to bed just after nine, Lucie had joined him shortly afterwards, and Céline had just left to visit a friend. The two boys were sitting in the living room, each with a beer, watching an American sitcom on television. A sleepy quiet had settled over the house. The only movement came from Boff, who was lying on the rug furiously chewing his claws.

Was it the alcohol? Or perhaps the absolute boredom that had set in after half an hour of watching drivel on TV? Whatever it was, Henri turned suddenly towards Charles and, in a kind of disengaged tone mixed with a hint of impertinence, said: "I know everything, Charles."

Charles looked at him quizzically.

"I'm telling you, I know everything."

"What are you talking about?" Charles asked impatiently.

"You know very well what I'm talking about. I know everything, and I've known it for quite some time."

And he began telling Charles exactly how he had been keeping track of his movements, and what he had learned and deduced from them.

"You get them from the pharmacy, right?" he added, triumphantly. "I don't know what you're handing over to your pusher buddy, but if I were you I'd give it up, now, because sooner or later you're going to find yourself in the soup, my friend, and it'll be as hot as hell."

Charles looked at him, astonished, dumbfounded, and furious. Slowly he placed his beer on the carpet and stared down at it, as though waiting for the solution to the terrible fix he was in to rise up out of the bottle. Then, looking up again, he ran a hand over his face. A trembling hand.

"You miserable little piece of shit," he said, with such suppressed anger that the smile of satisfaction vanished from Henri's lips. "I never thought you could be such a complete idiot. You make me sick. What are you doing, messing around in my business? What have I ever done to you? Do you have any idea why I'm doing what I am? No. You don't know anything about anything, and yet you play around at being the little detective and then come to me with your shit morality! You prick! Go ahead, turn me in! The four of you will be a lot better off when they come to arrest me."

Shame and indignation fought for control of Charles, and he was overcome by a series of convulsions that brought tears to his eyes. In a stricken voice he told Henri about the two tumultuous meetings he'd had with his father, when he'd tried to save the hardware store, and about the deal he'd finally been able to make with him after so much painful effort.

"I had no choice. Don't you understand that? Don't you? What did you think, that I was doing it to make a few extra bucks? For what? For fun? You tell me some other way of getting my hands on two grand in six months. Could I borrow it? Who from? Brother André? Ginette Reno?"

He assured Henri that as soon as he'd saved the two thousand (plus a little cushion against any unforeseen eventualities) he'd give up selling drugs for good.

"You really think so?" Henri jeered. "You think your pusher will let you do that? He's got you by the short-and-curlies. He won't let you walk away just like that."

They continued their conversation in low voices, from time to time casting anxious glances at the door to make sure they weren't being overheard. Henri got up and got two more beers, then two more. Boff reacted to the tone of Charles's voice and the look on his face by coming over and licking the boy's hand, but was pushed away.

Henri, who was getting a little drunk, began to back down. He even felt a certain admiration for Charles, although he continued to tell him that what he was doing was pure stupidity. Finally, around midnight, he suggested they go out to a restaurant where they could talk more freely. Over an all-dressed pizza he agreed to keep Charles's sideline a secret. But only on condition that he keep him up-to-date on the smallest details, and that he promise to break the whole thing off with De Bané the minute the hardware store was out of danger – a time that he regarded as an unlikely, utopian turn of events.

13

The 11th of October was Charles's seventeenth birthday. It got off to a bad start. In the morning, on his way to school, he saw Marlene on her way to work. He went up to her with the idea of inviting her out to a movie the next evening, and then spending the rest of the night in her room making love, but she turned him down flat, saying she hadn't heard from him in three weeks and now she could barely remember his name, and anyway she was seeing someone else. Then she turned on her heel and marched off to her grocery store.

When he got home that afternoon, he found a note on his desk, hastily scribbled in Céline's hand:

René

URGENT!

It could only mean René De Bané. Charles had expressly told him never to call the house. Decidedly ticked off, Charles called him from a restaurant.

"Sorry about that, Charlie boy, but it's a case of *force majeure*. I've got to go away on a little trip for the next couple of days – an urgent matter, you understand – but there are a few deliveries that have to go out tomorrow. So I need someone who's one hundred per cent reliable to make them for me, and you're the only one I know who fits that description, old chum. You don't have the time? Hey, I'm prepared to offer you three fat twenties for your trouble. . . . Hey, Charlie boy, don't take it like that! You know my customers can't wait two days. . . . It's my reputation at stake here. If I let them down once, they'll lose all their faith in me, they'll find someone else, you know what I mean? Five little deliveries for sixty bucks! You've got to admit that ain't bad pay. Son of a bitch!"

After trying a few more times to beg off, Charles accepted the assignment, although against his better judgment. He agreed to meet De Bané in half an hour across from Place Frontenac, on rue Ontario.

Irritated and mistrustful, Charles made his way to the location. What sort of trip was De Bané going on? Or was he afraid that something about these deliveries would go wrong, and he'd decided to lay low and let his faithful little puppy take the flak? Or was it even more complicated: had De Bané sensed that Charles was going to quit – De Bané might dress like a joker, but he was one of the sharpest cards in the deck – and was trying to draw him in a little deeper, block off all the escape routes?

He almost stopped and turned back. But the fear of complications, or even of reprisals, made him turn up at the rendezvous spot. The meeting didn't take long. De Bané didn't even get out of his car. Smiling broadly, he handed Charles a fat envelope through the window.

"The stuff, the addresses, and the sixty bucks, it's all there, buddy. I owe you one. . . . Ciao!"

He waved and drove off. Charles watched him go, then, engulfed in a cloud of exhaust fumes, stuck the envelope into his school bag.

His birthday dinner had been set for seven o'clock in order to give Lucie time to make the final preparations, since she couldn't leave the hardware store before six.

She was struck by Charles's worried scowl as soon as he came in the door. She put the finishing touches to the lasagna Alfredo (one of his favourite meals), then finished decorating the cake she'd made the night before, mocha chocolate with butter icing, all the time wondering what it could be that was eating at him. She tried to draw him out two or three times, but he evaded her questions, and when all she got for her efforts were grunts and impatient sighs, she gave up. Try as they all might to be festive, Charles's bad mood put a damper on the evening. He gave the impression of being there only out of politeness. Every now and then Henri looked at him sharply, almost questioningly.

He cheered up slightly when it was time to open his gifts. Since business at the hardware store was picking up, Fernand and Lucie gave him a magnificent brass reading lamp. Charles looked at it with genuine pleasure, pretending not to notice the card that came with it, which expressed the hope that maybe from now on he'd be more inclined to lead a settled life. Céline, blushing becomingly, gave him the second and final volume of Maupassant's short stories, which had cost her any number of sacrifices. Henri merely shook his hand.

"I've already given you my gift, remember?" he said, with a meaningful smile.

Charles wasn't sure what Henri meant. He sensed more arrogance than friendliness in the gesture, and also found it a bit threatening. He couldn't wait to make the last payment to his father, so that he could at last get a good night's sleep. When that glorious day came he might even move out of the Fafard household, even though he'd been happy there. But to have a small apartment of his own, and to be able to live in peace! Only a month ago Marlene had told him there were places in the area that were going for less than a hundred dollars a month. If he could find someone to share it with, he could almost afford it.

He was careful not to let these thoughts show, and from then on he forced himself to look cheerful.

"Another piece of cake, Charles?" Lucie said, putting her chubby arm around his shoulder. "It's good, eh? One of the best I've ever made. I think it's because I put an egg in it this time. And I kept my eye on the oven. It hasn't been working properly, the blasted thing! I no sooner turn my head than it gets as hot as a forest fire."

"It's like you in bed," threw in Fernand, warding off her jab in the ribs.

And he burst out laughing at his own joke, despite Lucie's frown. He might still have been underweight, with a fringe of salt-and-pepper hair, but he was getting his old self back.

■ ■ ■

Five addresses. Four of them were relatively close, but the fifth was much farther east, on Sherbrooke near the famous Orange Julep, where Charles's father had taken him once when Charles was six. In one case, his instructions were to open the door to the apartment, which would be left unlocked, and to leave the envelope on the carpet, where the customer would collect it later. De Bané would collect the money himself.

Charles worried about the deliveries half the night and nearly the whole of the next day, which earned him a stern rebuke from his math teacher. Monsieur Boisclair despaired at seeing one of his best students, who had jumped so promisingly out of the starting gate at the beginning of the year, falling farther and farther behind, and ending up back among the also-rans. Charles was trying to imagine how he would respond if he were ambushed (his flick-knife figured largely in that particular scenario), or what he would reply to searching questions, or what the best reactions would be to crackpots or crazies who might attack him, and he told himself that all he could do was keep his eyes peeled, maybe add a couple to the back of his head, and be ready to pick up the slightest suspicious movement and run as fast as he could out into a public space, where he could lose himself in a crowd after having dumped his merchandise.

In other words, he was scared to death.

He left the school at a quarter to four before the end of the last class, and made his way to the first address. It was on rue Fullum, not far from the CBC building. Four doors down from the Armoricain Restaurant was a brick building dating from the beginning of the century, like most in the area. A nice enough building, carefully renovated. He rang the downstairs bell. For the first time, he was going to see what it was like at the bottom of the food chain. He had already looked into the eyes of the people he'd been robbing of their medication. Now he would see those people whom he was making sick.

A young man opened the door. He had a large mouth and thin lips, the top lip jutting out slightly, and a huge nose, wide at the bridge and pointed at the tip. His eyes were sunken below a large, high forehead topped by short, chestnut-coloured hair, close-cropped at the sides. The whole face gave the impression of the man being determined and cruel.

"Yeah?"

"I'm here from De Bané."

"Yeah?"

He stood in the doorway, immobile, unperturbed, waiting for Charles to make the next move. Charles reached into his bag and handed him a blue envelope. The man took it, slipped a hand into his shirt pocket, and produced a small roll of bills wrapped in an elastic band. Then he nodded briefly and shut the door.

At the second address Charles was greeted by a man in his sixties, with a pink, fleshy face, an abundance of white hair, and thick lips. His expression was kind; he looked like a fat, slightly sad woman. He invited Charles in for a coffee. Charles refused politely, gave the man the envelope, asked for his money, and left.

So far things had gone smoothly, and his nervousness began to slacken. The flashes of heat that had sweat running down his back and in his armpits began to come farther apart. De Bané had been right: if things kept on this way, it would be an easy sixty bucks. But he still told himself he would never earn it this way again.

On rue Darling he opened the door and left the envelope in the hallway, as per his instructions. A small dog yapped furiously from an inner room, but no one appeared.

He looked at his watch. It was almost dinnertime. To avoid the questions that would inevitably come if he went home late, he decided to finish the deliveries later that night.

"Where were you?" Henri asked in a low voice when they were having their dessert.

Charles looked at him and frowned. Henri guessed what was up and gave a faint smile, complicity mixed with something else, something troubling. Charles felt hatred boiling up within him.

He went to his room, worked on his chemistry homework for a while, then stretched out on his bed looking at Hachiko, still at his post on the dresser. Boff had twice tried to knock him down, and each time had earned himself expulsion from the bedroom for a week. The way the statue remained sitting up, resting solidly on its two massive forepaws, its muzzle thrust forward, made the bronze dog appear to be waiting for a signal from its master to leap into service. Its entire attitude proudly proclaimed its blind loyalty to the Japanese professor who had taken it into his home when it was a two-month-old puppy. Charles had tried to model himself on Hachiko. Which was why, in order to protect the man who had taken him in as a son, he had – against every rule of proper behaviour – become involved in criminal activities that risked causing that same man the most grievous sorrow. And if that happened, then Fernand, unswerving in his adherence to principle and honesty, would fly into such a volcanic eruption that its fury would probably carry him right out of the house, forever.

He got up and left to make his last two deliveries. The fourth customer lived on rue Rachel, not far from La Fontaine Park. Charles walked quickly, since the distance was considerable and he was walking into a cold wind. A man with long, black hair carrying a package tied with string came out of a sidestreet and turned in Charles's direction. As they passed, the unknown man gave him a crisp smile, vaguely menacing, exposing as it did the man's long, yellow, widely spaced teeth. Charles stopped and looked after him, surprised. Why had the man smiled at him? Had he perhaps recognized a fellow criminal? Or had something amused him about the way Charles was dressed? He looked down at his clothes, saw nothing remarkable about them, and continued on his way, perplexed.

Ten minutes later he arrived at a two-storey building of grey stone fronted by a tiny square of grass, at the centre of which grew a young apple tree, already half bare of leaves. A long, curved stairway touched the top of the tree. He climbed it and rang the doorbell of an apartment on the second floor.

He waited for a moment, checking his list of addresses to make sure he was at the right place, then the door opened and a young woman stood before him. She was wearing a blue satin dressing gown and looked at him sleepily. She seemed to him the very embodiment of Scandinavian beauty, almost a cliché: long blond hair, blue eyes, straight nose, large mouth with prominent lips sensually curved. Only her slightly plump figure kept her from being the perfect Hollywood icon.

"I've come from René De Bané," Charles said, intimidated.

"I know. Come in. I'll get the money."

Her voice, her pale, languid face, expressed such sweetness that he was frozen in place.

"I'm sorry to have kept you waiting," she said, drifting into the somewhat sparsely furnished living room. "I was asleep."

She disappeared. Charles stood in the doorway, looking about the room. Red sofa and chair, coffee table, candle-holder, all clean, modern lines. It looked like a photo in a decor magazine. The sanded hardwood floor, with no rug or carpets, sounded a note of sadness. Charles wondered if the extraordinary softness that seemed to dwell in this beautiful woman came from the drugs she was taking. Who could tell? He certainly wasn't foolish enough to ask her.

She reappeared with an envelope in her hand, gliding lightly across the floor in the loose undulations of her dressing gown. He noticed her feet, shod in tiny pink slippers with tiny blue buckles; he imagined they were ravishing.

"I'm a bit short," she murmured with a smile behind which lurked a tender supplication. "I'll make up the rest next time, I promise."

"All right, no problem," he said, turning red, even though De Bané had expressly told him never to give credit to anyone, even if he had to take back the merchandise.

He took the money.

"Have you been working for René a long time?" she asked, absently tightening the cord of her gown.

"Yes, long enough," he said, lifting his hand to the doorknob, impatient to be on his way before his blushing became unbearable.

"Good night, and thanks," she murmured, smiling again.

He went down the stairs and breathed in great gulps of fresh air, relieved to find himself alone again. He was one of her enemies, he told himself, and she was so kind, so gentle, so disarmingly vulnerable. No one was forcing her to take drugs, it was true, she'd made her own choice; but he was helping her to do it. And for what? For the most selfish of reasons: to make money.

A passage from a novel he had read a few months earlier came back to him suddenly, one in which a woman was compared to an angel. The image had made him smile. He'd found it exaggerated, sentimental, old-fashioned, almost ridiculous. He'd seen a few girls and women in his life, and none of them, no matter how desirable or gentle they had been, had made him think of an angel (assuming such a thing as an angel existed). Well, tonight that was exactly the word that came to mind. He felt as though he had just spoken to an angel, a fallen angel, true enough, and one that he was helping to keep down. He suddenly felt like returning to the apartment, giving her back her money and taking the envelope he'd given her, persuading her to give up the deadly habit that would surely ruin her life and hasten her death.

But he kept hurrying down the street, head lowered, eyes focused on the dead leaves, the cracks in the sidewalk, the bits of cellophane and plastic and paper that swept by and reminded him that everything was headed for dissipation and destruction.

He made the last delivery and was home by nine o'clock. Céline was just taking her coat from the hall closet to go out on an errand.

"Where are you coming from?" she asked him.

He usually liked the affectionate, open smile she always gave him, but tonight it seemed tense, and her eyes were worried. Was his face betraying his thoughts? Had Henri been talking to her? Surely not. There was no reason for him to do so. But she sensed something was wrong, that much was clear. Sooner or later she would learn everything. Better that she learned it from him. "I've just come from killing an angel, Céline," he said to himself. "It's one of my favourite hobbies. And if you only knew how well it pays!"

"Where was I?" he said, looking away and taking off his coat. He paused, then said, "I'll tell you one of these days."

With Boff at his heels snorting with excitement, he went into his room, where his school books awaited him, and shut the door. He tried to concentrate on homework, but the Blond Angel kept appearing in his mind. In her own way she had made an impression on him as vivid as that of the Black Goddess when he was fourteen. But this time it was remorse that tortured him, not love. He had to talk to someone. Should he call Blonblon? How would he respond to his moral decline? But who, then?

He was in this state of hesitation when there came a light tap on his door.

"It's me, Céline. Am I disturbing you?"

"Come in," he called, surprised and slightly annoyed.

"You're studying? Sorry, I can come back later."

"No, no. Come in, it's okay."

She sat on the edge of the bed and rubbed Boff's head when he came over to greet her.

"Papa and Mama have gone out to a movie. I don't know where Henri is. I felt like talking to someone."

"She feels the same way I do," Charles thought. He smiled, intrigued. This didn't sound like her. "She's here to find out where I've been." His promise to tell her "one of these days" must have seemed too vague.

"Are you finished your homework?" he asked, not knowing what else to say.

"Almost. I still have my French to do. It'll only take me fifteen minutes. French is one of my better subjects. Like it is for you."

She sighed, looking down at Boff and scratching behind his ear. The dog sighed too, and pressed against her leg, eyes half closed in ecstasy.

"I feel at loose ends tonight, I don't know why. I don't like it."

"Me too. It happens sometimes."

Her openness touched him. There was something else, as well, something physical that pushed the image of the Blond Angel to the back of his mind and replaced it with a new mixture of pleasure and nervousness. For the first time he clearly pictured himself taking Céline in his arms, hugging her and kissing her passionately. He had to cross his legs.

"Whenever I feel like this," Céline continued, without seeming to notice his discomfort, "I run a really hot bath, slide down into the water up to my neck, and try to clear my mind of all unpleasant thoughts."

Now he imagined her lying in the tub, her lovely legs stretched out, her arms floating gently, her face perfectly relaxed, eyes softened in a dream state. Ravishing.

"Hmm," he said, also feeling the urge to confide. "I have a different method. Two different methods, in fact."

He told her about Amélie Michaud's Christmas Room. He'd never told anyone about it before, except Blonblon, and Marlene one day when he was feeling low. Céline listened to him, entranced by the strange story. She made him describe the room in minute detail and begged him to ask Amélie if she could see it.

"And what's the other method?" she asked.

This one he'd never told anyone about, and he hesitated to speak of it now. But she urged him with such insistence that he gave in and opened one of the secret doors in his heart, being careful, however, to describe it as one of his childhood methods, one that he hadn't resorted to for a very long time. He told her about the little yellow dog, the heroic efforts he'd made to save its life at the daycare; he described its death, and the cherry tree under which he'd buried it fourteen years ago. When things had become really unbearable (not often, perhaps, but unforgettable when it happened), he'd gone to sit near its grave, and the gentle presence of the dog – he imagined it, of course, he wasn't crazy enough to believe in its actual presence – seemed to hover about in the empty yard, and each time he had felt mysteriously comforted by it. Under that cherry tree he'd always found the solution to whatever problem was troubling him.

Céline's face took on a thoughtful expression that he hadn't seen before. He was flattered. She asked him the address of the daycare and said she would visit the little yellow dog the next day – as long as Charles didn't mind, of course.

"You don't need my permission." He laughed. "I don't own the place, after all . . ."

They went on talking for a long time. Céline told him about things that happened at school, what she was reading, about her friends and what they were into, often quite different from the things that interested her. She talked about her plans for the future (she wanted to become either a nurse or a schoolteacher, but really dreamed of being a doctor). Then she told him some of the things that caused her concern: she was very worried about her father, and the fact that her mother was becoming more and more irritable as her work at the hardware store wore her down, and the state of open warfare that existed between herself and her chemistry teacher. Charles thought she was leading up to asking him questions and was immediately on his guard.

But all she did was ask him how he was feeling, and she put the question with such faith and affection that his suspicions soon faded away.

"Me? Hmm. Things could be going better, I suppose, but I guess they aren't so bad. You know what? For some time now I've been thinking about living alone, in an apartment by myself. It's not that I don't like living here, but I sometimes need to be alone, I don't know why. It's just a gut feeling I get."

She looked disappointed and sad.

"What would you live on?"

"I don't know."

It was getting late and she had to get back to her homework. She said good night and was leaving the room when he caught her arm, then leaned towards her and kissed her on the cheek.

They looked at each other and laughed, both of them turning red, and then she left.

When he went to bed he felt a delicious contentment pervading his body, as though he had just accomplished something difficult and good. But when he woke up in the middle of the night the Blond Angel was back in his thoughts, smiling at him with an air of gentle reproach. "What am I supposed to do?" he asked himself, exasperated with his own sense of guilt. "I'm not forcing her to take those bloody pills!"

His tossing and turning woke up Boff, who looked at him worriedly.

"All right, go back to sleep, old thing," he said, petting him. "You're not the one who's done something wrong."

After an interminably long discussion with himself, during which he alternately agreed with and violently opposed his own rationalizations, he fell into an exhausted slumber, just as a thin shaft of sunlight was falling on Hachiko.

■ ■ ■

A few days later he met with René De Bané to settle his accounts; the sudden trip must have been a profitable one, because De Bané looked happy, relaxed, even seemed to have put on weight, and was his usual amiable, cheerful self. Charles told him with some trepidation that the young woman on rue Rachel owed him money, but to his great surprise De Bané didn't become angry; all he did was give a sigh of resignation.

"Brigitte, Brigitte," he said. "Always the same old story. . . . Okay, I'll go see her. What can you do, eh? She's an artist, for Chrissakes."

Charles asked about her and learned that her name was Brigitte Loiseau and that she was an actress. Like most performers, she was struggling frantically to rise above obscurity, and in the meantime was living a very hard life.

"An actress?" Charles repeated. He felt a surge of admiration.

The Blond Angel's wings had suddenly become much larger in his mind. Brigitte Loiseau . . . what a pretty name! He imagined she must be enormously talented, have a profound and complex sensitivity, be obsessed by an ideal that was all but impossible to reach. Poor woman! With all the discouragement of all the things that got in her way, no wonder she took drugs. But he believed that success waited around every corner. If only he had had more courage he'd have gone to her and smothered her with encouragement, assured her that a woman as beautiful and talented as she was would sooner or later be adored by everyone.

■ ■ ■

Weeks passed. De Bané began leaning on Charles – ever so lightly, of course – to bring him more and more merchandise. Autumn was coming on, he said, and with the shorter days the need for his product became greater among his clientele. His accomplice, however, far from acceding to the pusher's request, had started cutting down on his deliveries. Something in the way Henri Lalancette was behaving, a certain specula-tive expression that came over him at times, an indirect question here and there coming out of nowhere, had recently aroused Charles's suspicions. And then last week he'd caught the pharmacist going through his coat pockets – "Just looking for some matches," he'd said, reddening, his boss who didn't smoke. Charles was convinced that, despite all his care, his days as a sweet-swindler were numbered and he would soon have to close up shop. Not that he would be all that sorry, since he had already reached the limits of his own self-disgust.

Once he even felt the chill of catastrophe pass over his head. He had delivered three dozen Valiums (after having replaced them with fakes) to an old woman on rue Bercy, a woman who was known for the generosity of her tips and her somewhat senile gentleness, and just as he was leaving she called him back.

"Sorry to take up so much of your time, young man, I meant to mention this to you earlier but it completely slipped my mind. . . . I wonder if you would do me a small favour."

"Of course, ma'am," Charles said, courteously.

"It's just that . . . well . . . oh dear, how can I put it? I don't want to cause Monsieur Lalancette any trouble, but it's just that . . . these pills, for some time now I've not found them working as well as they used to. . . . They don't seem to be doing me any good when I take them, if you understand me. . . . I always take two before going to bed and usually sleep right through until morning . . . unless I drink too much fruit juice during the evening, which I know I shouldn't. . . . Anyway, lately I've been having the devil of a time getting to sleep, and last night, well, I could hardly even close my eyes . . . I must have checked my alarm clock three hundred times . . ."

Charles listened to her without comment, but his throat grew suddenly very dry and scorched, like asphalt under a hot sun.

"So would you be kind enough, my dear young man, to ask Monsieur Lalancette to give me some better pills the next time? Not *different* pills, you understand, just *better* ones?"

Charles gave her a big smile.

"Yes, ma'am, I'll tell him as soon as I get back."

He left, feeling very worried. If the old woman had called Lalancette instead of talking to Charles, he would have been in trouble up to his neck.

He went back to the woman's apartment and told her that there had been a mistake on the label, that he had to take back the pills he'd given her and bring her a different bottle. Very surprised by this, she gave him back the envelope, still sealed, and launched into a lengthy tirade about the dangers of allowing one's attention to wander. Fifteen minutes later he brought her back a different envelope and apologized profusely for the mistake.

When he returned to the pharmacy half an hour later, Henri Lalancette gave him a lingering look. Charles didn't dare ask him any questions. Maybe it was just a coincidence? But from then on he felt as though he were walking on a rotten plank across a deep crevasse.

14

One November afternoon, Charles and Blonblon were having a smoke in the student cafeteria by the main entrance to the school. Blonblon had two pieces of news to announce:

1. He was having a tooth filled in two days.
2. After having gone through a long emotional desert, he had just fallen in love again.

Both were making him feel frightened, but the second was much worse than the first. He was afraid of being disappointed again. Charles chided him gently for his fearfulness and told him jokingly that he should take something to relieve his anxiety.

"Keep your bloody stupid jokes to yourself," came Blonblon's terse response, and he turned away with such a tight-lipped expression that Charles had to laugh.

"Come off it, Blonblon. You're acting like an old maid, for Chrissakes. What've you got in your glass there, holy water?"

"I'd sooner drink a hundred gallons of horse piss than do what you're doing, pal. . . . You've got a hell of a nerve laughing at me. You should be ashamed of yourself. I've told you this before and I'll tell you again: this is not going to end up well. I'm warning you."

Charles was angry, but he told Blonblon that in a few weeks he wouldn't have to listen to his sermons any longer. He was going to tell De Bané that their little deal was over. All he needed was another five hundred dollars to give to his father.

Blonblon shrugged.

"If you think your pusher is going to let you go that easily. . . . Does the word 'blackmail' mean anything to you? Or how about 'kneecapping'?"

"What, a little pipsqueak like him? Piss on him! Anyway, I'm quitting my job at the pharmacy soon."

But he thought better of giving his reasons for coming to that decision.

"Really?" said Blonblon, relieved. "You're giving it all up? When do you see your father again?"

"Soon. And after that it's goodbye, asshole. I never want to see him again. I'll have earned a bit of peace!"

"Are you going to get him to sign something?"

"Saying he promises he'll never do anything bad again?" laughed Charles. "Get real, Blonblon. I think I've found a much better way to make him keep his word."

Blonblon conceded that with people like Wilfrid Thibodeau a signature wasn't worth much, and he asked Charles what better way he had found.

"There are people who like nothing better than doing little useful favours," Charles replied with a sardonic smile.

Blonblon was careful to hide his indignation. In his most affable, conciliatory manner, to which he owed his status as schoolyard peacekeeper, he acknowledged that the most important thing for Charles was to get as far away from this quagmire as he could before he drowned, and he offered to go with Charles the next time he visited his father.

"Won't be necessary, old chum. As soon as I give him the dough he'll be as gentle as a little lamb."

■ ■ ■

Lately when Henri Lalancette looked at Charles, the boy saw the word "MISTRUST" emblazoned in flaming letters across the older man's forehead. Why hadn't he been fired ages ago? Charles asked himself that question every day. Then the answer came to him, in two separate episodes.

One night, on returning from making a delivery, he'd gone into the pharmacy through the rear door and interrupted a conversation between Lalancette and Rose-Alma. He'd heard only a few words, but they were enough: the cashier was defending him warmly, based on the indelible impression he had made on her since he'd first started working there, and about which she could not be wrong.

The next day, a Saturday, Monsieur Lalancette had called Charles into his office just before closing time.

"I need to have a word with you, young man," he'd said in a solemn tone, and pointed to a chair facing his desk.

Charles turned pale and sat down silently, certain that he had been found out and he was going to be squashed like a worm on the sidewalk.

"The College of Pharmacists has just sent around a directive to all its members," Lalancette continued, still speaking gravely. "As we do every year, we're required to warn our employees about pharmaceutical products."

Charles could feel himself turning red. He'd been wrong; his skin was worth less than a worm's.

"I haven't done it in your case," Lalancette went on, "but I've decided recently that we'd better follow the rules, hadn't we? So that if anything goes wrong I needn't blame myself."

Then, in a neutral, professorial tone, and using what he called a "totally hypothetical" example, he gave Charles a long list of the disastrous consequences – for legitimate patients who relied on the drugs, for abusers of drugs, and also for anyone caught supplying the latter with illegally acquired medications – attendant upon the trafficking of pharmaceutical products.

Charles understood what Monsieur Lalancette was saying. He was unable to rid himself of his suspicions concerning Charles's honesty, but neither was he able to prove that his suspicions were grounded, and so he was issuing a desperate warning under the guise of fulfilling some fictional directive. His subterfuge was motivated by friendship, perhaps even a feeling of tenderness. Charles heard him out in silence, deeply touched, forcing himself to maintain control over his emotions. His guilt became more and more acute, but he couldn't allow it to make him alter his conduct. He had undertaken to save Fernand and Fernand's business and he couldn't go back on it now. There was something else, too. He took a certain amount of pleasure from his successful trickery, from the subtle, simple pulling of wool over another person's eyes, a practice that was new to him but which he was now perfecting with the attention and passion of an artist.

He resolved, however, to be even more cautious. From then on he would switch only two or three pills per subscription. Business fell off sharply, and De Bané complained loudly.

"You want to go to prison in my place?" Charles retorted angrily.

"I hear you, chum, but it seems to me you could do a tiny bit better, eh?"

"I do what I can. I'm being watched like a hawk, I tell you. I'm going to have to quit my job at the pharmacy. My nerves are shot, they have been for some time. I'm not sure how much longer I can take it."

Charles's declaration had an extraordinary effect on De Bané's mood. He became solicitous. He begged Charles not to make any decisions on the spur of the moment. He promised to be more patient, adding that his concern was not solely for any loss of revenue he himself might suffer, but also for Charles. He even offered Charles a few odd jobs to get him by until things at the pharmacy returned to normal, such as, let's see, making a few small deliveries here and there, which would keep the money flowing for Charles and also give De Bané a bit of breathing space. For the past few weeks he'd been working on a very promising project that was eating up all his time.

"Never again," Charles told him. "Once was enough."

The discussion ended on that note for the moment.

But De Bané returned to the offensive a few weeks later, and by then Charles was less adamant. What had happened was this. Wilfrid Thibodeau's demands for more money had increased with his need for more alcohol, and he was beginning to get impatient with the tiny amounts his son had been bringing him. One day, after an exasperated Charles had explained once again that his source of revenue had begun to dry up and there was nothing he could do about it, the carpenter growled at him.

"If you don't live up to your end of the bargain, I don't see why I should live up to mine."

"You'll get your goddamned money, every last penny of it!" Charles shouted furiously. "It's just going to take more time, that's all! You can make all the threats you want, it won't make anything happen faster!"

Thibodeau blanched. He picked up an empty beer bottle from the kitchen counter, and a violent convulsion seemed to go through his body. Instinctively, Charles threw himself to one side, but the bottle never left his father's hand; Thibodeau stared at Charles for a second, then gave a strange smile, and for a time father and son stared at one another in silence.

"Watch your manners, sonny boy," the carpenter eventually said in a low voice, black with rage. "You remember what happened the last time you forgot yourself? Eh? You maybe don't live with me any more, but you're still my son, don't forget that!"

He put the bottle down, and, having regained his calm, spoke in a cold, detached tone.

"Do what you want, it's not my problem. But if you come here ten days from now with less than two hundred bucks, don't bother coming at all."

Charles nodded and left the apartment, feeling more humiliated than he had ever felt before in his entire life.

When he met with De Bané the next day, there was a short discussion that ended with De Bané understanding that Charles would work for him two nights a week delivering merchandise to his customers, but that there would be a maximum of five or six customers per night. On the other hand, De Bané would pay him no more than thirty dollars a night, and his territory was expanded considerably.

"What do you want from me, old buddy? Business ain't so good as it was. . . . When things pick up, you'll benefit as much as I will."

Despite his pride, Charles asked De Bané for a two-hundred-dollar advance, to get his father off his back. De Bané agreed so readily that Charles was taken aback. "He thinks he's got me on his hook for good," he thought as he walked home. "Well, my good man, you'll soon see who's in control."

■ ■ ■

Steve Lachapelle was bored to death living in Pointe-Saint-Charles. His boredom had been getting worse and worse since spring. He no longer went to school unless he felt like it, which wasn't often, and he compensated for his lack of classroom learning by devoting most of his time to honing his skills in the arcades and pool halls of his neighbourhood. But they didn't come close to filling the void that was consuming him.

Louisa, his Haitian girlfriend, had broken up with him the previous week. He thought it was funny, how it happened. The night before, they had made love like a colony of rabbits, after which Louisa, at Steve's request, had left him her pretty pink slip with the lime-green lace trim, saying with an obscene gesture and a snigger or two that she had a pretty good idea what he was going to do with it. Then she had given him a long, hot goodbye kiss.

"It's going to be a long night without you, my beautiful little teddy bear," he'd whispered in her ear. Then she'd left.

As far as Steve was concerned, it had indeed been a long night, and he had finally been obliged to make use of the slip.

The next afternoon he'd called her to make a date. In a quiet but cool, clipped voice she'd told him she was busy, without giving him any details.

"How about tomorrow?"

"No, not tomorrow. And not any other night, either."

He'd thought at first she was joking, and he gave his long Apache cry, like a wolf howling at the moon, a signal that he wasn't going to let her treat him that way. But after a few minutes he had to admit to himself that she had really tossed him into the garbage like a sack of rotten oranges. He therefore dredged up all his oratorical skills and finally managed to get her to agree to meet him in a restaurant for ten minutes – ten lousy minutes were all he could get for his efforts.

She was waiting for him, a pained expression on her face. She looked a little contrite, he thought, but with an air of having come to a decision. That worried him. She was as pretty as ever, wearing a fabulous pink dress that he hadn't seen before, and she kept her hands folded on the table, looking at the tips of her fingers as though they held the secret to the cause of their breakup. He took one of them in his and noticed that she was also wearing a ring with an enormous diamond on it – a fake, of course, but a high-quality fake. He'd never seen the ring before, either. He asked her where it came from. She answered vaguely, looking away, then in one breath she told him she had found someone else. The news nearly knocked him over.

"Since when?"

"Not that long," she replied, looking more and more uneasy. She refused to tell him another thing.

After a few minutes, not having pried another word out of her, he got up, picked up his helmet, and tapped the tip of her nose with the visor.

"Poor little Louisa. You've been whoring around, haven't you? You should be more careful. You never know what you might pick up."

And he left the restaurant. She came out on his heels. There was a huge brute with a red crewcut waiting for her in a Cadillac. She climbed in beside him, looking pathetic; he put his arm around her shoulder and gave poor Steve a tiny but ironic nod. Steve knew that he stood about as much chance against this guy and his money as a snail against a bulldozer. He contented himself with a few obscene gestures, shaking his rear end at them and mimicking a sodomite reaching an orgasm. The man burst out laughing and the Cadillac took off with a deep, contented purr.

■ ■ ■

The street on which Steve lived was remarkable for the number of bottles, cans, wrappers, and other detritus that littered it, but it was even more encumbered than usual this year by an astonishing number of Christmas trees, which, despite the lateness of the season, were sticking out of the melting snow that lined the sidewalks, pathetically waving their bits of tinsel in the breeze.

Steve considered them for a moment, made a disgusted face that lowered his left ear a fraction of an inch, and decided he definitely needed a change of air. He'd pay Charles a visit. He hadn't seen him for a long time and it would be good to talk to him. But first he had to put something in his stomach. He hurried into his house, where his mother was talking on the telephone (on a good day, she could have supplied the entire telephonic network of Montreal with conversations); he managed to get her off long enough to take it into the bathroom and make a private call. Céline answered the phone. Charles was off making deliveries, she said, but he'd be home for supper.

"I'll surprise him," Steve decided.

He gave the phone back to his mother, who resumed her interrupted conversation, and made three enormous peanut-butter-and-banana sandwiches – two of which he ate himself and the third he kept to eat on the way – and headed for the metro.

When he showed up at Charles's house, they were just finishing supper. He thought he could have been made to feel a tad more welcome.

"Bad timing," Charles told him. "I've got more deliveries to make."

"For the pharmacy?"

"No."

"I'll come with you," Steve said, intrigued. "We can chat as we go."

Charles shook his head. "I'm afraid not," he said in a low voice. "I'd be too ashamed."

"Ashamed? Ashamed of what?"

Charles cursed himself for having let that slip out, and tried to think of some way to divert Steve's suspicions, but nothing came to him.

"I'll tell you some other time. I'm not up to it at the moment."

"Hey, don't go shushing me up, old buddy! What's the matter, are you dealing drugs or something? Peddling your ass? Eh? You wouldn't be the first of my gang to get into it, but I'd never have guessed it of you!"

Charles stared at the floor in silence, more and more embarrassed. Then he sighed and shook his head as though ridding it of a tormenting thought.

"No, some other time."

"Okay, okay. . . . Keep your little secrets locked up in your little heart, sweetie. I doubt if I'd find them that interesting anyway."

"I have to go alone, Steve. It'd be too complicated with someone else there. . . . Don't make faces at me! Okay, I've got a bit of time. Let's go somewhere for a Coke. But I warn you, fifteen minutes and I have to go."

He sighed again. The two boys walked towards rue Ontario.

"Things aren't going so well for me, either," Steve confided when they were seated at a table. "I had a load of shit dropped on my head this afternoon."

And he recounted the story of Louisa's betrayal. Charles waxed indignant: the sick feeling that had been churning his insides for days seemed to have let up a bit.

"Count yourself lucky, Steve. If she can be bought that easily she couldn't have been worth much. You're better off without her."

"That's what I keep telling myself, but still. . . . What a girl, man. I really thought she was the one, you know, deep down? She was the best, you don't know how good she was. Oho! Hey, sourpuss, I just realized why you've been sitting there wheezing like a broken accordion: it's because of that actress of yours, isn't it?"

Charles hadn't been able to keep from telling Steve about Brigitte Loiseau, to whom he was still delivering Valium.

"You're out of your gourd, you dummy," he said, half telling the truth. "Stop interrogating me. You haven't got a clue!"

Still full of roast beef from dinner, Charles drank his Coke slowly, more out of solidarity with Steve, who, with tears in his eyes, had gone back to fulminating against the faithless Louisa. Charles tried to console him, telling him that a guy with his silver tongue would find another girl in no time. Then, glancing at his watch, he said he had to be going.

"We hardly see each other any more," Steve said. "And when we do, lately anyway, you've had a face on you like a funeral director. Get yourself straightened out, man. I'm worried about you. I don't have so many friends that I can afford to lose one."

Charles shook his hand – a solemn and unusual gesture in their circle, and one heavy with significance.

"Call me the day after tomorrow. We'll play some pool at the Orleans."

He returned home, slipped along the side of the house, and went into the backyard. It was already almost dark. After making sure no one was watching, he opened the shed and took his delivery bag, which he'd hidden under an old tarpaulin, and quietly went back the way he had come.

He had three deliveries to make. He was saving the Blond Angel for last. The last time, she'd invited him to stay for a coffee. They'd talked for a while; she hadn't said anything particularly extraordinary, but she'd been so relaxed, so soft and confiding, that he'd felt almost honoured to be in her presence. He could have sat for hours letting her voice wash over him, watching the graciousness of her movements, the purity of her face that contrasted so sharply with her deadly habits. She'd told him about her life as an actress, which she loved but was thinking of giving up because there were so many hurdles. He'd tried to dissuade her, speaking so eloquently and admiringly of her talents that she'd smiled, touched and amused and almost comforted. Then she'd asked him about his life, what he liked, who his friends were, and he'd told her things he hadn't thought he would, the kind of confidences one makes only with strangers who have made a real impression. The phone had rung. She'd got up, said a few words in a low voice, and when she'd returned there was something in her face, a vague embarrassment, that had told Charles it was time for him to leave.

The night was warm and humid, the breeze redolent with the mingled odours of the city and the first hints of summer. He felt wrapped in them as he walked rapidly along the street, suddenly filled with a kind of luminous joy. "By the time the weather turns hot," he told himself, "I'll be finished with this disgusting business for good."

The first customer lived on rue Préfontaine, not far from Hochelaga and a few doors from the metro station. He was a fat, bald man with soft features, as though he were melting; he took the envelope Charles gave him with a weak hand and gave him back a handful of warm coins as a tip, which was unusual since De Bané's pills didn't come cheap and almost never inspired generosity on the part of his clients.

The next customer lived not far from there, on rue Dézéry. Charles rang two or three times, waited in the hall shuffling his feet impatiently, then left muttering curses: he would have to come back the next day without knowing if anyone would be there then, either, since De Bané never gave him his customers' names or phone numbers.

That left only the Blond Angel of rue Rachel. He quickened his pace, hoping she would ask him in for another conversation. Although he'd been a long way from La Fontaine Park, he made the trip in twenty-five minutes.

"Damn it!" he muttered when no one answered her door either.

Maybe she was sleeping, as she had been the first time? He rang again, then twice more, then paced back and forth on the landing, waiting, for what, he didn't know. A huge tabby cat with wide jowls ran out from behind the building, started up the stairs, and then stopped, meowing quietly and staring up at Charles, not daring to continue. "Maybe it's her cat," he thought. He knelt down and called to the animal, rubbing his thumb on the tips of his fingers as though he had some food for it. The cat took a couple of cautious steps up, then, seized by some undefinable fear, turned and ran back the way it had come, uttering cries of lamentation.

Charles stood up, surprised by its reaction, and tried to see where it had gone. He was suddenly overcome by a strange presentiment. He rang the doorbell again, and when there was still no response he tried the knob. The door opened. He stepped into the vestibule and called out. There was no sound from the darkened apartment except the echo of his own voice; he felt a chill come over him. "Odd she didn't lock the door when she left," he said to himself, taking a few more steps inside.

Then, in the living room, where the light from a street lamp came faintly through the venetian blinds, he saw a figure lying on the sofa in a strange position, one arm flung across her face and the other trailing on the carpet.

His heart began pounding so furiously in his chest that he could barely breathe.

"Mademoiselle Loiseau," he murmured, terrified and befuddled.

She didn't move. Her stillness filled the room like a thick, viscous liquid on the point of bursting through the walls. He leapt forward and seized her hand. It fell back to the floor, absolutely lifeless.

But then she emitted a faint groan. Quickly, almost violently, he removed the arm from her face. Her mouth was half open, her skin pale. She had sunk into a terrible sleep, the kind from which it seemed there would be no return. He shook her with all his strength, shouting at her to wake up. Her mouth opened again and another groan escaped her lips. Her face was hideous.

"Oh God," he cried, standing back. "She's dying and it's my fault."

He stared at her, appalled. Her forehead glistened with sweat, and he saw her eyes begin to flutter. He must call an ambulance. But not from there. It was too risky. He hurried out the door, down the staircase, and began running along the street looking for a pay phone. As he ran he kept repeating to himself: "I killed her. The Blond Angel, I killed her!" His tears mingled with the sweat that stung his eyes.

He saw a phone booth at the corner of a parking lot. In an instant he was talking to a 911 operator.

"Address? Just a minute!"

In his distress he couldn't remember it. Fortunately he still had De Bané's list. He fumbled furiously in one pocket, then another, uttering a string of swear words punctuated by sobs. Finally he found it.

"Hurry, for Chrissakes! She's dying. Dying! My name?"

He almost gave it, but a scrap of lucidity held him back. He hung up the phone and ran away as though the police were already on his heels. He ran all the way to rue Ontario, then stopped, out of breath. He thought about returning to the Blond Angel's apartment to make sure that the ambulance was there and she was being taken care of. But he was afraid of drawing attention to himself. What could he do?

He could drink. He could drink a lot, to settle the turbulence that was coursing through his head. He thought of going to the Orleans, and headed in that direction. Nadine would sell him a beer under the counter, he was sure of it. And maybe De Bané would be there. He'd be very happy to run into De Bané! It would be his farewell to Montreal. The city didn't need an angel-killer.

15

It was nearly one o'clock in the morning. Fernand and Lucie were sleeping, and Céline was watching television, sitting on the rug close to the set, which was turned down low. *Rosemary's Baby* was on, a Polanski film that one of her friends had said was terrific. Since she couldn't sleep, and her math class the next day was cancelled, she thought it was a good chance to stay up and watch it.

It started out as a story of a young couple in love but soon began to take a sinister turn, and she was beginning to feel afraid. She would have liked Charles to have been there with her, or at least Henri, but they had both left the house after supper and God alone knew what they were up to.

How horrid she would feel if she found herself in Rosemary's shoes! Carrying a thing in her belly for nine months that came straight from Hell! She couldn't watch. She wanted to turn a light on, since the living room was lit only by the glow from the TV screen and seemed almost as frightening as the movie.

Suddenly she heard the knob on the front door squeak and someone coming into the vestibule. Which of the two had come in? She obviously hoped it was Charles, and turned to watch the gap in the living-room door to see who passed it. And it was Charles. In the split second it took him to pass the opening she could tell that something was wrong. His head was bowed and he seemed to walk with a shaky step.

She jumped to her feet. Just as she came out of the living room she saw his bedroom door close.

"Charles," she said, bringing her mouth close to his door. "It's me. Can I come in?"

There was no response from within.

"What's the matter, Charles?" she whispered, more and more concerned. "Is something wrong?"

She heard a deep sigh coming from her parents' room, and the bed gave a dry, imperious squeak, as though ordering her to be quiet.

Frightened, she waited a moment; then, in an almost inaudible whisper, she called Charles again. This time she heard steps approaching the other side of the door.

"Leave me alone!" the young man said in a hoarse and curiously guttural whisper, as though he were choking back sobs.

Céline stepped back, suddenly chilled. She remained in the hall for a few moments, wondering if she should overcome her fear and go into the room, then she went back to the living room instead. She turned off the television and went to bed.

But it was a long night! She slept for five or six minutes, then suddenly opened her eyes, her mind as clear and racing as though it were mid-afternoon. She listened, jumping at the tiniest sounds, trying to figure out where they came from. She thought of Charles, and only of Charles. A plethora of details passed through her mind, some she hadn't paid much attention to earlier: his sudden bursts of irritability over the past few weeks, especially aimed at Henri (when he'd always been so easy to get along with), and his secretiveness and mistrust, the way he went out nearly every night. According to Fernand he was simply "out on the prowl," and Lucie, more elegantly, said he was old enough now to be interested in girls, and added that she hoped he would find one who would please him and stay with him. Henri didn't say anything. All he did was roll his eyes, or snigger behind his hand and look away.

Céline didn't put much stock in Charles's supposed amorous adventuring, partly because when someone runs after a lot of girls it's usually because none of them is very interesting. But she also thought there was something else going on; there was the way he talked to her now, so different from how a brother talks to his sister! But mostly it was the air of unhappiness that had hardly left him for the past few weeks: that wasn't at all how a boy behaved when he was chasing after girls. Of course she wasn't naive enough to think that he hadn't had his adventures. . . . Steve Lachapelle, whose mouth sometimes worked faster than his brain, had let something slip a while ago about a girl named Marlene. Céline had been instantly jealous. But Charles had never brought anyone to the house, never spoken of anyone, and for several months now hadn't seemed to be seeing anyone special. In the end, Céline felt nothing for this Marlene person but indifference.

No, there was something else afoot, something serious, and she was sure Henri knew what it was. She'd tried a few times to worm it out of him, but he hadn't responded with anything but vague stories he was obviously making up, or an abrupt order to mind her own business. What could be going on? Nothing really terrible, she was sure, because she didn't think a person like Charles would get mixed up in anything like that. It must have something to do with his father. With that man, anything was possible. He could be forcing his son to do something he didn't want to do. If only she had the courage to talk to Charles directly, or if he would come to her to confide in her, share whatever it was that was tormenting him, everything would be out in the open, and the two of them could surely find a solution.

Two or three times she got out of bed and tiptoed to the hallway to listen. Once she thought she heard a strangled sob, but with her father's deep snoring she couldn't be sure. His room was across the hall from Charles's.

Then she was suddenly overcome by exhaustion and fell dead asleep. She woke up feeling that she had climbed out of a deep, cotton-filled chasm, and that it had taken all her strength and left her with a feeling of deep sadness; she was almost sick to her stomach. How long had she slept? It was nearly morning. Then she suddenly sat straight up in bed. Something had happened, something she could sense only confusedly. But it had to do with Charles.

Her intuition was confirmed when she heard slight creaks coming from the hallway, followed by the squeaking of the door lock again: someone had just left the house!

She jumped out of bed, ran to the vestibule, and, pulling aside the curtains on the door, saw Charles disappearing around a corner with his backpack. His backpack? Where the devil was he off to? And why so early? According to her watch it was only twenty after five. She ran back into her room, took off her pyjamas, and climbed into her jeans.

Lucie appeared in the doorway.

"What's going on?"

"I'll tell you later," she said, pulling a sweater over her head. "I don't have time right now."

"But where are you going? Don't you realize what time it is?"

Without even looking at her mother, Céline ran out the door. An instant later she was dashing down the street, and then she was gone. To Lucie, it was as though the city had swallowed her up.

She ran for a minute, maybe two, hoping to catch up to Charles, but she couldn't see him anywhere. She stopped. Where could he have gone? Maybe he was waiting for a bus on rue Ontario. At this time in the morning they didn't come very often.

Retracing her steps she came to the corner and swept the street with a glance. Two city workers were tinkering with a fire hydrant, making a lot of noise, but there was no one else in sight. Had he flagged down a taxi? She turned around in circles, feeling more and more helpless, and then had an idea. It was a long shot, but for the time being it was the only shot she had.

She ran towards rue Dufresne, turned south as far as rue Lalonde, crossed it, and came to a stop in front of Charles's old daycare. It had long been converted into a woodworking shop. There was a sign on the front door:

GODIN & GOSSELIN
Furniture of all types
Specializing in kitchen cupboards

She had come here the day Charles told her about the little yellow dog. Whatever else was going on in his life, it was certain that he was going through great distress: maybe he had come here to find some peace beside his dog?

The gate to the yard was locked at that hour, so she climbed over the iron grating. Then she ran alongside the building into the yard, where piles of boards and beams were covered with large, flapping tarps to keep them from getting too much sun. At the back, to the left, now flanked by a kind of plastic garage, stood the old cherry tree under which Charles had buried the little yellow dog. Someone had tried to trim it, or had attempted to cut it down and given up, but despite the mauling it had received, and even though it was reduced now to a twisted shrub, it was still responding to the spring by valiantly sending out a spray of blossoms.

Céline uttered a cry of disappointment; there was no one under the tree. Her intuition had failed her. Then, in the pale, blueish haze of dawn, she saw someone slumped against the tree trunk on the opposite side. She moved forward, holding her breath, ready to run away at the least sign of trouble. She saw a pair of legs, and recognized the black leather boots as belonging to Charles. She kept moving ahead slowly, craning her neck forward, her eyes wide, trying to figure out what he was doing. His head was bent over his backpack, his arms were crossed, and he seemed to be staring off into space. A piece of cardboard, no doubt picked up in the yard, protected him from the wet ground.

"Charles," she said softly.

She fell to her knees beside him and put a hand on his shoulder. He looked up, apparently not surprised to see her.

"So," was all he said, raising his shoulders. "So it's you the little yellow dog has sent me.... How did you know I was here?"

She smiled timidly.

"I knew."

Then she added, "I've come to help you."

"Henri told you, then?"

"Henry didn't tell me anything. But just seeing you last night, I knew that something terrible had happened."

"Henri doesn't know anything . . . about this, anyway," Charles went on, as though talking to himself. "No one knows . . . yet . . ."

"What is it, Charles? And where are you going like this?"

"South America."

"South America?"

"Yes."

"How?"

"I'll hitchhike."

"But you don't have a passport."

"I'll get one. There are ways."

She tried to say something, but her voice cracked and her eyes filled with tears.

"Have you gone crazy, Charles? I . . ."

"Yes. Crazy."

She started to cry.

"Charles, listen to me. Please, Charles, try to calm down a bit. . . . Tell me what happened. I'm sure we can work something out. . . . All we have to do –"

"I killed an angel, Céline."

She looked at him, stunned, wondering if she'd heard correctly.

"I killed an angel," he said again, with bitter conviction. "We can't work that out. It's done. I have to go away. I can't live here any more. Ask your parents if they'll look after Boff. And thank them for everything they've done for me."

A moment went by. She kept looking at him, not knowing what to say, wondering if he really had lost his mind.

"What angel, Charles?" she finally murmured. "I don't understand."

Feverishly, speaking a mile a minute, as though he had no time to lose before removing himself forever from human compassion, he told her the lamentable story, right up to the terrible conclusion she had witnessed the night before. Caught between the demands of his father and the terror of pushing drugs, he had gone through moments of deep wretchedness, but the death of the Blond Angel had been worse than any of that. It had dirtied him forever, and the only way he could put it behind him and be forgotten by everyone was to leave the city, like the hero of some romantic fable.

She listened calmly and closely, holding back the surprise and fear that his story produced in her. All the while he was talking she was trying to think of a simple and practical idea, something she could put together with other ideas to come up with a plan of action that would pull Charles back from the brink of despair.

When he finished talking, exhausted, he stared down at a small bump in the dirt in front of him with a pitiful, bitter smile.

"I'm rotten, eh?" he said at last.

"No, Charles, you're not rotten. You're the opposite. You've shown what a generous person you are, trying to help Papa, more generous than anyone has ever been. It's just that you picked the wrong way to go about it."

He laughed bitterly.

"Easy for you to say! There was no other way."

She said nothing. She followed Charles's gaze to where he was staring at the ground.

"What are you looking at?" she asked after a moment.

He seemed not to have heard, lost as he was in despair. Then a shiver passed through him; he raised his voice, turning towards her.

"This morning I was on my way to the port to try to get a berth, so I could get the hell away from here as soon as possible. But while I was looking for a cab I thought I'd come here first, to say a final goodbye to my little yellow dog, because I knew I'd never see it again. I hoped it would do me some good, because it always has in the past. I felt so messed up, Céline, so sick of myself, I didn't know how I was going to make it through the day. So I came here and sat down with what's left of this pitiful tree and I tried to get calm again. I leaned against the trunk and tried to put my thoughts into some kind of order – but it was hard after what happened last night, and I could feel the cold rising up my legs. And then I saw . . . Céline, you won't believe this, but I'm telling you I saw . . . it only lasted a few seconds . . . I saw a kind of yellow vapour rising up out of the ground, out of that little bump you can see there: it looked like a kind of cloud in the form of a small dog . . . please, Céline, you've got to believe me, I wasn't imagining it! . . . it rubbed against my leg and then *pffft!* where it went I don't know. But from that moment I knew that something would happen, so I waited, and . . . you arrived. It's amazing, don't you think?"

What Céline thought was that Charles was a deeply troubled soul. "Those blasted pills," she thought, "he must have taken some of them himself."

But she told him she hadn't the slightest idea what had happened; what was important was that they were together and that they would find a solution, that really difficult problems were always easier to solve when there were two.

He nodded his agreement and his face brightened a bit.

Encouraged, Céline told him what she had been thinking. The first thing they had to do was find somewhere where Charles could rest, even sleep, because he didn't seem to be in any condition to make decisions at that point. Then they had to find out exactly what had happened to Brigitte Loiseau. In his befuddlement he was behaving as though she were dead, but how could he be sure? If she were still alive, it would change everything.

Charles shook his head like a stunned boxer.

"Either she's dead or as good as. . . . You didn't see her, Céline, you didn't see . . ."

"Listen to me! You've got her dead and buried already and she might be walking around as alive as you, maybe even more so! Let me at least find out, and stop being so damned stubborn."

He shook his finger at her.

"Do not ever call the police! I absolutely forbid that. That would finish me!"

"Come on, Charles, what do you take me for, a turkey? I'll find out, don't worry."

That Charles was even listening to her plans was encouraging. But they had to get out of the yard before the workshop opened and they were discovered. Where could they go?

Charles, all of a sudden, seemed to have pulled himself out of his slough of despair. He walked as though on firm ground, his step back to its normal assurance. Seeing him gather his wits about him so quickly filled Céline with boundless joy. Her love for him grew stronger, if such a thing were possible. She laughed and kissed his cheek. He didn't respond, lost in his own thoughts.

"There's a small hotel at the corner of Mont-Royal and de Lorimier," he said suddenly. "They'll probably let me have a room. Let's go there. I'll go in alone, though; you look too young."

She looked at him a little crossly and was on the point of asking him how he knew about this hotel, but she thought it wasn't a good time to be challenging him.

Twenty minutes later they were there. Charles hadn't said three words the whole way, having slipped back into his despondency. The Blond Angel was surely dead, he knew it. He could feel it. All Céline's kindness and resourcefulness wasn't going to change that. Her presence at his side was comforting, of course it was, but it didn't erase his crime. And even if Brigitte Loiseau were alive, he was still what he'd always be: a miserable dope peddler. He could never forgive himself for that.

"Wait for me in front of that fruit stand, okay?" he said to Céline. "I'll be back in two minutes."

She crossed the street and went up to the window of a fruit stand. Inside, a man with a black moustache and a thin, brown face was washing the floor with wide swipes of his mop, his eyes still half closed. He looked up and saw her, and gave her a smile. Another good sign. She felt bubbles of goodness welling up inside her, ready to burst out of her body and float off in all directions, to do battle against all human misery. Charles would be the first to feel the benefits. How wonderful! A feeling of intense happiness invaded her, and she had to lean against the window frame and tap her foot on the pavement in her excitement.

Charles came out almost immediately and crossed over to where she was waiting, making a small sign with his hand to indicate that everything was settled. He seem calmer, relieved.

"You were right, it will do me good to get some sleep. I'm dead on my feet and my brain feels like mashed potatoes. I'm in room 206. Come and get me whenever you're ready. I've told the clerk to let you up."

And he kissed her on the cheek.

"I'll make a few inquiries first," she said, blushing with pleasure.

He gave her Brigitte Loiseau's address and warned her again to be careful. She left, full of excitement but not having the faintest idea how she would go about achieving her mission.

"I'll just play the innocent little know-nothing," she decided after thinking about it for a moment.

■ ■ ■

A few minutes later she was ringing the door to the actress's apartment. "There might be someone there who can tell me what happened," she thought. When there was no response, she rang the bell of the apartment below. A woman with a large, wrinkled nose opened the door. She had a knife in her hand, and her hair was tied back in a nylon net; she smelled strongly of spaghetti sauce.

"Poor little thing," she said, "you should'a phoned before coming all this way, dear. She's in the hospital, is our Brigitte, and she won't be getting out too soon, if you ask me. . . . They had to take her in an ambulance last night."

"An ambulance?" cried Céline, feigning surprise. "What happened to her?"

"How should I know? And even if I did I wouldn't say nothing," replied the woman, with a caution that contrasted sharply with her earlier loquacity. "I don't know who you are, do I? It's everyone for himself in this world, dear. That way no one gets in trouble, eh?"

She turned and went back into her apartment, where her spaghetti sauce was calling.

After a few more inquiries, Céline learned that the actress had been taken to Notre-Dame Hospital. That was all she'd really hoped to find out. She left, feeling encouraged. If the actress were still alive, a terrible catastrophe would have been averted. Now Céline had to find out if that were the case. She ran into a restaurant and telephoned the hospital, pretending to be a friend. She was told that Mademoiselle Loiseau could not receive any visitors at the moment, but she was out of danger and was getting better.

"I can't wait to give this good news to Charles," she said to herself when she'd hung up the phone.

She made a second call, this time to her mother, who was sick with worry but had had to go to the hardware store anyway, as she did every morning. She greeted Céline's call with a volley of reproaches. Céline tried to reassure her, but it took some doing.

"I'm with Charles, Mama. He's not feeling too good, but I think he's coming around. He doesn't want to see anyone right now. . . . Yes, Mama, of course we're in Montreal, where did you think we were? . . . No, he doesn't want anyone to know where he is. . . . Yes, I'll tell you everything, I promise. Even better, he'll tell you himself. Why am I mixed up in this? Don't worry, you know me, I've always behaved responsibly, haven't I? I'll call you back later in the day to fill you in on what's happening. Tell Papa not to worry, there's nothing bad going on, nothing to get worked up about. Tell him that, okay? And can you call the school, tell them we're not coming in today? You're a dear. Hugs and kisses. See you soon!"

She was eager to get back to Charles, but she thought it better to let him sleep since he was in such a pitiful state. She also realized she hadn't had anything to eat and her stomach was growling. She asked for a hot chocolate and an order of toast, which was brought to her by an old, grumpy-looking man whose chin was covered with grey hairs, and who was chewing his lips distractedly, trying to discern whether or not his son had been telling him the truth about his car accident the previous night.

She'd never eaten with such appetite. She had just enough money with her to leave a tip, albeit a large one. Through the window she saw rue Rachel bathed in a joyful, wavering light, as though it were shaking in the warm wind that had begun blowing over the city. She left, saying a cheerful goodbye to the old man, who barely acknowledged it.

Nothing remained of winter but a few long, thin crusts of grey ice melting in black rivulets along the pavement and flowing down the rain gutters. She was walking slowly towards the hotel, taking singular pleasure in flexing the muscles in her thighs and calves, when the troubling thought suddenly occurred to her that Charles, far from sleeping, was probably waiting for her, stretched out on a bed in a hotel room that only the two of them knew about. Still thinking that his actress had died! She was sorry she'd stopped to eat; it was cruel of her not to have hurried back to his side. He'd been counting on her more than anyone else in the world. The thought filled her with a boundless joy and renewed strength, and convinced her that she would overcome any obstacle between Charles and his happiness – and, a small voice added tenderly, her own happiness with him. The blow he had just suffered had robbed him of his peace of mind, and she was suddenly annoyed with herself for taking such a selfish pleasure in helping him to recover from it. "You're nothing but a little egotist," she thought. "He was about to run off to South America, and here you are bathing in the milk of human kindness. You should be ashamed of yourself. Hurry, now! Get back to him! Can't you see he's suffering?"

■ ■ ■

Ten minutes later she was in the lobby of the hotel, completely out of breath. It was a small room, with walls covered in pink wallpaper that was peeling in several places. Behind a huge counter with flaking veneer a man with a crisp, mobile, and joyful face, and hair carefully combed over the top of his head to hide his bald spot, was speaking on the telephone; he smiled at her and gave an acknowledging nod of his head.

Stunned and almost put off by his welcome, she climbed a beautiful, massive oak staircase, sumptuously carved but lacking all its banisters. Her erstwhile joy began to fade and turn to dust, crumbling into nothing. What kind of place was this? Were the rooms rented by the hour? How did

Charles know about it? Had he brought girls here? She almost turned and left the building, but her legs continued up the stairs despite her feelings of disgust. She had to tell him about Brigitte. She couldn't let him run away to the ends of the earth over a misunderstanding.

Suddenly, her mind changed again. Now she couldn't care less what kind of place this was, or if Charles had brought a hundred or ten thousand girls here. Only one thing mattered: that she see him, take him in her arms, reassure him, console him, and tell him how important he was to her.

The next minute she was standing in front of the door marked 206. Despite the pounding in her ears she registered the silence of the dusty, shabby corridor with its dented walls. At the far end a window was filled with light, which made the place seem slightly less horrid. She waited until her breathing returned to normal, raked her fingers through her hair a few times, and gave three light taps on the door.

She heard bedsprings creaking, then the dull thud of bare feet on the floor, crossing the room; the door opened and Charles was standing there wearing jeans and an undershirt, his cheek marked by a diagonal pink crease. He looked half asleep and still troubled; the sun crowned the dishevelled hair on his head with gold. He seemed to her more handsome than ever. Her mind emptied of every other thought.

"Come in," he said, yawning.

He closed the door behind her, yawned again, and picked his shirt off the back of a chair and put it on without buttoning it up. Céline looked around the room. It was quite small, but clean enough, with cheap furniture that had been badly treated by a long list of careless clients. The curtains were faded green, and the linoleum floor was doing its best to look like ceramic tiles.

"Well?" Charles said, becoming anxious again. "Any news?"

Céline smiled. "Yes. And it's good news. Your Blond Angel isn't dead, Charles. She's in the hospital, and they say she's getting better."

She leaned tenderly into him.

"And so *you* can start getting better, too. You looked so forlorn when I left you. But that's over now."

He remained silent, responding weakly to the pressure of her arms. He rested his head on her shoulder. Céline felt warm tears running down her neck.

"No, no, Charles," she said softly. "It's all over now. Now maybe life really can go back to the way it was."

■ ■ ■

The next thing they knew they were wrapped in a passionate embrace, standing in the middle of the room, whose spareness had suddenly taken on a kind of solemnity, soon dissipated by the shafts of brilliant sunlight that poured in through the window. Then, without knowing exactly how it had come about, Céline found herself in the bed, being smothered in kisses and caresses. She laughed ecstatically, and a bit fearfully.

They continued to kiss, parting from time to time to exchange wondering looks and to murmur the thousand little nothings that come to lovers' lips when they are making love. Outside they could hear the constant hum of traffic, the honking of car horns; the steady noise seemed kind to their ears, and slightly mocking.

"You will be careful, won't you Charles?" she whispered in his ear. "I'm not very used to this."

He smiled tenderly and, taking her chin between his thumb and forefinger, kissed her lips.

"I'll do whatever you want me to do, and only what you want me to do."

A long time passed.

The sky had begun to darken; the shape and colour of objects in the room softened in the shadows of evening.

At five o'clock Charles had left the room to find a restaurant, and had come back with two white boxes tied with string, each containing a club sandwich buried under a pile of steaming french fries. Now both boxes were on the floor beside the bed, empty.

Céline was asleep, curled up against Charles's side. He was lying on his back, staring up at the darkened ceiling, careful not to move a muscle for

234

fear of waking her. Occasionally a frown passed over his face. The contrast between the horrors of the previous night and the bliss of the one that had just begun was so violent that he was finding it too painful to contemplate.

■ ■ ■

Henri was curious when he saw that Charles wasn't in school that day. He expected to run into him at home at lunchtime and find that he'd been home sick in bed, or off doing God-knew-what. Henri himself would have dearly liked to know what. But Charles wasn't at home, and he had left no word of explanation for his absence. Henri hadn't seen him since the previous night, and he remembered that Charles had left the house right after supper with that chimpanzee, Steve Lachapelle, whom he'd started hanging around with again. Charles had had that impatient, pre-occupied look that he'd been carrying around for the last little while. Was the chimpanzee involved in Charles's drug business? Maybe Charles had spent the night with Marlene. Or someone else. Or maybe he'd got himself in trouble.

He ate his lunch, a bowl of soup and a piece of pâté, and went back to school. At one o'clock Charles still hadn't shown up. Henri became more and more alarmed, and wondered what he should do. By rights he should tell his parents, or at least his mother. He waited until the afternoon break and called the hardware store. It was Lucie who answered. He learned that Céline had called earlier in the afternoon to say she was with Charles, who wasn't in very good shape. The news rocked Henri: not only was Charles sinking into the black pit of his drug business, but he was dragging his sister down with him! He mumbled a few indistinct words to his mother and hung up, to Lucie's consternation. Her surprise increased two hours later when Henri turned up at the store looking fraught.

"Where's Papa?" he asked.

"In his office. What's the matter? Henri, tell me what's going on, for heaven's sake!"

"I have to talk to Papa."

He left without another word. His interview with Fernand lasted half an hour. Henri told him everything he knew about Charles's doings, and about Wilfrid Thibodeau's role in the whole affair. At the mention of Thibodeau, Fernand's face contorted into a look of ferocity reminiscent of certain African masks, and his eyes turned into burning coals. But he remained silent. When Henri was finished, Fernand stood up, as imposing as a statue, with his powerful hands leaning on the edges of his desk.

"Thank you for telling me about this, son," he said. "I would have liked to have been favoured with this information a little sooner, it would have made things a lot easier, but I can see how it was hard for you to do anything at the time. The next time I hope you'll be a little more forthcoming."

And he gestured that Henri could leave.

When she saw her son leaving the store looking pale but relieved, Lucie hurried into the office.

"Is someone finally going to tell me what's going on around here?" she said angrily.

If she was going to say anything else, the words caught in her throat. She was stopped in her tracks by the expression on her husband's face. A moment went by. From the store there came the sound of a customer laughing.

"Come on, Fernand, talk to me, for the love of God," she whispered.

"Charles has been acting like an idiot," Fernand replied heavily. "He has been for months, now."

And he told her briefly what Henri had told him.

Lucie tottered on her feet, and if Fernand hadn't had the presence of mind to push a chair under her she would have sat on the floor. She didn't move for a moment, merely sat there with her arms dangling and her head down, as though knocked senseless; then she began to sob, her shoulders shaking, crying with all her heart while pressing the Kleenex Fernand had hastily handed her to her mouth and nose so as not to be heard by the customers.

She wiped her eyes and patted her face and took two deep breaths, and appeared to have regained her calm.

"Céline is with him, he won't do anything rash for the time being. There's no need to worry about that now."

"Yes, you're right. Céline has a good head on her shoulders," Fernand said, nodding.

"She told me they'd be home later tonight."

"Good. Meanwhile, I'll go and take care of someone else."

"Who?"

"Wilfrid Thibodeau," her husband replied, pulling on his jacket. He raised a hand to silence her.

"No," he said. "Not a word. For now I've got to concentrate on settling his hash."

He left the hardware store, slamming the door so hard that a light bulb above the cash register burst and sent sparks flying everywhere, something that had never happened before and was talked about for a long time.

16

Wilfrid Thibodeau was in a particularly gallant mood that day. He was helping Liliane unhook her brassiere when the doorbell rang. The lovers exchanged surprised glances. Neither of them was expecting anyone, and in their uneventful lives sudden visitors rarely bore good news.

"Don't answer it," Liliane advised him, adjusting her straps.

The bell rang again. Then the carpenter remembered that one of his buddies from the tavern had promised to drop by that day to pay him the fifty bucks he owed him. He knew from long experience that if he were ever to see that money he'd better answer the door right away.

"I'll go see," he said, pulling on his trousers.

"Don't answer it, I tell you. Sure as shit it's my husband."

Wilfrid looked at his watch.

"Your husband's having his treatments right about now."

He went to the door, pulled the curtains, and looked out. He saw no one.

Even as he was unlocking the door he had a vague presentiment that he was making a mistake, but curiosity and the idea of the fifty dollars won out.

The next second he found himself face to face with Fernand Fafard, who was glaring at him with his eyes bugged out of his head.

"Are you alone?" Fafard asked, stepping inside with a strange smile on his lips.

Without waiting for a reply, he pushed his way to the centre of the kitchen.

"There's someone here," the carpenter said angrily after a second's hesitation.

"Get rid of whoever it is. I've got something to say to you, man to man."

When the carpenter didn't move, he placed a massive hand on the man's bony shoulder and repeated what he'd said, only this time more loudly.

"Go tell your visitor to leave."

"And what if I don't want to speak to you, eh?" said Thibodeau, looking up at Fernand with a fearful yet impudent face.

"It's all the same to me. But you're going to hear what I have to say. I've got a few things you might find interesting."

And turning Thibodeau around, he marched him rapidly across the room.

Liliane came out of the bedroom, her hair dishevelled, her lower lip thrust forward, as though she didn't know whether to bite or cry for help. But the sight of Fernand soon told her that caution was required.

"Who's he?" she growled in a low, vicious voice.

"No one. I'll see you later. I need to talk to him."

She snatched her bag from the kitchen table and, as she passed Fernand, shot him a ferocious look. With her mouth tightly shut and her upper lip curled up, her expression was so comical that Fernand couldn't help but smile.

The door slammed shut. Just then the sink emitted a kind of gurgle, as though it had been drinking beer with Thibodeau and his girlfriend and was feeling the effects deep in its bowels.

"Okay, so what do you want?" the carpenter demanded, throwing himself onto a chair without bothering to offer one to his guest.

"You're going to give me back the money Charles gave you. All of it."

Thibodeau gave a long, silent laugh. "What money?" he said.

"I'm a busy man, Wilfrid. Don't waste my time."

And he took a step forward.

"I don't know what you're talking about," said Thibodeau, but there was a slight tremor in his voice.

Fernand stared at him for a moment, gave a slight grimace, and then calmly grabbed him by the waist and lifted him, as easily as if he were a screwdriver or a box of toothpicks. He carried him over to the stove and sat him down on it. Thibodeau kicked his feet like a little boy in a dentist's chair.

"Where's the money?" shouted Fernand, squeezing Thibodeau's shoulders until he cried out in pain. Making a vise of his thighs, he immobilized Thibodeau's legs.

"Someone's been telling you fairy tales, Fernand," exclaimed the latter, his voice sounding pathetically sincere. "I don't have any money. All I get's my unemployment insurance."

Fernand stared at him straight in the eye, waited a moment, then said, "Right. I see you need a little inspiration."

And reaching behind Thibodeau he turned a dial on the stove.

"Don't be crazy, Fernand! Stop! Turn it off! Turn it off, for Chrissakes! *Ow*, Jesus, you're burning my ass, *Ow, ow*! You have no right to do this! I'm gonna call the. . . . Okay, okay! Lemme down. Okay! Take your money and for Chrissakes leave me alone!"

Fernand released him and he jumped down from the stove, slapping at his buttocks. The smell of burnt cloth filled the room.

Fafard crossed his arms and watched with amusement as Thibodeau feverishly checked to see if his nether parts had been fried.

"Okay, enough fooling around, Wilfrid. You've still got all your manly parts. Now get the money. Where is it?"

"I . . . I spent most of it, you know," Thibodeau said, giving him a look of hatred and fear.

Fernand grabbed him by the belt.

"You want me to put you back up on the stove, Wilf? I know a great recipe for braised bollocks."

"All I got is twelve hundred!" Thibodeau cried, pushing Fernand's hands away. "That's all I got left! I'll let you have it right now. It's in my dresser."

Fernand accompanied him into the bedroom, where he took the thick pile of banknotes. He counted the money carefully and put it in his pocket.

"You should be ashamed of yourself, taking advantage of your son like that."

"He came to me, after all. He's old enough to know what he's doing."

"And what about you? Aren't you old enough to know this money wasn't falling out of the sky?"

"I don't know nothing about where he got it."

"Give me a break. You make me sick, you do. Your mouth is like a sewer talking to me. . . . I'm going to give you two little pieces of advice, Wilfrid."

He pushed Thibodeau back on the bed and sat down beside him. Then he grabbed his cheeks, stretched them as wide as they would go, and brought Thibodeau's face close to his.

"First: you have nothing more to do with Charles. At all. Understood? Get that into your thick skull. And two: don't ever come anywhere near my store. Never mind the wide innocent eyes, I'm not as stupid as you think I am. And if you're ever unfortunate enough as to forget what I just told you, I'm going to come after you, you snivelling little rat, and when I catch you I'm going to *personally* shove my hand down your throat and pull your guts out through your mouth. Are we clear about that?"

And to give added force to his words he smacked Thibodeau across the face so hard his nose began to bleed.

17

Charles and Céline had returned to the house. Lucie pretended she didn't notice their amorous looks. She was equally discreet about asking her daughter what she had been up to.

When Fernand came home he took Charles and Lucie into the living room and closed the door. They were in there for a good hour. Boff stretched himself out in front of the door and scratched at it from time to time. Finally, losing patience, Henri seized the dog by the collar and took him outside for a walk.

When Charles came out of the room he looked chastened but happy again, almost serene. Lucie's eyes were red from crying, and Fernand looked as haughty and beneficent as Jupiter, ruler of Olympus; it was hard to believe that this was the same man who, ten months earlier, had slit his wrists.

After consulting with Parfait Michaud, Fernand and Charles agreed that the twelve hundred dollars would be donated to the Portage Rehabilitation Centre. Charles quit his job at the pharmacy, and Henri Lalancette was circumspect enough not to ask any questions. René De Bané, whose business had expanded significantly over the previous few months, was visited in the middle of the night by the police and became an overnight guest of the State, spending a lot of time being interviewed. Three days later, a ten-thousand-dollar bail bond put him back on the street while he awaited trial, but Montreal seemed to have lost much of its appeal for him, and he fell into a fit of melancholy from which neither pool nor beer could lift him. He decided to find a new line of work; he had a fertile imagination and an inexhaustible supply of energy, and he was sure that several avenues would suggest themselves to him before too long.

Charles returned happily to his quiet, regulated life; everyone in the Fafard household acted as though the episode involving the trafficking of prescription drugs had never taken place. His love for Céline was new and delicious and went a long way towards easing his feelings of remorse. They flared up occasionally, however, and when they did, nothing and no one could relieve his mind.

"You needn't beat yourself up over it too badly," Blonblon said to him one day when he was feeling particularly depressed. "After all, you did what you did for a good reason."

"That doesn't mean anything! If a man kills his wife with a butcher knife because she's been unfaithful, you can say he did what he did for a good reason, but he's still a monster!"

Blonblon smiled and patted him affectionately on the shoulder. Despite his fondness for Charles, he was having trouble understanding the reason for his sadness. After a disastrous love affair, he too had taken up with a new girlfriend, and everyone knew that new love went a long way towards calming the soul.

Blonblon had only recently discovered the pleasures of sex, the cement that bonded two hearts together, and the euphoria in which he bathed from morning to night had somewhat removed him from the troubles of humanity. He forced himself to listen to Charles, but all the time he was thinking of Isabel, the young Chilean student he'd met in a department store. He was fascinated by the beauty of her eyes. Her father had been a gynecologist in Chile, but as a political refugee he was now driving a taxi until the Quebec College of Physicians deigned to allow him to practise his profession.

Blonblon was proud of his conquest and had wanted to introduce her to Charles more than once, but Charles always backed out of the dates Blonblon tried to set up for the four of them.

"I'm not in the mood tonight," he would invariably say. "Maybe next week."

And he would stay home with Céline, or go out with her to visit one of their friends, who would lend them their apartment.

"Charles, listen to me," Céline said to him one day. "It's over. Let it go." It worried her to see him fall so often into these bouts of sadness. "Why do you keep going back to it? Turn the page, throw the book away, get on with your life. Charles, I'm begging you. . . . When I see you like this, I feel as though I can never make you happy."

"Oh, no, Céline, it's not that at all. Believe me," he said, taking her in his arms and covering her with kisses. "What you do for me isn't nothing! Quite the contrary. If you hadn't come looking for me that day, where would I be now? I might not even be alive!"

"And where would I be?" Céline said. "In a nuthouse, probably, crazy as a loon. Charles, Charles, you're too hard on yourself. . . . You can't accept that you made a mistake. How are you ever going to live with yourself?"

The young man's face darkened.

"If you'd had a father like mine, you'd understand."

"But he's *not* your father any more!" she cried, exasperated. "He hasn't been for eight years!"

"Yes, you're right," Charles sighed, taking her in his arms (and on the verge of tears). "Be patient, Céline. I've been through so much. It's bound to take time."

But summer came and Charles found that time wasn't healing any wounds. He finished his fifth year of secondary school with honours, and an essay he wrote on "Future Choices for Quebec" had been circulated among all the teachers. Céline adored him, and his love for her deepened each day, assuming an intensity that amazed and delighted him. And yet the episode of the Blond Angel and the life he had fallen into continued to torment him.

One night he felt he had to talk about the whole thing with someone who would give him good advice. Not knowing any psychiatrists or psychologists, he decided he would go and see Parfait Michaud.

■ ■ ■

He found the notary home alone, sitting with a glass of port, wearing blue jeans and a flowered T-shirt, thumbing through the *Grand Robert* dictionary looking up the origin of the expression "knight of industry," which had come to his attention earlier that evening. Amélie had left a week earlier for a month's stay in a health spa, one that specialized in thalassotherapy, energy transfers, deep breathing, and other forms of holistic medicine that were supposed to bring about the total rejuvenation of one's being to anyone who had the means to pay for the treatments.

It would be an exaggeration to say that the couple were getting along well.

Michaud had been given all the details about Charles's misadventures, but, being a discreet man, he had judged it best not to intervene directly. He knew that Fernand and Lucie had things well in hand. He would have liked to have seen Charles, to whom he had always felt a deep attachment, and he was sorry that the young man's friendship for him had seemed to weaken over the years. And so his welcome to Charles was so joyful it gave the latter the courage to bring up the delicate subject he wanted to discuss.

"Madame Michaud is well?" he asked, as a way of easing into the conversation.

"Oh, you know her, Charles. She's only well when she isn't thinking about herself. . . . As soon as she turns her attention to her health everything goes off the rails. Deep down, she only lives to be sick. Her health is killing her."

He told Charles that he'd been a bachelor for a week and would be until the tenth of August, and that, all things considered, he wasn't minding it much at all.

Charles gave a knowing smile and began to take unexpected pleasure in their "manly" conversation. Michaud, encouraged by Charles's smile, began making more and more obvious allusions to the kind of freedom his wife's absence was affording him.

"Marriage, Charles," he concluded cleverly, "is the most noble of institutions. The only problem with it is that it goes totally against human nature."

Charles laughed, although such a remark a few years ago would have scandalized him. Now he was fortified by the indestructible love between himself and Céline, as well as by the example of Fernand and Lucie. He could laugh because he knew the notary was wrong.

Michaud, curious about Charles's visit and wanting to put him at ease, brought out the port bottle and another glass, which he filled to the brim.

Charles had never tasted port before and found it delicious; the notary refilled his glass. Two red patches warmed Charles's cheeks, and his eyes became bright and ardent. He found his old friend more charming and humorous than ever, and he was sorry he had been avoiding him for so long. How many good times had he let slip through his fingers? He promised himself that from now on he would visit the notary more often.

"Monsieur Michaud," he said suddenly, "I have a question to ask you."

"Call me Parfait, Charles, please, as I've asked you many times before. That is, after all, what I am."

And he burst out laughing, as though his old joke had just leapt to his lips for the first time.

"You know about everything that's happened to me, don't you?" Charles went on, becoming serious.

"Is that what you came here to talk about?"

"Yes."

"And so?"

Charles hesitated and glanced at his glass. The notary reached for the bottle of port.

"No, thanks. I've had enough to drink."

Michaud uncorked the bottle anyway and refilled his own glass.

"Are you sure?"

"I'm sure."

The notary took a sip and swished the port around in his mouth with a small smile, his eyes half closed. His visitor waited in silence.

"And so, Charles?"

"Well, what I'd like to know . . . is . . . well, what do you think of me, Monsieur . . . Parfait?"

"You mean, as a result of this business?"

"Yes."

Michaud brought the glass to his lips again, but hesitated a moment before drinking as he thought about his response.

"Well, to be honest with you, Charles, I think you behaved . . . ahem . . . like a complete asshole. Pardon my language, but there's really no other word for it."

The pink patches on Charles's cheeks turned pinker, bordering on red, and he sucked in his breath quickly.

"That being said," Michaud went on, "everyone sooner or later behaves like an asshole. I've even acted like an asshole a few times myself, and I can't swear it won't happen again. What's important, however, is that you learn something from your own stupidity. And I think that's what you've done, haven't you?"

"I can't stop learning from it," Charles sighed.

"Only imbeciles don't learn from their mistakes. They're like fish who manage to get themselves off the hook by thrashing about like mad, and then five minutes later chomp down on another hook. Well, it's their own tough luck, I say. And of course what's also important, in my view, is the question of motive. Are you sure you won't have another drop of port?" he said, interrupting himself. "Just a drop to dampen the bottom of the glass?"

Charles held out his glass and the promised drop became a cascade.

"In effect, it's all there, my dear boy," continued Michaud after refilling his own glass (by now his hand had become rather heavy). "As I mentioned earlier, Fernand and Lucie have told me your story. If I'd learned that you had become involved with trafficking simply to make a fast buck, I'd've been mightily disappointed in you, I don't mind admitting it, because I would have had to say to myself, 'Charles has turned into one of those little street urchins that every Montreal neighbourhood turns out. What a waste. I thought he was going to make something of himself some day. I was wrong.' But that wasn't the case, praise God."

"Do you think Fernand and Lucie have the same opinion as you do?"

"I'm sure they do. In fact they told me so themselves, in their own words. In any case, if they thought you were a criminal you'd know it by now, and you wouldn't have come here tonight to ask me that question."

"And yet, I almost killed a woman."

"Without meaning to, Charles, without meaning to! Hmm . . . I'm not happy about the way you're seeing this. . . . Let's look at the thing as it really happened, shall we? It was she who seems to have wanted to kill herself. But she failed to do so. And to whom does she owe her life? To you, Charles. To you. That's what you must not forget. I hope you will always bear that in mind."

Charles jiggled the glass of port in his hands, staring down at the gently dancing liquid. He saw the actress talking to him, sitting across from him, wearing her blue silk dressing gown, her long hair tied back with a ribbon to which she'd pinned a tiny bouquet of dried flowers. He heard her deep, resonant voice echo in his ear, warm with the friendship she had been offering without even being aware of it.

And for the first time in a long time, instead of grimacing at the memory, he smiled.

"I think the moment has come for you to learn something from life." The notary stood up, slightly wobbly, from his desk. He walked over and stopped at the shelf on which were ranged the most beautiful editions of the literary masterworks. "I think, young man, you're ready for an intensive treatment of *The Human Comedy*. You are familiar with *The Human Comedy*, are you not?"

"By Balzac? I haven't yet read anything by him."

"Well, the time has come, young man. It'll open your eyes and shore up your soul for life's approaching battles, as our old spiritual leaders used to say. You've already had one battle, but there'll be others."

He took down five huge, red tomes bound in stiff canvas boards, and placed them on the floor at the young man's feet.

"I just bought it in the Pléiade edition. These here are part of the 'Intégrale' collection, brought out by Les Éditions Seuil. They're quite lovely too, but I find them a bit cumbersome, although the price was right. Are you going straight home?"

Charles nodded.

"Good. Take them with you. A present from me."

Charles was speechless. When he found his tongue he protested that he didn't deserve such a gift.

"Nonsense, nonsense, it's nothing. No need to thank me. But read them soon – all of them, no skipping! You'll have your preferences, as I have mine; parts of them will strike you as slightly boring, but others will sweep you away like a hurricane. I defy you to read through the whole of *The Human Comedy* without coming away with a more self-assured and intelligent view of life."

He leaned against the bookshelf. The tiring day, combined with the port, had suddenly turned his legs to rubber.

"That's one of the benefits of great books," he went on, his chin raised high as though he were addressing a vast audience. "The most important, of course, is the pleasure we derive from them. Oh yes, Charles, read *The Human Comedy* and it won't let you down, I promise you. You'll learn to appreciate the effects of passion, greed, ambition, egotism, and hatred thrown into fierce hand-to-hand combat with virtue, love, friendship, genius, integrity, and what have you!"

His voice, carried away by an access of lyricism, became nasal, trembling, and rose at times to its highest pitch.

"Literature, my dear, young friend, is concentrated life served to its readers in the comfort of their armchairs (to paraphrase Musset). It is the fruit of a million experiences, a tenth part of which one wouldn't normally live long enough to have. Through literature we participate in a sort of eternity; it makes us like God: omnipresent, existing everywhere and in every time! Literature doesn't necessarily make us wiser – that would be asking too much, and it depends, does it not, on what we carry around in our heads – but sometimes it can help us to be a little less stupid."

He continued in that vein for several minutes. Charles listened with a slight smile on his lips, but gradually the notary's fervour broke through his reserve and he recognized in it his own love of books, expressed though it was with an eloquence and precision he himself could never have attained. From being mannered and a bit ridiculous, the notary had become sublime.

"Right," he said suddenly, wiping his forehead with the sleeve of his jacket. "I guess I let myself be carried away. Whew! It's tiring! I'm not twenty years old any more. Let's deal with more tangible things for a moment. I'll go find you two large plastic bags to take your books home in. But first, a last little drop of port!"

This time Charles declined strenuously. Whenever he had too much alcohol he had the disagreeable impression that reality broke down bit by bit, and he felt obscure forces sloshing around within him trying to gain ascendancy. It made him think of his father, and he was overcome by a sense of horror that immediately rendered him sober.

Michaud drank a last glass of port and sank into his chair, feeling suddenly calm, almost melancholy. Then he got up, left the room, and returned with two bags.

"I have a great deal of faith in the Balzac treatment," he said to Charles, placing his arm around his shoulders and conducting him to the door. "You are an intelligent young man, and also a very sensitive one. Balzac will do wonders for you, I'm certain of it."

"So am I," said Charles. "I still don't know how to thank you." He seemed unable to express his gratitude except by being exceedingly polite. "I'll start reading the *Comedy* first thing tomorrow morning, I promise. And I'll ask Céline to read it, too."

The notary smiled with delight and patted Charles several times on the back.

"Come more often, Charles," he said with a sudden show of gravity and emotion. "We hardly see each other any more! If you knew how much pleasure. . . . No, no, don't worry, I won't get drunk on port every time you come by. Tell me what you think of Balzac. I'll be all ears, dear boy. In the meantime, to bed with me, old butt of Malmsey that I am! I'm half asleep already!"

Charles had just stepped off the porch and was heading down the street when the door reopened and the notary's head appeared, worried.

"Oh yes, I forgot to ask you. . . . Your father, Wilfrid, I mean. Have you heard from him since the . . . er . . . incident?"

"No," Charles said simply.

"It's just . . ." He stopped, troubled, apparently regretting his question. Then he added: "Maybe he's left the city. . . . He could be a long way from here . . ."

"Could be. Did he say anything to you?"

"No, no, of course not. He definitely did not speak to me." And with that he closed the door again.

Intrigued, Charles walked off down the street, his euphoria gone.

■ ■ ■

Charles never saw the Blond Angel again, and never tried to see her. He had no desire to stand by watching helplessly while she slid into the depths (didn't he recall reading some lines in a poem by Victor Hugo about that?), and he preferred to believe that that dramatic evening in Brigitte Loiseau's life had been like a warning to her, and that, after having come so close to death, she had decided to take herself in hand. Once, walking along rue Rachel, he had glanced up to the door of her apartment; a "FOR RENT" sign was hanging from one of the posts of the balcony, and he found the sight comforting. The woman who lived downstairs came out to shake out a rug and told him that the actress had gone back to her family in Chicoutimi to convalesce. "Ah," thought Charles, "I hope she stays there, far away from predators like De Bané. I hope she regains her strength and pours it all into acting." Fame awaited her, he was sure of it.

Sometimes he talked about Brigitte to Céline, but he soon realized it was not one of her favourite topics and he determined to avoid bringing it up in her presence. In any case, his new love for Céline pushed thoughts of the Blond Angel farther and farther into the darkness of the past.

Lucie, who had a nose as sharp as a fox after a three-day fast, had twigged to the relationship between Céline and Charles. There were a thousand little signs. But since she could do nothing to stop it, she decided to turn a blind eye, leaving it up to the two principals to make the announcement themselves, but also hoping against hope that they didn't end up with a baby in their arms. She said nothing to her husband, who as yet hadn't noticed any-thing, preoccupied as he was with keeping his business afloat and, in any case, happy to see that Charles's misadventure seemed to have had a salu-tary effect on him, and that he had returned to his former good-natured self. But in the end everything became obvious to everyone. Charles and Céline couldn't take their eyes off one another. They sat together in inter-minable conversations, went out on long walks, went to movies together, and disappeared from time to time without telling anyone where they were going. And often they were caught smooching in dark corners.

Like Lucie, Fernand's feelings about the affair were mixed. Charles's trafficking days had left him with some doubts about the boy's character. But his strong affection for Charles helped him keep an open mind.

"Céline is as solid as a rock," he said one night to his wife, "but by the same token she knows what she wants, and we can't just make her do what-ever we want her to do. She'll be a good influence on Charles, and will keep him from getting into trouble again. And he's a good lad. His heart is in the right place. I'm sure he'll treat her with the utmost respect. Still, we should keep an eye on them, don't you think?"

One night shortly after the end of classes, Steve Lachapelle called to say he'd landed a summer job at a cheese factory in Anjou, and that there were two or three positions still open. Charles went down the next day and was hired. A few mornings later, he and his friend found themselves wearing white smocks, hairnets, and rubber boots up to their thighs, shovelling cheddar into an immense vat that reeked to high heaven. The work was exhausting, and carried out in a somewhat hostile environment, since the factory's other employees were non-unionized and forced to work under stupefying conditions, and they looked with envious contempt on the students, whom they saw as pampered little middle-class kids out on a lark to make some extra pocket money.

Charles got home each night at six, quickly ate his dinner, and went to bed. After sleeping for an hour or two, he got up, took a shower, and spent the evening with Céline. Or with Balzac.

Fulfilling his promise to Parfait Michaud was not a problem for Charles. He began reading the different volumes of *The Human Comedy* at random. After being disappointed with *The Country Doctor*, which he thought for a while he would never get through, he picked up *Splendours and Miseries of the Courtesans*, then *Lost Illusions*, and finally *Old Goriot* and *Cousin Bette*. With these he became a devoted Balzacian. Characters such as Vautrin, Lucien de Rubempré, Esther and Eugène de Rastignac became part of his daily life. He talked about them constantly, and in his proselytizing zeal went out and bought several paperback copies of Balzac's novels and tried to convert Céline and Blonblon – without much success, it must be said. But it was when he tried it out on Steve Lachapelle that the real disaster occurred.

■ ■ ■

One night he had insisted so fervently that Steve read "at least a bit of Balzac" before he passed on to his greater reward that when Steve left he took with him a collection of the great novelist's short stories, promising to return it within a week. Still under the influence of Charles's enthusiasm, he opened the book in the metro and took a run at "An Incident During the Terror," a tale of courage and goodwill. All through school he had never read any more than he'd absolutely had to, relying on his memory, guesswork, and the notes he'd borrowed from his fellow students. But after a few pages he found that the story was taking a run at him. "An Incident During the Terror" became mysteriously transformed into an incident during the drowsiness that slowly overcame our novice reader, who, with the book resting on his lap and his head bent over it, started his night before arriving at his home.

He was awakened by a sudden jolt. He looked wildly around the empty carriage. The ceiling lights were blinking on and off and a low rumbling was coming from under his feet, giving the impression that the earth was cracking open everywhere and soon he would be swallowed up.

"Holy shit!" he cried, leaping to his feet. "I'm in the garage!"

Through the window he could see he was in an immense cavern, darkly lit in places by blue and white neon lights. The ground was covered by an intricate lacework of rails and electric cables.

Suddenly the carriage stopped and he was engulfed in complete silence. The prospect of spending the night in such uncharming surroundings suddenly gave him the energy of a bull. Gripping the sliding doors with both hands and exerting all his strength, he managed to force them apart and he jumped out of the carriage. He was cautiously making his way through the darkness, looking for a way out, when he was stopped in his tracks by a loud yell.

"*Hey!* You there! Stop where you are!"

The voice came from behind him. He turned and saw two shadows moving in his direction. A beam of light played over his body.

"What are you doing here?" the voice demanded menacingly.

"I . . . I fell asleep," Steve stammered.

"Yeah, we know all about that, you guys who fall asleep," the other man said, as they both continued to draw closer.

The one who had called first was a tall, muscular man, wearing a mechanic's overalls and sporting a handlebar moustache. He had enormous, glistening teeth that made him look vaguely like a beaver. His companion, shorter but equally sturdily built, had a jacket draped over his arm and was carrying a lunch pail; he favoured Steve with a ferocious smile.

"They fall asleep," said the beaver, "then suddenly they wake up and start scrawling filthy words on the sides of the carriages with cans of spray paint."

They stopped when they reached Steve and the beaver began roughly patting his clothing.

"No cans," he grumbled. "He must have got rid of them when he heard us calling him."

"But I told you," Steve protested, becoming increasingly alarmed, "I fell asleep, for crying out loud!"

"I'll just take a look," said the short man, moving off.

"What's this? Some kind of book?" asked the beaver, taking the short-story collection from Steve's pocket.

"It's mine," barked Steve.

The employee held the book close to his eyes.

"An Incident During the Terror," he read slowly.

The short story Steve had been reading was the title story.

The man looked again at Steve with a strange pursing of his lips. The book's title seemed to have had a galvanizing effect on him, although he hadn't been able to make out what it meant.

"Ron! Come back here. Never mind the cans . . . I think I might've got that wrong. Looks like we landed ourselves a bigger fish . . . I think we got us a terrorist or something like that . . ."

Steve was taken to a police station and interrogated for a long time. He found himself suddenly an ardent defender of literature and the right of each citizen to read whatever and wherever he wanted. He defied the police who were holding him, calling them thick-skulled illiterates (a word he used for the first time in his life). His sharp tongue didn't help his case any. The police roughed him up a bit, but they couldn't find any solid reason to put him in jail; to get back at him, they kept him stewing in a small room for a couple of hours, with only a bare electric light bulb, a cabinet, and a wooden chair with no cushion for company. At three in the morning he found himself back on the street, his book confiscated and a dollar twenty-five in his pocket. He had to phone his mother to ask her to have some money ready when he got there in a taxi. Madame Lachapelle paid the driver, then gave Steve a piece of her mind, of which a little went a long way.

"Don't you dare mention Balzac to me again," he fumed to Charles the next day. "Or any of your other bloody writers, either!"

18

Charles was experiencing a new period of happiness. He was devouring Balzac, he was truly in love for the first time in his life, and, despite the unlooked-for turn of events he had gone through, he felt he had paid at least part of the debt of gratitude he owed to Fernand and Lucie by having saved them from a huge danger. For how long? Almost certainly forever, since Thibodeau, having been frightened out of his wits, had decided to seek his fortune in Manitoba; that at least was what Liliane, Thibodeau's mistress, told Lucie when Fernand sent her as a spy to check out Thibodeau's neighbourhood, a role that Lucie, with her good manners and apparent naïveté, was able to fill quite easily.

"There's been a huge boom in construction out there," Liliane told Lucie during a long conversation about the high cost of living and the difficulty of bringing up kids. "People are making money hand over fist. And since he's perfectly bilingual he thought he'd get a jump on it. He said he's gonna send me money for a plane ticket one of these days, so I can go out to see him. It'll be okay by me, I guess, I've always enjoyed travelling."

"I hope he starves to death out there, that goddamned piece of crap," grumbled Fernand when he heard the news. "Manitoba can have him and good riddance. We've put up with him long enough."

Charles was more relieved than anyone by his father's departure, but his deliverance still didn't inspire in him the kind of exuberance that others might have expected. We get used to happiness, and after a while it begins to seem ordinary to us. If only we could take as much pleasure from our good health as we suck misery from our sicknesses! But for us, everything eventually becomes stale and flat, and we seem to be condemned to dissatisfaction.

His love for Céline monopolized his attention and distorted his view of things. He more or less forgot the suffering his father had caused him, and welcomed the latter's disappearance with a slightly absent-minded joy. He thought only of Céline. He couldn't believe he had lived in the same house with her for so long without loving her to distraction, as he did now.

"How is it possible? How is it possible?" he said to her over and over. "Was I blind? Was I insane?"

"I've always loved you," she would reply, looking serious. "I loved you when I was still playing with dolls. My heart sang every time I looked at you, long before I knew that that was what love is. My teacher was right: girls aren't made the same way as boys. We fall in love more quickly than you do."

She read *The Duchess of Langeais* and was swept away by the story of love and pain – to the great delight of Charles, who now found his own alter ego in her (as Parfait Michaud was more of a master than a kindred spirit). Carefully choosing books for her that conformed to her tastes as much as possible, he gave her *Modeste Mignon*, then *Cousin Pons*, and *Old Goriot*; she took little pleasure from the last title, although it did set her heart to racing.

One night Marlene called him. He hadn't spoken to her for a long time, and he spoke to her now with a lightness and indifference that humiliated the poor girl, although Charles was unaware of his cruelty. Even the Blond Angel would have had trouble rekindling the fascination he had once had for her. Whenever the two lovers found themselves alone, far from anyone's prying eyes, they tore off their clothes and made love, lying in each other's arms for hours afterwards in a chaos of bedsheets, marvelling at one another and murmuring sweet nothings into each other's ears.

"I've never seen a girl as beautiful as you, not in person or anywhere else, I swear," he told her over and over. She would laugh, flattered, and shrug her shoulders. "You're so beautiful you drive me crazy! You could be a supermodel, or a movie star, you could marry a millionaire. . . . And yet you love me!"

The passion we feel for another person always embellishes that person in our eyes, but in this case passion had little to do with it, since it was true that Céline had become a ravishing beauty. Charles was amazed that Fernand and Lucie, with their thick, fairly ordinary bodies, could have produced such a marvel of perfection. Her face had a kind of Asian delicacy, with a lively and determined expression, and deep, twinkling, superb black eyes; her limbs were graceful, almost frail, almost like those of a child; her perfect breasts were as smooth and white as porcelain, but with nipples so sensitive that they trembled voluptuously at the slightest touch; her tiny feet seemed made to be kissed, which Charles delighted in doing passionately, although never as much as he liked because she was a bit ticklish. Her temperament perfectly disposed her for love, and her apprenticeship in that art proceeded effortlessly. She mildly chastised Charles for having created insatiable needs in her, needs that she condemned him to satisfy for the rest of his life, on pain of unbearable tortures. At which Charles laughed, smugly, pleased with himself, as if the credit for her perfection were all his.

■ ■ ■

Charles finally accepted Blonblon's invitation to meet Isabel, certain now that she would be little more than a pale imitation of Céline. And so she turned out to be. It was a double date; they went to see Truffaut's *Confidentially Yours,* then for a spaghetti dinner at Da Giovanni's, a restaurant famous for its high prices. With her mocha-coloured skin and small nose with its slightly flared nostrils, Isabel was pretty in an oddly comical way, and her Québécois accent, lightly oiled with Spanish, was extremely charming, even Charles had to admit it. Céline watched his reactions closely, but finding no reason to be alarmed decided that Blonblon's friend was a very nice person.

Steve had met Isabel a few times already, and to him she seemed to be a bit of "a suck" – a category he had a great deal of difficulty defining but which included people he felt should be avoided if at all possible. Of course, Blonblon was Charles's friend, not Steve's. Steve found him too "out of it," there was something "spaced out" about him. He needed to "get it together," although he wasn't so bad, Steve hastened to add, as to fall into the dreaded "wuss" category. But he definitely hadn't got it together, which was the nicest way Steve could think of to put it, as he came up with obscurely fashionable words to describe him. And anyway, hadn't Blonblon always been a ferocious adversary of smoking cigarettes? So what was he doing working in a tobacco shop, where his bland affability was raking in the customers like gangbusters?

"It's a question of principles, Charlie boy," Steve explained. Steve was already a pack-and-a-half-a-day man, although it didn't stop him from energetically manhandling his cheese shovel at the factory. "I mean, would a guy going to AA take a job at a liquor store? Would a vegetarian work for a butcher?"

"Why not?" Charles replied. He felt a deep, visceral affection for Blonblon, reinforced recently by the fact that he was reading and enjoying *César Birotteau* in his spare time behind the counter. "You make your living the best way you can. Not everyone has a choice. What about you, do you love cheese all that much?"

"You better believe I love cheese! I've always loved it! Mind you, it's beginning to turn my stomach. The way they make us sweat in that retarded goddamn factory of theirs is enough to kill anyone's appetite!"

Charles had gone back to visit the notary a few times, and Parfait Michaud was amazed by the effect *The Human Comedy* had had on him. One night Charles confided in him that he sometimes thought of becoming a writer.

"Hmm ... now there's a dangerous occupation, old man. Like anything involving the arts. I suppose you could do what so many others have done, take a stab at it in your spare time, wait for success to come knocking – as it does sometimes, although nobody knows exactly why."

"I think our young friend has pulled himself out of it," Michaud announced to Fernand and Lucie the next day, when he paid them a visit. "I've never seen him so full of beans. And all thanks to good old Balzac! What a marvellous thing literature is, when you think about it! It can change a person's life, believe me!"

"Uh-huh," said Fernand with a somewhat skeptical frown. "But there's also the fact that he's sleeping with my daughter. They seem to be finding that a pretty marvellous thing, too."

"Of course they are, of course," agreed the notary with a smile. "The recipe for happiness has a long list of ingredients. You don't make a good soup with nothing but carrots. Just as you don't make a woman happy just by making love to her . . ."

"Maybe not, but it sure helps!" exclaimed Fernand, giving Lucie a huge wink and bursting out laughing.

"So you think our Charles is back on the rails for good?" Lucie said with a somewhat worried solicitude.

"I'm ninety-nine per cent sure of it. He was telling me last night about his plans for the future. The distant future, at that!"

"And what were they?" she asked.

Michaud rose to take his leave.

"I prefer to let him tell you himself when he feels the time is right. You'll be astonished . . . unless of course he changes his mind in the meantime. In any case, don't forget the lad is only seventeen years old!"

"No one could ever accuse you of being a blabbermouth," Fernand said, as he saw him to the door.

"I probably talk too much for a notary, but I have a pretty shrewd notion of professional privilege."

"Well, God bless you anyway."

And he shook Michaud's hand so vigorously that the notary's eyes bulged and he all but let out a cry of pain.

■ ■ ■

Charles was shovelling cheese relentlessly, making love to Céline like a man possessed, ploughing through Balzac and, two or three times a week, playing pool with Steve and Blonblon – who had reluctantly allowed himself to be converted to the game and was showing such a remarkable aptitude for it that Steve sometimes seemed positively jealous. Fernand had officially forbidden Céline to join them because of her age – otherwise she would have been there.

In order not to run into De Bané, Charles no longer patronized the Orleans and the beautiful Nadine; they now went to a place on rue de Lorimier, La Belle Partie, run by a fellow named Albert Gouache, a small, chubby-cheeked man with long white hair and a huge, drooping, Asterix-like moustache. Gouache was born in Paris but had been living in Montreal for the past thirty years, and, like all good Montrealers, complained about the city with an unremitting fluency. Charles enjoyed teasing him, making a fuss over his hair – "just like Victor Hugo's," or "Santa Claus's" (depending on the season) – commiserating with him on how difficult it must be to master a Quebec accent, and constantly asking him about his plans for expanding the business, which Gouache had been talking about for fifteen years, and which by now had become part of the local folklore.

Despite his precautions, however, Charles did run into his former drug dealer two or three times on the street; each time, after a hard stare, De Bané gave him a wide berth and vanished into thin air. Then one day he was gone. Had he taken his business elsewhere, or was he mulling over the error of his ways behind bars? No one knew.

In short, the summer passed agreeably, despite the forced labour at the cheese factory, which resulted mainly in aching muscles and a fierce desire to be done with it. But no one seemed to be willing to hand him money for nothing, and so Charles allowed himself to give in to the harsher realities of life.

One night, after a long conversation with Parfait Michaud over two cups of delicious cappuccino (at which the notary still excelled), Charles walked home in an almost uncontainable state of excitement. He was overwhelmed by inspiration. He went into Céline's room and made passionate love to her, then went into his own room and began writing a short story. By four o'clock in the morning he had written twenty pages, and he fell asleep convinced that he had accomplished something worthwhile.

"Loving books doesn't necessarily mean you can write them," the notary had once warned him. "I'm living proof of that myself. When I was a young man I wrote a novel, two plays, and a collection of poems, all of which were published by Trashcan Editions!"

"No," Charles told himself as he tossed and turned in his bed. "Not me. I'm good! I know it! And I'm going to work and work at it until I'm better. The next thing I buy is going to be an IBM typewriter. Then we'll see what we shall see!"

Each morning, because of his job at the cheese factory, he was the first one up. Céline often had breakfast with him and then went back to bed. That morning he read her the first few pages of his short story, which he called "Skidding in Fourth Gear." She thought it was fantastic.

"Well, not yet," he objected modestly. "It's only a first draft. There are two or three good things in it, but I've got to rework the whole thing."

At work a few hours later, Steve remarked on the dark circles under Charles's eyes and his sluggish behaviour, and Charles had to confess to him that he'd been up half the night writing.

"Writing what?"

"A short story."

"It couldn't be too short if it took you half the night."

Charles explained to him what a short story was. His friend gave him a long, dumbfounded, not to say worried, look, and after thinking about it for a moment, said:

"If anything's going to keep me up half the night, I'd rather it was sex."

And he went back to shovelling cheese.

■ ■ ■

It took him a few weeks, but Steve finally convinced Blonblon and Isabel to smoke a joint, arguing persuasively that if they didn't try it at least once the entire twentieth century might end up passing them by untouched. Charles and Céline had also lent their support to the argument.

It happened one Saturday night in August, in a quiet corner of Park La Fontaine after an evening at the movies. There were at first a few shudders, a few dry coughs, a few wry grimaces, but after a few minutes the effects of the fabled fumes began to make themselves felt, and Blonblon settled into a quietly contemplative state while Isabel laughed herself hoarse. Their friends, a little more hip to the scene (if twenty joints in three years qualified them for that distinction), let themselves float off into their own foggy reveries. Steve, hunched desperately over to hide a preening erection, was scraping away at the gravelled path with a broken tree branch, making drawings that meant nothing to anyone but him. Charles was blown away by the growth patterns in the trees around him; the profound and inexplicable connections between them and him filled him with serene joy. His eye fell on Céline, who was leaning against the bench beside him, smiling at something invisible. A thin, pink halo flowed along the contours of her body; he found her furiously, gloriously beautiful. She took his hand. With the slightest encouragement from her he would have made love to her right there, on the bench. On second thought, it would be better to wait. Somewhere in an obscure corner of his brain he remembered that it was best to keep his cool, and to keep in mind that only assholes violated the established order of things.

An hour later they were sitting in a small snack bar on Sainte-Catherine, looking at a platter of poutine. The happy, lively conversation flew off in all directions at once. They talked in a jumble about a new kind of condom on the market, the civil war in Ireland, Martin Scorsese's most recent film, and Robert Bourassa's latest subterfuges. Isabel laughed until her eyes filled with tears at Charles's and Steve's description of their supervisor's head-first fall into a vat of cheddar cheese, while Blonblon and Céline compared notes on the potential marvels of computers. Charles ordered his third coffee. He wanted to tell his friends about Balzac. His friends stopped him, saying it was far too late. For a few minutes he sat there looking morose. Céline caressed the back of his hand, and his good humour returned as though a switch had been thrown on.

"We should go for a walk on Mount Royal," he said, jumping to his feet. "On the night the Parti Québécois was elected in 1976, Fernand and Monsieur Victoire stayed up there the whole night, singing and talking. They were up until sunrise. Not bad for a couple of old farts, eh?"

In order to save time, since it was getting late, they decided to take the metro, then a bus. The metro station at Berri-de-Montigny was only a short distance away.

As Charles passed through the turnstile, surrounded by the happy sounds of Saturday-night travellers, his eye fell on the huge slab of black granite set at the centre of the station to commemorate the Montreal Metro's inauguration in October 1966. It served as a bench in this kind of waiting room for lost souls.

Suddenly he was struck by a revelation. Followed by the surprised gaze of his companions, he moved towards the slab and stared at it, his jaw tightly clenched, as though he were going to try to lift it. Two young girls in sundresses, sitting directly in front of him, were drinking a glass of orangeade. They looked up at him and exchanged amused glances. He didn't see them. He had become Eugène de Rastignac in *Old Goriot*, the ambitious hero who, at the end of the novel, defies Paris before setting out to conquer it.

Céline came up to him. "What are you doing, Charles?"

"What's up, Thibodeau?" echoed Steve, coming up to grab his arm. "Are you having a religious experience?"

He didn't hear either of them.

The slab, the symbolic convergence point for all the metro lines that threaded through the city, had suddenly become for Charles the soul of Montreal, its brain and its will, the seat of all its urges, good and evil.

He stepped around the two young girls and jumped up onto the slab, transported by a feeling of power that all but obsessed his mind. People were looking at him with joy and alarm in their eyes. Enormous waves of energy were flowing into him from throughout the city, swelling, crackling with electricity. He felt the heart of Montreal beating in his breast. He tasted its acrid, raging, intoxicating blood.

"Montreal!" he shouted, arms outstretched. A ticket-collector began moving towards him, curious, his brows furrowed.

"Montreal! You're going to be hearing from me! I'm going to make your ears ring!"

END OF VOLUME TWO